JMУ

CARRYING ON

Matthew's friends wished him well and sat back to watch the outcome of such an unlikely marriage with malicious curiosity. To Matthew's face, they envied his good luck in finding such a pretty and agreeable wife; just what was needed. Behind his back, they made jokes about Svengali Craven and his Trilby. She was young, engaging, certainly beddable, but –

The marriage appeared, nevertheless, to be a success. The house was as clean as a convent, the dinner-parties never broke up before midnight. Even the tragedies – a splendid-looking crème brulée forever locked below a barrier of toffee which a security guard would not have spurned – gained charm from Laura's looks of comical despair and Matthew's affectionate laughter. They seemed to be devoted to each other; the tutor-pupil relationship appeared to have satisfied a mutual need . . .

About the Author

Miranda Seymour is the author of several successful historical novels, including THE GODDESS and MEDEA. She also writes children's stories, and is currently preparing a life of Henry James and his circle. She reviews regularly for a number of leading newspapers and literary journals. CARRYING ON marks her impressive debut as a writer of contemporary fiction.

Miranda Seymour lives in North London.

'I liked her book so much that I hope to be reading another soon'

Susan Hill
Good Housekeeping

'A fine depiction of a loveless boy becoming aware in a loveless adult world'

Books and Bookmen

'Those who relish bitter-sweet tragi-comedy, the flamboyantly selfish intoxications of youthful and not so youthful sex, the slow disappointments of glamorous marriage and ambition, the ironic dangers of physical charm, will welcome this story, not least for its asides, observant, often tart, yet affectionate'

Peter Vansittart

Carrying On

Miranda Seymour

CORONET BOOKS
Hodder and Stoughton

Copyright © 1984 by Miranda Seymour

First published in Great Britain in 1984 by
Hodder & Stoughton Ltd

Coronet edition 1986

British Library C.I.P.

Seymour, Miranda
   Carrying on.
   I. Title
   823'.914[F]   PR6069.E737

   ISBN 0–340–38840–4

Printed and bound in Great Britain for
Hodder and Stoughton Paperbacks, a
division of Hodder and Stoughton Ltd.,
Mill Road, Dunton Green, Sevenoaks,
Kent (Editorial Office: 47 Bedford
Square, London, WC1 3DP) by
Cox & Wyman Ltd., Reading

To my parents with love

Oh what a tangled web we weave,
When first we practise to deceive!

Sir Walter Scott
Marmion, can v. xii

Part One

1

The porter looked down at the pale, smartly uniformed child standing composedly under the clock on Platform One. "Here's your trunk, then. Sure they know it's Paddington you're at?"

The child nodded and unclosed a fist to offer a tarnished sixpence. "My mother will be here soon. She's always late."

He pushed the coin away. "Keep it for sweeties. First term at school, was it?"

Mortified, Matthew shook his head. "Second year. I'm nine and a half."

The man whistled silently. Funny sort of parents these rich kids had, sending the poor little beggars off almost as soon as they could walk.

"I had a little lad just your age."

The boy's bright green eyes rose to scrutinize him. "Why? Is he dead?"

"Five years back when the Jerries were trying to rub out London. The whole street went up. He and the wife were sleeping. Don't suppose they had time to know much about it." He still couldn't get used to the quiet where they had been. Bloody old war.

"I'm awfully sorry," the boy said.

"Garn. Better dead than only half alive, like some I've seen." He patted the child's shoulder. "You tell your mum to get here early next time. And don't you go running off before she gets here."

Matthew smiled. "You needn't worry. I'm used to waiting."

Whistling, the man pushed his trolley away down the empty platform to the exit gate. Taking a last toffee out of his blazer pocket, Matthew unwrapped it and began to chew as he watched the minute hand click from point to point on the station clock.

11

There was no cause as yet for anxiety. There had never, so far as he could remember, been any variation in the end-of-term routine, her unpunctuality, and the mixture of pleasure and dread at the prospect of returning to the house called home. Chester Square was for Matthew Craven a purgatory to be endured between terms. But that could never be said.

He was just beginning to wonder if he should telephone the house when he saw her hurrying towards him behind the friendly porter. Elegant as always, she looked spider-thin in the tailored black suit. A pill-box hat was tipped forward to screen her eyes with spotted net. High-heeled scarlet shoes clicked like a Spanish dancer's over the stone squares. Enchanted, he gazed.

"Matthew, my darling!" She was on him in all her loveliness and he was enveloped in the sweet flowery scent which came to her in tiny golden bottles from Paris. She had dabbed some on his neck once for a joke and his father had been angry and told him to go and wash it off straightaway, that minute. Through the half-open door, he had heard him shouting something at her about little pansies and wondered why it should matter what flower they used for the scent. They quarrelled about the silliest things.

Her lipstick was new, a sharp vermilion which matched her shoes. It suited her. He liked the way she always dressed up to fetch him. The other mothers didn't bother so much. He wished they could have seen her. Kissing her, he saw eyes green as his own, glinting like little smiling swords behind the net.

"Don't throttle me, Matthew." Her hand rose to pat her cheek where he had tried not to smudge the powder. "Poor sweet. Did you have to wait for ages? That wretched hairdresser kept me under the dryer for hours."

"It didn't matter. I told the porter that I knew you'd come."

"As if I'd forget my darling boy." Her smile flashed round to dazzle the man behind her. "Sweet of you to look after him for me. The car's just beyond the taxi rank. I know it's not meant to be there, but I was in such a hurry. I don't suppose they'll do anything too dreadful."

The porter touched his cap. "Lovely ladies usually gets away with everything bar murder here," he said. "Don't you worry. I'll see to it."

Despite her narrow skirt and high heels, Matthew had to run to keep up with her as she hurried down the platform. "Isn't he nice? He wouldn't take a tip, either."

"He certainly shouldn't be tipped twice." She gave him a little push. "Do hurry, darling. Listen, we won't tell Daddy I was late, will we?"

"What if he asks?"

"Say the train was late. It's only a white lie. They don't count."

"But I thought—" he began, confused.

"Then don't think," she said quite sharply and then, with one of her bewildering changes of mood, she bent to hug him. "Oh darling, I thought we were friends. Don't you help your friends when they ask you nicely, as a special favour? Please. It's only a tiny little lie. Yes?"

He nodded. But he wondered, as they hurried along, why she supposed his father would mind so much. She was always late when she went to the hairdresser.

She drove the car fast but well, talking all the time, asking questions which seemed to require no answers, speaking in a grown-up way which was both flattering and unnerving. London had become so boring now the war was over. Nobody gave parties and when they did, it was always the same dreary food. This wretched rationing. She'd had to go practically on her knees to get extra butter when the French Ambassador came to dinner. And the beastly man never even noticed.

"We have butter on Sundays at school. You could have mine."

She gave a little crow of mirth. "How? In an envelope with the Sunday letter?"

Blushing at his stupidity, he racked his mind for some startling piece of information or news to offer her.

"I came first in English and Latin and essay-writing. Mr Jacks said it was the best essay in my house this year."

"Goodness!" Yet she did not seem greatly excited. "Well, you certainly don't get it from me. I always came in the middle."

"I expect Daddy was quite clever at school."

"Not clever," she said. "Industrious. Now, what about that

13

nice boy Remington, the one with the lovely house near Grace-dew? Have you made friends with him?''

She was always going on about Remington. ''He's a prefect, Mummy. And he's three forms above me.''

''Still, you could try. After all, if Cousin Jack leaves Gracedew to Daddy, it'll be your home one day. You'd be next-door neighbours.''

Nothing, he thought, could be more awful than to live next door to large, bullying Remington who had once tipped an inkpot over his Sunday shorts and laughed when he was beaten for appearing in the wrong clothes. He would never be friends with Remington. He wasn't even sure if he wanted Gracedew to be his home one day, although he knew how much it mattered to his mother.

''Promise to try,'' she said. ''Word of honour?''

Glumly, he nodded. ''Word of honour.'' He cast about for a subject which would distract her. ''They did your hair awfully well.''

''My hair?'' For a moment she looked quite blank. ''Oh. Do you think so?''

He thought and shyly said that the rumpled black curls were very pretty. They made her face look softer, he reflected but did not add.

''It's sweet of you, but I look an absolute gorgon. I only hope I can find a decent coiffeur in Paris.''

Matthew gave a little bounce on his seat. ''Paris! We're going to Paris?''

''Do sit still, child.'' She patted his knee. ''We'll talk about it later, my angel. All right?''

He nodded, hopeful.

When they reached the corner house in Chester Square with its black shiny door opening wide and silent, he went straight up the pale blue staircase, past the delicate pen-and-ink flower pictures which were his mother's prized collection, to the room which was formally his. The books and toys had been tidied away into a cupboard to accommodate term-time guests, but a vase of roses stood on the windowsill and a book of poetry for children which he would not have chosen for himself lay by the bed. A teddy-bear, bright yellow, sat stiffly on the pillow, a button-eyed intruder masquerading as familiarity. They had, he thought, tried. He opened the cupboard and began the solemn ritual of taking out and rearranging all his toys, establishing ownership. Not until each one was in its habitual place would he know the room was his.

"Matthew!" His mother called to him from her bedroom at the far end of the passage. "Do go down and see Daddy. He's waiting for you."

Sighing, he washed his hands, combed his hair carefully sideways and went down to the great white drawing-room which always made him think of the North Pole. His father was standing by the fire, looking down at the carpet. It was odd how he seemed to shrink a little bit with the passing of each term. He looked very small today. The mirror behind him revealed a new salmon-pink area of skin on the back of his head. Matthew walked slowly across the white carpet, debating whether to offer a kiss or hold out his hand.

"Hello Daddy. Sorry I'm late."

"Your mother explained. The train was held up. Can't blame you for that."

Charles Craven looked down at the dark shining wing of hair, the eyes, so candid but of the same treacherous green as hers, the outstretched hand. Too old for kisses, he supposed. Well, he didn't want to embarrass the boy. He compromised with a genial shoulder-punch and a dreadful—to his own ears—"Well now, young Craven?" Matthew gave a polite giggle and pushed his hand back in his pocket. Men together. Oh well. It was, he imagined, how most fathers and sons behaved.

"Good results, I hear. Best essay in the house. That's rather good news, old chap." He felt in his pocket and, after a moment, produced two new half-crowns. "You see you keep it up. And try to do a bit better in French. Only thing I was ever any good at and it's served me very well."

"I'm afraid I'm not very good at languages."

He had forgotten how badly the boy reacted to even the slightest criticism. Elizabeth all over again. Bad look-out for his future if he didn't stiffen up a bit. "Don't look so down in the mouth. It's not the end of the world." He patted the dark hair.

"Nice to have you back. I missed you."

"I missed you, too." He felt a little uncomfortable about that half-truth. It was his mother he always thought of when he couldn't go to sleep. Not her face so much as her voice, the soft laughing whispering voice she only ever used when they were alone together.

They talked awkwardly about the train journey, the form report, the test match. Mr Craven glanced at the smart little carriage clock behind him and rubbed his hands.

"Tea-time, then. You look as though you could do with a bit of feeding up. Grub not up to much at school?"

He, too, had a special voice, Matthew thought, only it wasn't at all the same. A sort of boys-together voice. "Well, not too good," he said.

Silence fell. A maid came in answer to the bell. New again. He had learned from visits to the kitchen that their servants usually left because his mother ordered them about too much. This one was rather pretty. She pushed before her a rattling silver trolley displaying thinly cut sandwiches, sponge cake, a plate piled high with garibaldi biscuits.

"Bet you thought we'd forget the squashed flies. Think you'll manage to eat your way through that lot?"

Matthew smiled and said that he expected so. It was horrible, eating something with a name like that and trying not to think about it. But they were intended for a treat and must be relished as such. He must please if he was to be taken to Paris.

His mother never ate tea. She was afraid of getting fat. While his father and he dutifully attacked pale wedges of cake, she smoked and talked in her quick, breaking-icicle voice about the Paris posting—his father was in the Foreign Office—and of how lucky Matthew was not to have to go with them. Unbelieving, he stared at her, but she was turning the pages of a magazine and he couldn't catch her eye.

"I thought you said—"

"Eat up and don't chatter, darling." Swiftly she sped on, intent on making Paris sound as disagreeable as possible. If he only knew what it was like there in July, plagued with ghastly tourists, nothing to do, half the restaurants closed. Staring at his plate, he listened to them agreeing on his good fortune, telling

16

him how lucky he was. There was nothing he could do. It was clear that all had been settled in advance. His summer holiday was to be spent at Gracedew. Just like all the other summers. Cousin Jack was sending Mr Bates to fetch him in the Daimler on the following morning. Trapped in a conspiracy of smiles, he was mute. One tear slipped guard. Furtively, he scrubbed it into oblivion with the back of his hand. The Cravens looked at each other over his bent head, eyebrows lifting in silent signals. Better not to notice. Kinder.

They went to the theatre later in the evening. It was terribly hot and Matthew could feel himself prickling on the red plush seat as they waited for the crimson curtains to open. The play didn't seem to have much of a story. A small lady with very blonde curls and a huge spangled skirt sang a long song about love and how sad she was because the man she loved had gone far far away. Then the curtain dropped down and a row of tall smiling girls in silver bathing suits came on sideways in a row and kicked their legs as high as their heads and then they did the splits, all together, and everybody clapped and his father shouted Bravo! and then looked very pink. When the curtains opened there were a lot of palm trees and straw huts and a blue sky. The spangled lady came out of a hut in a grass skirt and sang about how happy she was to have got here and found love at last. With her was a small dark man with a very deep voice who didn't seem to want to do anything except kiss her hand and say how he would never leave her again. Just as he was going to kiss her, all the dancing ladies came back in grass skirts and the man pretended not to know which she was any more. Which was silly, because she had a different skirt and anybody could see which she was straightaway. Then they all went off and she started singing about how miserable she was. He started to count the bald heads in the front row, and then the next.

"Do try to look as though you were enjoying yourself, darling," his mother whispered as they went out for the interval. "Daddy spent a lot of money on these seats. You could at least smile."

"You could have taken the trouble to find something more suitable," he heard her say to his father as they returned for the second half. "I don't suppose you even bothered to ask what it was about." He wished she wouldn't use that cold cutting voice. It made her sound like somebody else. Taking his place between them, he touched his father's arm.

"Sorry if it's a bit boring, old chap. They said it was just the ticket."

"I like it. Honestly, I do. Awfully." Anxious to compensate, he grinned until his mouth ached through the rest of the performance and clapped his hands to numbness at the end. Treats were tiring things.

There followed the high point of the ritual, the dinner at The Ivy, with a conspicuous march across the acres of red carpet to the corner table always reserved for the first night of the holidays. Waiters bowed around them like willow branches. Womens' eyes flickered over his mother as she stalked slenderly along with a little shake of her black curls to acknowledge the expected attention. People often came up to the table and asked for her autograph. She had achieved the smile of the famous. He felt very proud of her.

The meal had been ordered in advance, prawn cocktail, scampi, fruit salad and cream. At his father's insistence, he drank half a glass of wine. His mother took out her little black and gold compact and dabbed at her nose, then stretched her lips out in the sliver of a grin she and her friends used when they were putting on lipstick.

"He won't like it. Get him a glass of orangeade."

"Never too young to learn. It's Chablis, Matthew. What do you think?"

He smiled cautiously. "It's—interesting." He wasn't going to be trapped into taking sides. "I don't think I'd want it very often." He pushed the orange sauce round in the glass bowl, trying to hide what he did not want to eat. The wine made him feel dizzy and odd. His father's face loomed up, pink and enormous, then shot away into a haze of specks and light. He put down his fork.

"Excuse me. I think I'm going—"

"Oh, my God," his mother said, very far away. "You are a fool. You never should have given him that wine. Get a waiter, Charles. Hurry."

Head bent, he followed the sneering young man to the ladies'

18

cloakroom. He was given water and told to sit down with his head between his knees. Soundlessly, he wept. Everybody must have seen. He had spoiled the evening.

"Over-excited, are we?" The old lady who had given him the water mopped at his face with a tissue. "That's better. First night of the holidays, is it? Well, I expect you'll be going home to bed soon. That'll be better, won't it, dearie?"

He nodded. Dimly, beyond her, he saw his own white face staring at him from a wall of glass. It wasn't really, he thought. Not home. More like a hotel, really.

The car purred him into uneasy sleep on the way back and he had to be carried up to bed. He was half-conscious of being lifted in his father's arms, of a glow of light as he held out his arms for the pyjamas to be put on, of a comforting envelope of bed-clothes being wrapped round him. The soft whiskery moustache brushed his face with a warm smell of tobacco.

"There you are, old chap. Snug as a bug. It wasn't your fault, you know. Happens to all of us. You go to sleep now."

He raised himself on one elbow. "I wish—" The kind blue eyes looked down at him inquiringly. It was no good. The plans had all been made. They'd only be cross and say he was being difficult. "It doesn't matter. 'Night, Daddy. Thank you for the play and everything."

He turned in the doorway. "I know, old chap. It's not been much fun for you. Still, there'll be lots to do at Gracedew. See all your friends in the village. They're awfully fond of you. I expect Mrs Bates has been cooking toffees for you. Your mother's right, you know. Paris is pretty dull at this time of year. I'm not looking forward to it much myself."

"I could," he said hopelessly, "stay here."

"All on your own? Don't be a little muff. Anyway, it's all arranged now. And we're keeping your mother waiting. That won't do, will it? Good-night, Matthew."

The night-light was turned on, the door closed. He waited until he heard his father's footsteps going heavily down the stairs before pulling the sheet up over his head.

Charles Craven went down to the drawing-room in which he always felt like a stranger among the pretty tables of trinkets, the

19

carefully arranged photographs in silver frames. Elizabeth on their wedding-day, smiling and confident in her beauty. She didn't look a day older. Himself. He glanced with distaste from the solemn young man to the reflection presented by the glass over the fire. No wonder she was bored. He looked like an old bloodhound. Time to lay off the drink or he'd end as blotched a wreck as Cousin Jack. Not yet, though. He poured them each a generous measure of whisky before taking up his habitual position by the fireplace, his back to the glass.

"I'm dying of heat." Her voice was fretful. "Do open a window, will you?" As if he were a servant. Dutifully, he pushed the sash up on to the half-lit square. There was no wind. The pale curtains hung still, like shrouds. White carpet—her choice as the best background to her black hair and peacock clothes—lay before him, a frozen sea. He glanced without interest up and down the columns of print in the evening paper while she turned on the light by the piano and began a fast ragtime waltz, rather loud. He loathed jazz.

"What about some Chopin? One of those nocturnes."

"I'm not in the mood." She dropped her hands from the keys and moved away to lie full length on a sofa, flicking over the pages of a magazine. He took courage from his second glass.

"I suppose it really is out of the question to take him with us? He does seem to have taken it badly."

"Darling, you've a heart like a butterball. Matthew always manages to get you on his side. Listen. The flat's tiny. We'll probably be out or giving dinner-parties almost every evening. You don't suppose the poor child wants to spend his entire holiday trailing around the streets with some dreary nanny?"

"And, of course, you'll have your own friends to see." He watched for the flicker of apprehension in her eyes. "Come on, Elizabeth, I'm not a fool. I know Ivan lives there now. You've been pestering me for months to take up this appointment. It's perfectly obvious why you don't want your son in Paris."

"Our son." She looked up at him. "Don't be beastly. It's not that I don't love Matthew. You know damned well I do. I'd do anything for him."

"Except have him with you for more than a couple of days."

She winced. "Straight for the jugular. You don't have to

hammer the point. You always could have married a doting mother type. The world's full of them.''

He saw that reassurances were necessary if peace was to be preserved. There had been too many quarrels. "Dear Lizzie, you were born to be one of the world's adornments, not an earth mother. It's only when I think of the little chap sitting all on his own for weeks on end with Jack and Lucilla that I get a bit sad.'' He caught the glint of anger behind a portcullis of spiked lashes. ''Perhaps you're right. He's probably best off in a place he knows.''

"Knows! Gracedew's practically home to him. And they adore him being there. You know how lonely Lucilla gets. It suits everyone so frightfully well. Doesn't it?'' Her nails snapped on the rim of her glass. She needed that confirmation from him.

"Oh, Gracedew's certainly convenient,'' he said slowly. "Living up to its name.''

"More than that.'' She leaned forward, drawing her knees up under her chin. His eyes travelled wistfully up the silk stretch of stockinged thighs. Forgotten territories. She didn't seem to care for that kind of thing any more. Not with him. He could look and the others—best not to think of the others. Bad enough his silent acquiescence to her lies, to the protracted lunches, the hurried murmur as she ended an unexplained telephone call to turn her smiling face towards him. Ah well. If he was a fool, at least he had become one knowingly.

She pulled her dress down, but slowly. He had been privileged. "After all, it's going to be his home one day. It's where he belongs.''

He drained his glass and took a cigarette out of his silver case. "You don't think you're being a little premature? Jack's never even mentioned the subject of inheritance.''

"Don't be ridiculous. Of course he'll leave it to you. Who else is there?''

"He knows I've never wanted that millstone round my neck. Frankly, Matthew knows Gracedew better than I do. My parents took me there twice, I think, and since we were married—well, it wasn't a great success, that visit of ours.''

She shrugged it off. "Oh, I know they can't bear the sight of

21

me. I can't think why. I admired the damned place until I was practically hoarse. I tried, I tried, I damn near died. God, the cold of that bedroom.''

"You were splendid.''

"Oh, you're awfully decent, my dear,'' she mocked him. "But it's true. Despite which, they haven't got anybody else to leave it to. And however much it may surprise you, I do concern myself with Matthew's future. The more they think of him as part of Gracedew, the better for him. It's his security. He knows who he is there. He knows where he belongs. That's all I want for him.''

"I just wish you'd stop ramming it into his head,'' he burst out. "Filling him with all these expectations. It's all very well to talk of his security, but there's no base for it. If they knew—''

"But they don't.'' She came across the room to place a cool kiss on his cheek. "And nobody's going to tell them, are they, my sweet?''

He turned his head away. Just for that, she would still kiss him, perhaps even go to bed with him if he pressed her. For his silence.

"Well?''

"Oh, you'll get all you want,'' he said. "You always do.''

She gave a strange little laugh and turned away her head. "Dear Charles. I only wish it was true.''

"Isn't it?''

"How should I know when I'm never sure what I want? Certainly, I'd like Matthew to have Gracedew one day. But myself? God knows. Whatever can't be had. What a spoilt bitch I sound. Am. Rotten wife. Rotten mother.''

"Nonsense.'' He felt the familiar mixture of alarm and helplessness as he saw her shoulders begin to shake. He always managed to say the wrong thing when she was upset. Perhaps she minded about leaving Matthew more than he had realized. Cautiously, he put an arm round her. "Don't you worry, old girl. He'll be as bright as a cricket once he gets there. Out of sight, out of mind. Children are like that.''

"What?'' She slipped out of reach before turning a haggard face towards him. "Oh. Matthew. Yes. I'm sure he will.'' Her long hands fiddled nervously with an unlit cigarette. "I wasn't thinking about Matthew. I've been meaning to tell you. I had lunch today with—''

''Don't,'' he said quickly. ''Really, Lizzie. I'd much rather you didn't. Better not. You'll only wish you hadn't. You know you will.''

''There's nothing to tell,'' she said. ''There was. Not now. It's over.''

Thank God for that, he thought. Someone at the club had told him she'd been seen with the fellow who did the cabaret at the Savoy. Freddie something. He'd gone along to take a look at him one evening with shame-faced curiosity. Awful-looking bounder. All teeth and haircream and eyelashes. Oddly, he had felt less anger than embarrassment. He didn't like to think of her making a fool of herself. She was so beautiful, so quick and clever. She could have had anybody she wanted. He never could understand why she had chosen to marry him.

''Well, saves me getting my gun out.'' A jocular tone seemed the safest one to take. ''Silly chap. Didn't know his good luck. Poor Lizzie. Was it very awful?''

She dabbed at her eyes with the handkerchief he held out. ''A bit. I wasn't expecting it. And then I was late getting to Paddington and everything was such a rush. I suppose it's only just beginning to hit me. Stupid to mind. It was never meant to be serious. Just fun.''

''I know.'' He should never have been deceived by that nonsense about the train. The thought of her coaxing Matthew to cover her tracks made him feel a bit sick. She was odd, that way.

''I don't suppose you let on to the boy?''

''I said I'd been held up by my hairdresser. He didn't suspect a thing.'' Her eyes flared wide with apprehension. ''You're not going to tell him?''

''Don't be an idiot,'' he said gruffly. ''I just don't like the idea of him telling lies. Not even for you.''

''You needn't look so pious. I had to say something. I thought you'd be furious.''

He could smile at that. ''When it's happened so often?''

''It's the last time,'' she said with all the force of the resolutions which she never kept. ''I swear.''

23

Until Paris, he thought. Perhaps it was just as well that Matthew should go to Gracedew. Safer. He knew how the boy idolized her. It showed in the way he hung about her, looking for any pretext to stay, sniffing at her scent bottles, hoarding old photographs cut from social columns in magazines. Poor little chap. Let him keep his dreams for now. He'd have to be disillusioned one day, but not yet. Not if Charles Craven had anything to do with it.

"Time for bed, old girl," he said gently. "A bit of sleep's the best cure."

"Yes." Her head drooped. She looked exhausted, white as a bit of paper. Awful to think a greasy little crooner could have done this to her.

"I could come along to your room if you like. You might want some company. Up to you."

"I'd rather be alone." She turned at the door to look back at him. "You're so kind to me, Charles. I wish I could stop hurting you. I'm sorry."

He offered a grin. "It'd take more than this to hurt me. Hide like an old boot. Off you go to bed. I'll do the lights."

With the method of habit, he began to set the room to rights, mindful of her passion for neatness. No servant was scrupulous enough to satisfy her; he had long ago decided that it was easier to do it himself when she was out of sight. He hunted down the ashtrays, put back the magazines, closed the piano and the music-rack, drew down the window and plumped out the cushions, restoring the air of cold formality which she thought so elegant. He had never succeeded in convincing her that a slight disorder added to the charm of a room. It was not her fault. She had never lived in rooms of that kind. He could still remember sitting as a bashful fiancé in Lady Clitheroe's Knightsbridge drawing-room, perched on the edge of a pale pink sofa below a pale pink ceiling picked out in gold, wondering if anything there had ever been allowed to stray an inch from its allotted place. Dreadful old woman, with her false family portraits and her dyed curls and her simpering giggle. Astonishing that Elizabeth could be the product of that and a red-faced biscuit-king, long-dead—from drink, he had always assumed from Lady Clitheroe's evasion of details. He could still hear her. "So nice to think she's marrying

24

somebody of a similar background." And then, leaning towards him confidentially: "I'm afraid some of my daughter's young men weren't quite us." Dagoes, she meant. Like Freddie. She hadn't explained the part they were going to play in his married life. Elizabeth's sexual appetites had been kept in check for that first year, and by the end of it Lady Clitheroe lay safely out of reach, by her husband, in Kensal Rise. Death had saved her from the embarrassment of the explanations she had never intended to offer.

He made a last careful tour of the room before closing the door and tiptoeing up the stairs, to peer in at Matthew, buried in a fortress of bed-clothes, to glance down at the light which shone from under his wife's door. No sound. At least she wasn't crying.

"Is that you, Charles? Come and kiss me good-night."

He went in and bent over the bed where she lay like some lovely hothouse flower, red lips parted, eyes like jade chips as his face came down to hers.

"You taste of whisky." She gave him a little push. "I hope I don't."

"Honey and roses," he said, honourably.

"Liar." She lifted a hand to pat his cheek. "But a very sweet one. You really are a dear, Charles."

At least there was that solace, he thought as he went down the narrow passage to his room. He had her affection. They were still, after some sad fashion, a couple with a charming child.

Waking, Matthew tunnelled his way out of the heap of blankets towards a bright finger of morning light and the distant steady roar of traffic. Sitting up and rubbing sleep from his eyes, he stared with dismay at the clock. Nine already. Only two hours left. Panic seized him. Pulling on his dressing-gown and thrusting his feet into cold slippers, he almost forgot to brush his teeth and comb his hair—she minded like anything about that— before making a breathless dash along the passage to his mother's room. The door was closed. He did their special code knock, two quick, one slow, and waited anxiously for a response. It was part of the excitement that he could never tell with certainty what

25

form it would take. He heard a rustle of bed-clothes, the clink of a cup being set down.

"In you come then, Prince Charming. Sleeping Beauty almost gave you up for lost."

Good. They were going to play games. Screwing up his face, he stamped into the room with a roar.

"Gracious, it's the monster from the black lagoon. Mercy! Mercy!" She pulled up the sheet and peered at him over the top with her eyes all merry and laughing like they used to be, only they were smudged with black underneath where her make-up had run. She had been crying again. For him? Because he was going away? Passionately, he wished it might be so.

"The monster has no mercy. Death to the princess!" He flung himself across the bed, to sprawl and grapple and hug and to press his nose into the warm sleep smell of her before he rolled over to lie curled in the crook of her arm, staring up at the drooping white arch of the canopy. It was the first moment he had felt completely happy. He savoured it, remembering how long it was going to have to last him.

"Can I have some tea? It's hard work being a monster."

"You should try being the victim. I was petrified."

"Bunk," he said, enchanted. "Were you really?"

"Scared to death, my darling." He saw that she was only teasing him as she laughed and sat up, smoothing down her tangled hair before she reached for the tea-tray. "Here. You can have the rest of mine. It's disgustingly weak. Even tea's on ration now."

"Still, it tastes very nice." He sipped at it delicately, as he had seen her do. "Where's Daddy? Is he up?"

"Hours ago. I expect he's having breakfast." Her eyes glanced away to the gilt and onyx clock. "You mustn't be late going down. Bates is coming for you at eleven."

"Only eighty-five minutes to go," he mourned. "I do wish Daddy had a job that didn't make you have to go away so much. I hate the Foreign Office."

"Selfish little beast." She poked him in the ribs. "You liked it in the war when he was in Intelligence."

"Except he never told me what he did."

"He couldn't, you silly boy. Intelligence is secret."

He surrendered one of his private fantasies to the cause of knowledge. "I suppose he was a kind of spy, then?"

"A spy? Your father?" She giggled. "Desk-work, my sweet. Safe, but not madly exciting. Better than being in a trench."

"Drenched in a trench." He had a sudden funny picture of his father jumping up and down in a ditch and waving an umbrella. Treacherously, he shared the picture with her and was rewarded by another shrill burst of laughter.

"Idiot. Not that sort of trench. What an idea. Still, it is rather funny." She sighed and ruffled his hair. "I shall miss you, my pet. You make me laugh so much."

He sprang at the opportunity, nuzzling against her. "Why don't you come with me to Gracedew, then? I've got no end of jokes. And they always have masses of butter there—"

"Stop it." She took a cigarette from the packet by the bed and lit it to blow out a thin stream of smoke. "You know I can't. I'm not going to go over all that again. You'll have a lovely time. You know you will. Think of all the boys who haven't got a Gracedew."

"Lucky them." He turned his head away. Her hand forced itself under his chin and twisted his head round until he faced her.

"If you only knew how horrid you look when you're being disagreeable."

"I'm not. I just don't like the smoke."

She was remorseless. "I expect that's the face you put on when poor old Cousin Jack has a cigar. Why do you have to be so difficult? You know how I'm always explaining the importance of being polite and helpful. They won't like you if you don't behave well."

He looked down at the pale tea. "I am polite. I always am. And I do try."

"Good." She stubbed out the cigarette and gave him a quick hug. "That's my boy." Glimpsing herself in the dressing-table mirror, she wailed and screened her face with her hands. "God, what an old fright I look. Mascara everywhere. You should have told me. Pull the curtains, darling. I don't want the whole square peering in."

He swished the pink flowered folds shut with a tug at the

tasselled cord and lounged back on the bed to watch with fascination as she fretted and dabbled among the little tortoiseshell pots of creams and powders. It was better than any play to see the creation of his mother's daytime face.

"I thought I heard you playing the piano last night."

"You probably did." Her hands massaged pink cream into her pale cheeks. "And did you think you heard anything else?"

"No." She sounded anxious. "Why, Mummy?"

"Questions, questions."

"Were you talking about me?"

"Perhaps." She smiled at him. "Come here, Master Curiosity. Let's make you look beautiful."

"You're trying to put me off."

Her smile widened. "But of course."

He could not make up his mind whether his chief feeling was of pleasure or embarrassment as he stood stiffly beside her, blinking as her cool fingers dabbed at his eyelids and swept across his cheeks with an arsenal of miniature sponges and brushes. "I'm enjoying this," she said. "There you are. Finished."

"Does it look nice?"

"Nice?" She leaned back to survey him. "You're ravishing. Good thing you weren't a girl. You'd have taken all the compliments from me, you little wretch."

"Rubbish. Nobody could be as beautiful as you." He bent to peer at an unrecognizable reflection. She had made his eyes look huge, like butterfly wings, and his mouth was red and swollen and peculiar. There was white powder all over his cheeks. He wriggled his tongue out of the corner of his mouth to lick at it. Scented. Not very nice. He felt sorry for the poor ladies like his mother who had to smear all this stuff on and wear it for a whole day. They probably couldn't even remember what their real faces looked like.

She prodded him. "Aren't you going to say anything?"

"I think it suits you better," he said carefully. "But it's very interesting. I don't look much like Daddy, do I?"

"What, with that face? Certainly not." She returned to her cream pots.

"No," he persisted. "I meant that I don't really look like him anyway."

28

"Of course you don't, darling. You're Mummy's boy. Clitheroe to the tips of your fingers. Go and rub it off now. You'll catch it from Daddy if he sees you wearing eyeshadow."

He was preparing to point out that it had not been his idea when there was a soft knock at the door.

"Morning post, Madam."

She jumped up, almost knocking him over. "Come in, Elsie. I'm perfectly decent."

The pretty new maid came in with the letters on a silver plate. She looked, unsurprisingly, a bit startled when she saw him. He stared back at her, daring her to laugh. Instead, to his relief, she gave a little nod and a smile.

"Morning, Master Matthew. Off on holiday today? Your father's waiting downstairs."

"Okay, I suppose I'd better—" He looked towards his mother, confident of being held back for a little longer, but she was examining the letters with a frowning worried look. A fat cream envelope was plucked out. The rest scattered where they fell as she squeezed and turned the envelope, feeling the inside of it. She looked ugly when she was upset.

"The little bas—oh, not you, my love," as she saw him staring. "Not you. Do go away, Elsie. There's no need to stand gaping like a frog."

The girl turned very red. She did look a little like a frog with her mouth open. His mother could be awfully cruel when she wasn't thinking.

"Sorry, Madam. I was just wondering if there was something I could do. You look as if you've had a bit of a turn."

"I told you to go. It's nothing. I'm perfectly all right. Matthew, do go and get dressed. I can't spend the whole morning playing silly games. Hurry up."

She didn't want him there. She was bored with him. Her stupid letter interested her more. He could see that she was dying to open it. He didn't care. He'd show her.

"I was just going anyway, as a matter of fact." He thrust out his hand at her. "I'll say good-bye now, shall I?"

She looked down at him blankly. "Now? Oh, for heaven's sake don't start sulking again. I'm not in the mood for it. Go and get your clothes on and have breakfast."

29

As if he was a stranger. Furious and desolate, he stalked out behind the maid.

"Your mother's got a funny temper. You don't need to take on so," she whispered in the passage. "Cheer up now. Give us a smile."

She was kind, but he wanted no comforting. There was no dignity in tears.

"My mother and I understand each other perfectly," he said. "There's nothing to make a fuss about." Turning his back on her pretty puzzled face, he marched down the blue carpeted stretch to his room and shut the door behind him.

She did not even come down to see him off. His luggage had already been stowed into the big grey Daimler. Mr Bates was waiting, his hands on the wheel. Matthew looked past his father into the clean silence of the house, willing her to come down the stairs.

"Don't you want to run up and say good-bye, old chap? She'll be awfully hurt."

He stiffened. "I've said it already."

"Probably having one of her migraines."

His father looked miserable this morning. He had hardly said a word at breakfast. Forgetful of codes, Matthew reached up his arms to hug him. "I do hope you have a lovely time in Paris. Will you send me postcards?"

"Oh, dear old fellow, of course I will. Every week. What do you want? The Eiffel Tower?"

Hugs were nicer than handshakes. He rubbed his face against the rough tweed jacket which his father always wore when he was staying at home for the day. "I don't mind. Honestly. Anything."

"You might like something to be going along with." He was pushed gently away and presented with two fists. "Guess which."

He looked for a glint between the fingers. "Left."

"Sharp fellow." The coin was deftly slipped into his breast pocket. "You behave yourself now. Remember that your cousins aren't as young as they were. No monkeying about. Try to make yourself a bit useful, eh?"

Bates put his small rosy face out of the window. "Don't you

worry about the young gentleman, sir." He gave Matthew a slow wink. "We'll keep him up to the mark. Up to scrub the floors at six, Master Matthew, or you'll catch it."

"That's the idea," his father said in a jolly voice. "You keep his nose to the grindstone. Gruel for breakfast and cold toast for tea. In you hop, young Craven. You're keeping poor Bates waiting and it's a long drive. Give them our love."

"I will." He climbed reluctantly into the back of the car. The door slammed shut. He turned round to stare out of the back window as Chester Square fell behind them. His father had climbed the front steps to stand stiffly waving, a small clockwork soldier under the pluming trees. For a horrified moment, Matthew saw a stranger, a little red-faced man whose military manner was ever so slightly ridiculous. He dug his nails into his palms, punishing himself for the treacherous thought. Fathers should be heroes. His closest schoolfriends were always swanking about what Major Jardine and Captain Jarvis had done in the war, about their brilliance in shooting parties, their munificent tips for school. He knew he ought to be like them. Only he was not. He never had been. It was the only sure knowledge of himself that he possessed, that he was somehow, and not altogether comfortably, different. Not so nice. Jarvis and Jardine never seemed to have mean black thoughts about their homes or their parents.

He should have gone up the stairs to say good-bye. She was probably sitting there now, waiting for him. Tears rose in a sudden gulp from his throat. He stuffed a handkerchief into his mouth and bit on it.

"What did your dad give you then?" Bates inquired after a quick glance at the back seat. "A bob?"

He felt the heavy coin in his pocket. "Half a crown."

Bates whistled. "Some of us have all the luck. Don't you go spending it on sweeties."

"I won't. I'm going to save it up."

"Anything particular in mind?"

Running-away money, he thought. "Not really."

"What about those cars you used to collect?" He peered in the driving-mirror at the boy's bent head. "I'm forgetting how grown-up you are. Don't suppose you've time for that kind of thing now you're such a big lad.''

"Only nine.'' He wished Bates would stop making him take the handkerchief out. It was almost impossible to suppress the sobs without it.

"Go on,'' Bates said to his mortification. "Do you good to have a bit of a cry. Not worth it, though. I wouldn't want to go to Paris if I was you. Horrible place. Never stops raining and not a decent plate of chips for any price you like to pay. Nothing to do but go up the Eiffel Tower or sit on a batty-much listening to all those Frenchies gabbling away at each other.''

"I wouldn't have minded any of that.''

"You would and all. You'd have been round the twist after two days. You're best off coming to Gracedew, Mattie. Mrs Bates made a special batch of her toffees for you. And there's a new family over at Chillingston. Treshams. They've got a little girl about your age. Someone to play with.''

"I don't much care for playing with girls.'' Remembering his promise about the hateful Remington, Matthew leant forward.

"There's a boy called Charles Remington who's at school with me. I don't suppose you know if he's in Nottinghamshire this holiday?''

"Remington?'' Bates tapped the side of his nose, a habit which he had caught from Cousin Jack. "Knaresfield Hall? The place with all those horrible stuffed bison sticking their heads through the walls? They went off to the Riviera yesterday. Cook told me. She's a friend of the housekeeper. You haven't met Cook yet, have you? Terrible woman, she is. Puts the fear of God in me just to look at her. Voice like a sergeant and a temper to match it. Your Cousin Lucilla's scared pink by her. As for her cooking, well, I haven't the words to describe it. A pig wouldn't touch the meals she serves up, not if he hadn't seen food for a week. This Remington lad's a friend of yours, is he?''

"Well, not exactly. I'm quite glad he's away.''

"Still, you could do with a few friends about the place.''

"Not ones like Remington.'' He sank back into the rich sickly smell of leather and petrol. Duty had been done. He could truthfully say that he had tried. The fantastically crenellated and green leaded roofs of Park Lane soared above him. Squinting up through the back window, he could turn London into a city of castles and shut out the grey ugliness of the streets, the weed-hung shells of bombed houses. It was better this way. He started to weave a story about a boy who did brilliant cat-burglaries from his roof-top hideout and was never caught. The Demon of Mayfair was what the police called him, and he was never discovered. He began to feel a little more cheerful.

"I'll tell you a story if you like."

Bates chuckled. "You will, will you? Don't frighten me into missing the turning like you did last time."

Matthew smiled. "I'll try."

2

"Nearly home, Mattie. Time to wake up."

"I wasn't asleep. Just because I had my eyes closed."

The car was sliding out of the high green cathedral of Parson's Woods. Below, snug as a little old woman asleep in the hollow of the hill, lay Gracedew village.

"Let's beat the record," Matthew said. "Bet you can't get to Church Corner in two minutes. I'll time you."

"She weren't built for a race-track, you know. Still—see what we can do and don't you go telling Mr Craven."

The sweet smell of bleached grass blew in as Matthew wound down the window and held his face up to the rush of air. "I do *love* going fast."

The familiar landmarks flashed across his eyes, quick as telegraph posts, Rectory, Cartwright's farm, the apple-cheeked walls of Craven Cottages, the smooth plain of the cricket pitch, bringing them in sight of the church, beached high like an old grey ship among the tidy gravestones.

"Ten seconds under by my watch," Bates said, slowing down. "That do you?"

"Lovely."

"Aye. She's not bad, for her age. Still, best let her cool down a bit."

Matthew looked up at the church as the engine sank to a purr. All those Sundays to come, trapped in the corner of the pew as Mr Flower climbed the steps of the great tiered pulpit to tell them how to save their sinning souls in his brisk jolly voice, as if it was like scoring goals in a football match. Afterwards, at lunch, there would be questions, to make sure he had taken it all in. Matthew sighed. Still, he had Sir Thomas to keep him company.

Sir Thomas didn't think much of sermons. He preferred talking to Matthew.

Sir Thomas Dobell lived above the family pew on a great grey monument where he and his wife knelt above two curly tailed greyhounds. He had built Gracedew. It had looked quite different then. Matthew knew because his mother had taken him to see the drawing of it in the British Museum. It had been as big as Buckingham Palace, but much prettier with its windows like six-sided stars and its roof hedged in by toy-sized pyramids. Gracedew had been confiscated because of something wicked Sir Thomas had done. Matthew knew it could not have been anything very bad, for Sir Thomas' face was as kind and open as the morning sun. He should have had a fat jolly wife, not Venice, whose eyes were sly as a ferret's above the high chapel of her ruff. She never talked to him. She pretended to be too busy praying.

"Do you know what happened to Sir Thomas Dobell, Bates?"

"The bloke who built the house? They hung him. Or was he burned?"

Appalled, Matthew leaned forward. "They couldn't have done that. Not to Thomas."

"Didn't take much to get you killed in those days," Bates said. "Pity they didn't get his wife. She was a right bit of mischief, from what I've heard. I reckon old Thomas was better off dead in the long run."

"Why?"

"Allus asking questions. Why this, why that. Because she was wicked, that's why. And don't you go asking me what she did or your cousin'll be having my guts for garters."

"I like wicked women," Matthew said. "Like Jezebel, you know. She was immensely wicked."

"Was she now?" He pressed the accelerator. "Put your jacket on and straighten up now, Mattie. We'll be there in a minute."

"I know. I'm ready." He lay back with a sigh as Bates jumped out to open the tall black gates which hid the Cravens' house from curious eyes. Wired across the wrought-iron was the big white noticeboard which promised prosecution to all

35

trespassers. Pretty silly, really. Nobody ever came to look at Gracedew.

Up the twisting drive, dark as winter below the walls of yew and laurel, with the shine of the lake glinting below them through the branches. The first tall chimney poked into sight and there, as they swung round the last bend, was Gracedew. He gazed up at the high row of chimneys, the intricate forest of pepperpot turrets erected by Cousin Jack's grand-father, the long veiled windows standing like mourners along the rosy walls. Giant Despair's castle in winter, all whispers, sighs and echoes, on a summer evening it looked more like a fairytale palace that had been enchanted into sleep. Nothing had changed, he thought, as the car drew to a halt before the pillared entrance. Nothing ever would. It was like the bit at the end of prayers. As it was now, so it ever would be. A world without end. He took some pleasure in the thought. Gracedew was, as much as any-where had been, his home.

"Matthew dear!" Cousin Lucilla stood above them on the porch steps, lank and smiling in a sunhat and a dress of pink flowered cotton, awkwardly clasping a pair of garden shears and a vast wicker basket of roses. "I thought I heard the car. How lovely to see you—and how you have grown! Gracious!" It seemed from her tone that growing was not altogether a desirable thing. "Well, come and let me kiss you, child."

Her thin bosom was all buttons and moth-ball smells. Her brooch pricked at his cheeks. He was grateful to be briskly released; Cousin Lucilla never wasted time on what she termed gush. "Tea-time, then," she said. "It's all ready. A good journey, was it, Bates?"

"Nothing to complain of, thank you, Madam." Matthew noticed with interest that he had a specially grand voice which he put on when talking to Cousin Lucilla. "The Daimler's running very nicely at the moment. No more of that engine trouble we were having last month."

"Oh, good. Splendid," she said with a vague smile which cut off the opportunity for discussing mechanisms. Lucilla had never reconciled herself to the noise and smell of motor-cars. Carriages had been so much more congenial to the proper pace of life.

Tea was set out in the long dark hall where Craven coats-of-

36

arms gleamed between leering stags' heads on the walls of varnished oak. A yellow cake occupied the centre of the table, vast, pale and unappetizing as custard junket. Matthew blanched as his cousin cut a generous slice.

"It's one of our new cook's special Victoria sponges. She made it specially for you, my dear. Be a good boy and have some. She'll be so pleased."

"Do I have to?"

"Don't be tiresome, Matthew. Eat what's put in front of you."

Conscious of her stern and anxious gaze, he took a small mouthful.

"Delicious."

Cousin Lucilla smiled. "Perhaps if you ask her very nicely, she'll make you another one."

Cousin Jack came in late as always, heralded by the slow familiar shuffle of carpet slippers up the back passages from where he had been closeted with his most prized possession, a television, the only one in the village. A small red-haired man, his principal fascination to Matthew's eyes lay in the number of whiskers which sprouted from his ears and nostrils. He was wrapped from head to toe in a crimson travelling rug, a daily attire which he warmly recommended to guests who were brash enough to complain of Gracedew's lack of heating. Halfway between door and tea-table, he stopped, peering forward into the gloom.

"I thought I'd get—" Frowning, he tried again. "I rather thought I'd get—"

"Tea, dear!" Lucilla cried. "Do have it in here with us. You've been watching that machine all afternoon. Little Matthew's arrived. You remember Matthew. Stand up, child. He can't possibly see you in this light."

His voice grew querulous. "Matthews? I don't know a Matthews. What's he want?"

He thought about his mother's admonition. Remember to be polite and helpful. It matters.

"Hello, Cousin Jack. It's very kind of you to invite me here again."

The carpet slippers shuffled nearer. Matthew looked up into

the veined blue eyes, almost as blank as a blind man's. A flicker of interest briefly lit them.

"Of course. Little Matt. Well, well. School all right, then?"

"Thank you, sir. I got quite a good report."

"That's excellent. You hear that, Lucy? Bright little fellow." His head jerked when he spoke, as if he had a steel spring in his throat. "Parents all right, then?"

"Oh yes. They sent you their love."

"I hear they're off to Paris. Gallivanting."

"He knows that. Do sit down and stop fidgeting, Jack. You're making the boy nervous."

"Nonsense." He glared at her. "Don't nag me, Lucy. I'm not well. Heartburn."

"Rubbish," Lucilla said firmly. "You're perfectly well. I expect you had too much to eat for lunch. Have some cake. It's better than the last one."

"Can't that damned woman make anything else?" He sank into his chair and looked with disgust at the floury slab which Matthew was dutifully handing to him. "Filthy stuff. Take it away, Lucy. I'm not touching it."

"It's very good for you."

"Just because you've the constitution of an ox."

"Iron if you must, dear. The ox and I have nothing in common."

"Except that you're both too damned stubborn."

Matthew giggled nervously. It had the sound of a joke, but Cousin Lucilla's face had gone quite red.

"Do try not to be disagreeable, Jack. It's so unnecessary."

"Damned if I can see anything to be agreeable about." Pushing the plate away, he slumped down, head forward on his chest. "Not so much as a slice of bread and butter."

"I did explain that to you, my dear. We can't have butter at breakfast and tea as well. It does go rather quickly."

"I thought that the whole point of employing Mrs Fletcher was that she could arrange things like that."

"I did ask her," Lucilla murmured.

"You don't use the right approach. Force. That's what she needs to feel." And he brought his fist down on the table with such a thump that the teaspoons sprang from the saucers.

"Then I suggest you try using it. I can assure you it won't do the slightest bit of good. We'll just lose another cook." Lucilla pushed back her chair so hard that the legs shrieked in protest on the stone. "It's time for you to go upstairs, Matthew. You'll probably find Mrs Bates in the Green Bathroom. Perhaps you'd like to come down to the library at six o'clock."

All as it was, is now and ever shall be. Boring, but somehow comfortable. Even the bickering at meals was just as it had always been. Groping his way up the dark stairs, Matthew wondered why it was that their quarrelling was less frightening than the more restrained hostilities of Chester Square. Perhaps because it had become a habit, a way of life, with his cousins. He had often seen Cousin Lucilla looking quite angry, but the old man's grumbling never made her sad. The rage was all in the words. There was no larger threat, no sense of something worse and unspoken behind what was being said. That was the difference.

Perhaps Paris would make it all right again.

The bath, a vast enamel tub on claw feet, breathed warm swirls of steam over the plateau of green linoleum. Mrs Bates was pulling the curtains shut when he came in, presenting him with the opportunity to creep up and take her by surprise with a tug at the dangling ribbons of her apron.

"Got you!"

She gave a most gratifying shriek before she turned to shake and then hug him. "Little devil. Want me to have a heart attack, do you? Well now." She looked him up and down with admiring eyes. "You've grown and all. Blest if you aren't taller than me. What do they give you at that school of yours—steaks for breakfast?"

"Not likely. It's usually bread and margarine."

"No harm in that." Her little black eyes twinkled at him with a hint of mockery. "Quite the young gentleman. Too old to be bathed, I suppose."

"Nobody washes us at school—don't!" he protested as Mrs Bates shot out an arm to seize his shoulder. "That hurts."

"Does it now?" She peered behind his ears. "I thought as much. These fine places. It's all eddication and no hygiene. Black as a tar brush. I shouldn't wonder if you haven't got nits as well.

39

Doesn't your ma give you a scrub when you get home?''

It would never have occurred to his mother to interest herself in his washing arrangements, nor had it ever occurred to him that she should. She wasn't that kind of mother. "She didn't have time," he said, loyally.

Mrs Bates sniffed. "Doesn't like chipping her nail varnish, I suppose. Into that bath now and no moaning. We'll have you as clean as a whistle before you go down."

Dutifully, Matthew peeled his clothes off and stepped into the scalding water to receive her fierce ministrations. He choked and spat as she scrubbed the waxy carbolic soap into his mouth and ears and eyes before pummelling him with the flannel until he ached in every limb. Reduced to a state of red rawness, he appeared to satisfy her.

"You'll pass for clean," she said. "Out you get—on the mat, not the floor. I'm not mopping up after you, my boy, not with the aches and pains I've got. Towel. Quick about it now. Pyjamas." Her duty done, she grinned at him. "Reckon I'd make a good drill sergeant."

"Reckon you're right," he said, imitating her rough accent. Secure in the knowledge that it was near to six o'clock, he could risk the expected inquiries after her health. Her smile widened in anticipation of the saga to be unfolded. Health was the subject nearest to her heart.

"Terrible, I've been, Mattie. Terrible sick. Your cousin, he thinks I can go springing up and down the stairs like an antelope and me with corns the size of pincushions on my toes. It's the mileage, sir, I keep telling him. I'm no spring chicken, you know, and we don't make old bones in our family. My sister Ruby was dead at forty-two and I shouldn't wonder if I don't go the same way."

"Well, you'll just have to try not to," Matthew said. "I wouldn't like to come and live at Gracedew if you and Mr Bates weren't here."

She squeezed him in her arms. "Bless the boy, I'm not dead yet. Don't go worriting yourself. You just put in a lift and I'll be right as rain for a score of years. There's the rheumatics, of course. I tell you, Mattie, that cottage of ours is worse than living in a bog-marsh come winter. I said to John last Christmas he didn't need for me to go washing his shirts. All he had to do was to hang them on the end of the bed and they'd wash themselves, there's that much wet in the place—"

The clock chimed salvation. "Well, I suppose I'd better go down," he said. "I'd like to stay."

"Oh, there's a few nights yet for chatting," she said. "A month, isn't it?"

"I think so."

A month. He trod out the stretch of days and nights on the threadbare brown carpet. Given the physical form of four flights of stairs, the time seemed quite unbearably long.

Having no children of their own—Jack Craven had not married until his mid-forties, by which time it seemed to him that a good housekeeper was of more value than a good breeder—the Cravens had never seen the need to alter the pattern which had been established on Matthew's first summer visit of four years ago at a time when Gracedew was the logical alternative to Chester Square, a safe harbour from the nightly terror of the air raids. Dimly conscious now that Charles Craven's marriage was going through a difficult phase—how, they wondered to each other, could it ever have been otherwise with a wife like Elizabeth Clitheroe?—they brought a kindly sense of duty to the preservation of routine. In habit, they felt, lay security. The child must be made to feel that here, at least, nothing had changed.

And so, when Matthew came into the library, he was settled into a corner of the shabby chintz sofa while Lucilla put on her spectacles and started to read a chapter of *David Copperfield*, just as she had done the year before. He would have preferred, but did not dare to suggest, the chance to read it peacefully to himself. Lucilla's flat cheerful voice, so well suited to the opening of church fêtes, robbed the characters of humour and eccentricity. The low insistent whine of Mrs Gummidge became a dull catalogue of complaints which provoked a yawn, hurriedly concealed as a cough. Nor was the narrative helped to flow by his cousin's conscientious pause at the end of each paragraph to question him on the more difficult words. Her own vocabulary was quite surprisingly limited; from behind *The Times*, Cousin

Jack roused himself to mock and correct her tentative definitions. Inconceivable that she could have reached the age of sixty-three without knowing the difference between infer and imply! Humbly, she bowed to the superior knowledge of the male. If Jack did not always know best, it was still prudent to seem to think so.

At half-past six, the book was closed and put away. The newspaper was folded and squeezed into the rack as Cousin Jack prepared to take his turn.

"Well then, let's see the proof of that report of yours," he said. "It didn't seem to show up in your reading. I knew every word in that book at your age. Every word."

"Now Jack, I'm sure you were older than Matthew," Lucilla murmured diffidently.

"Every word," he repeated, ignoring her. "How about arithmetic? You need a good head for that if you're ever going to run Gracedew. What's seventy-three times sixty-five, hey? Quick now. No finger counting."

Helplessly, Matthew stared at the carpet, wishing himself buried beneath it. "I don't know. Four hundred and fifty?"

"Christ in all his glory, don't they teach you anything?" the old man roared. "Try again. What's, let's see, seventeen times forty-two?"

High on the wall above Cousin Jack's head, Isabella Mary Craven glared down on her great-great nephew. Her mouth was thin as a knife. Her eyes were like little grey pebbles in her pinched white face. "Ignorant little boy," she said. "Imagine not knowing the answer to that at your age. You're a disgrace to the family."

"I—don't know."

Not until seven o'clock was Lucilla able to lay down her tapestry and suggest it was time for Matthew to go to bed.

Milk and biscuits had been set out in the pantry. He ate slowly, putting off bed-time while Cousin Lucilla watched him with one eye on the clock in the kitchen.

"If only he'd tested my Latin. I could have done anything about the battlefields of Gaul."

"I'm sure you could, dear. You mustn't worry. He doesn't

mean to sound cross. It's only because he's so fond of you. He
wants you to do well.''

"Yes."

"Drink your milk up, Matthew. I don't want to be here all
night.''

"Sorry, Cousin Lucilla.''

Slowly, he followed her down the black cold passage with the
wind whistling behind their backs, up the carved staircase where
moonlight glittered and heavy portraits menaced him with their
staring eyes, across the threadbare landing where dustsheets
masked a row of marble busts. He pulled at his cousin's hand.

"Am I in the same room as last year?''

"It's the room you're always in.''

"Couldn't I be in another one? Please.'' Her uncomprehend-
ing stare forced him to explain. "Cookie told me last summer
about the housemaid who hung herself in there. Grace Randall.''

Cousin Lucilla frowned. "Cookie was very naughty to tell
you such a silly story. I dare say she made it up. She was very
fond of telling what Bates likes to call Nanny-goats. I'm not at
all sorry she left us.''

"But was there someone called Grace Randall?''

"Perhaps. There were an awful lot of servants here. There may
have been one called Grace. Now do come along, Matthew.''

They climbed the last twisting flight of stairs. She opened the
door to the room where—he knew it was true, however much
she pretended not to know about it—that woman had hung
herself.

"There's a bottle in the bed, so you'll be nice and snug. Say
your prayers now like a good boy.''

He spun them out as long as he dared, adding elaborate
blessings for the sheep, the cows, the dogs, the postman—

"That's enough, Matthew. You can't bless everyone. Into
bed with you.''

The bottle was a stone one, cold as a dead man's leg under the
heavy sheets. He curled away from it, burying his face in the
pillow. "Please, can I have the light on? Please, Cousin Lucilla.
Just this once.''

She looked at him in vague astonishment. "You don't have a
light at school, surely?''

"Not exactly." Didn't she understand how little it mattered when Jarvis and Jardine were only a stretched arm's distance away on either side of him?

"Well then," she said and shut the door.

Silence swelled up behind her and breathed at him of invisible horrors. He turned his face to the wall and stared at the dark knots of paper roses, trying not to see the gnarled faces of witches in the pleasant garlands, the grasping fingers in the twining stems. He couldn't turn back again, not with the thought of her hanging there, staring at him.

Fearfully, he counted the clear hour strokes from the clock-tower. Only eleven. He was still safe. No terrible thing could happen if he was asleep before midnight. Softly, he started to whisper at the watchful darkness, willing it free of terror:

"Get behind me, Satan. Protect me, dear God, from all wicked things of the night. Matthew, Mark, Luke and John, bless the bed that I lie on and please don't let me want to go to the lavatory and have to go across the landing after twelve o'clock. Dear God, please, I'll do anything, only let me go to sleep—"

Unquestionably, the nights were the worst part of it. The long days presented only the problem of how to survive tedium with the appearance of enjoyment.

It wasn't easy.

A sleepless night did not prevent him from being first up, loitering, hands in pockets, at the side of the breakfast table, keenly aware of the distant scent of smoking sausages. Patience was the virtue which he knew he must practise; hunger was a nagging void unsatisfied by the stale biscuit crumbs shaken out of his bedside tin. The creamy curls of butter glistened and melted in the morning sun. One hand edged towards the toast rack and was snatched back as the clock struck nine and the breakfast gong imperiously sounded.

"Gracious, you are an early bird!" Cousin Lucilla came in and moved with brisk steps to the sideboard. Matthew moved with her. The silver-lidded dish was unveiled, to reveal four small sausages laid in a neat row. Three into four? He had been left out.

"Never mind, dear. There's plenty of porridge. You

44

wouldn't like poor Cousin Jack to find his breakfast all gone, would you?"

Meekly resentful, he supposed not. It was harder to restrain his anguish at the sight of the sausages being popped, with every appearance of enjoyment, between Cousin Jack's whiskery lips.

While no particular order was imposed upon his days other than his required presence, clean, neat and as silent as possible, at meals, there was such a catalogue of forbidden pleasures as to severely test his capacity for entertaining himself. No climbing of trees, no playing near the lake, no exploring of the roof. No mixing with the village children, no visits to the kitchen, no bringing muddy feet into the house. No certainty of punishment attached to the breaking of the rules, but they were established with a firmness which was persuasive enough to make him see the wisdom of observing them.

He generally spent the mornings in the back yard, watching Bates washing down the Daimler or tinkering with its engine. If rain kept him inside, he retired to the top of the house where a large glass-fronted bookcase offered a wealth of Victorian children's literature. He was supposed to ask Cousin Lucilla to unlock it for him, but he had discovered on his last visit that the key was always hidden on top of the postbox in the hall and that its absence was never noticed. Armed with a pile of cloth-bound books with brightly gilded pictures on their covers, he could shut himself into his bedroom to study the fate of disobedient children, the rewards of the virtuous and the glory of the British Empire. Charlotte Yonge and Rudyard Kipling, Arthur Mee and Andrew Lang, E. Nesbitt and Mrs Molesworth; these were the authors who led him into a private world where grown-ups became shadowy and insignificant. They were his friends.

The chief rule of the afternoons was that they must be spent outside, for that was healthy. He was usually asked to help Cousin Lucilla to weed the borders laid out by Isabella Mary Craven in the days when there were twelve gardeners on hand to carry out her instructions. Now, there was only Mr Bates. It was, as Cousin Lucilla frequently said, all very well to plan gardens. It was the upkeep of the plan which was wearing her down.

Released from duty, Matthew was free to play outside until

tea-time. Slowly scuffing his toes along the gravelled paths in the dank shade of the rhododendrons and laurels, he watched the sun stretch out the gold-armed hours across the sun-dial and waited for the great house-clock to summon him into the house.

He marked the passage of time by the appearance of the Paris postcards. There was the one of the Eiffel Tower from his mother in her beautiful italic writing to say that she missed him dreadfully and did hope that he was being good and helpful to dear Lucilla and Jack, to whom she sent her fondest love. His father, always the more reliable in correspondence, followed a busy street in Montmartre with Notre-Dame, both attended by a wealth of useful information. Matthew learned the height of the Eiffel Tower, the date of the rebuilding of Paris, the history of the Arc de Triomphe. He would have preferred to know whether they had eaten frogs or snails and what sort of car they went about in.

There were no more postcards after the second week, and no explanations. His cousins said only that the posts were very bad. He was too proud to show that he minded what he suspected to be the truth, that his parents had forgotten about him. They were probably very busy.

One night towards the end of the third week of his visit, there was a storm. Peering fearfully over the sheets, Matthew saw the curtains blow apart in a gust of wind. Lightning spat green fingers across the room as the rain lashed in through the open window. He saw—and for the rest of his life he was to swear that it had been no childish dream—the shape of a woman, dressed in a long black pinafore, suspended from the iron hook once intended for a lantern. Her feet were long and bare and white, and they were less than an arm's length away from his pillow. Screaming, he squeezed himself back against the wall, as far away from the thing as he could get. Nobody came. And as he continued to scream in a high, piercing wail of terror, he understood that nobody would. His cousins' room was on the floor below at the other end of the house. Nobody was there to hear him.

When, at last, morning came to fill the room with rain-washed light and the garden with the soft summer crooling of pigeons, it was too late for comfort. He had already made up his mind to run away. Anything would be better than to stay and endure another such night. With three half-crowns in his pocket, the world beyond the fences of Gracedew was there for the enjoying.

It was the most casual of escapes, made without the slightest idea of his destination or of how far his savings would take him. He left an explanatory note in the hall to say that he would not be coming back but they were not to worry about him, before he set off across the park in the throbbing heat of afternoon.

The fields were high in buttercups and clover, the air buzzed with the sound of insects and contented bees. The park was a good deal larger than he had imagined and his legs soon began to ache. Safely out of the sight of the house windows, he dropped from a trot to a leisurely amble which carried him to the western edge of the estate. A low wooden fence was all that stood between him and freedom. Beyond, lay the rough river meadows and the railway line; behind him, a certain world and the assurance of tea and a bed, however beset by phantoms. With one foot on the lowest bar of the fence, Matthew weighed his choices.

Far away, muffled in the depths of the hill, came the shriek of an approaching train, bringing to his mind the brilliant idea that if he could get to the track in time to be seen, the driver would stop and take him aboard. Hurriedly, he scrambled over the fence and set off at a breathless run over the hillocky turf towards the distant row of arches supporting the track before it swung out across the Trent. He was still running when the goods train burst into sight and thundered past him, shaking the ground into a roar of life before it raced away to the flat fields on the far side of the river with a low wail and a soft musical click of wheels sinking down into silence. Staring after it, Matthew watched the trail of smoke fade slowly away. Ahead of him, the fields stretched out, flat, vast, a landscape without horizons. It was hopeless. He would never get away. He had nowhere to go. There was nothing for it but to swallow his pride and return. Tears of rage salted his throat as he turned in the direction of the house.

"Hi-ya! You down there!"

The call seemed to be coming from somewhere up in the trees.

Astonishment opened his mouth to a gape as he lifted his head to peer up the wooded slopes.

Behind the trees, rearing out of the side of the hill, stood a castle of blackened brick, its turrets and battlements webbed in ivy, hanging like a giant bird of prey over the mouth of the railway tunnel. Perched on the battlements with legs swinging nonchalantly over a forty-foot drop was a girl with bright fair hair blowing about her face in the wind, a Rapunzel of the railway tracks. He was roused from stupor by the thump of a pebble close to his feet.

"Come up here, can't you? Are you scared of heights?" The sound of an oncoming train engulfed her yell of mockery. He watched the great clock-front of the engine burst like a cannonball from the black maw, its funnel driving up a jet of steam to wreathe the castle in vapour. Black-faced and spluttering, the girl came back to his sight, one hand imperiously raised to summon him.

"How do I get there?"

"Climb, stupid."

Used from school to obeying orders without question, he plodded towards the foot of the hill and started up its side. The hard clay broke to dust-shoals under his shoes; the long, loose-rooted weeds came away in his hands as he grasped at them. Painfully, he crawled on, wincing as the straggling briars ripped at his clutching hands. If it had not been a girl up there, vaunting her superiority, he would have given up and taken the long slide back to safety. But there she sat, giggling at him. Manliness must be displayed. Turning his eyes from a sick glance at the plunge down to the tracks, he scrambled on.

Close-to, the castle turned out to be a sham, a façade plastered on to the side of the hill. Behind the soaring battlements, there was little more than a foot drop to the reddish ground. The fairy princess was also disappointingly ordinary. She was almost ugly. Large freckles specked her round face with brown and when she smiled, he saw the glint of a brace on her front teeth.

"You took your time." She turned to look at where he stood, cautious and fearful, on the hill behind the battlements. "Scared, are you?" Her brown sandals swung casually over the void.

48

"Of course I'm not."

"Well then?"

With the taste of panic at the back of his throat, he climbed on to the parapet and, eyes tightly shut, swung his legs out to join hers.

"Nothing to it."

"Swank," she said promptly. "You're scared stiff, and you're not much of a climber, either." A sudden grin split her face like a cut melon. "I'm Alice. Actually, I came the easy way over the top of the hill, so you needn't look so miserable. You're not that bad, for a boy. Want an aniseed ball?"

"I wouldn't mind one."

Silence and the pleasant taste of aniseed rolling over the tongue bred a certain feeling of comradeship. He had begun to recover from his initial terror and to enjoy the adventure when she prodded him in the ribs.

"Have you got any money? There's a village down the side of the hill with a sweetshop and a lock for barges. We might buy some cornets. I've got a sixpence."

Matthew beamed. Here, at least, he could shine. "That's nothing. I've got three half-crowns. I'll buy you one."

"Attaboy," said Alice with a wide slow grin. "Why not ten, if you're so rich? Come on. I'll show you the way."

The sun lay on the rim of the hills when he reached home, bloated with ice-cream, full of satisfaction with his adventure. There were voices in the hall. With an abrupt plummeting of his spirits, Matthew remembered that there had been much talk at breakfast of visitors for tea. Somebody called Lady Livingston had invited herself and Sir Antony Makepeace was driving her over at four o'clock. Cousin Jack had been furious. He hated only one thing more than Gertrude Livingston, he had said, and that was her blasted poodle. Cousin Lucilla had murmured something about poor Gertrude being so lonely since her husband had died and how they really couldn't put her off again.

Visitors meant that he had to be extra clean and tidy. His eyes travelled down from his muddy knees to his earth-caked sandals. Well, he couldn't always be perfect. Taking courage from the thought of how Alice would manage such a situation, he marched into the hall.

"I changed my mind. Sorry I'm late."

Four pairs of eyes swivelled towards him. Poor anxious Lucilla, who had been picturing him drowned in the river or run down by a train, could hardly speak for shame. "Oh Matthew, how could you?" was all she could manage.

Lady Livingston, a big ruddy-faced woman whose stomach had been rumbling a demand to be fed for the past hour, advanced upon the culprit with a boom of disapproval. Seeing an angry battleship with guns all trained upon him—she was intimidatingly large—he dodged behind the tea-table. Her glare was very nearly as unnerving as Isabella Mary Craven's.

"Do you realize the worry you've caused to your cousins, young man? I'm sorry to see a boy with your good fortune in having such a lovely place to spend the holidays behaving in such an ungrateful, thoughtless way. I wonder if you know what would happen if you were in my charge?"

Matthew eyed the sharp faced little poodle trotting in her wake. He did not like Lady Livingston. Cousin Jack had been quite right. She was a nasty, fat, interfering woman and he wasn't going to be polite. "Of course I do," he said. "You'd put me in the kennels. Only you can't, because I'm not in your charge. And I certainly wouldn't want to be."

"Matthew dear!" Cousin Lucilla wailed, but Sir Antony Makepeace gave a little titter and waved about like a long grey reed.

"Well, he's certainly put you in your place, Gertrude. At least we can sit down and have some tea now the child's condescended to return. I'm sure we all need it. Lucilla dear, you look quite washed out. Sit down and let me pour you a cup. Jack?"

"Going to bed," Cousin Jack announced curtly. "Headache. So glad you were able to come over. Sorry you can't stay for drinks. Lucy, get on with the tea and tell Antony to stop dancing about and sit down. Matthew, stop cringing behind the table. The damned dog's not going to eat you."

Lady Livingston rearranged her face into an affectionate smile. "But you can't be thinking of deserting us when we came all this long way especially for the pleasure of seeing you, Jack dear. I'm longing to hear all your news."

"You have seen me and there isn't any news." He raised a hand in valediction. "Doctor's orders. Have a bit of our cook's sponge cake. It's rather good. Lucilla will give you some. As for you, young Matthew, you'll be hearing about this performance tomorrow. I'm not pleased. Not pleased at all. No."

Lucilla struggled to cover her dismay in smiles as he vanished with unhabitual speed. "Poor Jack. He has been most terribly ill."

"Looks pretty healthy to me," observed Sir Antony, waving away the proffered cake. "No thank you, my dear. Only at weddings. One has to exercise some restraint."

"I know I should," Lady Livingston sighed, "but I've lost so much weight since the rationing and I have to keep my strength up. I wonder if Pudsie might have a tiny piece? She loves a little treat, don't you, my dearest?"

"Oh, does she talk?" Sir Antony peered at the dog. "I had no idea."

"I'll hand round the tea," said Matthew, keen to escape the proximity of Pudsie's snapping jaws.

"You," Cousin Lucilla said with unexpected firmness, "will go upstairs, wash, and go to bed. Now."

Matthew knew his rights. "I haven't had my supper."

"Indeed you have not." Carefully Cousin Lucilla poured out the tea. "Sugar, Gertrude?"

"Thank you, my dear. Oh, you're absolutely right," Lady Livingston approved with a wag of her head. "It's the only way to teach them. He'll thank you for it later."

He would not. From the doorway, he took his revenge. "Actually, Cousin Jack isn't ill at all. He simply detests visitors."

Scurrying up the stairs, he had the satisfaction of hearing Lady Livingston choking on her second slice of cake. It was, he thought, less than she deserved.

He carried his indifference to bed with him like a talisman. It amazed him to think how such a punishment would have hurt him only a day before while now it mattered not at all. Loneliness was at an end, and the next morning he would be meeting Alice again, down by the railway line. Lying in bed, he re-lived the pleasures of the afternoon, the ice-creams on which he had licked his savings away, the bank at the side of the lock

51

where he had lain, watching the oily water slide up and down between the gates, listening while Alice told the most entrancingly awful jokes, the smiles of the lady in the sweet-shop as they had entered to spend his last half-crown on liquorice sticks candied pink and blue. Not once had his thoughts strayed to the postcards which had not come. And now, lying snugly in bed, the terrors of the previous night were no more than a shadow on his sleepy mind. For, according to Alice, all he had to do was to recite the Lord's Prayer backwards three times. "That settles them," she had said with the authority of one capable of beating down a hundred ghosts. "You'll see."

3

"You do keep yourself busy nowadays, dear," Cousin Lucilla said, not without relief; small boys were difficult to entertain.

He did not want to be entertained. He had all the entertainment he could wish for in his afternoons with Alice. She was a year younger than he, but she took from the start the role of leader, and Matthew was happy to be dominated. It was Alice who devised the plans of the day, who invented and undertook the dares, terrifying him by her courage. Where he thought, she acted. When he shook with alarm, Alice laughed and swaggered forward.

"Bet you don't dare strip naked in the vestry," Alice said, bright-eyed, bare arms flecked by leaflight under the tall beech trees.

"Bet you I do, then." He trembled at his audacity.

"All right. Tomorrow afternoon. Three o'clock."

She was there before him, sitting cross-legged and stark naked on a heap of clothes and sucking a gob-stopper. She was sleeker and fatter than he had imagined, astonishingly pink, the shade of someone who has just come out of a hot bath. Her round tummy stuck out in a way which struck him as so funny that he started to laugh.

"Sour grapes," Alice said, scratching her stomach with a look of great satisfaction. "That's better. Mosquito bites. Look at them, all round the middle. It's torture."

He squatted to peer at the row of red bumps which girdled her. Alice's skin smelt of grass and baby-powder. He sniffed at it appreciatively.

"That's enough, pop-eyes," she said sharply, pulling a grey aertex shirt across her lap. "Your turn now."

Slowly, he took off his jersey and socks and shoes, piling them neatly, a school habit. "What if Mr Flower comes in and catches us? What do we say?"

Alice's eyes glinted at him in the musty gloom. "That's the dare. Come on."

Obediently, he took off the rest of his things. Naked, he was embarrassed by her inquisitive stare. He would have liked an excuse to leave, but none came to mind. The curtained space was disagreeably hot; he could feel the back of his neck prickling. He felt silly, standing there with no clothes on with Alice staring at him.

"What are you looking at? I don't see what's so funny."

"Isn't your wee tiny!" She giggled. "It's like Piglet's tail. Come and let me look properly."

He crouched beside her, wriggling slightly as Alice's sharp fingers prodded and pinched. "That's not fair. The dare's over. We only had to take our clothes off. You didn't say anything about this."

"It's like squashing baby bananas," Alice observed, intent upon her exploration. "I'm glad I'm a girl. I'd hate to have something like that stuck between my legs. It must be awfully uncomfortable." She thrust out her legs like signpost arms. "You can feel my hole if you want. Only it's not so interesting."

Curious, he peered at the plump bulge of flesh with a long slit in it which curved up towards her tummy like a scythe. Alice giggled as he cautiously pressed a finger into the soft division.

"It tickles. That's where you're meant to put your wee. You can if you like. I don't mind." She lay back. It was clear from her expectant smile that she would mind more if he didn't. He wriggled his stalk of flesh against her for a time.

"Like this?" It was, he thought, a boring game.

"I think so." She shut her eyes. "It's meant to feel nice. Do you think it does?"

"Well, not particularly." He didn't want to hurt her feelings. "It doesn't feel nasty, anyway."

Alice lay with closed eyes for what seemed to be hours while he dutifully squeezed himself against her and did nine times tables to stop himself from going to sleep. "Well, that's that, then," she said at last, pulling her shirt over her head and sitting

54

up with a pleased expression. "We're lovers. You can put your shorts on now. Buck up or they'll catch us."

He found himself hurrying past the Dobell monument with unnecessary speed. It had only been a game, but he was not sure that he wanted to meet Sir Thomas' tranquil gaze just at that moment. Alice felt no such compunction.

"Gosh, she looks a bad-tempered old witch." Hands on hips, she squinted up at Venice Dobell. "I bet she was constipated when they did that. I always am. I have to have syrup of figs every morning. It makes me pretty bad-tempered, I can tell you."

"They used to live in our house."

Alice looked awed. "I didn't know it was as old as that. Have your family always been there?"

"Quite a time." He liked impressing Alice. "It's going to be mine one day. You can come and stay. Bring your family with you."

"Not likely," said Alice. "How big is it?"

He spread out his arms. "Gigantic. Bigger than a cathedral."

It took Alice a moment to recover from this information. "Pity," she said with a sniff. "I prefer little houses, myself."

"Well, well, and what seraphs are these loitering in church on a Saturday afternoon?"

Matthew jumped as though shot as he saw Mr Flower, the young vicar, emerging from behind the curtain of the bell-tower to sweep towards them.

"Do you think he heard?" Alice hissed.

"We were just looking at the monument, Mr Flower." He could feel his face becoming hot and red. "Did you know about Sir Thomas building Gracedew? It's awfully interesting."

"Oh, I know quite a bit about Thomas," Mr Flower said. "Great pity nothing's been written about him. Perhaps you ought to have a go when you're older. Fascinating character. I've never been able to make up my mind whether he was a sinner or a saint."

"Sinner," said Alice. "Sinners are more interesting."

The vicar rubbed his chin to hide a smile. "Still, it's not quite so easy to decide. We could say that it was wicked of him to use his wife's dowry to build the house. We could say that it was a wicked ambition to want to make such a big home for himself.''

"I know," Matthew interrupted. "Mummy showed me the picture of it. Was that why they killed him, for having a house as big as the Queen's?"

"I don't think the Queen minded that so very much," Mr Flower said. "Done the Elizabethans at school yet, Matthew?"

He shook his head. "We're on *The Road to Rome*. But unfortunately I'm still in Mesopotamia."

So then Mr Flower explained that Sir Thomas had been a Catholic and that it had been as bad as being a traitor not to be a Protestant in those days. And how he had been brave or wicked, depending on how you looked at it, to make patterns based on the Trinity all over Gracedew to show how proud he was of his faith. And how he had hidden two of his wife's cousins in the house, knowing they were Catholic priests, to save them from being caught by the Queen's spies.

"Brave," said Alice.

"I don't see what was wicked about it," said Matthew.

"Well, it certainly wasn't very wise," Mr Flower answered. "He was caught, you see, and then the house was taken away and poor Thomas died at the stake."

Matthew looked up at Thomas' kind smiling face. "It's all right," Thomas said. "It was very quick. I can't remember much about the pain now. Anyway, I didn't care much about living after they took my home away from me."

"What about her?" Alice inquired. "She looks wicked. I mean, really bad."

Mr Flower coughed. "Her wickedness was of a very different kind. I'm afraid poor Thomas' marriage was not a happy one." He bent down until his head was at their level. "Which reminds me to tell you both that it's not an awfully good idea to go scampering about in God's house with no clothes on. I wouldn't do it again if I were you."

Alice became tremendously interested in the buckles of her sandals. Matthew peeped through his fringe at the vicar's face. He didn't look very angry. The corners of his mouth were turned up.

"Lecture over," Mr Flower said briskly. "Off you go now. My regards to your cousins, Matthew."

"Yes, Mr Flower. Thank you, Mr Flower." Thankfully, they scuttled towards the door, Alice in the lead.

"What do you think he meant about their marriage?" Matthew asked, catching up with her at the lych-gate. Alice looked at him with scorn.

"Lovers, of course. She went off with other men. They don't teach you much at school, do they? She was an idolatress."

"Adulteress," Matthew said. "Actually. Can I come with you?"

"Come where?"

"Well, wherever it is you live. I've got an hour before tea."

She looked at him reflectively. "I'd cut along home, Matthew. They don't like strangers in our camp. Killings have been known to take place."

"Camp? You never said you were a gypsy."

"You didn't ask."

"I've never seen a gypsy camp. They wouldn't hurt me if I was with you."

Alice rolled her eyes. "Wouldn't they just? Gypsy Joe'ld tear out your liver and lights as soon as look at you. He's my uncle."

He looked at her wonderingly. "Are you sure? Holy Bible?"

"Strike me dead if I ever tell a lie," she said. "See you tomorrow—ninny."

Walking home, he wondered about the familiarity of the phrase, liver and lights. Wasn't that what the convict had said to Pip in *Great Expectations*, Alice's favourite book? And yet she had sworn. He could not doubt her. A gypsy girl. He was more than ever entranced by his new friend.

Lucilla, more worried by the dearth of news from Paris than Matthew could have supposed, decided that their small cousin needed some diversion to keep his mind from parental indifference. It was a pity that the Remington child was away. There were, however, the new neighbours at Chillingston to be appraised. Prudently, she issued the invitation before informing Jack.

"Very sensible idea, Lucy," he said when, in mildly defiant tones, she told him what she had done. "Good for the boy to meet someone his own age. Cheer him up."

But on the morning of the Treshams' visit, a sudden and troublesome cough prevented him from leaving his bed.

"Nothing more selfish than inflicting one's illnesses on strangers," he said when Lucilla returned from the breakfast table to harangue him on his duty. "Don't worry about me. I'm quite comfortable."

"You look it," she said, surveying the calm mound of blankets. "There's nothing wrong with you that a spoonful of Gees won't cure."

"Horrible stuff. You've no sympathy for people when they're ill."

"I'd have more sympathy for you if I didn't know you so well." From force of habit, she plumped up the pillows and straightened the covers. "Well, I dare say we'll manage without you, but it's very tiresome. They're perfectly nice people—didn't you have an Oliver Tresham at school with you?"

"Gresham," he ruminated. "Gresham's dead. Only fifty-eight. Drink. Pity. Nice chap, Gresham. Nothing to do with Tresham."

"Oh, go to sleep, you old trout," she said, not without affection.

He bounced up in bed as she went through the door. "Don't forget to show them the garden—and the flowers on the piano need changing. And you might tell Mrs Fletcher to send up a little more tea—"

"It's all right, dear. I'll remember." She went rather slowly down the stairs, wondering if all wives had the same moments of blank depression, and why it was that she always surrendered to Jack's caprices and criticisms. Habit, she supposed. It was always easier to concede. If he would only help her a little more, not fuss quite so much about everything being just so—well, he was probably right. Standards had to be kept up, the standards set by Isabella Mary Craven in the last century. She did sometimes feel he was a little unreasonable to expect her to maintain them with only the Bates couple and Mrs Fletcher to support her. Keeping Gracedew running smoothly was like captaining a royal yacht with a crew of three. Still, it was worth the struggle. She had never doubted that.

Matthew was lying on the library floor with his nose in a

book. He read more than was healthy for a child.

"Finish the page and then you can come and help me cut a few roses," she said. "It's much too nice a day to be spent inside."

His head remained bent. "Was there a postcard for me today?"

"Not today. Never mind."

"Oh, I don't mind," he said quickly, closing the book. "I just wondered. It doesn't matter."

She considered making some sympathetic remark and decided against it. His pride would be hurt. Best to let him think she was deceived by his indifference. "I've got a treat for you today," she said brightly. "There's a little girl coming to tea with her parents. Perhaps you'd like to play hide-and-seek with her in the garden if the weather stays fine?"

Matthew nodded glumly. Alice apart, he did not greatly relish the company of little girls. Brief experience had taught him that they were mean, vicious, and unforgivably treacherous. Catch them ever owning up or taking the blame when they could gain credit by dint of a few strategically timed tears. Besides which, visitors meant losing an afternoon down by the railway with Alice, and he had only three days left to go before the return to Chester Square for the last two weeks of the holidays. He realized, with surprise, that he was for the first time sorry to be leaving Gracedew.

"It's been an awfully nice visit," he volunteered. Cousin Lucilla seemed pleased, if startled.

"Has it, dear? I thought it must be so dull for you with stuffy old people like us."

"Well, you can't help being old," he said generously, and was dismayed to see his cousin's eyes brimming with tears.

"Hay-fever," she said, dabbing at her cheeks with a handkerchief never meant for use. "Wretched thing."

Grown-ups were nothing if not unpredictable. Why on earth should anyone as ancient as Cousin Lucilla mind about being thought old?

Colonel and Mrs Tresham were tall tweeded creatures who strode and bayed and looked as though they would be much more at home on a tennis-court than ranging among the uneasily disposed sofas and tables of the Gracedew library. Lucilla twisted her pearls as she eyed the large diamond spray so conspicuously pinned to Mrs Tresham's jacket lapel. Not used to the country, evidently. Still, they must be civilly treated. One had a duty to be friendly, and the new owners of Chillingston House could hardly be ignored. Neighbours were scarce and it was the nearest place of any size.

Lurking in the doorway with downcast head was their daughter, a furious-faced blonde child who appeared to have out-grown both her socks and the prettily smocked and ruffled dress which failed to conceal scarred and grubby knees. Lucilla looked down with silent sympathy at the corkscrew curls which owed nothing to nature, and at what appeared to be a painfully tight sash of sky-blue organza. She remembered the feeling of shame which accompanied such clothes.

"So this is dear little Alice. Come in, child. Don't be shy. Matthew's been so looking forward to meeting you."

Matthew stared. His Alice? His gypsy maid? This glaring poodle in frills? Behind her mother's back, she made a sudden face of indescribable hideousness at him. He was slightly reassured.

"I didn't—" he began, but Alice looked at him so ferociously that he swallowed the rest of the sentence.

Tea was an awkward and protracted meal, punctuated by many exclamations over the Victoria sponge, and the frequent replenishing of tea-cups. Alice and Matthew bent studiously over their plates. Mrs Tresham, who talked enough for all of them, explained that now her husband had retired from the army, he was hoping to run for Parliament. He had always been tremendously interested in politics, of course. Lucilla, who did not think politics were best discussed at tea, murmured faint interest. The Colonel heard his cue. Setting down his cup, he began to arrange the running of the country on sensible regimental lines. Mrs Tresham smiled her agreement. Lucilla wondered what she ought to offer them to drink after tea. They were bound to want whisky. That meant asking Jack for the key to the cellar, and he was sure to be difficult about it. Perhaps she could make a point of saying they drank only sherry.

"What does Alice like doing?" she asked as Colonel Tresham paused for breath.

"Oh, she's a real little bookworm, aren't you, darling?" her mother said complacently. "Tell Mrs Craven what you've been reading, darling."

Alice rolled her eyes. "Story of Moses and how he read out the ten commandments thou shalt not kill thou shalt not commit adultery thou—"

"That's enough, Miss," her father said. "I don't suppose Mrs Craven cares to hear about that kind of thing."

"Oh, please don't stop her," Lucilla said, fearful of a return to the merits of Conservatism. "You like the Old Testament best, do you, my dear?"

"I never seem to get tired of any of the Bible," Alice said, gazing at the Victoria sponge with an adenoidal expression of sanctity. "I can do Mary Magdalene if you like."

Matthew choked.

"Well, perhaps another day," Lucilla said, caught in the cold floodlight of Colonel Tresham's stare. "Why don't you run about in the garden with Matthew?"

Out of their sight, Alice pulled off her sash and rammed it into the middle of a laurel bush. "That's better. I thought I was going to burst in there."

"You might have told me," Matthew reproached her.

"About bursting?"

"About being at Chillingston."

"Didn't feel like it," said Alice. "And who cares anyway? It's just about the most boring place on earth."

"I bet it's not as boring as this."

They had reached the end of the garden. Alice looked down the serene stretches of lawn, dipped in early darkness by the spreading elms. The grave high walls of the house were rosy and warm in the last light; Lucilla's long lavender borders edged a jubilant cloud of yellow roses in front of the library windows.

"Well, I think it's lovely," she said. "I wouldn't mind living here. You're jolly lucky to be getting it."

"I suppose so." He wondered if he should tell her to stop scuffing holes in the gravel. Cousin Lucilla would be sure to blame him. "The trouble is, there's nothing to do."

"Are you coming back next summer?"

"I don't know. Perhaps," he swaggered. "I'll be going abroad with my parents. We travel a good deal."

"I've never been abroad," she said, impressed. "I hope you do come back. For a boy, you're all right."

He grinned at her. "So are you, except for that dress."

"It's not my fault. She chose it."

"Who?"

"Alice! Alice!" Mrs Tresham prowled forward through the rose-beds, hands cupped for a hunting whoop. "Come heah!"

"Her. The old foghorn. What's your mother like?"

"Beautiful," Matthew said without hesitation.

"Imagine her producing a creep like you," Alice said. "You might meet me tomorrow. Usual old place."

"Okay."

He stood with Cousin Lucilla on the porch steps to wave them off, straining his eyes for a last glimpse of Alice's jauntily flapped hand as she was carried round the curve of the drive.

"Odd child," Cousin Lucilla observed. "Very plain, poor little thing. The brace is rather bad luck."

"She's quite nice, really. For a girl I mean." He felt a wish to defend her from any form of deprecation. "When you know her. She's pretty tough."

She'll need to be, Lucilla thought, as she smiled vaguely and said: "Is she, dear? I'm so glad. Well now, I think it's time for our reading." She walked ahead of him into the darkened library with stiff steps, and sat down with evident relief on the fire-settle.

"You won't have so much to do when I've gone back to London," he said as she turned the pages.

She gave him a little squeeze. "That doesn't mean I want you to go. You know how much we both enjoy your visits."

"But I won't—" No, that sounded too rude. "Will I be coming every year, then?"

"That depends on your parents, my dear," she said. "We'll just have to wait and see."

They did not have to wait for very long.

When Matthew came down to breakfast the following morning, he saw a letter addressed to Cousin Lucilla in his father's hand lying by her plate. Looking more closely, he saw that it bore a London postmark.

"Look!" He waved it in front of her as she came in. "They're back!"

Her smile was infuriatingly placid. "I've told you before, Matthew. First breakfast, then letters. Remember the rules. Cousin Jack's having breakfast in bed today."

"Why? Have we got visitors?"

"Don't make silly jokes. It's childish."

"I am," he said, "a child."

She poured out his glass of milk without answering. "Sit down. If you behave well, I'll open the letter."

He sat like a mouse, his eyes fixed on the magic envelope with such earnestness that she laughed and pushed away her toast. "Oh, very well. Now, let's see."

The envelope was slit, the paper held up close to her eyes. Nothing was said. The line between her eyebrows deepened.

"Well?"

"Well." She folded it and replaced it in the envelope before looking at him in a way which struck him as peculiar. Her eyes seemed to have shrunk into their sockets. "Come here, darling."

That was equally odd. She never used endearments. He went towards her. She put an arm round him, holding him close.

"Well Matthew, your father's coming here tomorrow night. Isn't that a nice surprise?"

"What about Mummy?"

She shook her head. "No, dear. She'll be staying abroad for some time. Your father wants me to try and explain things to you a bit. Your parents won't be together quite so much in the future, you see. It's not that they aren't fond of each other, but sometimes people find their lives going in different directions." Her arms tightened as he started to shake. "Try to be brave. Your father's just been offered a new job, a very interesting one."

"Where?" he asked through his teeth. "In London?"

"Belgium."

He stared at her. "And what about Chester Square? What about me?"

"I expect he'll tell us about the house when he comes. And you—dear Matthew, this is always your home. You know how fond we are of you. And Daddy can't look after you if he's working in Belgium, can he?"

He floundered in a sea of disbelief and terror. She sounded so normal and ordinary, but what she was saying was so awful that he couldn't hold the sense of it in his head. "You mean they want to get rid of me."

"It's a question of place and convenience, dear. If you're at school in England, you need an English home for the holidays. And Gracedew is home. Westerham isn't very far away. Bates will be able to drive you there when the term starts. Perhaps you'll be able to show him the school."

He was not going to be diverted. "What about my trunk? It's in London. With all my school clothes. Mummy always does that. Nobody else can."

"Well, somebody has. Your father says it's being sent directly to the school. Now, you think about how lovely it will be to see him tomorrow. You don't want him to see a sad little face, do you?"

He could not make any words of response.

He scarcely saw his father during the visit. He was only there for two hours before he returned to London, and most of his time was spent closeted with Cousin Jack in the library. Mrs Bates took their tea in and came out with pinched lips. She pretended not to see him perched on a chair in the corner of the hall but hurried out towards the kitchen. Stealing closer to the library door, he wondered what she had heard to make her look so fierce. He couldn't make out the words, but Cousin Jack was shouting a lot. He was probably saying what a beastly thing it was, to have left Mummy abroad on her own.

His father came out alone. He looked even more shrivelled up and ill than when he had gone in. For a moment, Matthew felt quite sorry for him.

"Hello, Daddy." He thrust out a hand to hold off the proffered embrace. "Congratulations on your job."

His father stuffed his hands back in his pockets and seemed to be trying to smile.

"It's not so bad, you know. I shan't be away for ever. And

64

your mother will come and see you at school. Nobody's deserting you. We'll be all right.''

"I want to go back to London," Matthew said.

"What, to stay with me at the club? Chester Square's being rented out, you see. I've nowhere to put you, old chap. You're best off here.''

He stared at the floor. "I don't want to be here.''

"Keep your voice down. We don't want to hurt anyone's feelings.'' A coin was produced and pressed into his hand. "Here. For tuck. Don't lose it.''

Very deliberately, he flung it across the hall, as hard as he could. "I don't want your beastly money. You can have it back.''

His father looked into his eyes. "Tell me what I've done to hurt you, Matthew.''

"You left her. And now you're leaving me.'' He flung his griefs like javelins. "You don't care. You and your job.''

A faint smile touched Charles Craven's lips as he remembered the horrors of the past three weeks, Lizzie's flippant shrug when he had begged her to stay for the child's sake, the man—just another Freddie with a bogus title—whom he had seen waiting for her in the street in his tinny little sports car, the loathing he had suddenly felt for them both and for the hot careless imperative of Lizzie's desire. Love? She chose to call it that. Uncaring, she had gone. Well, not quite.

"You won't do anything silly like telling them,'' she had said, just before she left.

"I might,'' he had answered.

"I'll never speak to you again,'' she had flashed.

"I doubt if you'll have the chance.'' Cheap, but his only moment of satisfaction in a loser's game. It was the only thing she still cared about, Matthew's inheritance. He could hurt her there.

And now the thing had been said. And, awfully, the innocent child would suffer more than her from his revenge. It was unbearable to look at him and see her in miniature, the eyes, the Asiatic cheekbones, the high candid forehead, the winging black hair. All her. All here. Gently, he touched the boy's face.

"It hasn't got much to do with jobs, old chap,'' he said. "Or with not loving you. But I don't think there would be much point in my trying to explain things to you now. I'm not even sure that I could."

"Charles dear, you're not really going again already?" Lank and flustered, Lucilla broke in on them. "Can't you stay the night?"

He drew himself up, a shadow of the solid military figure she remembered coming to Gracedew with his young wife, so obviously in love with her, so anxious that they should share his adoration. How dreadful to think of her behaving like that. Poor, poor Charles. "Do," she repeated earnestly. "We'd like it so much."

"Afraid not, Lucy. It's very kind of you, but there's a dickens of a lot to be done before I go." He put a hand on Matthew's head. "Look after him for me—for us. He's not a bad little fellow."

Matthew was swallowed by a wave of desolation and fear. Limply, he trailed his father to the door.

"I didn't mean it."

"I know." Charles Craven twisted his hat in his hands, trying to think of some comforting lie. He had none to offer. "Chin up, Matthew," he said gently. "Put on a brave face and the battle's half won. We've both got to learn to do that." And then he was gone, driving the car away into the leafy darkness beyond the arches.

"Matthew?" Cousin Lucilla called.

"Coming in a minute." Heavy with the weight of unshed tears and unsaid words, he stared out into the blackness. All as it was and never could be again.

There was some comfort in finding that his new situation made him an object of interest. Sitting under the Dobell monument on the last Sunday of the holidays, he was conscious of being observed and scrutinized. The nudges and whispers in the front rows had little to do with Mr Flower's sermon. The prayer for those in distress prompted a ripple of sighs and glances.

It was not the interest of the villagers which he minded but the sense of exclusion in the house. The passages were full of whispers and mutters. Conversations stopped when he came into the kitchen.

"What's a painted harlot?" he asked Cousin Lucilla the evening before his return to school.

"Gracious, what an extraordinary question." Flustered, she started to polish her spectacles with exaggerated care. "Where did you hear that?"

"Mrs Fletcher was talking to the milkman about it. I just wondered what it was."

"I'll tell you. Your mother's no better than a damned prostitute and the sooner you know it the better." Jack Craven folded up his paper and lay back in his chair. "Don't look at me like that, Lucy. You know I'm not one for beating about the bush. I'll tell you something young man." He raised a magisterial finger. "Stop squinting and blinking. Nobody's going to eat you. Look me in the face."

Lucilla gave him a little push. "Go to your room, Matthew. Quickly now. Cousin Jack's only playing games. Off you run."

"Over my dead body do you tell him," he heard her say, his ears riveted to the other side of the door. "You can say what you please when I'm in my grave, but not before. There's no need. Not yet."

Even the geniality of Mr Bates could not ease the dread he felt on the journey back to school. They were sure to ask questions. What could he tell them? Oh God, he prayed as the grey walls of Westerham came into sight, don't let them ask.

"Where did you spend your hols, Craven?"

He hesitated for a moment.

"Paris. It was rather jolly. What about you?"

He had always been good at making up stories. As the questions persisted, he relied, with increasing confidence, on imagination to save him from exposure. He fabricated holidays abroad, embellished with details culled from his parents' letters. He spoke of a splendid château in France where his mother and father resided in hedonistic splendour. Intoxicated by the ease of deception, he came almost to the point of believing in his own lies. His masters, aware of the possible stigma attached to being the only child in his house with divorced parents, decided to overlook Matthew's resort to fictions. His conduct was impeccable, his scholastic results excellent. Nobody wanted to risk the boy's chance of missing a good scholarship. If fantasizing helped him to survive—well, public school would shake him out of the habit.

The Westerham years were survived in a fortress of lies. He arrived at Eton with a photograph of his father and mother which he ostentatiously placed on top of his locker. Recklessly, he embarked on the stories which had won the envy of his Westerham peers. The sight of Remington's broad back in chapel on Sunday gave him a moment's pause, but he shrugged uneasiness off. Remington was in another house and two years above him. There had been no revelation at Westerham. He saw no reason to fear one now.

Matthew had reckoned without the fagging system which acts, among other things, as a highly efficient intelligence network. Remington's fag that year was a small golden-haired child called Rufus Deardon. And Rufus Deardon came into the classroom one rainy Sunday afternoon when Matthew was describing life at the French château to an enthralled group. Deardon, who had come to borrow a pen, stayed to listen.

"That's absolute rot," he said in the clear piping voice of truth as Matthew paused for breath. The heads turned towards him.

"Who says, Deary? You?" There were a few sniggers at the idea of Deardon's knowing anything of importance.

"Remington says," he said with calm assurance. "Remington says your mother ran off with a nightclub owner. And there isn't any French château, only some potty cousins in a crummy old house in the Midlands. And they only have you 'cos there's nowhere else for you to go. Remington says you're jolly lucky he doesn't report you for being such an awful liar."

In the ensuing silence, one of the boys giggled.

"Look at Craven. He's blubbing."

"Poor old Craven."

They circled round him, peering and laughing. With his hands squashed between his knees, Matthew sat on the desk and wept. Not for the discovery, although that was bad enough, but because discovery hounded him out of the sustaining world of his fantasies. If they would not believe, he could no longer pretend to himself.

*   *   *

68

The shame which had seemed as frightful as a brand on his forehead at twelve years old, shrank slowly, almost imperceptibly. He was left with a faint but lasting residue of bitterness against the parents who had rejected him. His affection for his mother remained; the old unqualifying love could never be regained. At seventeen, he could feel some pity for his father, but of a kind nearer to contempt than to compassion. Understanding now what a sham their marriage had been, he scorned his father's weakness and misconceived the helplessness of love.

Even now, watching Charles Craven's ashes being ceremoniously laid to rest in Gracedew churchyard, two weeks after his second heart attack in Brussels, he could find no tragedy in the occasion. It was, as they say, a merciful release. His father had never got over the shock of the divorce. He had been dead in all but body for seven years. Standing in the Belgian crematorium, a tabernacle of hygienic anonymity, Matthew had watched the coffin slide down through black curtains with only a flicker of anger against his mother for not having sent so much as a wreath, before emotion was overtaken by boredom at the prospect of the forms to be completed before he could take possession of the urn. He had even found himself grinning at the ludicrous situation in which he found himself at the airport, until the shocked murmur of an old Frenchwoman reminded him to look decently afflicted.

And yet, standing in the chill of the church while Cousin Jack stammered and coughed and spluttered his way towards some weak recollection of Charles Craven's virtues, he had felt rage. The hesitant phrases might have been used of anybody. There was no warming perception in them, no understanding. His father had not been a remarkable man, but he had been a decent one. If he could be cruel enough now to see some kinship between his mother and the pretty, smiling, faithless wife who knelt in feigning piety on the Dobell monument above his head, he could with equal readiness credit his father with the gentlemanly tolerance which seemed such an attractive trait in the letters of Sir Thomas Dobell.

The grave was covered over. The villagers dispersed. There would, he supposed as he followed the shrunk figures of his cousins back to the house, be bound to be some talk of Gracedew's future now. It was a prospect which he found both unnerving and exhilarating. Steeped in accounts of Gracedew's past and the ambitions of its Catholic builder, he was increasingly attracted to the idea of trying to restore some of its glory. To bring it near to Sir Thomas' conception, a house to rival the intricate splendours of Wollaton, the lovely shining lines of Hardwick—that would give a splendid purpose to his life.

What a curious thing it was, the attachment of men to houses. Chester Square, now technically his although it would remain in trust until he was twenty-one, meant nothing to him. Emotionally, he had become bound to Gracedew simply by being there. It was a shrine of past experience, a vault of memories. At seventeen, he could look back with amusement on his childhood terrors as he walked under the branches and glanced down to the bright stretch of the lake beyond a sweep of curtseying willows. (He might take Alice out in the boat if she came over.) Coming into the hall, he could use every object in it as a kaleidoscope of fragmented memories. Each held a part of him. The table, for example. Picture one. Five years old, making a robber's cave underneath it with a couple of car rugs. Picture two. Being beaten with a slipper when he was caught scratching his initials on the side. Picture three. Sitting with Cousin Lucilla, not daring to say that he didn't like the cake. Picture four. Crying and hitting its shining surface with his fists after his father had driven away into the night. And now? He slid an affectionate hand across an ugly reproduction of a refectory table, cracked and pitted, as full of his past as a dower chest of treasures.

"Very tasteless stuff, this packet ham." Cousin Lucilla eyed her plate with distaste. "Just like the stuff we had in the war. I shan't go to that supermarket again. Very confusing. Nobody helps you. I wonder if we should have asked the Flowers to lunch. I thought he did the service very nicely, didn't you, Matthew?"

"Forty-eight. No age at all. Still, his heart was never very good." Cousin Jack ruminated. "He should have looked after himself better. Poor old Charles. He'd never have coped with running this place. Not enough energy."

It seemed an appropriate moment. He looked up from his plate of whitish-pink rectangles. "I was thinking about that on the way back from church. I suppose it's time I started learning a bit more about all that side of it. I've got three months before I go to Cambridge. It would be quite interesting—if you thought—that is—" He floundered into embarrassed silence as the old man blinked at him.

"I'm not dead yet, you know."

"Oh, I'm sure Matthew didn't mean—"

"I know bloody well what Matthew means." He pushed his plate away. "Well, young man, you'll just have to wait. I'd rather run my own house while I'm still able to crawl from one end to the other. And when I need advice, I'll ask for it. Damned impertinence. Where are you off to now?"

"Out. I've lost my appetite."

"Oh Matthew, I'm sure he didn't mean anything. He's just trying to get used to the idea of anyone else ever running Gracedew. Daddy's just the same. I've done everything at Chillingston ever since my mother died and he still thinks I'm just competent to boil an egg."

"That's ridiculous. You're the most efficient person I know."

"Well, I have to be. Daddy may be good at making speeches in the House, but he hasn't a clue about running his own. Politicians aren't expected to. They don't have the time."

"That's no reason to turn you into an unpaid servant. You could have gone on to university if you'd stayed another year at school instead of rushing back to minister to him."

Alice shrugged. "It doesn't bother me as much as you think. I'm not clever, Matthew. I'd much rather spend my afternoons like this, lazing about in boats, than sit swotting over textbooks. And I quite like cooking for the dinner-parties. Hey-ho, shan't I make someone a perfect wife?"

"Remington, for example."

She giggled. "Imagine having that menagerie of stuffed bison at Knaresfield around you on the wedding-night. Some thrill. No, thanks awfully, dear. I'd rather marry you."

"What a compliment. Still, you might give me a kiss to be getting along with," he added, rather audaciously, he thought.

She leaned forward from the prow of the little skiff and pressed her soft round mouth to his. Matthew slid the oars back into the rowlocks to free his hands. "Oh no, you don't," Alice said and slid back to her place. "Not when you've just buried your poor father. It's not proper. Actually, it would be quite nice, marrying you. Comfortable, anyway."

Naïvety or temerity? With Alice, he could never be certain. "Shall I propose?"

She pulled a funny face at him. "Come on, I was only joking. You're fated to marry a literary female and turn Gracedew into the Bloomsbury of the Midlands. Like the place that Morrell woman lived in. How's it going, by the way, all the writing?"

"Oh, I scribble along." He didn't want to talk about it. Not to Alice. She was a darling, but she got so solemn and anxious when she talked about books and if he made fun of her she got upset and started apologizing for being stupid.

Dear Alice. Sliding the boat through the dappled shade of the willows, he watched her as she fell into a trance over a family of ducks. Her clothes were frightful, baggy green jeans and a blue check shirt, demurely buttoned but tight enough to show where soft bumps of flesh squeezed up from an outgrown bra. The sight filled him with embarrassed tenderness rather than desire. Her lack of self-consciousness or vanity was absolute, and she would have mocked at the idea that she looked beautiful when she laughed.

"You ought to put your hair up," he said, watching her.

"Oh really? Like this?" She scooped up a bundle of sunny fairness, piled it high and let it fall. "Can't be bothered. I hate hair. I'd shave it all off for two pins."

"My mother used to do hers in a sort of chignon sometimes. It was awfully pretty."

"So you've frequently told me. Anyone would think you were in love with her, the way you go on. I'd better be off."

He had erred and annoyed her. "I thought you were staying for supper."

"Can't. Charles Remington's taking me to a film in Derby at six."

"Snogging in the back row." He was furious. "I can't think

why you bother. I bet he won't even pay for your ticket. Just because he's got a car."

"All right," she said, reddening. "I won't go, then. Only it is a bit boring talking to your dotty old cousins and having to behave like something out of the nineteenth century."

"I have to put up with it."

"But I don't. Still," she relented. "I will stay. If you insist."

"Don't be idiotic. I really don't give a damn who you go to the cinema with."

But he did. The thought of Remington slobbering and pawing her about made him feel quite sick with rage. Watching her swing away up the bank to where her bicycle lay on the grass, Matthew wondered if this was what being in love was like. If so, the poets had greatly over-rated it. Legs straddling the machine, she turned to call back to him.

"He has got one virtue. He doesn't make me feel stupid."

Childhood had been purgatory; growing up was hell.

4

"Well? Do you think it's any good? I'd rather you were honest."

"I'm seldom honest and as for its quality, with a hangover like mine even the blessed J. Donne would make me throw up. Now shut up like a dear fellow and get me a glass of something very unalcoholic."

Matthew scoured the chaos of his room and produced a plastic cup from under a chair.

"Only Cambridge tap, I'm afraid."

"Alas, it is familiar." Delicately, James Erskine sniffed at it. "Château Colgate, I surmise. A highly recognizable bouquet."

"Sorry. The sulphureous Remington annexed all my glasses. I did have some tonic water." Without hope, he peered under the bed. "Somewhere."

"Keep it for your wild nights of work. Which reminds me." James took off his spectacles. "I actually came here to tempt you to a literary lunch, not to appraise your prose. It's about time you met the bunch now you're a famous author."

"It's only one story in the *London Magazine*," Matthew muttered.

"But my dear, it's print, and it isn't *Granta*. Don't be modest. None of us has broken out of the grisly bonds of academe. We're positively swimming in jealousy."

"Very funny." He hoped he was being successful in disguising his pleasure from the shrewishly perceptive eyes of *Granta*'s new editor. The moment was one of sweet triumph. James Erskine had been two years ahead of him at Eton, a prince of Pop and the author of some murkily satanic poems which

Matthew had thought immensely brilliant. His first year at Cambridge had been spent distantly worshipping the shrine cultivated by James' select band of disciples, but his chance of joining them had seemed as remote as a voyage to Baghdad until the publication of his story. "Curves and Smiles" had raised his status and, while he now despised the story, he understood that it could alter his solitary and industrious life into something richer, stranger, indisputably better. A queer thing, success. It would have been inconceivable a year ago that James Erskine would be sprawled in his room, reading his work and bestowing invitations with the princely air which coloured every aspect of his life with interest and exoticism.

It was a life designed to be observed, the sort of life likely only to find acceptance at Cambridge or Oxford. A loving reading of Huysmans and Firbank had produced an artificial gloss of languour which almost disguised the fact that Erskine was shrewd, tough and ruthlessly manipulative of his friends. Matthew as a quiet scholarship boy who avoided politics and punch-ups as rigorously as he declined dances and dinners was of no interest. Matthew Craven with his name among the prestigious in an illustrious magazine and with, it transpired, a literary ambition to match his own, was quite another matter. He would add lustre to the coterie. He might, one day, be useful.

"Unless, of course, you're quite booked up?"

"Not to the hilt," said Matthew, whose only future assignments were with his tutor and a dull first-year girl called Emily Hitchens whose stream of invitations he found some difficulty in continuing to refuse. "When is it?"

"One o'clock, in my room. Ned Foley's bringing a bottle of champagne, so I hope you're not feeling terribly puritanical."

"Today? Oh damn," Matthew said, forgetting to be casual. "My mother's coming."

"The delectable Principessa?" James rolled his eyes. "All the better. Bring her along. She might quite enjoy it."

Matthew lay back on the bed. "She's not exactly literary. And she's ceased to be a principessa. That was the Italian period. It's Polish now, I think. Or is it Hungarian? Somewhere oppressed. She did tell me."

"Gracious, what an exhausting life. Do you have to meet them all?"

Matthew shook his head. "She always came to Eton alone, if you remember. I don't think the idea of confronting glowering adolescence was quite Giorgio's idea of heaven. As for this one, I gather he's in Chicago, selling something."

"Perhaps your dear mamma. She seems to be a fairly marketable property. Sorry. That's not in very good taste, is it?"

"Not terribly. I hope you won't say it twice."

"Touchy little fellow, aren't you," James said with a grin. "You should hear what I say about my mother."

"I have." Mrs Erskine had recently, to her son's extreme and well-advertised mortification, remarried herself to a prosperous meat-dealer, an act which was taken by James to be a slight on his (somewhat obscure) ancestry and which was recognized by his friends to be a means of allowing an adored only son to live in the style to which his mother intended him to become accustomed. The butcher might be an object of mockery but he was a generous subsidizer, and James' elegant little gatherings were silently understood to be funded by good Scotch beef.

"Anyway," James said, sliding away from the subject with some haste, "I'm grief-stricken that you can't come. Still, family first. You are so endearingly conventional, Matthew."

"I haven't seen her for more than a year," he defended himself. James had let drop the manuscript into his lap. Nervous, he lit a cigarette. "Did you like it?"

"This?" He flicked at the sheaf of pages. "It's not bad. Historical fiction isn't quite my line of country. I liked 'Curves and Smiles' better."

"It isn't fiction," Matthew said, irritated. "Dobell's no invention of mine. Call it faction, if you like. I did a hell of a lot of research on it last summer."

"Up in the stately manse?"

"At Gracedew, yes."

James smiled knowledgeably. "Give it to your relations. They'll love it. It's not quite *Granta* material. Not sparky enough. Now don't go looking gloomy. You do some more stories like the other one and I'll publish you *avec plaisir*, my old dear. But not this one." Lounging to his feet, he peered at the reflection over Matthew's gas-fire. "Christ, I do look decadent. Forty at least. Still, an interesting face. Dorian in middle period with just a touch of the Baron Corvos, I'd say."

"You usually do. Unhealthily self-engrossed."

"One's self is always so much more interesting than other people. And don't tell me you've heard that before. You're sure to hear it again. Too good not to repeat, I'd say."

"Only it's not your invention."

"It would have been, had I been alive in time. All the best lines were made to be borrowed." James smiled agreeably. "Well, dear *confrère*, I must desert you for my little gathering. Tell your mamma it's very tiresome of her to choose today for her visit." Swinging open the door, he came into the arms of Countess Kiernatowski, the former Elizabeth Craven.

"I'm frightfully sorry. It must be the wrong room." She backed away from a position of disconcerting intimacy. "I'm looking for my son, Matthew."

Composure recovered, James offered a flourish of a bow. "Fortunate Matthew. We have met actually. I'm James Erskine."

Behind the door, Matthew flung a cover over the bed and pushed a pile of dirty plates underneath it.

"Have we?" She wrinkled her unlined forehead. "How awful of me to forget. Are you one of Matthew's friends?"

"A brother of the spirit," James said gravely. "I, too, write in my modest way. Nothing like 'Curves and Smiles', of course."

"Curves and what?"

It was necessary to effect a rescue. He crushed his dressing-gown into a reasonable imitation of a cushion and put his head round the door.

"She hasn't read it, James. Hello Mamma. Come in. I'm afraid the place is in a bit of a mess."

"Darling boy! As if I'd care." She offered her cheek for a kiss. "Now don't tell me. I know I look awful. It was a frightful rush to get here and the traffic was simply appalling. I haven't had time to do a thing to my face."

He smiled at the familiar plea for praise. Her make-up was

flawless, her hair a brilliant auburn which, after the initial shock, was rather becoming. For a forty-five-year-old woman on her third marriage, she looked unnervingly young. Only at the edge of her eyes did a curious tautness to the skin indicate that the surgeon's illusory art had been employed since their last meeting.

"You look absolutely magnificent."

"Dear Matthew. Isn't he sweet?" Thickly coated eyelashes fluttered an appeal to James.

"In all but introductions." He lifted her hand to his lips, a gesture which looked stupidly affected to Matthew but which was received with regal gravity by his mother.

"James is on his way to a lunch."

"No hurry. I don't need to go quite yet, dear boy."

"I think you should," Matthew said gently. "They'll never survive without you."

"Alas, you may be right. Enchanted to have met you, Madame. Not for the last time, I hope."

She withdrew her hand with a little sigh. "What a pity you can't join us. Perhaps we can capture you for my next visit."

"Well, what a charming boy your friend is," she cried as Matthew closed the door. "Do tell me, is he one of the Scottish Erskines?"

Her thirst for pedigrees never failed to entertain him. A racehorse trainer would, he thought, make an excellent consort for her. Backgrounds and bloodstock, a rich solid diet of genealogies. "James' ancestry is one of the best-kept secrets in Trinity. Probably for excellent reasons. I don't think it's a start-lingly illustrious line."

Her eyes lost some of their glitter. "Still, he seemed very nice."

So much for James, fallen from grace for want of rank. Just as well. He didn't want to spend lunch discussing James' charms. He watched her glance about the room with the apprehensive smile of an empress thrust into the gorbals. "Well, this is cosy. And what a lovely bedspread. Did Lucilla give it to you? And look at the fire! I haven't seen one of those for years."

He intervened to spare her the effort of further insincerity. "I got some ham and pâté, or would you rather eat out?"

She gave a pretty little shrug of her shoulders. "I don't think I really want to balance a plate on my knees, darling. Is there some little restaurant nearby? It would be more fun, don't you think."

Kiernatowski was reported to be a man of substance. Without too many qualms, he led her to a restaurant often frequented by dons in the early and more expensive days of dalliance. Red check tablecloths and a motley assortment of windsor chairs gave it a deceptively unpretentious air; he had heard that a Dover sole could cost as much as fifteen shillings. Following her as she threaded her way between the tables with an occasional flick of her long fur stole, he was reminded of the old days when he had watched her entrances and exits with enchanted eyes. More conscious now of the theatricality, he could still relish the performance and her evident pleasure in conquering a new audience. There was, he thought, something disarmingly childish about her vanity. Had it been possible, he would have clapped her as she sat down at the window table with a little glow of triumph on her cheeks.

He smiled at her. "It's lovely to see you. Marriage seems to suit you, or is it that you always look your best in black? Not for one of Johann's family, I hope?"

"Jozef. I did tell you." Her face translated itself into madonna-like grief. "I'm surprised you need to ask why I'm in black. Your poor papa."

He blushed for his folly. "Of course. I'm terribly sorry. I hadn't thought. Still," he added after a decent interval, "it is well over a year since he died."

"It seems like yesterday to me. Poor dear Charles."

He was not going to become an accomplice to an extravaganza of her unfelt sorrows. She wore black because it suited her. She made a public show of mourning because she considered it to be appropriate.

"You did leave him," he said brutally. "And you've had two husbands since then. You can't be as devastated as all that."

She dabbed at her eyes. "He loved me. I shall always remember that. And he was a wonderful wonderful father to you. Generous, kind—"

"I know." He cut her off. "At least I went to the funeral."

79

"I would have gone. I wanted to. Jozef's frightfully jealous."

"Of the dead?"

She put her hand over his. "Don't let's quarrel, Matthew. I don't begrudge his leaving Chester Square to you. I don't resent the fact that Cousin Jack never bothers to answer my letters. All I care about is your happiness, darling. Nothing else."

He was silent. He had been unnecessarily unkind. The tears on her lashes were real enough.

"I noticed Remington as a name on your staircase," she said as the quenelle plates were removed. "The same one?"

He nodded.

Her face lit up. "Isn't that a remarkable coincidence? Westerham, Eton, and now the very same staircase at Trinity! I suppose you see quite a lot of each other in Nottinghamshire? I was thinking how nice it must be for Jack now that you're old enough to take a real interest in the place. And of course he's been so helpful about your father's trust and Chester Square. We must never forget how much we owe to your cousins, darling. It's such a relief to me to know that I needn't worry about you—"

He listened with half an ear as she began to elaborate on her favourite theme, the legacy of Gracedew. It still puzzled him why it should mean quite so much. On her rare Eton visits, it had always been the first question on her lips. Was everything all right? Was he on good terms with them? It was her one concern. She had never displayed more than perfunctory interest in his literary beginnings or scholastic successes. For her, the house was all.

It was a passion which put distance between them. He lacked the will to tell her how little time university life left for thoughts of Gracedew's future, how great was his distaste for the idea of currying favour as a kind of insurance. The old man's rebuff had been too absolute to be forgotten. His understanding was that he should concentrate on the present, on his work and on his writings. Gracedew remained a comforting background, a soothing image. He had only to close his eyes to repossess it, summer light glancing up the walls, velvet-striped lawns sweeping out to where a row of mays flung stars across the grass, a grey flutter of pigeons crooling in the elms. It was his home, and he loved it, but to contemplate the future in practical terms was to feel security tightening to a shackle on his freedom. How could he explain to her the dread he sometimes felt when he foresaw himself becoming as much its prisoner as its owner, his choices prescribed by Gracedew's needs, his ambitions pared to suit its economics? It was a prospect which no aspiring young man could be expected to view with unqualified pleasure. But she would find such a remark incomprehensible. Better to say nothing.

The window-light unkindly shone in on a fine net of powdered wrinkles as the Countess Kiernatowski leant forward to re-apply her lipstick. Perceiving them, she snapped the compact shut and moved to place herself in shadow.

"What a spoilsport you are, darling. You haven't said a word about gels." (Only in her ringing pronunciation did she expose the age so artfully denied by paint.) "Do tell me. I'm itching with curiosity. Is there anyone special?"

"Apart from you?"

"Silly boy." The most transparent of compliments could be relied upon to please her. "I bet they're mad about you. You're awfully good-looking, darling. I always knew you would be." She tapped his hand. "All right, I won't pry. Just a teeny bit of advice. Never let her think she matters too much to you. Tell her you can't live without her and she'll drop you like a stone."

He raised his eyebrows. "So, if Papa had been more of a bastard, you would have stayed."

"I didn't leave, darling. It was mutual. We just didn't get on."

He decided to let the lie pass. He had no wish to make her unhappy. "I see. So the best kind of love is based on uncertainty?"

"Oh dear, it does sound rather cynical. Yes, I suppose that's what I want to say. Listen." She leant forward to cup her hand round the flame of his lighter. "Jozef's in Chicago. If I thought he wouldn't look at another woman while he was there, I'd find it a bit boring. But the uncertainty makes it all so wonderful, so exciting. Do you see?"

He understood that, in her convoluted way, she was saying precisely the opposite to what he was hearing. He's left me alone. I'm getting older. I'm terrified he'll find another woman. For God's sake, reassure me. He had found the reason for the tension round her eyes where no wrinkles formed.

"Well, it sounds marvellous. But you may have to resign yourself to growing bored, dear Mamma. He won't find another you in a hurry." Smiling at her, he bent over the menu as his eye caught the outline of a familiar figure pushing towards their table. "The chocolate remoulade sounds good. Or do you think the lemon mousse?"

"I can recommend the chocolate. They've got some rather good port here, too. Taylors, 1927."

Trapped, he produced a smile. "Hello, Charles. You haven't met my mother, Elizabeth Kiernatowski. Charles Remington."

Bonhomie gave way to a stare of dismay before Remington recovered his manners and extended a hand.

"Jolly good. Awfully pleased to meet you. I used to see you on sports days, didn't I? Wonderful hats. My mother admired them so much." (That dreadful Craven woman's here again. Do let's go and talk to your house-master, Charles. I'm always terrified she's going to pounce on me and announce she's coming to Nottinghamshire. I really can't face it. The stories one hears. Not that one should listen to gossip. Do hurry, Charles.)

"Charles Remington! Why, we were just talking about you, weren't we, Matthew?"

Remington gave his big jolly empty laugh. "Nothing bad, I hope."

"Sugar and spice and all things nice. Actually, I always thought those hats were a little out of place. It's such a relief to know your dear mother liked them. I have met her, you know." She looked up at him appealingly. "She didn't think I overdid it?"

(I can't imagine how anyone in her position has the nerve to turn up looking like that. You know the prince turned out to be some sort of a night-club owner? Too awful. Poor Charles Craven.) "God, no. Not for a minute." He pumped her hand to emphasize his sincerity. "I'd better get back to Sarah. She hates sitting alone in restaurants. Jolly nice to have met you, anyway. Perhaps we'll see you in Nottinghamshire one of these days."

Uncommitting. He had managed it well. Tricky situation. Secure in the sense of having behaved decently, he leant confidentially towards Matthew. "Don't suppose I can touch you for a couple of quid? I haven't got a penny left for the tip and Sarah's train. Rather embarrassing."

"Only the rich never carry money." He felt in his pocket. "And the poor. Sorry. I can't help."

"Really, darling, you mustn't let people think you're a pauper. What will your friend think of me?" She held out two crisp notes. "There you are. And do give my very fondest wishes to your dear mother."

Heavy with the sense of bribery, Remington shuffled the money into his pocket. "Very kind of you. Most grateful."

"Now he is charming!" she cried before Remington had lumbered out of earshot. "So friendly and easy and natural. Just the kind of friend your father would have wanted you to have."

It was, he thought, the chief flaw in her character, the clue to that dismal trail from English gentry to pseudo-prince to a most dubious count. She had, would always have, an anxious reverence for rank which made her as blind to the faults of the gentry and nobility as a mole in sunlight. It was not Gracedew she wanted for him. It was the position of an English country gentleman.

Gently, he helped her to her feet and put her stole around her shoulders. It was strange, but the moments at which he loved her best were those when he most clearly saw her faults. He bent to kiss her cheek. "It really is lovely to see you. Come on. I'll show you round the colleges."

Matthew was always inclined to regard the take-off of his writing career as a piece of phenomenal luck.

The book started life as a skit on county life, written to amuse the English Society during the long summer vacation of his third year at Cambridge. He sent the manuscript off to Screeby's with every expectation of getting a rejection slip by return of post. A letter from no less a personage than the managing director offering four hundred pounds outright for April publication so staggered him that he assumed that it must be some curious kind of a practical joke. The second letter confirmed that Screeby's were in earnest. They proposed a contract for his next three novels and increased their offer to four hundred and fifty pounds. Matthew's swift acceptance was, as he later perceived, naïvely prompt and unduly grateful. Screeby's were not known for their altruism.

His struggle to seem indifferent to the book's fate deceived his friends somewhat, himself not at all. He dreamed of glory. He lived in terror of being dismissed, or, worse still, ignored. Learning from James Erskine that only ten per cent of hardbacks ever got reviewed—James could always be trusted to produce disagreeable statistics—he fell into a mood of calm despondency. His would be the unmarked grave. Well, better a blank than to bear a stigma. He returned to revision and to contemplating the virtues of the Roman stoics.

Anxiety overcame any attempts at indifference on publication day. He was outside Heffer's bookshop at nine o'clock, peering through the windows with eager eyes. Pritchett, Powell, Priestley, Amis. No Craven. He retired into the obscurity of a coffee shop to fret until opening hours. Embarrassing enough to be caught by one of the coterie in the act of checking, it would be worse still to learn from them that his book was nowhere to be found. At ten o'clock he was through the doors and at the cash desk.

"Excuse me. I think you may have a novel by me somewhere around, if you could—"

"Certainly sir," the young man said with a smile. He raised an authoritative hand. "Lucinda dear, just check if there's a Mee on the fiction shelves, will you?"

Matthew collapsed. Craven by name, craven by nature, he reflected savagely as he returned to his room. A novel by me—he had made an absolute fool of himself. Ridiculous to get into such a state over a stupid book. He kicked a lamp-post to demonstrate mind over matter and limped the rest of the way.

A nervous perusal of the daily press did much to raise his spirits. *The Times* called him a force to be reckoned with, and praised his acid wit. The *Guardian* looked forward to his next work with lively interest. He read both at least three times before throwing the papers into a drawer. It would not do to appear concerned. Insouciance was the creed to adopt.

Finding himself a success, Matthew understood that he had

been altogether too casual. Screeby's wrote to inform him that they would be reprinting. James Erskine did some rapid calculations which led him to opine that Screeby's had already doubled their investment.

"You don't think you'd be better off with an agent? You really aren't awfully practical."

He shrugged. "I'd rather cut my own throat if it has to be slit."

"Your choice of funeral, sweetheart," James sighed. "But please don't say your friends didn't warn you."

He minded what could only be a speculative loss of income far less than the letter from his mother. It arrived, for which he was more thankful than grateful, on the last day of the finals. He had sent her a copy of the book in the fond supposition that his success would gratify her. Any expectations of praise were dashed by the first lines. How, she wished to know, could he have been so vulgar, so callous, so stupid as to write such a thing, let alone publish it? Did he really value his cousins so little as to make them the subject of cheap mockery? Anybody, even a blind deaf mute, could recognize their portraits. How could he have done it? She had hardly been able to finish the last chapter, so great was her wretchedness. The only thing was for him to go to Gracedew immediately and apologize.

"Signed, 'your grieving parent', I presume," James said. "I'm surprised she didn't tell you she burnt it after reading it."

"She probably has. It's so ridiculous. I invented the Rathbone family. They're nothing to do with my bloody cousins."

James yawned. "Well then, there's nothing to worry about. You can't go on being a good little mother's boy for ever, you know. Running off to apologize will only make a situation where, probably, none exists except in the countess' fevered brain."

"Still, perhaps I ought to go home for a bit. Just to keep the peace."

"Caution, caution," James mocked. "Christ, Matthew, it's the great moment. End of finals. Start of life. Freedom. Discovery. Drama. If you want to be a writer, you've an absolute duty to savour the cup of experience. You aren't going to get that by sipping tea and discussing houseplants or whatever

85

it is they talk about. It's the rich tapestry of life you're after, not the petit-point on the family hassocks.''

"Point made and carried. So what do you suggest?''

"A month of cerebral hedonism,'' James said with a sedate skip which gave him the look of a bespectacled deer. "In Greece. We shall gaze upon glories. We shall revel madly.''

"I'm quite keen on revelling,'' Matthew said. "Which reminds me, I've got to go and book a room somewhere. I've got a girlfriend turning up for the King's Ball at any moment.''

"The divine Alice?''

"She doesn't have much of a life. I thought she might enjoy the experience.'' And he couldn't think of anybody else to invite.

"And she'll be so awfully grateful that she'll surrender herself to you without ado?'' From the door, James sent his sweetest smile. "Well, good screwing, angel. But don't let her drag you back to the murky Midlands. You're committed elsewhere.''

The prospect of playing the bold seducer was both alarming and appealing. Apart from a few evenings spent wearily grappling with the innumerable hooks on Emily Hitchens' broad cold back, a prelude to the strokes and cautious pinches which appeared to gratify her, Matthew's sexual experiences had been limited to masturbation and observation of the mammary wonders exposed by *Playboy* and *Penthouse*. It was a situation which should be remedied and would be, if only he knew how to set about finding a co-operative victim. It was possible that he would get it wrong. The thought of Alice convulsed with mirth was no encouragement.

Matthew's principal feeling on discovering that he was to be the seduced party was a gratitude which came very near to love. Alice was, as he could have anticipated, wonderfully practical about it all.

"Well, I'm going off to stay with an American family and look after their brats next month,'' she said, pulling off her dress and lying back on the bottom of the punt. "So I thought I'd better get this out of the way first. I mean, I wouldn't like it to be any old Yank. God, this is so uncomfortable. Whoever said punts were romantic?''

Matthew knelt above the fine white lines of her body. "Here. Have my coat. Actually, there is a bit of a problem. Like an idiot, I haven't brought anything with me. Still, so long as I don't—"

"Don't be silly. That's the whole point of it. You really are so vague, Matthew. Here." She pushed a packet into his hand. "I got them at the station."

He laughed. "The amazing Alice. You look awfully pretty."

"Only because you can hardly see me." She reached up to touch his face. "Dear Matthew. How satisfactory that it should be you."

It was all very quick. He knew something had happened somewhere, but he was not entirely convinced that he had been inside her. Her smile suggested that he had.

"Well, what did you think?" she inquired, sitting up.

"Lovely." He pushed away a mild sense of disappointment at the rapidity with which she was reassembling her clothes. He had understood that women lay about in a pleasantly languid fashion and talked above love after the event. He would have preferred it to be a little less of a scientific experiment.

"I've got blood on your coat," she said, peering. "Sorry. Can you get it dry-cleaned?"

"I shall keep it exactly as it is. In memory." He kissed her, trying to recapture something which had gone. "How long are you going to America for, my love?"

She wriggled a protest at the endearment. "Long enough for Daddy to learn to manage without me. Probably three months. Maybe more. What about you?"

He pulled his trousers up. "I think I'm going to Greece for a bit."

"You don't think you ought to go to Gracedew?"

Something in her voice prompted the memory of his mother's letter. "What's up? Did they say something about my book?"

"Not to me," Alice said sleepily. "I shouldn't think they've done more than look at the cover. But Lucilla looks rather ill. I wondered if there was something wrong. Serious, I mean. Still, I don't suppose anything's going to happen in a month. And now, dear Matthew, I'd like to be escorted back to my respectable single bed."

"So you shall be." He helped her to her feet. "It's funny, but I feel as though I ought to be thanking you."

Alice laughed. "We might as well thank each other and be done with it. Anyway, it wasn't too bad, was it?"

"Not bad at all," said Matthew.

The holiday with James was a qualified success. It was rather arduous to be intellectual all of the time. Fascinating though it was to theorize about the cult of Dodona, the oracular utterances at Delphi, the narrow line between the myths and history of ancient Corinth, Matthew found himself thinking with increasing wistfulness how pleasant it would be to spend more time investigating the night life of Athens where bazoukis tinkled the allurements of a harem, and less in trekking off to obscure sites where they could think themselves lucky to find mattresses and a plate of tepid beans. He had no wish ever again to see a bean or a chopped sausage floating in oil. Small wonder that those the gods loved died young if this was their diet.

There was also the problem of sex. He supposed that he had been naïve not to realize that James' emphasis on the pleasures of male companionship had to do with more than literary conversation. There was a disquieting night in Athens which provided illumination of a kind he could happily have foregone. They had managed to laugh it off the next day, but the embarrassment remained and, with it, a certain constraint. For Matthew, there was the memory of male flesh, hard and imperious, of James whispering that he was going to be broken in gently and that he was going to love it, simply love it. For James, there was the shrinking horror of Matthew's recoil as he freed himself and said in an unsteady voice that he was going to the bathroom. Where he spent the rest of the night, miserably hunched beside a dripping cistern, watching the cockroaches line up like starlings on the shower-rail. It was a memory which made the resumption of friendship awkward, if not impossible.

It had been Matthew's idea that they should go to Corfu. It was, he remembered, an island splendidly lacking in archaeological sites. It had, in Edward Lear's journal of his stay there, sounded a lively and engaging place. It was still lively. Every tourist in Europe seemed to be holidaying there. The hotels were packed, the streets glistened with sun-baked flesh and peroxide mops, the beaches drifted high in cellophane bags, hopping flies and ice-cream papers. James, remembering Byron to have said that the Albanian louse was the largest of the species, developed a playful running joke from the supposition that their pension's manager was a frustrated Albanian wreaking vengeance on his clientele. The lice remained virulent; the comedy palled. Matthew, writhing in the scratchy cotton sheets, thought of the long sweet summer days at home, the smell of beeswax, the shading vellum blinds.

"I think," James said on the third morning as they strolled through the bustling arcaded streets, "that I shall investigate boats to Sicily. One more night in that verminous dump and I shall go gently staring mad. Anyway, I've always wanted to see Syracuse. You'll like Sicily."

"I'm sure I will," Matthew said meekly. His stomach was churning, his head ached from lack of sleep, his ears rang with the shrill voices of the milling crowd of pleasure-seekers. He would have settled for Finland, if there had been a ticket available. James, egotistical but not unkind, gave him a pat on the shoulder.

"Go and get yourself some coffee on the promenade. You look like death. I'll meet you there."

Sitting under the acacia trees at one of the spindly iron tables around which the Corfiotes carried on business, flirtation and baby-minding over cream cakes and innumerable cups of sweet black coffee, Matthew found himself being scrutinized from under the brim of a floppy straw hat. He looked back. Straight blonde hair, a smiling mouth and heartshaped dark glasses. Age indeterminate. He decided to smile at her and see what happened.

"I thought you looked rather bored sitting all on your own. And since I seem to be on my own, too—" She sat down, crossed honey-coloured legs and dropped her glasses beside the newspaper on the table. She was older than he had thought, at least twenty-five, but there was a girlishness in the wide smile which reminded him of Alice.

"You shouldn't be on your own," she said, probing. "I've never seen so many pretty tourist girls around as this summer. How did you manage to escape?"

"Perhaps I wasn't looking." He wished he was better at flirtatious conversation. "You live here?"

"Some of the time. My husband's gone back to England, but I rather liked the idea of being on my own for a couple of months. Swimming, reading, lazing about."

"It sounds delightful."

"Oh, it is, it is," she said. "A bit lonely though. My name's Celia. Celia Rivers."

He blushed with embarrassment. "Of course. I should have recognized you. I saw you in *Othello* last year. How stupid of me."

"I don't come here to be a celebrity," she said. "Just to lead a quiet, very private life. The house is miles from anywhere so it isn't too difficult. Now you tell me your name."

It would have been delightful if she had known it, but she only said, "Matth-ew. How nice. And what brings you here, Matthew?"

Her voice was warm and humorous. Her eyes were of the kind to invite confidences. He found himself telling her about James and of the reluctance, which was creeping up on him by the minute, he felt about going to Sicily with him.

"Well now," she said. "Perhaps you shouldn't go. Perhaps you ought to stay here. It's an awfully big house for me to keep all to myself. There's not a lot to do, but it's by the sea and I've got a nice little sandy beach which the tourists haven't found. And I could take you for drives. I love showing the island to people. What do you think?"

"It sounds like paradise," he said. "Only—what about James?"

"Nothing about James," she said sweetly. "I'm afraid I haven't got room for both of you. Tell him you met a friend." Her smile widened. "Well, isn't it true? I'll come down this evening at around six to pick you up. Same table. All right?"

"Terrific."

He watched her swing away down the promenade, moving through the crowds with a pretty high-headed walk. She was awfully attractive. James would be furious. Still, he had come to Greece to discover life. Celia Rivers promised to show him a more engaging side to it than he was likely to discover plodding around Byzantine churches and the desolate quarries of Syracuse. He picked up the newspaper she had dropped on the table and flicked it open. He found himself looking down at Lucilla Craven's obituary. The paper was two days old.

"Screw that for a laugh," James said bitterly. "I spent two hours queuing for those tickets. Can't you just pretend you never saw it? Nobody expects one to read *The Times* on holiday."

"It would never occur to my cousin Jack that I didn't. I really am awfully sorry, James. I'd better go and try to get a refund on the ticket and see if there's a flight this evening."

"Oh certainly. We must keep in favour, mustn't we," James said rudely. "Wouldn't do to fall out with your cousin and lose the blessed heritage, would it? Be a good little baa-lamb and scamper home for the funeral then. Mummy *will* be pleased."

Matthew felt in his pocket. "How much do I owe you for the ticket?"

They left the table by opposite directions.

"Well, that is a shame," Celia sighed. "How very inconvenient of the old dear to choose the very time I meet you to pop off to the blessed land. Do you really think her corporeal form's going to mind whether you're there for the burial? I'm sure she'd want you to enjoy your holiday."

She wore a short sleeveless dress of pink silk cut down to the pale curve of her breasts. Her blonde hair was moon-pale in the dusk light, her long pretty hands lay near enough for his to touch them on the table.

"You can look down on the sea from the bedroom window," she said. "It's a lovely sound to listen to when you're falling asleep. There's another flight tomorrow noon. I've got a friend in the airways office who's terribly helpful. I'm sure one day wouldn't make any difference."

Her long silver ear-rings chinked as she leaned forward. Without exactly peering, he could see the little pink tips of Celia's breasts edging into view as she lifted her hands to enclose his face.

"Why don't we go and change the ticket?"

Her throat was like a long river of honey flowing down to the

91

delectable land she offered him with a smile. He pushed back his chair.

"Why not?"

Lying in pink flowered sheets under the eye of a brightly observant moon, Matthew tried to do to Celia what he had, without total success, done to Alice. Celia laughed, very gently, and said that was very nice but wouldn't he like to find out how it could be nicer still? And then she showed him and Matthew agreed that, yes, it was a good deal nicer. At about four in the morning, he wondered if Celia was ever going to get tired of educating him. At five, lovingly buttoned into Mr Rivers' blue silk pyjamas, he was allowed to sleep.

She let him drive her white Alfa to the airport the next day. Her head rested on his shoulder. Her hand held his between her legs. On the straight stretches of the road, she opened her thighs wide to let his hand slide up and touch her. He was pleased to find himself alive with desire after such a protracted night. Celia lightly bit his neck and said he was a wonderful lover.

"I'm going to remember you," she said. "We might meet in London when I'm back."

"What about your husband?"

Celia smiled. "I can always lunch out with a friend."

She was tremendously sophisticated. He was glad he hadn't taken the earlier flight.

He arrived at Gracedew at six in the evening. The house seemed deserted. Mrs Bates eventually answered his anxious tugs at the bell-wire.

"Mr Craven don't want no callers. You'd best write."

"It's me," he shouted. "Matthew. Do hurry."

The bolts ground back. "Well," she said. "You're a bit late, dearie. The funeral was this morning. It's all over. Come in, Mattie, and let me shut t'door. You look terrible peaky, poor lamb."

"Just tired. What happened? If only someone had told me."

"Now don't you take on so. You couldn't have done much by being here." She stooped to thrust the heavy bolts home. "Rusty old brutes. She slipped away like a baby. Never a murmur. Mr Craven, he was sitting by the bed and he said she

92

just shut her eyes and went out of herself. Not that there hadn't been pain, mind. But she never let on what was wrong with her. Well, it wasn't her way. Just a bit tired, Mrs Bates, she said. Not a word about it being leukaemia. You didn't know?''

He shook his head, remembering the times he had noticed her face drawn hard and fine as a death-mask and never looked for reasons.

''Well, no more did Mr Craven. He'd not have driven her the way he did if she'd let on. He's not taken it well, Mattie. You'd best watch your step.'' She gave him a motherly pat. ''Still, it'll do him good to have the company. I'll make dinner up for two. Macaroni cheese tonight. Your favourite.''

He managed a grin. ''Spoiling the prodigal son.''

Or was he the lamb to the slaughter? Slowly, he walked across the hall to the library.

The old man was standing at the far end of the room, looking out through the long windows to where the sun seeped down like an open wound, smearing the hills with red. Glancing around, Matthew saw every trace of her gone, the overflowing bag of embroidery wools and canvases, the gardening magazines which she had loved to peruse, the stiff wedding photograph framed in leather. Only her budgerigar still sang its two-note strain, cheep-chip, cheep-chip. He dropped the cover over the cage to silence it.

''So you're back, are you? Had enough of buggering around the continent?''

''I came back as soon as I could. I would never have gone if I'd realized. Nobody told me.''

''And now you're back for the pickings. You thought you'd find out what's in it for you.'' Hands behind his back, he turned. ''Come to offer to help run the house, have you? Or did you think I'd hand it over as soon as Lucy was underground?''

Matthew flinched. ''I'm ready to do anything I can to help, of course,'' he said quietly. ''You'd have a good deal more cause for bitterness if I took no interest at all.''

''It's a damned funny interest that led you to set us up as guys in that piece of tripe you wrote behind our backs. Paid you well for it, did they?''

''Not very. And it wasn't about you.''

93

"Don't you try to wriggle out of it. I don't want your excuses. You killed her. She never got over it. I hope you're pleased with yourself."

"I thought she died of leukaemia."

"Bugger that. I don't give a damn what the doctors say. I know the cause." He shuffled across the room until he stood at Matthew's shoulder. The sour smell of whisky came off him like the scent of hate. "You're twenty-one," he said. "I've done pretty well for you on your trust and now I'm handing it over to you to do what you bloody well like with. You're no pauper, I can tell you, so there's no need to start snivelling about your hardships. Nobody's asking you to live on your damned scribbling. You've got the house in Chester Square. I'll see that all the transfer deeds are made out by Gudgeons."

He could feel the blood draining away from his face. "You're throwing me out, then?"

"I never asked you in. I put up with it for Lucy's sake, but I'm damned if I can see any need to have you hanging round my neck now she's dead." His red eyes squinted up at Matthew's face. "Taken the sunshine out of the homecoming, have I?"

"Home?" He picked his rucksack off the floor. "You needn't worry about my troubling you. I'll leave now."

The old man looked discomforted. "There's no need to act wildly, Matthew. I just wanted to have the situation clearly understood. Nobody's forbidding you to come to Gracedew."

"So now we sit down and have a glass of sherry and pretend nothing has happened?" He smiled. "Thanks, but I'd rather not. I'd run the risk of seeming in your debt."

"I'll telephone for a taxi."

"Not for me, you won't," Matthew said. "I'll walk. Without obligation."

The flat landscape left no opportunity for the sentimental gesture of the last glance back. Trees drew a dark curtain across the house, screening it from any vantage-point for prying eyes. Which was, he thought, just as well. Tears were close enough already without any further need to induce them. It was another kind of sentimental instinct which led him to stop at the church and push open the door. The Dobell monument glittered pale in the dusk. He walked forward to stand below it, looking up at Sir

Thomas' tranquil face, the wise half-hooded eyes. He had, Matthew felt sure, gone to his death with the same contemplative smile. Contemplating what, he wondered? The folly of aspiration? The pain which a practising Catholic would have been taught to embrace?

"Well, Thomas," he said. "I would have tried. I don't know whether I could have succeeded, but I would have tried." And since there was nobody to see him do it, he stretched up to kiss the cold stone cheek before he went back down the aisle and out into the night to start the six-mile walk to Nottingham station.

Part Two

5

"Are you sure that's what the book said we have to do?"

"Positive." Earnest-faced, she looked up. "Why, didn't you like it?"

"I don't see why we have to go in for all the gimmicks. I thought it was quite nice without them."

"Quite nice isn't good enough," she said. "Quite nice is what I'm trying to emancipate you from. There's no point in having a one up and one down love-affair. Now, you lie on the edge of the bed with your feet on the floor. I have to stand for this. I'm meant to wear high-heeled boots. Do you suppose shoes would be all right? They have got heels."

"It's a commando course you need, not me," he said. "Celia, I hate to say it, but that is extremely painful."

"It is a bit. Damn." She disconnected herself, with some difficulty. "I'm sure that's what the bloody book said. I bet the man who wrote it never tried out half these things. I'll go and check again. It's in my jacket."

He caught her wrist. "Forget the book. Come back into bed and let me fuck you, you idiot. We're not auditioning for a circus."

She complied, but with an expression of such resignation that his desire waned with embarrassing suddenness, leaving him limp and apologetic and unreasonably annoyed with her.

Celia was delicious company, but he was tired of being a guinea-pig for her sex manuals and Celia deprived of her tricks and experiments was as frigid as an ice-cream buried in hot chocolate. He wondered how to ease the relationship on to a less physical level without offending her. Apart from anything else, she was visiting Chester Square too often for him to feel easy. He did not want to be beaten up by an outraged husband. He did not altogether like the idea of sleeping with a married woman. He could not make her see the difference between a holiday fling and an unlicensed affair.

"Not that I don't want you," he amended as Celia's soft mouth began to tremble. "But it's almost three. I thought Robert was picking you up at Peter Jones."

"It can't be!" She rolled over to peer at the clock. "Christ. I'll never manage it. Chuck my stockings over, will you, sweetie? Skirt. Sweater. Jacket. That's it. Almost." She sprayed herself liberally with scent, brushed her hair back to a shining bob. "There. The perfect wife."

He looked on with admiration and amusement. "The fastest dresser in the business. You didn't start life as a stripper, by any chance?"

"Reckon ah jest had mahself a lot of practice, honey-pie," Celia said. "Well, guess ah might jest drop in tomorrow."

"I'm out all tomorrow, worse luck," he said, untruthfully. "What about Friday? I could pick you up at the theatre. We might have a late dinner somewhere in Soho."

"You know perfectly well I can't. Robert would be sure to find out. I've told you before. No publicity." She turned from the mirror to face him with an anxious stare. The strain took all the prettiness out of her face, he noticed, cruelly.

"Getting the boot then, am I?"

Directness always undid him. He didn't want her to cry. He was not even entirely sure that he wanted to end it. Indecisive, he compromised. "Of course not. Come for lunch on Thursday and I'll conserve my energies."

"Perhaps. I'll let you know." Her eyes were disquietingly bright. "See you, sweetie. I'd better run for it."

A note on lilac paper arrived on Thursday morning. Celia shared Mr Jingle's predilection for dashes, he noticed. Terribly fond of him—realized that it was a difficult situation—different lives and interests—better not to see each other for a while—perhaps lunch in a couple of months—she would never be sorry. Stylishly carried through, it ended with a splendid flourish of a signature and, an afterthought, a face ornamented with two currant eyes and a crescent moon grin to signify her happiness.

Matthew tried to summon a proper sense of regret and sadness and discovered only a feeling of pleased relief. Clever Celia to have taken the initiative. He liked her better for it.

She deserved a measure of gratitude. The hole which Grace-dew had left in his life had been very adequately filled—if that was not too vulgar a pun—by his affair. She had helped him to face the sense of loss with equanimity and to come to terms with his obscure guilt. She had teased away some of the gloom which descended on him with the weekly arrival of his mother's long, reproachful letters. She had found his nostalgia for a crumbling unheated house in the drabbest part of England hilariously funny. As far as Celia was concerned, his expulsion from Gracedew could only be regarded as a blessing. Thoroughly urban in her tastes, she could not conceive of anyone preferring a damp country house and hunting neighbours to a house in Chester Square with a gourmet delicatessen and two splendid restaurants less than a stone's throw away. London was life. The country was living death.

Celia had almost convinced him. She was certainly right about his mother. However deeply she might feel the loss of Grace-dew, he could not spend the rest of his life apologizing for something which was no fault of his. Her lack of interest in any other part of his existence was chillingly apparent. Her screeds were devoted to her own life and to the one part of his which absorbed her. Everything else was excluded. He read her letters with increasing haste, and answered them at leisure as his life settled down to a new direction.

He was perceived as a success by his friends. There were times when he could almost believe that he was one. His second novel had described the rise and fall of a young politician in a sufficiently lively and scurrilous way to attract speculation as to his sources (always excellent publicity) and praise for the lightness of his style. He read of himself as one of England's finest young comic talents with annoyance. His satire had been intended to bite home. He had succeeded only in amusing. Still, as his friendly editor said, comic books sold better. He had better stick to them.

He took his manuscript about Sir Thomas Dobell out of a drawer, read it and replaced it in a folder marked "Ideas and

Unfinished Work". It was good, but without Gracedew he had lost the inspiration which lay behind it.

Introduced to a number of pleasant and forceful young women, Matthew found himself irrationally alarmed by their organized, energetic lives.

He wanted a woman who would look up to him. He wanted the respect and admiration denied to his father. He was now of an age to understand the humiliation which Charles Craven had silently endured, the terrible price in self-respect he had paid to keep his wife as she tripped with feverish eyes from one affair to the next, returning only for the assurance that her charms, for one man at least, remained as great as ever. And his father had put up with it, just as Thomas Dobell had wearily tolerated the infidelities of his treacherous Venice. Good men were there to be made fools of by their wives, it seemed, in all ages. Well, his eyes were open and he was not going to fall into the same trap. When he married, he would take a wife he could be sure of possessing and holding, a woman who would return his passion and loyalty in kind. Wherever she might be.

He thought with increasing wistfulness of Alice, his straight-limbed Eve in a lost Eden. She had prolonged her American visit, but her future was depressingly predictable, marriage to a Charles Remington, a country house, dogs, pearl necklaces. Walking down Ebury Street to the fortnightly gathering of Cambridge friends at La Fontana, he wondered what Alice would make of his present style of life. Not much, he thought. He had become a little tarnished.

"What you need," Ned Foley shouted across the table, "is a fourteen-year-old nymphet. A pupil to be cherished and guided."

"Talking of which," Matthew said, "what do I say to eighteen-year-old girls about the state of the novel? I've let myself in for giving a talk at Albany College on Thursday and I've no idea what they want me to say."

"My, aren't we modest. Tell them how to write a best-seller in three weeks," James Erskine said. "How much are they paying you?"

"I haven't asked."

102

"Well, you don't need to, do you?" Ned Foley said. "Unlike the rest of us. Lucky sod."

He would have been wiser not to mention it. "I'm hardly in the millionaire range. And you can't accuse me of not working for my living."

"No need to get riled about it, Matthew," Ned Foley said good-naturedly. "We all know you work away like a beaver. It's the fact that you don't have to which makes a bit of difference between you and the rest of us. Nobody's holding your private income against you."

Until he stopped footing the bill. Well, if he chose to play Gatsby to them, he could expect to invite a certain amount of envy. Money didn't buy friends, but it assured him of company and he had little inclination for his own when the day's stint of writing was done.

Did money make the difference, or was it that they had grown apart? He glanced round the table at the flushed faces, the smiling mouths and dead eyes. Extraordinary that a couple of years in London could have transformed the band of aesthetes into this Hogarthian assembly of young men middle-aged before their prime. He found a grim comedy in the memory of the same group ardently reading Yeats' late poems in Ned Foley's Cambridge room. Their literary input nowadays was mostly culled from the books page of the *Guardian* or *The Times*, he suspected. All had achieved some measure of success, but not of the kind which any of them would once have found pleasure in contemplating. Ned had just started directing some comedy series for television. Will Lazlett did a monthly column on restaurants and wrote celebrity profiles for one of the Sunday colour supplements. James Erskine commissioned vast glossy books of the kind to be seen and not read, for Wickenfield and Vyson. Good jobs all, but none had the stamp of glory on them.

Perhaps security bred the selfishness which he perceived as their common quality. As a group, as a generation, they had not suffered enough to look beyond their own interests. No sacrifice had been required. They had never been asked to justify or act upon the beliefs which were bandied about at these lunches. It was all very well to pontificate about the last throes of French imperialism in Algeria or the horror of the new wall built across

Berlin. Which of them had ever faced a gun or used one except to shoot a few pheasants? War was a school-room memory of rationing; they had been too young to be affected by the horrors of Hungary or the Suez crisis. Untouched and uncommitted, there was something troubling about them all—he included himself—in their candid pursuit of self-promotion, self-enrichment. Strip a Thomas Dobell of the grandeur of his designs, the passion of his faith, and you achieved this, ambition void of aspiration.

"Planning to put us in the new masterpiece, dear boy?" James Erskine inquired, his knee touching Matthew's under the table. "Or has the thought of nymphets transported you away?"

He removed his legs from reach. "I was just thinking."

"Thinking!" James cried. "Lunch is about talk, dear boy. Breakfast's the meditation hour, if you must have one."

The conversation moved on to the difficulty of persuading women not to raise the subject of love on the morning after the night before.

Lunch at Albany College offered no incentive to make a second visit to the concrete groves of urban academe. The food consisted of a small scotch egg resting on a grief-stricken lettuce leaf. The company was equally unpromising. The small and fiercely intense lady to Matthew's right had the most vigorous elbow his ribs had ever encountered, while the genial Yorkshireman to his left seemed determined to lend veracity to his assertion that he was only there to teach scatology to the little lasses. Still, robust vulgarity was more enjoyable than a refined discussion of Pound's influence on *The Waste Land*.

"No need to worry about giving them intellectual stimulus when they're full of stodge," the Yorkshireman said, chewing his orange egg with a look of enviable enjoyment. "Give them a slice of your love-life. A few jokes about fucking and you'll have the little poppets eating out of your hand. Trouble is, they do tend to take it all for gospel truth." He leaned across Matthew. "Isn't that right, Mary? Remember Rosie Dalton's essay on Coleridge seeing the piss in his pot and how it could be described as the first perception of inscape?"

"I certainly remember having heard you tell the story. Many

104

times." She gave Matthew the winter of her smile and the edge of her elbow. "Mr Rumbold tends to carry his love of the picaresque into conversation."

"Better than pummelling the poor chap with Pound, if you'll excuse the alliteration," the Yorkshireman said sourly. "Silly old prude," he added, not quite under his breath. "No fucking sense of humour. No fucking her either. Wedded to the Anglo-Irish poets, our Mary."

"You'll have to excuse Mr Rumbold's curious sense of humour," the intense lady hissed with an inflamed stare at her colleague. "He's what you might call a charity case in the department. Do have some salt."

"To sharpen my wits?"

She leant closer. "To get rid of the taste of the mince. Cat. It has been known to happen once or twice."

He wished that he could believe she had a sense of humour.

Entering the lecture room with a weight of sodden and possibly feline mince lying heavy as doom on his stomach, he was filled with panic by the row of smiling, expectant faces turned towards him. He turned back.

"I'm not sure I feel up to it."

"Stick to the jokes and tell 'em they're pretty," the Yorkshireman muttered. "In you go. They'll love you. Look out for Clarissa."

His voice suggested excitements in store which were hardly borne out by the round, pleasant and distinctly ordinary faces of Albany's second-year English students. Introduced in glowing terms by the head of department, Professor Samuel Jenkins, Matthew approached the lectern with a nervous smile. Amenable though the girls looked, they were the first audience he had ever confronted as a teacher. They looked disconcertingly earnest, pens poised for his first sentence.

"Satire isn't easy to define." Down went the pens, briskly scribbling. Christ. It was worse than being witness for the prosecution. "Still, I'm going to have a bash at it in the next hour." Laughter. But he hadn't made a joke. Oh well. Better get on with it. At least he hadn't lost his notes.

Established on a comfortable jog-trot from Firbank to Amis, alarm gave way to gloom as he watched them diligently inscribing every word. They were, he thought, an audience of born secretaries; at least two of them were taking him down in shorthand. By way of experiment, he informed them that Joseph Conrad had paved the road to modern satire. Down it went. Evidently, the lecturer's word at Albany was law. He had better look to his responsibilities and stop seeing how far credulity could be pushed. "Not in any serious sense, of course." Thank God for that. They were crossing it out.

He had reached the halfway mark when the door behind him opened and slammed shut again. At the far end of the room, Professor Jenkins opened one eye and glared the disapproval of a cyclops. Not that he supposed it would have any effect on the wretched girl. Clarissa's unpunctuality was the only predictable thing about her. He entertained a suspicion that she cultivated it to make an impression on visiting lecturers. It had to be said that she was very successful.

Matthew lost his place as he watched Lolita's lovelier older sister drift past in a cloud of scent, sweeping back a curtain of blue-black hair and dropping a languid "Sorry" with a dip of her eyelashes. He had never seen legs so long or eyes so luminously blue. Sprawling behind a desk, she dropped her hands over its front like the broken white wings of a bird. He gazed. She smiled. Pens remained poised. Saucer-eyes grew respectful—pauses indicated the approach of a key statement—and then puzzled, as no statement came. The clock noisily recorded the passage of unfilled time. Professor Jenkins gave a small warning cough. Matthew jumped.

"Anyway, as I was saying about *Black Mischief*, the comedy really lies in the juxtaposition of episodes."

The girl lifted a frail hand to stifle a yawn. His heart plummetted. She was right. His talk was abysmal, a total failure. To win a smile from those burnished copper lips he must abandon his notes and dazzle with all the brilliance he could command.

"And now for another form of satire. I want to take a look at the tragi-comedy of sexual passion in *Lolita*."

The girl gave him a speculative look and reached for her pen. He had caught her. Recklessly, he improvised and elaborated his feelings about Nabokov's tale of deception and self-deception, of the need to justify a sexual crime as a necessary redemption. It did not seem difficult to argue the seducer's case with conviction as he looked at the girl. He passed the hour with the sense that he had only just got into his subject. Professor Jenkins' vote of thanks cut him off, kindly but firmly, in mid-sentence.

The students shuffled out. The girl remained, twiddling a red pen between long white fingers as she stared at him. He felt as gauche as a schoolboy.

"Did you like it?"

"It was pretty good," she said. "But I wouldn't bank on their asking you back. *Lolita*'s a banned book on the Albany curriculum."

"Oh, lord. I should have known."

"I shouldn't worry about it. You wouldn't want to come back. Albany's a real drop-out hole, as you might have noticed."

"It's not totally beguiling. I hope you won't think me rude, but I can't quite see what someone like you is doing here."

"Me? I wanted to be in London and they offered me a place. So here I am, surviving. Just. It's a pretty grim course. I'm thinking of switching to Political Science next year. I like politics."

"What kind?"

"The revolutionary kind." She sauntered up to the lectern and put her elbows on it, propping her chin with her hands as she smiled up at him. Her eyes really were extraordinary, turquoises fringed with lashes that reminded him of Victorian feather fans. "Wondering what a nice girl like me can know about that kind of thing, Mr Craven?"

"Matthew," he said, transfixed.

"Well, Matthew," she said. "If you were to give me a meal, you might find out. If you're interested."

He blinked. "How about dinner tonight? Seventeen Chester Square. Eight o'clock."

"Okay by me, buddy." Her smile widened suddenly. "You were good, you know. Better than the others we had this term. And a lot better looking." Swinging away to the door, she turned. "You never asked my name. I'm Clarissa."

Torn between the desire to beguile her with exquisite food and beautiful music and the nervous apprehension that neither they nor his house might be to the taste of a revolutionary spirit, Matthew compromised on two slices of quiche, a workmanlike slab of cheddar and Handel's organ concertos turned down very low. Jeans and an open shirt, red sneakers, a copy of the *New Statesman* flipped open on a chair; well, at least he would pass as being ripe for reform. He picked out the Marseillaise with one finger on the piano.

Clarissa arrived at ten o'clock with a large raffia bag swinging from her gaberdined shoulder. Below her in the square, Matthew caught sight of a strikingly beautiful red-headed boy glowering at him through the windows of a blue Deux-Chevaux before it zipped furiously away towards Victoria.

"Who's young Swinburne?"

"Jake? He's a pal. It's dyed, actually. I once told him red hair was terribly erotic." She grinned. "And now he's stuck with it. Am I late? You look cross."

He stood aside to let her in. "I'd given you up."

"Early days," Clarissa said cheerfully. "Punctuality isn't my strong point."

"It's the least important," said Matthew, who regulated his days with the precision of a quartz watch. "Lovely you're here. How do you manage it? I thought Albany girls got locked in at night."

"Where there's a will, my dear," Clarissa said. "Getting back in is a little more difficult."

"That shouldn't be a problem. The one thing this house doesn't lack is spare bedrooms."

"Do they come with a teddy-bear?" She looked at him blandly. "I do hate sleeping on my own."

He glanced down at the skirt and sweater protruding from her carrier-bag. "You *are* resourceful."

"Put it down to experience," she smiled.

He watched her strip off her coat and shake back a mane of hair. Black jeans clung like a wetsuit to her legs up to the soft split of her crutch. Her small breasts made punctuation marks in a very under-buttoned shirt of red silky stuff. "Nice, aren't they," she said. "Leather." He adjusted his gaze.

"Very nice."

Immensely alluring, she was also mildly alarming. Girls tended to be impressed by the chilly splendour of Chester Square. Clarissa's eyes glittered with amusement as she came into the drawing-room.

"Well. This is elegant."

"The garrets were all taken. Wine?"

"Pepsi." She turned from the cushions fringed and tasselled in harmonious shades of pink to the chaste array of silver trinkets on the piano and the pallid smiling portraits flanking the fire-place mirror. She prodded one of the cushions. "Pretty stuff."

He put the glass in her hand. "You don't have to be polite. My mother always had it like this and I never got around to changing it." Which was odd, now he thought about it. He had always disliked the room. Celia had said it reminded her of an American funeral parlour.

"A maternal shrine." Clarissa's eyes narrowed. "Now, that is interesting."

He saw Freud coming, and ducked. "Hardly. She's very much alive and kicking. In Rapallo. Husband number three. My parents got divorced years ago."

"Did you mind?"

"Very much."

Clarissa stared up at the portrait of his mother. "I was really glad when mine split up. I used to lie in bed and pray for it every night. I thought it was all my doing when she went. God and I, hand in hand. That was my religious phase." She sprawled on one of the high-sided white sofas and stretched, sliding one black heel down the side of her calf. "Would you believe me if I told you I used to wear a night-shirt stuck full of pins to show my love of God?"

"I hope he appreciated it."

"Not so it showed. *Ergo*, I gave him up."

"For?"

"Carnal delight," Clarissa said. "This is my favourite music. How did you guess?"

"Hunch." He gloated over his good fortune as Clarissa rolled to one side and looked up at him with the opaque stare of a beautiful Siamese cat. "I've got a little hunch myself," she said. "I think you and I might have a lot more in common than a taste for Handel. Are you tied up with anybody?"

109

"No. Still, don't let's be too precipitate."

She held him with her curious unflickering gaze. "I only make up in conversation what I lose by clocks, Matthew. You ought to try. It cuts a lot of unnecessary corners."

He smiled. "I quite like the corners myself. Still, perhaps you'll persuade me over dinner."

Her conversation turned into more general channels at the meal, to his relief. She told him about her family—Italian mother, father a lecturer in French history; she saw little of either—and of her beliefs. Bakunin was her hero, closely followed by Trotsky on whom, she said with confidence, her friend Jake was a great authority. She was keen to be involved in political action, but was at present having to satisfy herself with pressing pamphlets on people in Oxford Street. When Matthew rashly made some mention of Gracedew and the past, Clarissa's eyes brightened with fury, but not on his behalf.

"I find that sort of thing appalling. Think how many families you could house in a place like that. Men like your cousin are the parasites of the country, stuffing themselves with caviare and port while the poor starve on their doorsteps."

Oh dear, Matthew thought. One of those. "Steamed puddings and tepid tea would be nearer the mark," he murmured.

"Don't swing red herrings about. It doesn't matter if the old bugger lives on cornflakes. I mean, you couldn't live with a clear conscience in twenty rooms thinking of all the homeless families in Nottingham and Leicester. You'd have to do something about it. There's a moral obligation."

"Fortunately, it's not one that I'm likely to have to meet." Nor, although he was not in the mood to discuss it, did he share her view. The answer to Britain's housing shortage was not to be found in squeezing ten families into Gracedew. Despoiling the past did not resolve the problems of the present. He turned the conversation back to Clarissa's political aspirations.

Revolutionary ardour appeared to satisfy her physical appetites. She ate only a handful of nuts, picked at the quiche and crumbled a piece of cheese in her fingers. Cast in the role of listener, Matthew could not fail to notice, with slight irritation, the number of times that Jake's name was quoted at him as an authority. Carefully nonchalant questions produced the

110

information that he worked for the *Morning Echo* and was a serious and committed person. Capital letters were implicit. He began to think he had over-rated Clarissa's intelligence.

"You've no idea how trivial he makes me feel," she sighed. "He's right. I haven't done anything that could be called significant."

"Perhaps you should set about converting me for a start," he suggested, humouring her.

She looked at him and broke into a sudden laugh. "You should have stopped me. I've been boring you rigid. Tell me about you instead. That's going to be interesting." She propped her chin on her hands. "All I know is that you're rich, you've written two very successful books, you like Nabokov and you'd like to go to bed with me. Anything else?"

"Why don't we stick with the last?"

"Insufficient."

"For what?"

"I don't fence about futures," she said quickly. "Don't let's play games. You know quite well what I mean."

Was he being propositioned? He smiled at her. "I'm not terribly sure we're a perfect match, if that's what you mean. I'm not politically committed. I'm very selfish about my privacy. I'm told that I'm quite neurotic and difficult."

"It's not how you strike me. Who says so?"

"Plural. Irritated females."

Her eyes sharpened. "Any in particular?"

"None so pretty and sharp off the mark as you."

"You're certainly good at indirect answers. I'm not sharp, though. Soft as a little butterball."

"Dropped in ice." He grinned at her. "Sorry, but I find that the most unlikely proposition of the evening."

"Even more unlikely than my hunch?"

Back to that again. Still, she was astonishingly seductive-looking. One white wing of a hand was pushing a veil of hair away from her face. The curve of her turned cheek had the quality of one of those mysterious girlish profiles painted on Japanese screens. To be precipitate was not, perhaps, such a bad thing.

"I quite like your hunch," he said.

"Enough to take it seriously?"

"Not yet." He drained his glass and stood up. "The only thing I'm ready to take seriously at the moment is the idea of getting some sleep. I'm glad you came, Clarissa. Now, pick up your bag and we'll find you a bed."

She came into his arms with a half-smile and lifted her mouth to his. "Your bed. Then we'll talk about sleep."

"I begin to see the charm in cutting corners in conversation," he said as she started up the stairs. She swung round, laughing down at him. "Oh, you've an awful lot to learn yet."

"Have I indeed?" He felt a moment of unease. "About what?"

"You'll see. Which way now?"

Naked, with black hair flicking about her narrow hips, she reminded him of a splendid wild animal as she prowled about the bedroom, looking at his books, glancing over the letters on the windowsill, peering into his cupboards with shameless interest. He knew that women usually made thorough inspections of a new lover's bedroom, but he had never heard of it being publicly carried out. Unsure whether to rebuke her or laugh, he decided to help her along by opening all the drawers. Unembarrassed, she peered in.

"I don't somehow think I'm going to find the key to Bluebeard's chamber here. Christ, you're so tidy."

"Or careful. With you around, I might need to be."

"How irritating." She turned into the circle of his arms. "Just when I was looking forward to getting to know more about you."

"You seem to be doing quite well."

"I'll do better." She locked her hands behind his neck. "Well now. Do you like me? Do you want me?"

He laughed. "Do you always talk like a whore in men's bedrooms, Clarissa?"

"I talks as I inclines," she said. "Fifty pounds, sir, and I'm yours for the night."

"Done," he said. "So come to bed."

"Not yet." She pulled away. "I want a bath. Come and have one with me. Let's get to know each other a little better first, hm?"

112

Uncomfortably squeezed against the taps in a hot trough of scented foam, he submitted to Clarissa's ministrations for the pleasure of feeling her flesh touching his, her breasts soft against his shoulders as she soaped and stroked his body. He wanted to have her there, kneeling between his legs, but she frowned and slid out of his wet hands with discouraging agility.

"Why all the hurry?"

"Desire waits for no man," he said hopefully.

"Glad I'm not a man," she said, deftly winding a towel round her body and dropping a kiss on his forehead. "You wait. Good for you."

When at last, in bed beside her, he turned out the light and reached for her, she shrank away from his greedy hands with a sigh.

"I'm quite sleepy."

"Never mind."

"But I do mind," she said coolly. "Sorry, Matthew." And she turned on her side away from him and firmly went—or so it seemed—to sleep.

Clarissa visited him three times during the following week. Wearing clothes which seemed to have been expressly designed to inflame him, she talked about sex with a racy frankness which left him feeling that his affair with Celia had been decidedly tame. As liberal with kisses and caresses as in her conversation, she continued to fend him off with excuses. There had, she said mysteriously, been a very upsetting experience. He would just have to take things very slowly. Short of raping her, he seemed not to have a choice.

Accustomed to being the pursued party, Matthew was dismayed to find himself being reduced to a ball of putty by Clarissa's games of advance and retreat. She began to occupy his thoughts to a degree which he found indefensible and infuriating. Caution suggested that desire and jealousy—he was never allowed to suppose that he was the only man in her life—were unlikely to lead to contentment. He was not happy with her. He was nervous and bad-tempered without her. Amusing though she often was, she maddened him with her gibes at his mildly reactionary political views, and her constant references to Jake's nobler beliefs. He was dismayed to find himself envying her

her serene sense of commitment. Listening to Clarissa, he was painfully aware of the lack of nobility in his own aspirations since the fading of his dream of restoring Gracedew. He felt the truth in her accusation that he was indifferent to the sufferings of those poorer than himself.

He wanted Clarissa to commit herself to him. He wanted to lead her about, to parade her for the envy of his friends, to put a pretty leash around her neck. Most of all, he wanted her to stop seeing other men. He was tired of saying that he respected her freedom. Freedom meant that she was free to run away.

She remarked one day on the boredom of having to carry clothes and make-up about with her. Cunningly, Matthew suggested that she could keep a few things at Chester Square. He would clear out a few cupboards. Nothing easier.

"Well, I'll think about it," Clarissa said kindly. On her next visit she brought with her three large carrier bags and a kitten called Lois. The kitten ran away. The bags were joined by a box of Clarissa's books and a pink quilt of venerable appearance. Matthew gave her a door-key.

"Not symbolic," he said.

"Of course not," Clarissa said. "Better give me two. I'm not lucky with other people's house-keys."

Once installed, Clarissa took over the house with a rapidity which was mildly disquieting. The portraits of his parents were taken down and replaced by six large unframed posters proclaiming Clarissa's political affiliations. He agreed with her that it made the room a lot less formal. Finding his study piled high with her text-books and files, he retreated to one of the spare bedrooms. ("Sure you don't mind?" "Of course not.") The cleaning-lady struggled womanfully for a time to preserve the kitchen's neat order from an encroaching army of ketchup-stained plates, greasy saucepans and overflowing ashtrays, before deciding it was a battle she could best end by abandoning the field.

To all this Matthew submitted. It seemed worth losing a kingdom, let alone a kitchen, if he could gain access to the heaven which lay locked between Clarissa's white thighs. And eventually, wonderfully, heaven was his. The sweetness of desire achieved and consummated seemed adequate compensation for a lingering sense of faint disappointment. It would, he thought, get better.

It didn't. Clarissa didn't enjoy sleeping with men so much as making them agonize for the moment when she would bestow herself on them. Her power lay in her detachment. She would promote and exploit frustration by any means that came to hand in order to keep her lovers barking at her heels in a constant state of tension, uncertainty and jealousy. Living with Matthew did not lessen her relish for playing games. She would leave his bed in the middle of the night and return to Chester Square the following day without explanation. Questions would be met with smiles and evasions. Some weeks later she would refer to an occasion they both knew about when she had spent the night with someone else.

"You didn't tell me, as a matter of fact."

"Didn't I?" She laughed. "Well, it probably didn't seem important."

"Who was it?" A stupid question.

"Lordy, lordy, here we go again. It doesn't matter. It doesn't affect the way I feel about you."

"Then why—"

"Let's go and fuck," Clarissa said. "I've got ten minutes before Jake picks me up."

"Jake can bloody well wait for once," he said savagely. "If I want a slot machine, I'll go and buy one."

"We'll let him wait then," Clarissa said, smiling gently and starting to unbutton his shirt. "Coming?"

Through Clarissa, Matthew learnt that paradise and hell were one and the same place.

Sometimes, sitting alone at night over a novel which had, since Clarissa's arrival, become a protracted jeer at the sentimental face of love, he contemplated a return to the placidly selfish order of his solitary life. But when, the next day, his long-legged Clarissa sauntered through the door with an opaque smile and a bunch of roses to tell him he was the only man in London worth talking to, he found himself postponing decisions until the next week, and then the next. He must, for his peace of mind, bring it to an end. Lying on her, he had fantasies of squeezing her breath away with his weight, of twining her black hair round her neck and pulling it tight.

"You're hurting me, Matthew," she said, her eyes smoked with pleasure.

"Sorry."

"No need. I like it."

Did she? He could never be sure. Even with his mouth on hers and her legs crushed between his, he had no sense of possessing her. Doubt and apprehension clouded the moment he had spent the whole day looking forward to enjoying.

"And who is Alice?" She stood below him in the hall. A letter dangled from one white hand, a photograph from the other. "An old girlfriend of yours? I don't remember hearing about her."

"Only because there was nothing to tell." Smiling, he came down the stairs, trying to hide his irritation. "I do wish you'd leave my post alone, sweetheart. I'd much rather open my own letters."

"You ought to be flattered by my curiosity. She looks quite interesting. Pity her nose is so big." She dropped it on the table and swung out of the door. "See you when you're in a better temper," she called sweetly from the steps. "Good writing."

He heard the guttural splutter of Jake's car. Only for convenience and so as not to put him to any trouble, she always said, wide-eyed. She wouldn't dream of letting him ferry her to and fro for her tutorials. And Jake didn't mind. Oh no. Jake certainly didn't mind. A month ago, he would have put himself through the unnecessary torment of peering out of the drawing-room window to watch Clarissa slide into the car and lean across to kiss the driver's mouth before stretching a familiar arm behind his shoulders as they drove away. Not now. He had grown quite clever at protecting himself.

Lighting a cigarette, he went slowly back to the kitchen to read one of Alice's infrequent letters with the mean wish that she might also be suffering. Nothing so cheering to lowered spirits as the knowledge of someone else's despair.

Alice sounded annoyingly contented with her life. His idle predictions about her future could not have been further from the mark. She had married a Californian script-writer called Buck, become the mother of two boys, and had acquired a red Mustang and a pretty Malibu beach-house. She wrote now to say that she had seen a novel by him in the local book-store and wondered how he was enjoying being famous. Three exclama-ation marks. (Matthew sighed as he thought of the half-written chapter upstairs, buried, doubtless, under a heap of Clarissa's clothes.) She had told Buck all about him. It would be really lovely if he could ever come out to California. A bed was always ready for him. Et cetera.

Homesickness crept in only with the last page. Didn't Gracedew seem a different world, looking back? Did he ever go there now? She had heard from her father that there had been a bit of a quarrel and that old Mr Craven was more of a recluse than ever, spending all his time shut up in the back of the house while everything went to ruin. She supposed that Mrs Craven had always been the real mainstay. Still, she hoped that everything would come right in the end. She knew how much the house had meant to him. And it was such a splendid place.

Her words gave him pause for a moment. Perhaps he should do something. He could write and propose himself for a visit. It was dreadful to contemplate Gracedew's slow decline, the old man sitting like Miss Havisham in shuttered rooms, forgetful and forgotten. Remembering the viciousness of that final conver-sation, he hardened himself. There was no point in being sentimental. He would only lay himself open to further humilia-tion. In time, perhaps. Not yet.

He returned to the letter, now babbling to an end. Everything in California was different, the pace of life, the emphasis on the new, the importance of always seeming to be successful. Still, it was marvellous. Buck was a dear, the children adorable, the neighbours almost too hospitable. She wouldn't change her life for anything.

She did, he thought, protest a little too much to be entirely convincing, but the photograph of a brown, thin, brilliantly smiling Alice with her fat babies looked jolly enough. Lucky Buck.

It occurred to him that he could have been very happy, married to a girl like Alice.

117

Too late.

"I've got news for you, my darling," Clarissa said one day at the beginning of the autumn term. "I'm pregnant."

Joy. Alarm. Doubt. Curious that one could feel all that, simultaneously. "I thought," he said carefully, "that you were on the Pill."

"Right. I forgot a couple of days." She stood in the middle of the black and white marble hall, swinging her bag of books to and fro. Her face was puffy and sallow. Lank hair straggled on the shoulders of her dirty anorak. She looked frightened and very young. "I know what you're thinking. It is yours, Matthew. Honestly. I checked the dates. I suppose I could have an abortion but I haven't got much cash. You have to pay in notes."

"You don't have to worry about that." He hesitated. "I mean—do you want to?"

She didn't, or wouldn't look at him. "Not much. Not really. Shades of an RC upbringing, I suppose."

"Well, we could," he said, "get married. If you liked."

"Nightingales and moonlight," Clarissa muttered. "Oh my love, if I dared to think, if I could hope that you—" She stared with intensity at the chequered marble floor. "Nice if it was like that. Never mind. What do you think?"

"I don't feel capable of much thought at the moment. It isn't the worst idea in the world. But no more Jake. Or anyone else."

She grinned up at him with some of her old flippancy. "I see. Going to lock me up in purdah, are you?"

He looked at her soberly. "I'm quite keen on fidelity."

"We all are, in theory," Clarissa said. "You shouldn't have too many problems when I'm the size of an elephant. Well, I'd better buzz off to my lecture now that I've got that bit of news off my chest. I wish I didn't feel so damn sick."

"Stay here and go to bed," he said. "I'll bring you something to eat. You might need a bit of looking after."

"You're sweet." She turned at the door. "I do love you, Matthew. You're much too nice for me. I wish I could promise that I'll make you happy."

"You will," he said. He wanted, very much, to believe it.

Clarissa opted out of her degree course two terms short of the finals. They were married very quietly, at a registry office, in January, when Clarissa was four months pregnant. Matthew sent a brief note to Cousin Jack to notify him of the event, and a slightly longer one to his mother. The first elicited no response other than a handsome gilded card from Mr and Mrs Bates, wishing him all the best and hoping to see him and the young lady in the not-too-distant future. The second, as he had wearily anticipated, brought back a tirade of questions and reproaches. Who was she? And why was it all so hole-and-corner? She could well imagine. Had he nothing better to do than to bring disgrace on his family? It occurred to Matthew, as he unwrapped her present, an etching of Gracedew which had belonged to his father, that his mother had a remarkably convenient memory when she was in a righteous mood.

John Cunningham, the bride's father, came with them to the registry office. A small anxious-looking man with a handlebar moustache, the principal feelings he exhibited were of gratitude at having a troublesome daughter taken off his hands, and envious wonder when the newly-married couple took him back for a drink—several, in Clarissa's case—at Chester Square. The house was, he murmured, very fine. When Clarissa had mentioned a novelist, he had somehow expected—his small pink hands flapped in the search for the correct expression—well, nothing like this, he lamely concluded.

Matthew smiled. "I'm afraid Clarissa doesn't share your enthusiasm. Still, she's very busy giving it a less formal air, as you can see."

Dr Cunningham's eyes glanced timidly towards the poster faces which menaced from the walls.

"Not for the better, in my opinion."

"Dad's one of yours," Clarissa announced, waving a glass at them. "You've got lots in common. It's his dream come true, isn't it, Dad? Tell him your mother's a countess, Matthew. He'll like that a lot."

"Only by virtue of her third marriage. Poland's counts aren't too hard to come by. Not that it's of much consequence," Matthew murmured.

"I'm so sorry they couldn't join us—do be quiet, dear," Dr Cunningham said as Clarissa hummed "Here Comes the Bride" with a hand on the barely perceptible curve of her stomach. "You're embarrassing both of us."

"Good," Clarissa said and emptied her glass on the floor. "That's what I think of countesses." Her voice slurred. "My deah Matthew. Words cannot express the concern I feel. After all that has been done for you. I had hoped. Silly old cow." Swaying, she clutched the side of a sofa and felt her way down it to the safety of the floor. "I feel so sick."

"Hardly surprising," Matthew said. "When did you start drinking? Breakfast?"

"Spirit of celebration," Clarissa murmured sadly, and collapsed.

"Nerves," Dr Cunningham said, red to the roots of his hair. "She was always highly-strung. She was a very religious child. Loretta was Catholic, of course. We sent her to the Hastings convent school. She was their star pupil."

"So she told me." He bent over her slumped form. "She isn't used to drinking, that's all. I should have stopped her. Don't worry. I'll put her to bed."

Standing in the winter wind on the doorstep, Dr Cunningham shook Matthew's hand with excessive warmth.

"She has got splendid qualities, you know," he said plaintively. "An excellent brain, if she'd only make use of it. What Clarissa needs is firm guidance."

Matthew smiled, pitying him. "Don't worry. I'm sure we'll be very happy."

Dr Cunningham pressed his hand again. "Don't let her take you over, Matthew. That's all I have to say. Her mother was a woman of unusually strong character."

Closing the door after him, Matthew felt a chill on his flesh.

Clarissa had a bad haemorrhage at the end of the month. The child was miscarried. There were to be no more pregnancies. Matthew found room for as much relief as regret. His paternity would have been a matter of hope rather than certainty.

Clarissa's attitude to fidelity was not markedly changed by marriage. Matthew often wondered why he put up with her behaviour. He supposed it was because he loved her. Every month brought a new name into his life. Dan, Trevor, Roddy,

Adam—he learned their habits and characteristics as he imagined that they learned his. Only Jake remained a constant. He stopped asking questions after the first year. It was, marginally, preferable to live in ignorance.

Things improved a little when he persuaded Will Lazlett to commission Clarissa to undertake a couple of interviews for one of the Sunday colour supplements. She did them adequately and was encouraged to do more. Matthew gave her a few tips on style. Sometimes he wrote the pieces for her. He praised, quite extravagantly, anything she wrote herself. Clarissa accepted it as her due and complained of the agonies of producing creative work. Matthew sympathized and encouraged her to struggle on. Clarissa partially occupied was a little easier to live with than Clarissa frustrated and with time on her hands, blaming him for her wasted life.

He was writing a good deal. He was extremely unhappy.

6

"More tea. It's Earl Grey. Your favourite, I seem to remember."

"Darling, how clever you are. But no milk. I'm trying to lose weight. I've been eating too many chocolates."

He looked at the wasted face to which rouge gave an odd feverish brightness. "You're very thin, Mamma. I thought the Poles liked good solid food. Potato cakes."

"Not Jozef. Well, he left when he was seven. You keep forgetting. Petits fours are more to his taste."

He poured the tea and sat down opposite her. "What does he do now? You said he'd retired."

"Jozef gambles," she said after a pause. "Quite a lot. Well, more than I like."

"I'd have thought you'd rather enjoy a flutter on the tables."

"I don't find it madly amusing. Nor would you." She sipped her tea. "Now, that *is* good. I cannot get Luisa to make it properly. Still, she makes a wonderful expresso. He starts at lunchtime. And finishes around four in the morning. It's an addiction."

"Lucky he's rich."

"He isn't," she said. "Not any more."

Matthew made a second survey of her clothes. She had struck him as looking her usual elegant self when she arrived at the restaurant for lunch. In the harsh light of Clarissa's frightful overhead lamp, a splayed octopus of black steel, he saw the threadbare patches on her skirt, the dents of good use on the polished tips of her shoes.

"Look," he said awkwardly. "If I can help—I get quite well-paid for the television work. You know, the book programmes. I could write a cheque." No. Better just to do it. He took out his cheque book and made out the sum of a thousand pounds to her. "Here. And don't argue about it. Present." He opened her bag and pushed it inside. Being a woman and his mother, she immediately examined it.

"Oh darling—are you sure you can afford it?"

Not really. Clarissa's views had not changed with four years of marriage, but she showed as much relish for spending as any good capitalist wife. The only difference he could see was that she spent more time in justifying her extravagances.

"Of course I can. Has he gone through all your money, Mamma? You may as well tell me."

She touched her lips with a gluey red stub. "Quite a bit of it. Well, yes, most of it. He isn't terribly lucky, poor Jozef."

"Can't you stop him?"

She laughed, without humour. "Have you ever tried stopping a gambler? I had to hide the money for my air-ticket, I was so frightened he'd find it. Don't worry. I'm quite used to all that. I will pay you back, Matthew dear."

"You needn't." He leant back on the sofa. "Well, what do you think of it all? Quite a change."

"Yes." She looked from the octopus lamp to the (very expensive) hand-plaited green straw rug from China spread before the fireplace. "Clarissa's a modernist, I see."

He lit a cigarette. "The perfect modern wife."

"You smoke too much. Can I have one?"

"I'm all bad habits." He lit it for her. She exhaled rapidly, coughing. "Very strong. Doctor Perroni says I'm to give it up."

"Why don't you?"

"I will." She drew heavily. "I will. Where is Clarissa, by the way? I'm dying to see her."

In bed with Jake, probably. "She always goes shopping on Thursday afternoons. She'll be back soon."

She looked at him thoughtfully, lidding her eyes against the smoke. "You are happy, darling?"

"The working man's a happy man," he quipped.

"That's not what I meant. I know you're terribly successful and well thought of. I meant Clarissa. Are you happy with Clarissa?"

"About as happy as you are with Jozef."

"You could always divorce her. I mean, it was wonderful of you to marry her when she got pregnant, but nobody would think the worse of you. She sounds to be quite capable of fending for herself."

"She is. But I'm not going to." He smiled at her. "It's not wonderful, but it's not intolerable. Let's say that we respect each other's independence."

"And Gracedew?"

Matthew sighed. "I thought we were going to get around to that sooner or later. I don't want to talk about it. There's nothing to be said."

"Don't be so difficult." The voice of command was, he noticed, returning now she was launched on to her favourite subject. She leaned forward, legs poised to one side, head at a birdlike angle of inquiry, the favoured style of the 'forties woman. "What did he say that time exactly, dear? Was there anything in particular?"

He thought for a moment. "Not really. A general stream of venom. Some of it against you, I'm afraid."

"Miserable old brute. After all those letters I wrote."

No need to tell her that they had been thrust, unread, into the waste-paper basket. "Gratitude isn't his strong point."

"Still, he didn't actually say he'd cut you out of his will?"

He blinked in the floodlight of her stare. "I took that as read. If he didn't do it then, he certainly has by now."

"Why?"

"Because I haven't been to Gracedew for well over five years." He rose to give the fading coals a prod with his foot. "Let's talk of something else. It's sad, I know, but it's part of my life that's over. Finished." He looked down at her. "Really, I don't mind."

"Still," she persisted. "If you did go there—he didn't say anything in particular? I often wondered when poor Charles went there for the last time—they didn't mention anything at all?"

He was struck by the nervous intensity of her interrogation. Taking her thin hands in his, he lightly chafed them. She was cold as death. "What is it, Mamma? What's the skeleton in the cupboard, hm?"

She stared up at him. "There is no skeleton. Only—"

"And here, at last, I am. You must be Matthew's mother. Oh Matthew, you are useless. You could have got a few biscuits out."

His mother old. His mother young. Black hair swinging, eyes too wide for innocence, a yellow scarf tied too high round her neck for fashion. Jake and his bloody love-bites. How had that extraordinary likeness between them escaped him for so long? Hypnotized, he looked from one to the other, wondering which would be the first to acknowledge it. The recognition, if there at all, was suppressed. They offered wary smiles. Clarissa bent for a kiss. An extended hand put her in her place.

"How very nice. Matthew gave me the most delicious lunch. Wheelers. Such a pity you couldn't join us." Her social voice achieved the wail of a police siren.

"I don't eat fish," Clarissa said coldly.

"Clarissa's become a vegetarian," Matthew explained. "A very strong-principled one."

"Well, I suppose I'm a sort of vegetarian, too. Jozef and I almost live on *linguine alle vongole*."

"Clams," Clarissa said. "You can't eat clams."

"Oh dear." She produced a pretty display of fluttering embarrassment. "You make me feel terribly guilty."

"My mother can eat what she likes," Matthew said, seeing that Clarissa was preparing herself for combat. "What about getting some of those biscuits you mentioned, darling?"

His mother affected to glance anxiously at her watch. "Goodness! It's so sweet of you, but I must go. I promised to be back for early dinner with Margot. You remember Margot, don't you, Matthew? You used to go ride a cock horse on her knee."

"Ride a cock what?" Clarissa inquired.

"The horse, dear. It went to Banbury Cross. You must know." Quavering, she sang the opening lines in a high little girl's ghost of a voice. "I sang quite well," she said apologetically as a fit of coughing overcame her. "Once."

"You certainly did." Worried, he bent over her. "You're tired. I'll ring and make an excuse for you. We can get a bed ready in no time."

She pulled herself to her feet. "So kind of you, darling, but I think I will go. I stayed there last night. No point in moving all my things. And Margot does love a bit of company now she's on her own again."

He registered the note of desperation behind the excuses. Well, he had never expected them to like each other. The evening could only, at best, have been a scant maintaining of decorum. Still, he was curious to know what she had to reveal or explain about Gracedew.

"I'll drive you there."

But she said nothing about it in the car. She only said: "Oh, dear, darling, I do understand. And I'm so terribly sorry for you."

"You'll have to remind me of the way," he said, and added, *sotto voce*: "Stop it, Mamma. It's not your concern."

Standing on the doorstep of Margot Talbot's Kensington mews house, she put her thin hands on his shoulders.

"Promise me you'll go to Gracedew soon, Matthew. And if you do hear anything, please, try not to be too hard on me. I did everything I could."

He kissed her. "I know. And of course I won't. Don't be such a goose. And don't stay away so long next time."

"Awful thing, cancer," Clarissa said sleepily from her pillow later that night. "You should have warned me."

"What are you on about now? You haven't got cancer."

"Not me. Your mother."

"What?" He switched on the light to stare at her. "Is that meant to be a joke?"

"If you find death funny. Come on. Anyone could see it. She's dying. That's probably why she made the trip to see you." Her face grew softer. "Poor Matthew. I didn't mean to blurt it out. I thought you knew." Her fingers brushed his face. "She's still very beautiful. I can see why you loved her so much."

He turned the light out on her and put his head down on the pillow, face turned out towards the dark.

"I don't believe you. Anyway, she would have said something."

"Nonsense, darling," his mother said on the telephone the

next morning. "Do you think I wouldn't tell you if something was wrong?"

He smiled his triumph at Clarissa.

"You see? She's perfectly all right."

"She's fooling you," Clarissa said. "Okay. Be fooled."

Elizabeth Kiernatowski died two months later. He flew out for the funeral, which was executed with all the richly emotional ceremony in which the Roman Catholic church excels. He was faintly disconcerted by the discovery that she had converted. Religion had not been a large part of her life.

"She only came to it at the last minute. A real joy and solace to us all," Jozef Kiernatowski whispered as the voices swelled and sobbed over the flower-decked coffin. "Such a wonderful woman, your mother."

In the villa, a modest building nestling behind trees away from the glare and shriek of the summer crowds of visitors, Kiernatowski showed an embarrassing wish to provide a detailed account of their married life. Kindly but firmly, Matthew stopped him.

"I'm sure you made my mother very happy. It must have been hard on you, these last few weeks."

Kiernatowski wiped his face with a handkerchief. "A tragedy. She was really devoted to you, Matt. Can I call you that? And that house." He shook his massive head. "Why, I believe I could tell you just about everything to do with Gracedew."

"Well, we won't start competing for superior knowledge. No time, alas. I have to get the train to Rome for the six o'clock flight."

The count's face fell. "You won't stay for dinner? I've got all Lizzie's friends coming along. It'll be quite an occasion." He put a finger between Matthew's ribs. "And maybe a little black-jack later, eh? No disrespect to the dead. Your mother liked her fun. Oh, we had a wonderful time, she and I. A real ball."

He had nothing to say to that. "All the same, I really can't stay. I imagine she left most of her things to you." He glanced around the characterless white room. "Still, I'd quite like to have something to remember her by."

"Sure. You take what you like, Matt." He looked embarrassed

for the first time. "There won't be much of a cash legacy. Life out here's more expensive than you'd imagine. We—uh—spent as we went along."

"So I gathered." He tried not to sound as savage as he felt. "You needn't worry. She told me the situation."

"Is that so?" Kiernatowski rolled a cigar between yellow thumb and forefinger and lit it, thoughtfully puffing. "Well, Lizzie was always a good story-teller. I can bet she only gave you half the picture. The amount of clothes she bought—why you could start a fashion store with just her dresses. Still, a great girl. Full of fun."

"I'll take this." He had found a crystal paperweight lying on a table of ornaments. It had sat beside her bed when he was a child. He remembered staring into it when she held it up to the light, watching the glitter of the trapped quartz fragments.

"That's all?"

"All that I want." He hesitated. "By the way, my mother didn't mention any kind of a family secret to you, did she?"

"Secret?" Kiernatowski pondered. "Certainly can't put my finger on one, Matt." He chuckled. "Maybe it was too bad to tell, eh? A real slap-up scandal."

He shrugged. "Perhaps. Well, we're unlikely to hear any more about it now."

Better so. *Do mortuis nil nisi bonum.*

At the age of twenty-nine, Matthew decided that the only way to endure his marriage was to accept that pain was good for him. He had never imagined that pain could have so many thresholds, that every time he told himself he could bear no more of it, he would find himself capable of submitting to a new humiliation. He hated Clarissa. He remained, fairly wretchedly, in love with her. He understood that he would never possess her in the way that she possessed him. Like a miser, he reckoned up the brief moments of shared delight and told himself that they made all the sadness worthwhile.

The marriage was much admired by his friends. The Cravens glittered as a public couple. It was understood that Clarissa had other men in her life and that Matthew respected and praised her independence. Theirs was a modern relationship.

It was his own fault. He should have stood up to her long ago. Her father had warned him.

He should never have married her, knowing how ill-suited they were. They had nothing in common. She despised his work. He found her articles increasingly vulgar and crass. (People said they were awfully entertaining.) She found his friends boring. He was never allowed to meet hers. Clarissa said they wouldn't understand him.

It was not the best marriage in the world. It was not the worst. She had never betrayed him in front of his friends. She gave him time to write. She had even settled down to something approaching fidelity. There were now only two men in her life and although Matthew did not like the sound of Jake, he had come to feel a kind of comradeship with the most tenacious of Clarissa's lovers. Jake and he were evidently in the same situation, bound to an impossible woman by weariness and love. There was safety in the familiar rival. He did not think now, that she would leave him for Jake.

"Of course I wouldn't, darling," Clarissa said. "Come to think of it, he's never asked me."

"Perhaps you should ask him."

"Snip snap," Clarissa said, making scissors with her fingers. "Just what I was thinking."

"Go ahead."

"Christ, Matthew, you've got as much sense of humour as a crab-apple. Can't you tell when I'm joking?"

"I'd be very unwise ever to assume that you were."

"Well," she said after a pause. "I was. Run off with Jake. Christ."

This conversation took place three days before Clarissa disappeared. Matthew told himself that he was well rid of her and waited in anguish for a telephone-call or letter announcing her return. He heard nothing. She walked through the front door a week later.

"I picked up some croissants. How about a cup of coffee?" She shook her hair out of her eyes and dropped her bag on the kitchen floor. Her lower lip was cracked and swollen. Two red half-circles almost met on the side of her neck. "I'm starving," she said.

129

"Where the hell have you been?"

Clarissa took out one of the croissants and bit into it. "I thought you wanted to get on with your writing. You might have been glad to have a bit of peace."

"Peace? When I didn't know where you were or what had happened? You could have been murdered for all I knew. Or run over. You could at least have left a note to say you were with Jake."

She brushed the crumbs off her chin. "I just wanted to get away for a bit. It's so damned claustrophobic here with you moping about the house all day. I can't even get a cup of tea without you deciding you'd like one as well. Constant surveillance. Why can't you go and work somewhere else, like other people?"

He watched as she felt in her bag for a cigarette. "Damn. I must have left them somewhere. Have you got one?"

He pushed a packet across the table.

"Thanks."

"Nice to know I'm still useful for something."

She surveyed him through a cloud of smoke. "That suit looks as though you've slept in it for a week. Not very good at taking care of yourself, are you, darling?"

"I was worried about you." Carefully, he poured out the coffee. "Cream?" He must not lose his temper. He must not let her trample down the last shreds of his self-respect. "I'm sorry if it bothers you to see me working in my own house, but I really don't see why I should go and work in a public library or a hotel room so as not to get in your way."

"Fine. Okay. Although I can't see why it matters for the kind of writing you do. Surely anywhere would be much the same."

Matthew smiled. "Really? And what is my kind of writing?"

"You should know. Slick social comedy for the precious few who know what you're on about. The tiny gemlike flame of wit without depth."

"Do I detect the acutely critical mind of our friend Jake?"

"Have the other croissant," Clarissa said. "Sweeten you up."

"I had breakfast when I got up. Five o'clock this morning, to be precise."

"No wonder you look like death." Clarissa yawned. "Where? Here?"

"The Taj Mahal. Where do you think?" His temper was rising. "I might remind you that I earn the money to pay the bills. And I do feel entitled to work in my own house without being grudged the space. As for Jake, you can tell him to keep his criticism for the day he learns not to split infinitives."

"Just because he hasn't had the benefit of a Cambridge education."

"You hardly need to point that out."

She flushed. "At least he cares about what he writes."

"And I don't, I suppose?"

"You?" Hands on hips, she stared at him across the kitchen table. "You don't care about anything except getting good reviews. Not about me. Not about the house. Not about what's going on in the world. You're just negative, Matthew. Totally negative."

His control snapped. "God knows I'd rather be that than an uninformed mouth-piece for somebody else's views," he said with quiet ferocity. "I might be prepared to listen if you were capable of showing a pennyworth of originality. I'm damned if I'm going to put up with getting your lover's bright ideas trotted out as your own. If Jake wants to think of himself as a great writer, you might ask him why he never got beyond being a turgid, illiterate, repetitive hack for a newspaper nobody in their right mind would ever bother to read. And now, my love, you can make the most of having the house to yourself for the day. Perhaps you'd like to ask Jake around to take a few more bites at your neck if he isn't too tied up with writing the week's paragraph of great thoughts."

Clarissa looked at him with apprehensive eyes. "What are you putting your coat on for, Matthew? Where are you going?"

"You needn't worry," he said. "I'll be back."

And so at last, with no conscious motive other than the desire to escape from the present, he found himself driving north to Gracedew for the first time in eight years.

He was in a calmer state of mind when he arrived towards the end of the afternoon. A row of cars parked outside Craven

Cottages was the only immediate evidence of progress. The street was brown with caked dung. The airy branches of limes dappled the verges with shadow. The shock of change came to him only when he looked up at Gracedew's entrance arch and saw its splendour gone to crumbling brick and rusty iron, the old forbidding aspect mocked by ruin. The drive was so pitted with holes and ruts that he was forced to abandon the car and walk. Lichen covered the white fences; a slow-moving net of green slime webbed the lake below the house in a merman's cloak. He stared up at the broken row of chimneys, the windows streaked with birdlime. The bell-wire rattled high on the wall, its handle gone. He hammered at the heavy door. A flutter of startled house-martins rising from their nests in the porch was the only response. He walked rather slowly round to the west side of the house where the French windows overlooking the old croquet lawn had always, in the past, stood open and inviting until dusk. The shutters were barred. The scene before him was one of silent dereliction. From under the branches of the elms, a jungle of nettles had rampaged without check over the calm green lawns. The gravelled paths were throttled by ropes of bindweed and purple clematis. As for Lucilla's lovingly tended herbaceous border, the neat clumps of lavender, the trumpeting row of arum lilies, it was no longer possible even to guess where it had been. All that he had remembered was gone. The ugly face of neglect jeered at his dismay in the soft summer light.

If only he had known. No. He couldn't be allowed the indulgence of that excuse. It was years since Alice had written to say that the house was going to ruin. It was pride, the fear of a second rejection, which had kept him away, that and the ever-increasing gap between his past and present modes of life. It made no difference now. Even if he had decided to risk further humiliation, there was no reason to suppose that the old man would have softened or altered his view, allowed him any part in the running of the house. Nothing could be gained by regretting what had not and probably could not have happened. And now? Well, he was here. He could only try. Pushing away the sinewed laurel branches, he walked on past the south front of the house where butterflies spun brilliant wings across a wilderness of roses and hollyhocks.

There was, puzzlingly, music coming from the library, behind the yellow cloth blinds. The garden doors stood open and inviting. Rather hesitantly, he went in, dreading the shock of further change.

He was pleasantly surprised. Here, all was as he had remembered, the faded chintz sofas, the walls of brown bound volumes, the delicate swirls of a theadbare Aubusson carpet. He glanced at a bold arrangement of lilies and leafy branches on one of the tables with surprise. Lucilla had been the vase-filler, the prettifier of rooms.

Walking on through the double doors to the second half of the room, he saw a possible explanation. A young woman was seated at the piano, her back towards him, her hands moving with a fair degree of competence through the chinking cascades of a Clementi sonata. Mildly intrigued, he leaned against the wall to listen. No expert, she had a light pretty touch. Music, gentle yellow light, the slight nod of the woman's head as she completed a tricky phrase with success, all combined to soothe and ease. He realized that he had almost forgotten the pleasurable sensation of thoughtless peace.

The sonata came to an end with a fine resounding chord. The woman turned her head, peering into the room.

"Who's there? Is that you, Mrs Bates?"

The light clear voice was unmistakable. He came forward as she rose, taking in with admiration the new easy grace of her figure as she leaned on the piano, the prettiness of the heavy cluster of curls fastened loosely on the nape of her neck.

"You played that very delightfully, Alice. Hardly a Californian accomplishment. I thought macramé was more in their line."

"Matthew!" She came rapidly across the room, her arms outstretched to hug him. "Do you know, I was just thinking about you. And here you are, conjured up by the power of thought! Have you been there for ages? And I was playing it so badly." Glowing, she looked up at his face. "You're tired, so I won't ask any questions, although there must be at least a hundred I'd like to ask. Sit down. I'll see if I can find some tea for you."

"No. Stay here for a bit." Lightly, he held her back. "You look wonderful."

"Different, at any rate. So I should. It's been well over nine years."

"Nine years and two months."

"Good memory."

"Very good. Still," he added with a smile, "I suppose I should feign amnesia now you're a respectable married woman. Is he here with you now?"

"Buck? No." She paused for a moment. "I did mean to write and tell you. They aren't the easiest kind of letters to write. We're divorced. It was quite a while ago."

"Mutual?"

"Not really. He found someone else. Well, we'd been in a shaky state for quite a while. The girl was an actress. Very pretty. I hear they're getting married."

He admired the coolness of her voice, while noticing a sudden tightening of her face which suggested the considerable strain it might be causing her to maintain it. When the laughter left her eyes, she had, in repose, a melancholy kind of beauty which was new to him. She could have played a Chekhov heroine.

He touched her cheek. "Poor Alice. I'm so sorry. I wish you had written, although I don't know what I could have done. Something, anyway."

"Well, you've got another kind of life now. It would have been like confiding in a stranger."

"We were friends."

"It was," she said, "a long time ago. Although I must admit, seeing you again—anyway, I'm fine now. I'm a survivor. I had to be. It was awfully lonely out there. They were all Buck's friends. I didn't belong. My father said I could have the lodge house at Chillingston. It works quite well. The children love being in the country."

"And you?"

She looked into his eyes with the bright direct stare which he remembered always having liked. "I know who I am. And, oddly, that matters in the end. Feeling you belong. Well, you must feel that here, don't you? Time doesn't make much difference in that way."

"Perhaps not. I don't know." He was disinclined to be

trapped into describing his feelings about Gracedew. "And you come here when you want to escape?"

She nodded. "I've always felt happy here. And I seem to be one of the few people your cousin will allow to invade his privacy. Probably because I don't get in his way or try to see him. He's upstairs, incidentally, if you want to see him. I'm sure he'd like it."

"I'm not. He did chuck me out, you know. It wasn't that I didn't care about Gracedew or want to come here. He really did set out to make that pretty impossible."

"Well, I wouldn't worry too much about the past," she said. "He doesn't remember very well. He may not even recognize you."

"What does he do all day?"

"Watch television, mostly. Mrs Bates takes his meals in on a tray. I've often been here for a whole day without seeing him. It suits both of us. I like the peace. I do a few flowers to pretty the place up, polish the books. It keeps me busy."

He looked out at the decaying garden. "And keeps the ruin at bay. I hadn't realized quite how bad things had got. I wish I had come before. Although I don't know whether he would have allowed me to do anything about it."

"Probably not. Anyway, Gracedew wouldn't fit in with your life now. Novels and reviews and so on. And your wife. She doesn't sound the kind of person to feel much enthusiasm about Gracedew."

He laughed. "You're right there. Where did you hear about Clarissa?"

"Charlie Remington met you both at a party. He said she looked very beautiful and talked a blue streak about oppression in the third world. And that you looked rather gloomy."

"I probably had a hangover."

"Still," she said after a pause, "you don't seem very happy."

"It's not what you could call a happy marriage. Interesting, perhaps, but not happy."

"I see. Poor Matthew."

Silence thickened with suggestion and the possibility of confidences. Her glance was perceptive and commiserating. It would, he thought, be very easy to burden her now with all the bitterness he felt about his marriage and about Gracedew's ruin. To confide, however, was to establish grounds for a greater degree of intimacy, to invite a kind of complicity which he was not wholly sure that he wanted. Not yet, anyway. "Oh, things aren't so bad," he said, and the moment for frankness was gone. A shadow crossed Alice's face. She masked it with a smile.

"Well, I'd better be on my way. The girl who looks after the boys leaves at five and it must be all of that. Let me know when you're going to be here again. You might like to come and have lunch."

He had not wanted so absolute a withdrawal into social conversation. Perversely, he found himself hankering after intimacy. "Can't I give you a meal in London sometime? I suppose you're there now and then?"

She looked at him speculatively, then nodded her head. "Yes. Yes, I think I'd like that very much, Matthew. You can always get me through my aunt at Ebury Street. Zinnia Tresham. It's in the book. Anyway—" She pushed out her hand with a naïve fierceness which touched him. "Good-bye."

"Oh, come on," he said gently. "Don't we know each other better than that?" Bending to kiss her cheek, he found her mouth. His arms closed round her, pulling her body to his. He felt the pressure of her breasts and thighs hard against him before she drew away, unhurried, but faintly perturbed. The pink tinge on her cheekbones spread out across her face as she pushed back and repinned her hair.

"Don't, my dear," she said. "Don't do it to me."

"Why not?"

"Because I'm not so brave as I seem," she said. "If you want the truth, I'm frightened of loving anybody too much, after Buck. I'm not sure that I could cope with the pain, and I'm not awfully good at separating sex from love. I don't know many women who are."

He nodded. "My honest Alice. You haven't changed."

"Cowardly Alice," she said and laughed. "Don't you praise me for looking out for myself."

When Alice had gone, walking down the drive with her long swinging stride—she had mocked away the offer of a lift for a mile-long journey—Matthew went up the dusty staircase to find his cousin and present himself. The house offered too distressing a spectacle for him to contemplate leaving without some attempt at a reconciliation. He intended at the least to discover the grounds for the old man's inexplicable hostility and to try to reason with him.

He was rapt in front of the television. A comedy series appeared to be the focus of interest; the crackle of syphoned laughter filled the room as Matthew came in. Hunched under a tartan rug in the shabby armchair beside his bed, the old man looked like a shrunken tortoise with his head jerking and nodding wildly above the garish red and yellow covering. Crazy enough for Lear in his ruined splendour. Matthew wrinkled his nose against the acrid smell of unkempt old age. The room was clogged with dust; it rose in clouds over his shoes as he stepped forward.

"Cousin Jack?"

There was no movement from the chair. Deaf, probably, following only the flicker of movement with that feverish concentration. Contrite about his initial feeling of repugnance, Matthew gently placed his hand on the old man's bony shoulder.

"It's Matthew. Matt. You remember me, don't you?"

". . . and then what?"

"Well, then she turned it over and did the other side." Laughter again. He turned it off.

"I was enjoying it," the old man said peevishly. "Why did you have to do that? They're most entertaining. Put it on again at once, do you hear?"

"In a moment," he said.

The head jerked sideways. Veined blue eyes peered at him with what looked like a glimmer of recognition of a resentful kind.

"Where's Mrs Bates? Who let you in?"

He thought of mentioning Alice and rejected the idea. If the old chap was this senile, he could easily be distressed by the thought that she had been present in the house without his knowing it.

"The library door was open."

"Do you think that's an excuse to come barging in where you haven't been invited?" He seemed to be making an effort to

137

draw himself up with an appearance of dignity. "I don't like trespassers. Didn't you see the sign by the gate? Be off with you, or I'll call the police."

He forced himself to maintain a good-humoured tone.

"Dear Cousin Jack, you're quite at liberty to call in whomever you wish. But it does seem a bit hard to be treated as a burglar when I spent half my life here with you and Cousin Lucilla. Do you really insist on forgetting me? Charles Craven's son."

"Oh, that Matthew," the old man said slowly. "Yes, I remember him all right. Clever chap. Writes books about people like me and makes his name on it. Still, can't blame him. Hadn't got a right to his own name, had he?"

Matthew stared down at him. "Why not?"

"Not a drop of Craven blood in him, that's why not. Charles told me when that woman buggered off with her boyfriend. Came here and said it was his duty to inform me. He should have bloody well made it his duty before he sent the child here. I was damn near to letting that boy take over this place since Charles wasn't prepared to have anything to do with it. Well, it doesn't make much odds now. He's gone and they're dead. All dead. Except me. I'm still going." The thought seemed to give him considerable pleasure. He produced a chuckle, the rattle of pebbles in a tin can. "They shut me up about it, Charles and Lucy. Said I wasn't to upset the child. Probably right. He was a funny nervous little chap."

Silence roared like Pacific breakers in Matthew's ears as he stared down at the blank television screen. Sense was there, suddenly, in so much that had seemed strange about his life and his parents' marriage. He could have suspected it all so long ago, from the feeling of constant tension between them, the dim consciousness of the unspoken always just below the surface, their eagerness to have him out of the way, out of sight. His face must have been a perpetual embarrassment to Charles Craven.

"You never knew who the father was?"

"Didn't tell me. Didn't ask. Could have been anybody, from what I heard of her goings-on. She wasn't particular." He plucked at the rug with trembling hands. "Damn thing keeps falling off. You still there, whoever you are? Make yourself useful and pull it up, will you?"

Silently, Matthew arranged the folds of tartan high over the birdlike body. "Better?"

"It'll do," he said with a hard, suspicious stare. "I've nothing to give you. There's no money in the house, if that's what you're after. That's what they all want." He giggled weakly. "Well, they won't get it. Bloody parasites. Coming here with their benevolent funds and their charity boxes. Don't you waste your time on me, I tell them. You go and see my tenants. That's where the money is." His voice dropped to a confiding whisper. "That woman was always after my money. Smiling and simpering and hinting to Lucy about the future of the house. Thought I'd be leaving Gracedew to her little bastard. Damned lucky to get what he did from Charles, considering he wasn't entitled to a brass halfpenny."

"Did his birth matter so much? He did love the house. And he had been led to suppose—"

"He had not. I never mentioned the subject, not a word about it. Not my fault if that woman filled his head with ideas about inheritance. Oh no, you won't catch me apologizing, young man. I've nothing to feel guilty about. What's this rug all over me for?" Fretfully, he pushed it down. "I'm half suffocating."

"I'll open the window for you."

"And leave me to catch my death of cold in a draught? Well, who cares? Who cares? I'll tell you. Nobody. I'd be better off dead." His voice rose to a querulous wail. "Where's Mrs Bates? I want my tea."

"I'll tell her on the way out." He turned at the door on an irresistible compulsion to force a confession out of him. "You know bloody well who I am, don't you?"

Silence.

"Come on. It won't kill you to say it. You've had your bit of entertainment."

The old man turned his head and looked at him with a gaze of steady venom. For a moment, Matthew thought he had won. The eyes flickered, and shifted away.

"I don't give a damn who you are. Why should I? It's no concern of mine. Good-day to you."

It was, he understood, useless to persist. Bleakly, he went through the doorway and back down the echoing wooden stairs.

Bates, not his wife, was preparing the tea-tray in the large emptiness of the kitchen. His back was to the door, but the small wiry figure was easily recognizable.

"He wants his tea," Matthew said.

"What the hell are—?" Turning, he broke into an apologetic laugh. "Well. You gave me a fair start and all. I've not changed jobs, you know. She's in one of her headache moods, so I said I'd put things together this once." He held out a small polished palm. "Eh, but it is good to see you after all this time. Not changed much, neither. Brought the wife down?"

"No. I came alone."

"Not by invitation, I don't suppose."

"Hardly."

"Well, I reckon it follows, don't it," the chauffeur said. "You shouldn't have gone off like that, you know, not when she'd just died and all. I'm not asking questions, mind. I know there's two sides to every story."

"I don't know what story he tells."

"He told Mrs Bates you just flared up and went like a bat out of hell."

"He didn't say why?"

Bates poured the water from the kettle, set the blue and white milk-jug out beside the teapot. "Reckon that'll do him. No. And she didn't see fit to go asking for reasons. Well, it made sense you wouldn't be wanting to sit here with him for t'rest of your days. You'd your own life to lead. We read all about you in t'paper, you know. They've all your books in Nottingham library. There's a lot of respect for you in the village," he added gravely.

"I did want to stay here, you know," Matthew said. "I wanted to help."

"He wouldn't have taken kindly to that idea, not then. Happen he's changed his mind by now, though." He peered at Matthew. "Did you talk to him about it?"

"I tried. He pretended not to know who I was."

"Well, I shouldn't let that trouble you," the chauffeur said drily. "He doesn't know who I am half the time. It's the loneliness as does it. He's been like this since she died." He put a hand on Matthew's arm. "I know it's hard, but try to have a bit of

140

patience. He'll come round to it in the end, if you put it right to him. You always did have a way with words. Stay on a bit. See him in the morning. He's best in t'mornings. Tell him you aren't wanting to take over, just to see the place back on its feet again. If you could make him see sense—well, we'd work our guts out to see Gracedew back to herself again."

"So would I. It's awful, what's happened. As though he was willing the house to die with him."

"I think he is 'n'all. I told him last year I'd do the garden over for nothing rather than see it the way it is. He wasn't having any. Told me to mind my own business, near as nothing. Maybe with you here, he'd change his mind."

Matthew shook his head. "That's one thing I've learned today. He'll never tolerate the idea of my being here. It's too late to talk about saving Gracedew. I'm sorry."

The chauffeur studied his face for a moment. "Aye. Well. No more to be said then. Good-bye, sir. My regards to Mrs Craven."

"To—?"

"Your wife, sir."

"Oh. Clarissa."

Driving back to London down the motorway, he thought how peculiar it was that he should have been so slow to link Clarissa to her married name. Did he have so little sense of her as his wife? The thought produced a twinge of guilt. Perhaps he had over-reacted to her gibes. Negative, she had called him. He perceived some truth in the accusation. Waiting could produce a negative state of mind. There had, he acknowledged, always been a lingering assumption that Gracedew would take a place in his life again, that he only had to make the move, take the initiative. What was now impossible had been less than a likelihood for years, but it had, like an unfinished love affair, insidiously affected his attitudes and choices. There could be no expectations after today. The wise course would be to put the whole thing out of his mind, try to forget, avoid any temptation to brood on the past. The world knew him as Charles Craven's son. That was how things should stay. Only. Only. Angrily, he wiped his eyes with the back of his hand before swerving into the slow lane where lorries rumbled imperious displeasure and

141

flashed their lights until, blinded by tears, he slid to a halt on the hard shoulder. Slumped on the steering wheel, he wept, partly in a kind of rage against himself. Stupid! Stupid to be so affected by a house in decline and a story thirty years old. If only they had told him, not left him to find it out like this, to have her shame thrown in his face as if it was somehow all his fault.

A torch trapped his glistening face. "Feeling all right, sir?"

Weakly, he stared up at the bland young face and tried to grin. "Fine. Just a bit tired. Long drive."

"I'm afraid you can't sleep here, sir. There's a service station five miles on. My advice is to get yourself a cup of something and have a bit of a rest in the car-park. All right?"

"All right. Thank you, officer." Wearily, he started the engine and edged out into the stream of traffic.

The house was in darkness when he arrived back. There was a note on the table in the hall. It was from Clarissa. It appeared that she had left him. She offered neither an explanation nor an apology. She had simply packed her bags and gone.

To Jake, presumably.

He remembered once having read some article in a woman's magazine on the break-up of marriages. Women, according to the writer, were consistent in their obsession for leaving a clean house behind them when they deserted their men. No frenzy of hygiene appeared to have touched Clarissa in her going. Numbly, he went from room to room, emptying ashtrays, carrying out half-filled cups of cold coffee, stripping the tattered political posters from the walls. The unmade bed which he had infrequently shared with Clarissa bore evidence of recent use. He took the stained pink sheets down to the kitchen and crammed them into a dustbin which he carried out for disposal. Methodically, he washed up all the saucepans and plates which had been left stacked by the sink.

By midnight, the house was his again; all evidence of Clarissa that had not been burned or thrown away had been piled into a large suitcase at the back of the cellar.

There was nothing more to be done. A large tumbler of whisky failed to drive ghosts away. Silence gathered round him like a cloud of grief. A door banged in the wind. He found himself looking up eagerly, pushing the empty whisky glass out of sight.

Perfectly stupid. Why should she come back now? He didn't want her to come back. The bitch.

Alice Tresham had given him her telephone number before she left. He rang it, pleased to notice how steady his hand was. Nothing to worry about; he was perfectly in control.

"Yes? Hello? Who is it?" Her voice was blurred with sleep.

"Matthew."

"Oh. Isn't it rather late? I was in bed." She sounded remote. "Well, what do you want?"

"Just to talk. I wondered if you could manage to come to London for dinner tomorrow. Please."

"I don't think so. I can't leave the children. Why couldn't you ring up in the morning, like anybody else?"

He swallowed. "Clarissa's left me. Sorry if I sound a bit odd. It's been quite a shock."

There was a pause. "Hold on," she said in a gentler voice. "I'll just get a cigarette. Don't hang up."

He waited, and heard the click of a lighter.

"Poor Matthew. Is there anything I can do?"

"Not really." The salty lump in the back of his throat rose to block his words. Sobs broke his phrases into gulps of misery. Nothing but a failure. He might as well be dead. Clarissa gone, Gracedew ruined, books no good; appalled, he listened to himself whining for comfort and found himself unable to stop.

"Stop it," Alice said. "I'll risk leaving the children just this once. The girl comes in at breakfast. Just hang on until I get there, okay?"

"You're a saint," he said, and heard a laugh at the other end of the line.

"No such luck. I'll be there in a couple of hours."

She arrived looking pale and red-eyed in the grey light of dawn. Silently, he let her in.

"Coffee?"

"No thanks. Where do you sleep?"

Too exhausted to be bewildered, he led her meekly up the stairs and into the bedroom where, thank God, he had remembered to make up the bed. He looked on with

143

astonishment as Alice quietly and efficiently began to remove her clothes.

"I didn't mean that. What the hell do you think I am?"

"Lonely. I went through it myself. I do know." She turned her clear eyes towards him as she pulled off her cotton petticoat and put it neatly over the back of a chair. "I know you didn't mean this. I haven't any better comfort to offer. It's about friendship, not sex. So come to bed."

He slept gratefully and deeply with his arms wrapped round her warm body and his head buried in her shoulder. She had gone when he woke up. The note on the hall table in her large round hand simply said that she was always there when he needed her. And sorry about the dinner.

It was not long before Matthew received a short and disagreeable communication from Clarissa's solicitor, putting forward what seemed to him to be highly unacceptable terms for a divorce settlement. His own legal adviser was, while friendly and sympathetic, less than encouraging. Divorce laws, as far as Matthew could see, were laid down according to some fiendish feminist code by which Clarissa could represent herself as a penniless and homeless victim to whom he had a duty to hand over all the worldly goods with which he had so rashly endowed her in the marriage service. He pointed out that he was not a rich man, that the house was his only major asset, that he had paid for everything during the marriage. He drew attention to Clarissa's extravagance. It was useless. Chester Square would have to be sold, his few investments liquidated, and the furniture divided down to the last kitchen fork, all for the cupidity of a woman who had always claimed to disdain money.

Disillusionment seldom makes for good talk. His friends, while ready with expressions of sympathy, displayed the usual human distaste for misfortune. Matthew successful, charming and with an intriguing marriage was one thing; Matthew broke, sullen and talking too much of his own bad luck to add liveliness to a dinner-party was quite another. Invitations fell away faster than leaves from a tree in winter; the girls who had once been ready to drop all prior engagements for a dinner at Chester Square seemed always to be away or washing their hair.

He rang up Celia Rivers. But Celia was enmeshed in the throes of her own divorce from Robert.

"Darling, I'm here to listen," she said, gazing with limpid eyes across the candlelit table of a restaurant which, she had said, was blissfully quiet and which had turned out to be the favoured haunt of Celia's admirers and friends. "Tell me everything," she commanded him.

He spent the evening listening to Celia's woes.

"Poor sweet, you do look as though you've been through the mill," she said as he paid for the meal. "You used to look so young."

Courtesy forbade him to respond in kind. Besides which, it had to be said that Celia's traumas had left no visible scars. He understood that she had come to the dinner chiefly for the pleasure of delivering that gibe. It was Celia's way of getting her own back.

"We must do this again," she glowed, exultant, from her doorstep. "It's been such fun."

"Yes," he said. "Wasn't it?"

Anxiety wrinkled her pretty forehead. After the revenge there follows, inevitably, the moment of regret. "I don't think I'm doing anything on Thursday. We might—"

"I think not." He touched her cheek with his mouth. "Good-night, Celia."

Alice, dear dependable Alice, remained to buoy him up. He often wondered how he would have survived the post-Clarissa months without her support. It was Alice who produced a buyer for the house, who hunted through the property jungle until she found a pretty maisonette in Primrose Hill at a price he could afford. The arrangement of furniture, the choosing of wallpapers, the clearing of the rubble-filled garden, all were done by Alice with quiet, good-humoured efficiency. When he wanted comfort, he had only to pick up the telephone for Alice to be there, loyal, reassuring and attentive.

She begged to be used; was it wrong to take advantage of her kindness? He knew, however vehemently she chose to deny it, that her thoughts were turning towards a second marriage. Was he cruel in allowing her to focus her expectations on him? He was fond of her, he liked going to bed with her, he enjoyed and,

145

to some degree, depended on her company. Looking at her warm strong face and watching a smile tilt the corners of her clear eyes, he could even suppose himself to be a little in love with her.

He was not in love with her, but he found it disturbingly easy to act the lover's part when the cues were readily provided. She said she loved him. It was so simple to say he loved her, too. The pretence had its charm. The result was alarming. References to Gracedew and to the kind of life he should be leading came up almost every time they met. Alice spoke of the house with the concern and intimate interest of a future owner. He resisted telling her why he was not entitled to that expectation, not least because the last shared confidence would seem so great a pledge of trust. Deprived of knowledge, she very reasonably took the view that a reconciliation was only a matter of time and that the house would eventually pass to him. She linked her interest in Gracedew to his own. When he expressed some disinclination to give up his present style of life, Alice nodded and smiled with all the wisdom of superior understanding. The relationship was not, in this respect, a satisfactory one.

He tried to do as she sensibly suggested, to enjoy the present and stop feeling guilty about their undecided future. He took her to parties when she came to London and introduced her to his friends. The fact that this was not a success reflected no discredit on her. She was entitled to express her views; he would have been embarrassed to hear her mouthing his own. Clarissa's forcefully voiced opinions had caused him intense irritation; hearing Alice's ring out across a crowded room, he found himself torn between affection and dismay. He heard her telling a socialist shadow minister that it was high time his party stopped talking about ideals and looked to practical matters. Asked by James Erskine whether she liked Saki, she replied that she didn't much like any foreign drinks. Pressed by Ned Foley to agree with him that Henry James was a crashing old bore, she said that she didn't know about that but the only writers she really thought worth reading were Surtees and Whyte-Melville. Matthew, seeing Ned's eyes beginning to roll, broke in to change the course of conversation.

"Oh, I thought she was splendid," Ned said the next day when Matthew disloyally pressed him for his views. "Awfully practical and straightforward. I liked her. Still, I'm not sure that she's quite what you need. No sense in rushing into a second marriage when you're still recovering from the first one." He hesitated. "I know you were pretty wretched with Clarissa, but she did fit in. She wasn't—"

"Stupid? Alice isn't any kind of a fool."

Ned puffed on his cigar. "I'm sure she isn't. Still, a bit limited, in the nicest way. You don't really want to spend the rest of your life talking about hunting and Tory politics, do you?"

He shrugged. "I don't mind her political views."

It should not have mattered what they thought. He disliked himself for being affected by their opinons and for making so little defence of her worth, when he knew it to be so great. But what was the value of a piece of gold in a society which traded only in silver? Had she only been more flexible, more ready to take on new ideas, attitudes, interests—there was not much comfort to be derived from thinking that the fault lay in his selfishness quite as much as in her resistance to change. He simply could not face the idea of binding himself to an unbookish woman to whom he felt morally inferior. But of course, when he tried to hint that this was the case, Alice only laughed and kissed him and said he was talking utter nonsense.

There was, perhaps, no way out.

The divorce came through a year after Clarissa's departure. He was again a marriageable man. Alice, with ever so gentle a pressure, began to suggest that it was time for him to get to know her children. Perhaps he would like to come and stay? He foresaw the likelihood that Colonel Tresham would seize the opportunity to ask him to declare his intentions. Heavy-hearted, he wrote down a week-end date in his diary and prayed for a miraculous release.

It came like a gift from the gods. An invitation arrived from an American girls' college to spend a year with them as novelist-in-residence. The pay was negligible. The escape was absolute. He hesitated for barely a moment before writing to accept. He waited a good deal longer before breaking the news to Alice.

The time chose itself. He had taken her to a restaurant which had in some sense become "theirs", a pleasantly ordinary French bistro of the kind which had become fashionable in London in the late 'sixties. Alice was looking prettier than usual with her hair falling in loose curls which softened the angular lines of her face. They discussed the book he was writing on Elizabethan architecture which was to include a chapter on the building of Gracedew and which he had undertaken partly to please her and partly from a wish to make some public demonstration of his feeling for the house. Alice talked, with much laughter, of the week-end, two weeks away still, and of the need for him to read a few stoutly Tory articles before he encountered her father. There were jokes about where he was going to sleep and whether he would be able to reach her room without losing the way. She suggested that they might go over to Gracedew and take some photographs for the book. It would, she thought, be a splendid opportunity for him to make a further attempt at a reconciliation.

"I was thinking," she said. "Wouldn't it be nice to lay out a knot garden there again? There must have been one, originally. I'm quite good at that sort of thing. Well, we might think about it."

He noticed that she was running her sentences together as though, if she could only keep talking, she thought that she could prevent him from disclosing what had been on his mind throughout the evening. He put down his knife and fork.

"Alice?"

"Yes?" she said, very quietly.

"It's not that I can't come for the week-end. I'm just not sure that it would be the best thing for you if I did. I should have told you before. I've been offered some sort of a post at an American university. I've written to accept it."

"But that's wonderful news," Alice said. "Goodness. Success after success."

Wretchedly, he watched the tears gather in her eyes and spill down on to the plate as she bent her head forward. He passed his handkerchief to her across the table.

"Thank you. When do you go?" He could barely hear her.

"Pretty soon. And I really ought to try to polish this book off before I go. I'd like to try and get some work done in the evenings as well, if I can."

"It sounds very sensible. Will you be going for a long time?"

148

"About a year."

"I see," she said and went on with a brightness which almost broke his resolution: "Oh well, I should have guessed. I always knew it would be a mistake to go and fall in love with you. I told you, didn't I?"

He covered her shaking hands with his own. "Darling Alice, there's no woman in the world I—"

"Oh, please don't," she said quickly. "Please don't start being kind. At least you told me to my face. Buck just gave me a present and left a letter on the kitchen table. That was worse. I think it was worse."

"I don't think anything could be worse than what I'm doing," he said, rashly. "But I do think, honestly, that it's for the best. You deserve someone better than me."

The ghost of a smile flickered across her face. "I'm not sure I deserve those kind of clichés, my dear. I understand perfectly. It was stupid of me not to realize. You wouldn't want a wife like me. And whatever's best for oneself always has to be best for the other person. But don't ask me to agree with you. I can't, dear Matthew. Not yet."

He drove her back to old Zinnia Tresham's house and she wept, silently, all the way. Standing on the doorstep, he kissed her wet cheek.

"I'll call you as soon as I'm back and we'll have dinner. Perhaps—"

"Perhaps," she said. "Oh yes, there's always that. It's worse than nothing at all. Good-bye, Matthew. Good luck. I hope you find a more suitable person."

He had never felt more of a villain in his life than as he drove away, convinced though he was that he had done the right thing. He telephoned her as soon as he reached home, but she had taken the receiver off the hook. Perhaps it was just as well. There was nothing to be said.

He was free to go his own way. There was nothing now to hold him back to his early life. He wondered why the prospect filled him with despair. Sitting alone in the little sitting-room so pleasantly arranged by Alice, a glass of whisky at his side, a Mozart aria sweetening the silence, he started to plan out the next chapter of his book.

7

Laura Dare got out of the bath, wrapped herself in a towel and sprawled out on the bedroom floor to do her daily five minutes of Proust. Lack of education was something she was intent on remedying but, between work and parties, time was short. Ten minutes on Latin verbs, five on Bertrand Russell's *History of Western Philosophy*, fifteen on the history of England between the Wars; it was a modest schedule, but she had to start somewhere. She glanced up at the piece of paper she had pinned above her head—"The lyf so short, the craft so long to lerne, Th'assay so hard, so sharp the conquerynge." Lucky Chaucer, whose struggle with poetry could never have been so exhausting as hers with Proust. Sighing, she returned to the business of unravelling the massive clause-bound sentences which were going to enrich her life. Things had been brightening up yesterday with Marcel on the threshold of Albertine's bedroom. He was still there today, pondering the meaning of life.

"Do shut up and get in there, you old fool," Laura muttered. "She's probably sound asleep by now and I don't blame her either. Oh damn," she added as the telephone rang.

"Hello. Oh, Mummy. Yes, I'm fine. Reading my Proust for the day. No I'm not turning into a blue-stocking. It's quite fun. A philosophical Jennifer's Diary.

"No. I'm just going out. Screeby's Christmas party for their authors, God help us. You should just see them. Hampstead with pearls and horn-rimmed specs. No, of course I love working at Screeby's. I just meant—no, I don't take authors out to lunch. I'm not an editor yet, Mummy.

"This week-end? Goodness." She racked her mind for a

convincing excuse which would not hurt their feelings. It was part of Laura's plan for a new and better life that she should not go down every five days to the Dares' pretty house in Surrey, to hear how many rounds her father had done on the local golf course and how the country was going to the dogs under a Labour government. "Oh bother. Susie's giving a party on Saturday night. Yes, it is a shame. Still, soon. No, I can't say exactly when. I'll—I'll write. I really must go. Lovely to hear you. You too. 'Bye.''

Parents. Sighing again, she abandoned Proust for the more important business of choosing her clothes. The new red silk dress. Why not? Cheer the old men up a bit.

Swathed in scarlet, hair brushed down in a shining mass to her waist, Laura gazed into her mirror. "Pretty little idiot," she said affectionately. "Hey-ho. Come and find me, Prince Charming. I'm ready and willing.''

Matthew read through the day's work, typed it out, read it again and wondered if he felt energetic enough to carry on after a cup of coffee. There was, he noticed, a red ring around the date on his desk calendar. Screeby's Christmas party, he remembered with gloom. Hardly the literary event of the year. Still, as one of Screeby's most prominent authors, he had some duty to put in an appearance. To go or not to go—humming, he wandered into the kitchen to put on the kettle.

Perhaps to go. He had put no particular limit on his incarceration. It had been more than a month since he had accepted an invitation and he was tired of his own company. Screeby's parties were the least likely of any occasions he could imagine to lead him back into the kind of situation which he had determined, for a time, to avoid.

After his return from America seven years ago, Matthew had been through a succession of turbulent love affairs from which he had taken flight as soon as the desired prey became the predator. Pursued, a woman could seem all perfection; transformed into a huntress, she showed only her flaws. He had not, in his own view, behaved badly towards them. They had been given fair warning that he was not inclined to marriage, that he liked a degree of privacy in his life, that he was not to be seduced by having buttons sewn on his shirts or by allowing them to pay for his meals. Disbelieving, they persisted; persuaded, they retired in rancour to solace themselves with vituperative letters which Matthew dutifully read and sometimes answered.

Some fatal inclination towards the comfort of the known relationship had led him six months ago to renew his affair with Celia Rivers. They had met at a publishing party and had gone on to dinner together. A highly enjoyable evening spent in dissecting each other and forgiving the past had led to a light-hearted agreement that marriage was the last thing either of them had in mind. Matthew overlooked the fact that Celia was an accomplished actress. He looked forward to a pleasant relationship of an uncommitting kind. Celia's blondeness had become a little unnaturally bright and her body had lost its girlish smoothness, but she was good company and they had friends in common.

It had quickly become apparent that Celia wanted more of him than friendship. She spoke of the imprudence of marrying young girls with a vehemence which made it clear that she had an alternative in mind. He began to make excuses not to see her, to make the preliminary moves for a painless withdrawal. At the end of five months, standing in the middle of the pretty yellow bedroom of her pretty Hampstead house, Celia picked up her favourite Limoges vase and, intending it for his head, missed and sent it through the window. When, on being told that this disaster was entirely his fault, Matthew offered to pay for the broken glass, Celia screamed, very loudly, and said she never wanted to set eyes on him again, and that as for his (guilty) offer to paint her kitchen she would rather employ Rasputin.

He needed no psychiatrist to explain his behaviour. Insecurity about his birth, the fear of being deceived by women, a sense of deprivation leading to a need to possess, to establish power. To know this was not to know a cure. The simple, short-term answer was to banish women from his life and get on with his work.

Still, a month was a long time to spend alone. He would go to the party for half an hour, drink a couple of glasses of wine and retire, unscathed, to his solitary bed.

The event was quite as bad as he had anticipated. The wine

was thin, the canapés were of the kind which leaves crumbs on the floor and an unpleasant smell of fish paste on the fingers, a plump little lady-novelist was on hand to tell him that his books might be clever and witty but that he showed no knowledge of the female psyche. Matthew listened, smiled, and glanced at his watch. Half-past seven. He would leave in five minutes.

Laura Dare sipped her wine and gave half an ear to the love-problems of her girlfriend in the publicity department.

"He does sound a swine. Poor you. Susie, who's the tall man, by the fireplace?"

Susie obligingly squinted through her spectacles. "Him? You ought to know. We've been publishing him for years. Now there's a real swine for you."

"He looks quite nice," Laura said, looking again.

"Matthew Craven? Nice?" Susie shrugged her large freckled shoulders. "It's not what I've heard him called. He's clever, of course," she added grudgingly.

"And he's very attractive."

"If you happen to find snakes attractive. Can't say I do." Susie moved away. "I'm going to get some more wine. Coming?"

"In a minute."

Laura continued to look at him. He was tall and very thin, plainly dressed in a narrow black suit. His eyes, meeting hers through the dense wreaths of cigarette smoke, sharpened with interest. He smiled at her. He must, she thought, be getting on for forty. She liked older men. They had so many more stories to tell.

Well, why not? She made her way through the crowds.

"Hello," she said. "I'm Laura Dare."

He smiled again. "Hello Laura. Dare away."

"I thought," she said, "that you looked as though you were on your own."

"So I am. Or was."

"So am I," Laura said. "And I think I've had just about enough of the annual party. So would you like to come and have dinner with me somewhere instead? I'm quite good company. I've read all your books," she added as a cunning afterthought. "They're splendid. So subtle."

153

"Very nice of you to say so. Most women hate them. And which one did you like best?"

Laura turned pink. "The last one. Definitely."

Almost definitely, the girl was lying. Never trust a woman who looks you straight in the eye. She was extremely pretty. "I like that one, too," he said after a pause. "And dinner sounds a good idea. Why don't you go and get your coat and I'll meet you downstairs?"

Laura Dare was green-eyed. Her hair was reddish-gold and long. Her smile was quick and merry. Her body moved away from him with a leisurely sway, promising considerable pleasure. Forgetful of his resolutions, Matthew made his adieux and followed her to the door.

He took her to dinner in Charlotte Street at a dimly lit Greek restaurant where bazoukis genteelly tinkled and the seats wore the fading plush of old cinemas. They ordered an elaborate meal and hardly touched it. Laura, always prone to talking more as her courage receded, shredded her bread roll to crumbs and flew across every moment of silence with the speed of a dragonfly. They must, he thought, have covered twenty subjects in as many minutes. He wondered whether to tell her she had no need to be so nervous.

"If only I could talk in a nice orderly way," she said suddenly. "I can usually. I don't know what's wrong with me this evening." She looked at him with huge despairing eyes.

"It's all right," he said. "I like the way you talk. I like you. I'm very happy. Honestly."

"I got you here on false pretences. I haven't read any of your books. Not one."

"I know. I didn't come to dinner to talk about myself or to hear about myself. Cheer up. I've told lies which were more serious than that."

"You've got a special licence. Mendacity is the novelist's privilege." She had read that somewhere and saved it up. He seemed amused.

Her fingers plucked at the chain which dipped behind red silk on to her breasts. Quietly smoking, Matthew observed the electric frequency of Laura Dare's smile with a tenderness which

154

surprised him. Just turned twenty, she was young even for her age. A charming and desirable child. He would have to watch out.

He slid a covetous hand down the bare slope of her shoulder in the car. Laura swerved violently and avoided hitting a lamp-post by centimetres.

"Don't kill us quite yet, my love," Matthew said, taking his hand reluctantly away. He hadn't, he realized, so badly wanted to be in bed with a girl since he had first met Clarissa.

My love? Did he call all women that or did the words carry some special significance?

Deep in their separate fantasies, they drove silently on.

Matthew's home had deteriorated in his month of solitude. Celia's last revenge had been to coax his cleaning lady away to Squire's Mount and higher wages. The dreary business of hoovering and dusting had been put off from week to week. He saw Laura give a small shake to the chair cushions before she sat down. Still, the bed was made. Women were oddly fastidious about that. Clarissa had never given a damn, but Celia and her predecessors had given him no quarter for presuming to lead them to crumpled sheets.

"Coffee?" Had he any left to offer her? "Wine?"

Laura was kneeling, straightening a pile of books, peering at the titles, hungry for his life, his past. "Elizabethan Architecture? I didn't know you wrote about things like that." She looked at him anxiously. "I don't know anything about architecture."

Matthew gave her a reassuring grin. "Nor do I. I only wrote that one because of a house which I used to know quite well. I wanted to do something about it."

"Which was that?" She flicked through the pages. "Would I know it?"

He looked over her shoulder at the photograph of Gracedew. "That's the one." He smothered the familiar sense of melancholy which the memory of Gracedew always revived. The old bastard had never sent him a word of thanks for the book. Well, too bad. Too bad.

"Gosh, it's beautiful," Laura said. "Those chimneys! It's not yours, is it?"

"I suppose it might have been."

"Well, I'm awfully glad it's not," Laura said, shutting the book. "I'm not very keen on country life. Here, let me put these straight for you."

Matthew shook his head. "Stop tidying, pretty Laura. Come and tell me about your life instead."

"But I like tidying," Laura said earnestly. "Honestly. Do let me."

He could almost have believed it. But her red-gold hair stranded apart on shoulders as warm as apricot silk, and women who started by tidying always ended by wanting to be wives. "No," he said and twisted a gentle hand in her hair. "Look up at me." She murmured something about having to get home while her body made a slow undulating movement of anticipation.

"Come to bed, pretty Laura," he said and led her, unprotesting, up the dark and twisting stairs.

The squalor of the bedroom, when decently veiled by Matthew's pinkly shading lights, had for Laura a Bohemian charm. Intellectuals were allowed to live in filth; it showed that their minds dwelt on nobler things. Bending to undo her shoe-straps, she found herself gazing at the trailing end of a mauve chiffon scarf which lay under the bed.

"I forgot to ask," she said in a small and sorrowful voice. "I expect you're married."

Matthew, already in bed, smiled indulgently and cursed Celia's carelessness as he saw the scarf in Laura's outstretched hand.

"I was, and I'm not. That unlovely object probably belongs to my cleaning lady. Satisfied?"

Dropping her dress on the floor, she gave him an uncertain grin. "I never sleep with married men. It's the only rule I ever managed to keep."

Immature but very engaging, Matthew thought as he turned off the light and drew her towards him.

"No. I want to look at you. Let me." Smiling and naked, she knelt astride him and looked down at his face. "How beautiful you are."

She was rather more than engaging, he thought afterwards, placidly smoking his cigarette in the dark. Laura's head was

156

heavy with satisfaction in the crook of his arm. She had been docile and avid, a mixture which promised to charm for a fair while. She had straddled him with a sigh of satisfaction, stretched quivering and pleasure-hungry below him. And now, bless her, she lay silent, content and replete. He smiled as he remembered her saying with a laugh that he felt amazing, really astonishing, inside her, like that, and gazing down at him with eyes like the pools of Heshbron.

A sweet and desirable child.

"I love you, pretty Laura." Stubbing out his cigarette, he wondered if he had not almost meant it. Not that it mattered. She hadn't heard him. Her eyes were smudged by sleep, her lips curved in satisfaction. He had fucked his way into her dreams, he thought.

Mistakenly. Long after Matthew lay peacefully breathing, Laura remained awake and tense with desire. She was his. She had heard herself say it. He had wanted her to say it. His cunt, his body, his woman. For ever? She reached out to touch his back with a timid finger. He groaned, stirred and lay still. Sighing, she turned her face to the wall. Warm and secure in the velvet-curtained night, she began arranging a new future with Matthew, undisturbed by the fact that she knew next to nothing about him beyond his name and his easy assumption of the dominant role. She was quite willing to be mastered for a time, if it led to marriage. Mrs Matthew Craven. Laura smiled, yawned and fell asleep.

The relationship ran on lust-oiled wheels for the next few weeks. Conversation had little chance to jar when it could so easily be glided on to the trammels of their fascinating because seemingly insatiable desire for each other. They mapped out their past lives by love-affairs. Matthew told her a good deal about Clarissa, something of Celia, nothing about Alice who, he felt, deserved at least the loyalty of silence. Laura, pressed, admitted to having had seven lovers. Matthew, having long ago lost count of his own, pretended to be horrified. She, with a convent education?

"I thought Clarissa went to a convent. Anyway, it was never like this with them," Laura said, sighing, smiling, turning her head from side to side on the pillows. "Do that again."

"Or like this?" He drew his nails like claws along her ribs. "What do you want, sweet Laura?"

"You. Filling me. Now. Jesu, Matthew." Her eyes blinked open to stare at him. "I'm frightened."

"Of what?"

"Where all this is going to end."

Tenderly he kissed her eyelids. "Don't think about it. Go to sleep."

They started to learn about each other at leisure over the dinners which Laura claimed to have cooked for him at her Chelsea flat. Matthew was touched but not deceived. Celia had been a past mistress of the delicatessen dinner game. He ate Laura's bought quiches and mousses and listened to her woes and hopes, gratified and alarmed by her readiness to depend on his advice, her touching certainty that he was a great man. She was sweet, seductive, charming and she loved him. She was also young. He could do so much for her.

"Find a woman of your own age," said Ned Foley, whose young wife had just left him for a twenty-two-year-old musician. "I can see the charm of being her tutor, but she'll kick you in the teeth once she's learnt her lessons."

"I think she's absolutely charming," pronounced James Erskine who had brought his new boyfriend round to inspect her over dinner. "And Robbie thought she looked just like Lizzie Siddal. But I wouldn't go rushing into anything permanent."

"I hear she's only twenty and frightfully pretty," said Celia, playing the woman scorned, when they found themselves placed next to each other at a dinner-party. "And what does she call you? Daddy?"

He must, he thought, be careful. He tried to tell Laura that he was too old for her, that they were imperfectly suited, that he had made several women very unhappy.

"Well, you make me immensely happy," said Laura, green eyes shining.

He tried again. "Laura my sweet, I don't want you to think that because everything's lovely now, the future is in any way settled."

"Oh, I know that," said Laura. "The present's quite good enough for me."

Smiling in disbelief, he let the subject drop.

He would change, she thought. He was sure to change. He had only to learn to trust her and all would be well. And almost every night, locked in his arms, she whispered that she was his, utterly his, with the proud smile of a privileged woman. How could she not love a man who said she was the sweetest creature he had ever known and who held open the door to a new world?

Laura's own world was the principal reason for Matthew's uneasiness. She claimed to be no part of it. It was clear to him, watching her, listening to her, that she was still very much a product of the conventions she was so eager to condemn. A secretary-assistant at Screeby's, she had about fifty thousand pounds locked up until marriage in shares and an overdraft of undistinguished size at the bank. Her girlfriends were pleasantly jolly young women who regarded their jobs as hobbies to fill time until they got married. Like Laura, they went home every week-end and took as many hours off as possible during the week to go clothes-shopping.

Laura's parents lived on the edge of a Surrey golf-course in a mock-Tudor house where they gave Sunday-morning sherry parties. Mr Dare was a stockbroker. Mrs Dare was a magistrate and the president of two charitable organizations based in Guildford. They were both keen bridge-players. Their influence over Laura's life had, until now, been considerable. They had countered her faintly expressed wish to go to university with the confident assertion that university girls were dirty, difficult and unlikely to marry the right kind of people. Laura had passed from the fashionable convent school at which she was the only, and most disconsolate, Protestant, to a secretarial establishment. She had also, in some dilatory way, gone to dances in order to meet suitable friends. It was expected that she would marry the son of one of the Dares' Surrey neighbours before settling comfortably into her mother's role.

"But universities are crammed full of girls from your kind of home," Matthew said incredulously. "I don't want to sound rude, but your parents must have been off their heads."

"Oh well," Laura said. "None of my friends went. I know it sounds like something out of the last century, but they're just like that. Sons get educated. Daughters get married. *C'est la vie.* Can I have some more wine?''

He poured her some. ''Didn't you mind?'' She was sitting at his feet on the floor of his study. Now, she pulled her knees up under her chin and stared down at the carpet.

''Not then. I do now, awfully. More since I met you. I keep thinking that your friends are laughing at me for being so ignorant. They must think it very odd, you and me.''

He touched her bright hair. ''Of course they don't. Anyway, it's hardly your fault.''

She looked up at him. ''I do want to learn. Couldn't you teach me, Matthew? Be my private tutor. I'd like that.''

He laughed. ''All right. If that's what you want. How are you going to pay me?''

''By pleasing you,'' she said. ''You can teach me how to do that, too.''

And so, with some misgivings, Matthew set about the re-education of Laura.

He started her off with the simple rules of domesticity. The two spoons of sugar for his coffee. The toast to be lightly buttered. The prohibition of all serious conversation before nine in the morning. The sweet sexual litany of subjugation which committed her to his possession. She was quick to master these. Her enthusiasm for the telephone as an instrument of passion proved harder to reform. His sacred writing hours were interrupted rather too often by Laura's charming laughter and her passionate protestations of love. When remonstrances failed, Matthew was forced, to his mild irritation, to take the telephone off the hook until, frustrated, she grew more tractable. The resentment which she showed whenever he mentioned having seen another woman also promised to become tedious if he did not put a check on it. He did not prevent her from seeing other men if she wished—why couldn't she be equally tolerant?

''But I don't want to see other men,'' Laura said tearfully. ''It's you I love.''

''And I you,'' he said tenderly, guiltily, hating himself as he always did when Laura's distress became visible. ''So there's nothing to be upset about, is there?''

Laura studied her shoes. ''I suppose not.''

Covertly, she kept watch over his home for signs of her suspected rivals. Anxiously, she read the postcards—his letters were always hidden away—from women whose names meant nothing to her and who seemed to be on suspiciously affectionate terms with Matthew. Feverishly, she pictured his flirtations, the plans he might be making at the dinner-parties to which he went alone. To ask too many questions was to invite the reproach of being nagging and difficult; to be silent was almost impossible. Being in love was as painful as any medieval torture. She had wanted him to teach her about literature, philosophy, history. She was tired of learning how to be a perfect mistress.

"I'm sure he's wonderful, darling, but you don't look happy," Mrs Dare observed. "You're as white as a bit of chalk and your clothes are falling off you. Can't the man afford to buy you a good square meal?"

"I've never been happier," Laura said, ignoring the references to her appearance. "He's kind and sweet and clever and I love him. And I'm very lucky."

"So's he," her father said. "Got you running round in circles while he carries on saying he doesn't feel ready to commit himself. I've heard that one before. You may call it clever. I've got another name for characters like that."

"He is not like that. He's just had a very difficult life. I've got to get him to trust me. And you aren't being very much help."

"I'll trust him when I hear something positive," Mr Dare said, and her mother nodded.

"I do rather agree, Laura darling. Leopards don't change their spots, you know."

They didn't understand. She knew what she wanted. It was only a question of persistence and patience.

"Novel finished," Matthew announced one evening when she arrived. "Time for a treat. What do you say to a month in Italy, my pretty Lorelei?"

Laura's eyes shone with joy and expectation. He loved her enough to want a whole month alone with her.

"A holiday isn't exactly a proposal of marriage, you know," said her sceptical girl-friend in the publicity department when Laura announced that she was leaving Screeby's. "You watch out for youself. You've dropped all your old friends. What are you going to do when he drops you?''

"He won't. He said last night that he was thinking of giving up the bachelor life and settling down."

"Terrific," Susie said. "Well, don't say I didn't warn you and for Christ's sake, remember to take the Pill."

Laura looked at her with affectionate scorn. "The trouble with you is that you've no sense of romance."

"Put it down to experience," Susie said. "Still, if romance is all you want—I thought it was marriage you were after."

Blushing, Laura denied it. Her friend laughed and wished her luck.

The holiday was a success. Armed with a suitcase of guidebooks and an immense number of dresses which were never worn, they zig-zagged across Lombardy, Tuscany and Umbria in Laura's Renault. Matthew drove while obligingly ransacking his mind for the stories of gory Renaissance feuds of which Laura could never hear enough. His passenger slept or chattered with an enthusiasm to which Matthew, having been prepared to resign himself with grace, found that he was beginning to warm. In the golden afternoons, when the museums were closed, they laughed and struggled and whispered behind the shuttered windows of small hotels. Drugged with pleasure and heavy-eyed, they wandered through the jostling night streets. Matthew allowed himself to be dragged from jewellers to dress-shops in Laura's ravenous thirst for bargains. He bought her a fringed shawl of flaming silk to match her hair. She looked, he said, like an Augustus John girl; she must always wear it. And Laura laughed and spun it round her to make a circling orange sea for a pagan Venus. She was almost sure that he was going to ask her to marry him, but instead he laughed and said all things were possible, if they were not too frequently discussed.

When they returned to England, Laura packed her clothes and books, rented out her flat and moved to Matthew's home in Saint Anselm's Road. Now was her chance to show him what a perfect wife she would be, given the opportunity. Proust and Bertrand Russell were replaced by Robert Carrier and Elizabeth David. She polished the floors, typed out his lecture notes and reviews, cleaned the windows. Matthew had only to mention that he liked chocolate cake for Laura to produce a labour of culinary art before which the Prince Regent would have quailed. She mended his shirts, hemmed the curtains, tidied all the cupboards. It was wonderful. It was too much. He needed to escape and think things out. He went off to spend a week-end with Celia Rivers and told Laura that he had been called in on a promise to help an old friend with a bit of decorating. Laura, understanding that she had exceeded her role, wept. She had lost him.

A fashionably cropped hairstyle gave Celia's face a pinched, cross look. A new diet—she was always on a diet—had succeeded in shrinking her small breasts and sharpening her temper. She ate vindictively with angry little stabs at her plate. She talked expansively about the folly of chasing after little rich girls. The conversation which he had once found so entertaining was spiked with more malice than wit, much of it being directed at himself. Too wise to try smoothing her with flattering insincerities, Matthew smiled and waited until, her venom exhausted, Celia grew genial on her fifth glass of wine. Later, suffocating under her lace-edged sheets in a cloud of scent, Matthew failed to produce more than a flaccid testament to a desire he did not feel. Celia responded with a parrot-scream of angry mirth before starting to elaborate on the likely reasons for his sexual inadequacy. Wearily gazing up at the billowing heavens of a white lace canopy, Matthew was overcome by a passionate longing to be with Laura, who never criticized and was always desirable. He fled with precipitate haste after a cold Sunday breakfast and asked Laura to marry him two days later. She accepted.

Matthew was terrified. He had, he supposed, been looking for years for a young teachable girl, someone who would be bound to him not by love alone, but by obligation and need. Someone who would never leave him. But what when he had educated her? What monster of emancipation might she then become?

"She's pretty, she loves you and you say you want a settled relationship. Wherein lies the problem?" James Erskine inquired. "I can't see why you have to make life so difficult for yourself. Why not try being happy for a change? It won't be hard with your charming Laura. And she's certainly not going to run away.''

He muttered something about differences in age and remembered too late that James' Robbie was slightly younger than Laura.

"Look, dear boy," James said. "We can always find objections if we want to. But don't go out of your way to hunt them down. You had a bad time with Clarissa. Laura wants to make up for all that. Let her."

"I've never loved anyone as much as I do you," Laura sighed in his arms. "Lovely in bed, lovely to talk to, lovely Matthew. Oh, but it's nice to be happy." Her hands slipped like silken fish down his body. "Come on. Say yes, it is."

They were right. Happiness was to be seized and relished, not rationalized away. His hands gripped her shoulders, pulling her forward to lie on him so that he could look up at her laughing face, pale and mirthful as a Crivelli angel behind the rain of red-gold hair.

"God, you're the spitting image of Venice Dobell," he said, startled. "How extraordinary. I never could think who it was."

"And who was Venice Dobell?" She knelt back on her heels, bending soft mouth and lively tongue to his thighs. "Not another bit of your past?"

"Not a bit that should worry you. A lady on a monument. Rather a witchy lady. Doting husband, many lovers."

"Not like me. You," she said, "shall be all my lovers. Who'd want anyone else if they had you?"

Faced with such love, it would be perverse not to be happy.

Mr and Mrs Dare were displeased, but resigned. She was their only child and such a pretty girl; there were so many nice young men with whom they could have had something in common. To each other, they foretold disaster, but they unlocked her shares and gave her a pearl necklace and a fur coat. Matthew was presented with a set of Hume's *History of England*, originally purchased for their handsome bindings as an investment by Mr Dare. There was a stiff, but socially impeccable meeting at Mr Dare's club, during which there was much talk about fortune-hunters. It was intimated that a great deal of time and trouble had gone into building up Laura's small inheritance and that Matthew should, as her spouse, take care to husband it. Matthew laughed at the carefully rehearsed joke and gave his assurances. Patronizing old brute; the temptation to cut through bonhomie with a few home-truths was almost irresistible. Still, he had promised Laura to behave well.

"Splendid port," he said.

Matthew's father was, in the course of time, looked up and found to be a rather more respectable figure than Mr Dare had suspected. Gracedew, too, was tracked down. No children, Matthew the only cousin? It sounded promising.

"They spent the whole time going on about that house," Laura said after a week-end in Surrey. "They're convinced you're going to inherit it. Daddy said he couldn't understand why you'd been so modest. You are a bit odd about all that, darling Matthew. You've told me a bit about the Dobells and that book you started writing. And that's all. Is it a secret or were you just awfully unhappy? I would like to know."

"So you shall," he said. "But not just now. I've got those galley proofs to finish."

"Always excuses," Laura said crossly. "I've told you everything about me. It's most unfair."

Matthew hesitated. Surely, as his future wife, she should also be his confidante? She had poured out every detail of her own life to him with such readiness that it seemed ungracious to remain so guarded about his own. There was caution in doing so. His charming voluble Laura would be incapable of keeping intimate knowledge to herself. He had no wish to have his illegitimacy broadcast across London. There was also self-preservation. If he dropped the flood-gates and let all the bitterness and insecurity spill out, he would be exposing his most vulnerable side. Give her that power and he was indeed lost.

"You look very solemn," she said, rubbing her face against his. "Wherefore so? Thinking about all those skeletons rattling in the cupboard?"

"Just thinking." He smiled at her. "I'll tell you this much. The chances of my inheriting Gracedew are precisely nil. The old man can't stand the sight of me and I'm not overburdened with affection for him."

"Do you mind?"

"Yes," he said. "Yes, I mind."

"Silly you," Laura said, kissing him. "You're much better off here, writing your books, than repairing fences on the ancestral acres. And don't tell me you could do both, because I don't believe it. Anyway, I don't mind. Keeping dogs and planting out the borders? No thanks. It's just what you were sent to rescue me from."

The wedding was not of the kind he would have chosen. His suggestion of a quiet civil ceremony to be followed by a drinks-party for a few close friends was met with looks of frozen dismay. It was not, the Dares explained, quite what they had in mind. Laura's relations would be frightfully hurt if they were excluded. It would seem as though her parents were getting her married on the cheap. There was no need for him to concern himself. They would arrange it all. He looked to Laura for her support. Seeing her face pale and pleading above her untouched avocado, he gave in.

"Whatever you think is best."

Surrounded by a galaxy of Dares intended to compensate for a conspicuous absence of Cravens and hustled into position beside the cake by a Master of Ceremonies who bore an unnerving resemblance in his manner to the Westerham football coach, Matthew bitterly regretted his moment of weakness. Called upon for a speech, he heard himself thanking the Dares for a most extraordinary occasion and saw Mrs Dare's eyes turn to marbles under the foolish flopping feathers of her hat.

"Interesting choice of word," Mr Dare said, red with the effort to sound friendly. "I don't believe I've ever heard it used in a speech of thanks."

"I thought the occasion called for it. Above the ordinary."

"Ah. Interesting." Mr Dare sipped his champagne. "I rather had the impression you were making fun of us."

He smiled. "The last thing I had in mind."

The recompense came later when, in the soothing semi-darkness of Saint Anselm's Road, he lay back on the bed and watched his pretty young wife slowly stripping off her bridal finery before she came smiling towards him and put her hands on either side of his body, leaning down until the tips of her breasts touched his skin and desire for her shook him.

166

"I do love you so much," he said.

"And I you, Matthew," she said with a wide slow smile.

It was the first time she had been the second voice, the reassurer rather than the initiator seeking a response. It was, for Laura, a moment of triumph.

8

Matthew's friends wished him well and sat back to watch the outcome of such an unlikely marriage with malicious curiosity. To Matthew's face, they envied his good luck in finding such a pretty and agreeable wife; just what was needed. Behind his back, they made jokes about Svengali Craven and his Trilby. She was young, engaging, certainly beddable, but—

The marriage appeared, nevertheless, to be a success. The house was as clean as a convent, the dinner-parties never broke up before midnight. Even the tragedies—a splendid-looking crême brulée forever locked below a barrier of toffee which a security guard would not have spurned—gained charm from Laura's looks of comical despair and Matthew's affectionate laughter. They seemed to be devoted to each other; the tutor-pupil relationship appeared to have satisfied a mutual need.

Under Matthew's loving guidance, Laura pursued self-education with a tenacity which impressed him and an enthusiasm which was endearing. Listening to her dinner-party conversation, he entertained himself by placing silent bets as to which book had mastered her mind that day. He was, for the first time, engaged, happy, and full of love. Time would only improve her; the fruits would be his.

When the hunt after learning palled and Laura began to think she needed a vocation, Matthew suggested that she should start to write. A flood of poems about dark flights of swallows and murmuring seas and bittersweet love were returned with polite thanks and many regrets by Matthew's friends at the literary magazines. Laura wept and refused to be comforted by Matthew's assurances that all good writers had known the humiliation of being rejected. She cared nothing about other people's rejections; she knew only that she had failed and, even worse, that his friends had probably laughed at her efforts. Matthew made her some coffee, took her out into the garden and sat in sympathetic silence with his arms around her until the sobs seemed to be lessening. Perhaps, he said very gently, poetry was not the best vehicle for her talents. Had she ever thought about writing a novel?

"I couldn't," Laura said in a muffled voice. "I don't have anything to write about. I wouldn't even know where to begin. It's no use. I'd better go and run a children's playgroup."

"Nonsense," Matthew said cheerfully. "Look how good you are at inventing stories. I'd say you were a born novelist myself."

Laura lifted her head to look at him. "You're only saying that to cheer me up."

Matthew grinned. "Would I do such a thing? No, I do mean it. So stop sniffing and promise me that you'll have a try if I help you. What do you think you might like to write about?"

Sunlight dappled the little plot of grass. Matthew was at his most tender and persuasive. At the end of another half-hour, Laura was pinkly smiling at the picture of herself as an admired and successful writer.

Unwilling to expose her, and, to some degree, himself, for a second time to the gibes of his more literary friends, Matthew arranged for Laura to meet Max Moore, editor-in-chief of Rackitt's, a commercial and very successful publishing conglomerate. Max, he remembered, had a weakness for pretty young women.

Max was a large, well-fed figure of indeterminate Central European extraction, agate-eyed, with a perpetually smiling mouth. Women apart, Max's principal interests in life were money, sweet cakes and cemeteries. It was said that his favourite afternoons began with slow flirtation and Sachertorte, and ended with contracts in Kensal Rise, usually beside the tomb of a minor prince to whom Max let it be known that he was not unconnected.

He took Laura to a Hungarian restaurant in Soho and sweetened her on wild cherry soup while assuring her that he always fell hopelessly in love with red-haired girls. Laura sipped her Bulls Blood and smiled demurely, sure she could manage him. He looked to her unsuspicious eyes like a large and slightly shabby teddy-bear. At Max's invitation, she began to outline the novel she had planned. She spoke earnestly of Conrad and Virginia Woolf and thematic structures. Max lit a large cigar, smiled benevolently, and shook his head.

"Very nice too, dear. But where's the audience? And what are the reps going to put it over as?" He leant towards her. "A print-run of under three thousand isn't worth our time, you see, and frankly, my dear, I don't think your novel would make the three thousand after SOR."

"SOR?" Laura's eyes grew large and puzzled. She would have liked to say that she didn't mind if it only sold three hundred copies, but it seemed unwise. She sipped at her coffee. "I'm not quite sure that I understand."

"No reason you should." Max's smile was affable, paternal. "Now you listen to me, Laura, and I'll teach you how to write a book that moves off the shelves. You look a bright girl. I won't tell you twice."

Listening anxiously, Laura revised her opinion of Max. Screeby's had taught her nothing of commercial publishing. Authors were, she now saw, only grudgingly acknowledged as necessary accessories to the production of a Rackitt book. They did the writing. Max did the rest. He made the process sound as easy as baking a cake. At four o'clock, Laura left Kensal Rise slightly drunk on a mixture of Max's ancestors, Bulls Blood and the hope of a dazzling future. She had a plot, a finishing date, and the promise of eight hundred pounds if she did a good job. She was going to write something which Max laughingly referred to as a bodice-ripper.

"It sounds a bit like the body-snatchers to me," she had said, gazing down a sedate avenue of marble tabernacles. Max had not laughed. He never joked about work.

A bodice-ripper, she had learned, would call for a proud, beautiful and untamed heroine who would travel: "Plenty of colour and background. The South's always a good bet." She would meet a man who would master her and treat her brutally: "Just remember Rhett and Scarlett. It never fails." Eventually, he would marry her: "You've got to give them the weepies and

170

the wedding-bells." There would be wars and poverty, but nothing too depressingly realistic: "It's romance they're after, not statistics." Again, he had added with a wink, plenty of sex. "I'm not against details. Explicit as you like, but nothing with animals. Our readers don't go for perversion."

Encouraged by Matthew, Laura set to work with a will and produced four hundred pages of sex and adventure which appeared under the title *Red as the Rose*. It sold reasonably well. Max took her to Bertorelli's and Highgate Cemetery and outlined the next. Laura had found an occupation, if not a vocation. In the following three years she wrote enough to cover half a metre of public library shelf space, rather less in the review columns. Old ladies shakily wrote from retirement homes to praise her for the lovely stories she told. Laura underlined her answers with the flourishing signature which she felt her admirers deserved from a successful novelist. Bursting with confidence, she described her writing habits and aspirations to Matthew's friends. She felt that she was one of them at last. Matthew could be proud of her.

Which he was. He had, after all, helped to make her what she was.

Nothing rots the mind so efficiently as happiness and Matthew had become a happy man. The acid wit of his books had become a little too genial to please. The reviewers of his last novel had commented unfavourably on the complacency of his attitudes. One went so far as to suggest that he had passed his peak. Two important collections of criticism of contemporary writing failed to make any reference to him. Only Laura remained confident that she was married to a genius.

"We'll publish it, of course," said John Fellowes, his new young editor at Screeby's during the lunch to discuss his new novel. "April, I think. Not too much competition."

"Competition?" Matthew stiffened. "But surely this is going to be another Booker entry?"

There was a short pause. Fellowes refilled the glasses, wine for Matthew, Perrier for himself. "We've discussed that, of course. Nobody thinks you ought to go for the Booker on this one. It simply isn't good enough. Of course there are some splendid bits." He glanced at the sheaf of notes beside his plate. "I liked the airport scene. Very sharp. Very funny. But—well, to be honest, we were all a bit disappointed. Personally, I've always admired your work. I remember going to one of those marvellous Northcliffe lectures when I came down from Oxford. You really gave me a new way of looking at Forster."

"Madox Ford, actually," Matthew said.

James Fellowes clapped a hand to his forehead. "Ford. Ford. Slip of the tongue. Sorry about that."

Matthew sipped his wine without relish. "It doesn't matter. And now, like Ford, I'm old hat. Is that it?"

"I just get the feeling that you don't care about what you're doing in the way you did then. It's still good, your work, but a bit—"

"Slick?" He raised his hand for the bill. "Since I'm the pupil, the least I can do is pay for my instruction."

Slick. Was he? The word which had come unbidden into his mouth seemed, once said, to have become a judgement. The energy and the will to write the neatly topical social comedies on which he had made his name had left him. The facility remained. He had often derided the proposition that an unhappy life makes for better writing; reviewing his own past, he could not escape the fact that his best novels had been written when he was married to Clarissa.

"But those articles you've been doing for *The Sunday Times* are marvellous," Laura said when he admitted to a slight uneasiness. "Everyone says so. You can't be depressed just because that stupid James Fellowes wants to show off at your expense. It doesn't mean anything."

"Perhaps not." He leant back on the sofa, eyes closed, as the Kyrie of Mozart's last Requiem rose pure and triumphant as an angel's trumpet. Written, he remembered, in a period of poverty and with the apprehension of death. Damn.

Laura curled up beside him. "Why don't you go on with the Dobell history? You always said that would have been your best work."

He smiled. "Just because I said you were like Venice Dobell. You didn't give a button about the book until then. Anyway, I can't. It's too bound up with my feelings about Gracedew. No house, no book. Not that book.''

He was forty-one years old, and he felt empty, unfulfilled. To Laura's eyes—dear Laura—he was a man of achievement, a success. To himself, he was becoming a man who tended to avoid meeting his own eyes in the bathroom mirror. Always and increasingly, there was the plucking awareness of that other life, that other man he might now have been but for the mischance of his birth. The house came often into his dreams, broken-windowed, gaunt in its neglect. He went so far as to write a long and impassioned letter to the old man, and tore it up. There would be no change of heart. The most he could look for in response would be some crazed spate of self-justification.

He had lunch with Will Lazlett one day. Will, one of the most successful of the former Cambridge group at promoting himself, had recently been made the managing editor of one of the Sunday colour supplements. There was for Matthew some irony in the discrepancy between lunching with Will at the Ritz and being offered a thousand pounds to give a first-hand account of the life of a Russian dissident writer. He accepted nevertheless. He was to go with two other writers and a journalist. It was an opportunity to do something worthwhile and to regain self-esteem.

"Fantastic. I've always wanted to go to Russia,'' said Laura.

"No wives. Will was very firm about that.'' He kissed her. "Cheer up. It's only five weeks.''

She had been alone for three weeks. With no Matthew there to admire and praise her industry, Laura felt little inclination to work on her new novel. She crossed off the days on the calendar and frittered away the hours between. She decorated the house with Liberty print curtains and cushions, rearranged the furniture and asked her former friends to lunches. Matthew's circle politely kept their distance. She really must come and visit, they had urged in his presence, but they did not press her to do so when he had gone. Laura reviled them in her diary and wrote about the pleasures of solitude. She became conversant with the goings-on in *Coronation Street* and *Crossroads* and began to look forward to her morning chat with the postman and the milkman. Matthew's return seemed an eternity away.

The telephone rang one evening. She sprang at it.

"It's too ridiculous that we've never met, my dear," Celia Rivers said. "I expect Matthew told you all about me. He's certainly told me all about you."

"Has he?" Laura gazed at her dim reflection in the mirror above the telephone. He had never said anything about having seen Celia again.

"I thought it might be fun to have a gossipy lunch," Celia said. "What about Odin's tomorrow? One o'clock?"

She was thin as a razor, expensively dressed. Her forty-five years were cunningly masked by cosmetics. She had brought with her a spray of orchids for a present. Laura heard herself beginning to babble. She lit a cigarette with a shaking hand.

"Oh, should you, my dear?" Celia's peacock-painted eyes travelled down Laura's Indian dress and paused significantly at the midriff. "I'm terribly sorry. Perhaps you aren't?"

"Certainly not," Laura said. Catching sight of her scowling face in the glass behind Celia's elegant head, she tried to adjust it to a collected smile. "I don't expect you're used to these sort of clothes."

"Oh, but I think it's such a pretty dress," Celia cooed. "It reminds me of an old favourite of mine. I got it in one of those Oxfam Christmas sales. No, it was that gorgeous skin of yours that made me think you might be—well, never mind. You're still very young. You must be almost twenty years younger than Matthew and I. I expect that makes things a bit difficult for you sometimes. He's not an easy man, is he, between ourselves?"

Laura said stiffly that they were both very happy and that she had never found Matthew in the least bit difficult. And no, she didn't at all mind being on her own. They both respected independence.

"You mean Matthew wants you to respect his, my dear," Celia said with a reptilian smile. "I must say that in your shoes I'd wonder—" She knew how to make a pause full of rich and disagreeable implication.

"Wonder what?" Laura carefully rolled pellets of dough and arranged them round her untouched food. She wished that curiosity and loneliness had not persuaded her to come.

"Well, I'm the last person to want to sow little seeds of

suspicion," Celia said. "Tell me now, have you met Alice Tresham yet? Or Clarissa?"

Laura stiffened.

"I never could understand why he didn't marry Alice," Celia purred, seeing that she had caused some consternation. "She sounded so charming. But I expect the relationship's a more comfortable one now. A habit, at any rate."

"There is no relationship," Laura said. "Alice is an old friend. I think he may have seen her about twice for lunch in the last four years."

Celia's pencilled brows rose. "My mistake. How odd. I don't usually make mistakes about things like that. And Clarissa—have you met her?"

"It's hardly likely since she lives in Rome," Laura said. "I've seen photographs of her, of course. Matthew said that she's got quite fat and middle-aged looking."

"Naughty Matthew," Celia smiled. "She certainly has changed. For the better. Clarissa has the kind of beauty that seems to devastate men. She certainly devastated poor old Matthew." She sipped at her Perrier with a pensive smile. "Strange that she never got married again. I always thought it was because she hoped Matthew would come back to her. But of course he won't. He's got you, hasn't he? Poor Clarissa. Still, I'd be careful, my dear. She's awfully clever and persevering."

Somehow, no matter how hard Laura tried, the conversation swerved always towards the unspoken probability of Matthew's infidelities. She felt naïve for not having assumed that they existed. Celia seemed odiously certain of her facts.

"Still, we're none of us perfect and Matthew seems as happy as a sandboy now that he's given up trying to be the genius of our time," Celia said, shifting her attack as she saw Laura's lower lip beginning to tremble. "Frankly, I always did think his books were over-rated. Marvellous how far you can get with a few friends in the right places, isn't it?"

It was the cruellest stab of all. Nothing had so sustained Laura in what had often seemed to be a most demanding marriage as the thought that she was living with a man who was honoured and esteemed, a great figure. She had closed her eyes to the carping reviews, refused to listen to Matthew's own doubts.

And now, with frightful accuracy, this woman had slipped through her guard and struck at her most secret fears. If Matthew was not the great writer she had believed, it was impossible not to reflect on the degree to which she had built her life around his needs, submerged her own personality in his.

Silently, she looked at her plate.

"Still, you knew that when you married him," Celia said brightly. "And I'm sure you do a splendid job of boosting his ego. Poor Matthew. I mustn't be unkind. I'm sure he's a wonderful husband." She stood up, brushing an invisible crumb from her pencil-grey skirt. "Let me take you home. You look a bit washed out."

She drove Laura back in a silver Alfa Romeo. She expressed enchantment at the Liberty prints.

"Silly Matthew to leave such a pretty wife alone. I must say I wouldn't blame you for getting your own back. You mustn't let him have all the fun. Well, good-bye, Laura dear. I hope you didn't mind the intrusion. It's always so fascinating to see who one's friends marry. I couldn't resist finding out for myself." She brushed Laura's cheek with powder and the scent of richly fading flowers. In proximity, the mask of youth became a wrinkled web of malevolence.

Her parting-shot came from the car window.

"You must send me one of your own novels. My cleaning-lady adores them."

Matthew telephoned two hours later to say that he would be back in three weeks, not two. The enterprise was going splendidly, the food was unspeakable, the nights were lonely. Their interpreter was pretty but taciturn.

"Keep trying," said Laura. "I'm sure charm will win through in the end." He sounded drunk.

She sounded edgy. Perhaps he should not have mentioned the interpreter. "Anyway, how's my lovely Lorelei?"

"Fine. I've been seeing your friend. Celia. You never told me that you were still seeing her."

"You never asked me. Darling, I didn't ring up to talk about Celia."

"I'm sure you didn't. Still, I'd quite like to, if you don't mind."

There was a pause. She heard him strike a match. That meant he was nervous.

"Fire away."

Laura swallowed. "She talked a lot about Alice. And Clarissa. She said—I mean—have you?" She stopped. Pointless. Of course he would deny it.

"Have I what?" His voice was sharp with suppressed irritation. "Have I seen Alice? Yes. For lunch. I told you. I last saw Clarissa about seven years ago. And that's all there is to it. Celia does seem to have had a bad effect on your temper, darling."

"You don't," she said, "sound like a bowl of sugar yourself."

She heard him sigh. "Do try not to be aggressive. It doesn't suit you. I'll be back for breakfast on the twentieth. See you then." He paused. "Love you, darling."

"Love you, too," Laura said crossly.

"Be good." He put down the telephone. Damn Celia.

Laura picked up the biggest of the new Liberty cushions and flung it at the wall, bringing down the drawing of Gracedew in a shower of glass. "Russian dissidents," she said. "You miserable old hypocrite."

Celia was right. Why should she sit at home and pine for a man who had made her give up all her friends while he sneaked off to lunches and goodness only knew what else with his old mistresses? She had been virtuous and loyal. It appeared that he had not. Very well then. Quid pro quo. She felt better already.

Laura arrayed herself in a clinging scarlet dress, sheer black tights and jabbing stilettoes of the kind which Matthew detested. Sprayed with scent and crimson-mouthed, she thought she looked very like a Fellini whore. Swaying on her heels, she returned to the telephone to ring one of her schoolfriends from the Sacred Heart.

"Maria? Hello. Laura. I got the dates mixed. I'd love to come along to your party. Really? You're a dear. I'll be there in half an hour. See you."

Maria Galt's party was being held in a small and depressing flat off the Earl's Court Road. Looking round the room from the superior inches of her stilettoes, Laura was meanly pleased to see that the stars of the Sacred Heart had undergone a change for the

177

worse. The neat and pretty had grown dull and plain. Here, she could forget Celia's snide comments and boast of her literary connections, her clever successful husband, her enviable life. Her morale began to rise.

Nourished by confidence, Laura talked extravagantly and drank wine by the tumbler. Collapsing with a giggle on to a sofa, she found herself next to a young man with curly black hair and a soft red mouth. He gave her a speculative look under lashes like palm fronds.

"Well now," he said. "And how did a beautiful creature like you get out of purdah for the night?"

Laura twisted her engagement ring round to hide its sapphire blink. "I'm being a grass-widow for a week or two."

"He must be very trusting."

Laura smiled. "But I'm very trustworthy. Aren't you?"

"It depends."

His name was Edward, Eddie for short. He worked in advertising, had been married. His conversation was easy and flippant, full of suggestions which Laura was not slow to pick up. Mutual attraction was acknowledged in slow wide smiles. Laura's old friends slanted their eyes at each other—so that was what they got up to in the literary world. How blatant could you be? But she had never been one of them.

Laura went to bed with Eddie three or four times. He was an unremarkable lover. She noticed that his laugh was high and irritating, and that a light spray of dandruff covered the back of his jackets.

"Bet your husband doesn't fuck you like I do," said Eddie with a smirk. She looked at him with sudden and intense dislike.

"You're right," she said. "He does it a lot better."

Matthew was surprised and gratified by the warmth of Laura's welcome. At dinner, she told him about Eddie and, giggling slightly, about the denouement. It was, Matthew thought, easier to be amused than annoyed by the incident. It was not of consequence.

Matthew might have been more ready to make it of consequence had he not been guilty of a similar weakness. Celia's random shot had been uncomfortably close to the target.

Laura's brief infidelity and his own journalistic enterprise

178

marked the beginning of a new phase of their marriage. Will Lazlett was delighted with his piece and wanted him to do more articles on similar lines. He would be interviewing a number of eminent foreign writers and relating their work to their country. The series would appear under the title "A Man and His Country". All travel expenses would be paid. At a time when Matthew was looking for a reason not to begin a new novel, the idea seemed heaven-sent.

"It's not what you should be doing," Laura said.

"It's not going to run to more than six pieces," Matthew said. "And they do pay quite well, unlike Screeby's."

"Up to you," Laura said. She had only recently begun to understand that these discussions about Matthew's work bore no relation to the decision which would already have been taken. She was free to argue. She could not expect to influence.

The interviews meant that Matthew would be away for one month in every two over the next year.

Well, what did he expect her to do?

It was all so simple, once she had begun. She had only to mention Matthew's absence and look wistful for most men to transform guilty desire into a chivalrous duty to the abandoned wife. Laura perceived herself not as a victim of male lust but as a modern wife, an enthralling combination of Messalina and Lady Jane Digby, amorality wedded to romance. She was, by her own lights, loyal. She permitted no criticism of Matthew and conducted her affairs only in his absence. There could, she reasoned, be no harm in them since Matthew remained her master, her true love. The rest were underlings who, when she drew her final comparisons, must always be found wanting. The affairs were no more than games, played to pass and fill time, to feed vanity and bring her back, open-thighed and compliant, to her amused and forgiving husband, secure in the knowledge of his wife's continuing affection and desire.

Laura was not at all unhappy with her new style of life.

"And are you really forgiving?"

"Laura's very engaging in her penitent moods. Of course I'd rather she didn't have the affairs, but it's a bit late now to start making a fuss. And to be fair to her, she is alone a good deal.

She's discreet at any rate. She's never gone after my friends—where's the ashtray, my sweet?''

"Your side. You're too tolerant, Matthew. She'd probably be relieved if you seemed to mind more.''

"I don't believe in laying down laws. Marriage isn't a prison. I'm not going to stop Laura's little flutters so long as she loves me. It makes her happy and it means I don't have to worry about her feeling lonely when I'm away. Mutual convenience.''

"Mutual cynicism. And what if she falls in love with one of them?''

He thought about it. "I'd try to last him out. I wouldn't let her go easily. All being fair in love and war, I'd probably break the bastard's head in.''

"And yet you don't mind her having lovers so long as you aren't around?'' She shook her head. "You're a very odd man.''

"They just get her body. They don't get the part of Laura that belongs to me. That's the part I'd put up a fight for.''

"So you do love her?''

He touched her mouth with his fingers. "You aren't meant to ask that sort of question. Yes. I love her.''

"What she really needs is children,'' Alice said after a pause.

Matthew laughed. "There speaks the mother of two. She said the other day that maternity wards reminded her of mechanized dairies. Does that sound like fond motherhood to you?''

"Gracedew might change her mind. Country life's a great incentive to having families. There isn't much else to do except drink and survive your neighbours.''

"Gracedew isn't going to happen.''

"I wouldn't be so sure. Still,'' she added, "I'm quite glad it hasn't happened yet. After all, this would have been impossible in the country.''

"The Bedford Hotel on Saturday afternoons with tea and buttered toast. I don't know. It might have been quite jolly.''

"Sad,'' Alice said. "And squalid. It's pretty squalid as it is. Are you really sure that she doesn't know?''

He shook his head. "As far as Laura knows, Tuesdays are spent researching the backgrounds for my articles. Well, it's half true. I was doing that until twelve, in a state of happy anticipation.''

He stubbed out his cigarette and ran an appreciative hand along the strong white curves of Alice's body. She lay still, looking at him. "Perhaps we should have got married after all," he said. "We'd make a good couple."

"Bit late to think of that now. Anyway, I've had enough of emotion. Just coupling will do very well for now."

"Keep that joke for your country beaux. Still, I suppose I always could get divorced."

"What on earth for? You've got pretty Laura and you love her. To be perfectly frank, my dear, I've rather changed my mind since the old days. I did want you to marry me, then. Now, I'd rather settle for a faithful weekly lover than an inconstant husband."

Matthew laughed. He could always trust his Alice to give the right response. "What a beast you are. What's your watch say?"

"We've got another hour, unless you're in a hurry. It's a funny thing, amorality," she added reflectively. "We ought to be tortured by guilt. You say that Laura is."

"Spasmodically. She enjoys it. It's part of the pleasure, making me her confessor. I do have the occasional pang, to be honest."

"Well, I don't," Alice said firmly. "I don't sleep with anyone else. I'm a pretty good mother and a dutiful daughter. And I'm entitled to a little happiness once a week. It isn't hurting anyone. I'm not asking for love. It wouldn't be much use if I did, would it?"

"Dear Alice." He looked down at her strong sad face. "No bowing wall, you. You're the best imitation of an independent woman I know. I'd believe every word you said if I didn't understand you so well."

"Don't be so bloody smug," Alice murmured as he slid into the warm familiarity of her body. "Just because you've known me since I was eight doesn't mean you understand me. You understand exactly as much as suits you."

"Shut up, Alice," Matthew said. "And pull the blanket up. Your heaters aren't working."

"Don't be ungrateful. It was the nicest thing old Aunt Zinnia ever did, leaving me this house. I forgive her all its defects, and

181

so should you." She stared up at him. "Matthew, is it like this when you're with—oh, it doesn't matter."

"No," he said gently. "It doesn't. And it isn't. So let's not talk about it."

Driving back to Chillingston through the drizzling November dusk, Alice told herself that it was time to give him up, as she did every Tuesday evening, knowing that by Sunday she would have decided to postpone thoughts of renunciation for another week. She knew she was wasting her life. Life without him was too lonely to bear much contemplation.

They had walked almost literally into each other's arms just over a year ago at an exhibition dedicated to the preservation of the English country house. It was a subject on which Alice was well-informed and the initial embarrassment felt by them both was forgotten in discussing the role of the country-house owner.

"Still," she said. "Talking's all very well, but you're never going to do anything. It's an abstract concept to you, nothing to do with reality."

Matthew's face clouded. "You're wrong. Why do you suppose I came here today? To mock? I do care about Gracedew. Rather more than you might suppose."

"I don't suppose anything. I don't understand. I know you never go there. You've cut it out of your life."

He walked a few steps away from her before turning back with an uncertain look. "It wasn't my choice. Something happened. Are you going on anywhere, or can I give you tea in some very proper place?"

In the watery green surroundings of the Fortnum & Mason soda fountain, Matthew told Alice about his illegitimate birth and the curious mixture of indifference and responsibility which the thought of Gracedew produced in him. It was an extra-ordinary relief to have said it; he had never told Laura. Alice listened with no sign of shock or surprise. When he had finished, her hand moved across the table to cover his for a moment.

"Poor Matthew. I wish you'd told me before. I might have understood the situation better. Stupid old man. As though it made any difference."

"I can understand his feelings pretty well. He loathed my mother. The idea of her pushing to get her child accepted as the

182

heir, of being deceived for all that time—I can't forgive him, but I can't entirely blame him either."

"But it wasn't your fault. You loved the house."

"I still do. Still, no use in thinking about that now. It's too late."

Alice looked reflective. "I wish I could do something. I could try talking to him."

"No," he said. "I'd rather you didn't."

"As you wish." She stirred her tea. "And what about your real father? Do you ever see him?"

"I don't even know who he is."

"Now that is extraordinary," Alice said. "You mean you haven't tried to find out?"

He shook his head. "It may seem odd but I don't want to know. I had a rather strange letter about three years ago from Clarissa, full of hints about some man she'd discovered whom I might be very interested in meeting too for personal reasons. I didn't answer it. Knowing my mother's tastes, he's probably a very second-rate character."

"Still—your father."

"My father was the man who brought me up. He treated me as his son and I mean to carry on behaving as though I was. There's no point in exhuming the past when it's been buried for so many years." He leant back. "Anyway, that, my dear Alice, is my reason. I'd rather you didn't spread it around."

"I'm no gossip. You ought to know that." She spoke gently, but he winced as he took her meaning.

"I wouldn't have blamed you if you had. I didn't behave very well."

"Never apologize, never explain." She smiled at him. "Well, it's not a bad rule."

"It's very like you." He hesitated, feeling his way towards intimacy. "I'm so glad we met again. I thought about you a lot, but—"

"Don't explain," she said. "There's no point, as you say, in exhuming what's been buried. Tell me about your wife. Is she pretty?"

"I'm not going to be side-tracked into talking about Laura. It's true that I missed you. I still do."

183

Alice blushed the deep tea-rose pink which he remembered always having suited her. "So do I," she said in a low voice. "I wish to God I didn't."

"No need, now that we've met." He leaned forward to touch her cheek with his hand. "I'm not going anywhere this time."

"But you're married," she said gravely. "You don't suppose it could be the same now?"

He looked at her flushed anxious face. He knew that she was more than forty, but she retained the candid innocent stare which he had always found endearing and unnerving. Dear straightforward Alice, so black and white in her sense of what relationships were about. Adultery was wicked, marriage a pledge to eternal fidelity. So simple. He had shared that ideal himself once, before experience had taught him otherwise. The decent thing to do would be to go now and let her return to her orderly country life with a pleasant memory and, perhaps, a little regret.

"Still," he said. "It seems a shame not to see each other at all. Do you think lunch at Wheelers on Tuesday would be breaking any rules?"

It was, she thought, graceful of him to suggest a restaurant where they had never been together. To accept would be unwise. It would be the first step. There was no future for her here.

"Yes," she said. "Let's do that."

Matthew was too aware of her apprehensions to hurry her. He gave her lunch three weeks running, drove her home, gave her a good-bye kiss on the cheek. He talked just enough about Laura for Alice to realize that his wife did not share her own high ideals about marriage. Discreet questioning established that there was no other man in Alice's life. He had no wish to be the breaker-up of relationships; if there were none, he had less cause for guilt. She mentioned nobody and he knew that she was not given to concealment. After their fourth lunch, Alice invited him to come in to her Ebury Street house for a cup of coffee. After the coffee, he kissed her.

And so, on a pleasant summer afternoon a year ago, the affair had been resumed in the lacy billows of old Zinnia Tresham's bed with a quiet unhurried joining of bodies which seemed to Matthew more like married sex than anything he had experienced with Clarissa or Laura. They had been meeting on Tuesday afternoons ever since. And nothing had changed.

It was, she knew, a relationship without a future. He would never leave Laura. He had no serious thought of marrying her. Matthew described it, laughingly, as a connection of mutual convenience. And so, for him, it was. She was his lover, his confidante, his adviser. And she? Turning into the Chillingston drive, she glanced up at the lighted windows of the children's bedroom. Well, at least she had no illusions. She was free, if she wished, to end it and go. She knew that she would stay. Fed neither by hope nor expectation, she continued, against her judgement, to love him.

Driving home to Saint Anselm's Road, Matthew lashed himself for his weakness. He had meant to do something positive about bringing the weekly meetings to an end. As usual, he had done nothing. It was the same dreadful inertia which kept him from breaking the contract with Will Lazlett, from confronting Laura with anger instead of wearily tolerating the affairs conducted in his absence. He had contributed to the pattern of their London life. It was up to him to break and reshape it.

Of course he must end the affair. The thought of doing so filled him with sadness. Alice would be good about it, say that she understood, wish them to remain friends. She would never reproach him. Knowing that did not make the prospect any more agreeable. Perhaps in a month or two . . . .

Laura was curled up in the darkest corner of his study with her nose in a book. He turned on the light.

"You're going to ruin your eyes, Lorelei."

"Good cause."

"What is it? Proust again?"

"More fun. You." She looked up with a smile. "I'd forgotten just how good you were. James Erskine's right. He said at the dinner-party last night that you ought to get back to novels."

"So I will when I've got the time."

"We've heard that one before. You don't want the time."

He glanced at the clock. "Speaking of which, it's time to try out some of that new Muscadet I bought."

"You have some. I don't really feel like a drink."

Her voice was a bit odd, he thought. "What's up? Didn't the writing go well today?"

"Not too bad." Laura looked at her fingernails with interest. "How was the Reading Room?"

"Usual crowd of old buffers and cranks."

"It's funny," Laura said meditatively, "that you should choose to work in a place I can't come into, not having a pass."

Matthew felt a stirring of unease. "Want me to get you one? I'm sure it could be arranged. We can say you're doing a thesis on the American Civil War as that's the period of your book." He kissed the nape of her neck. "Want to come and work beside me? There's a splendid Italian coffee bar round the corner for lunches. Sit in there for a couple of days and you've got a ready-made novel."

"Calm down," Laura said. "I'm quite happy working here. Only it seemed a bit odd that you should have been in Ebury Street at two o'clock. Ned Foley saw you. With a blonde lady."

"Ned's as blind as a bat."

"Alice Tresham lives in Ebury Street," Laura said. "I looked it up in the directory. Thirty-two."

"Caught," Matthew said after a pause. "Still, it's not criminal to have lunch with an old friend."

"I don't trust old friends."

"I'm not too keen on your new ones, for that matter."

"Quits," Laura said with a small grin. "All right—but were you? Just lunch? It's a long way from Bloomsbury. I don't mind. I'd just like to know. I do always tell you."

"There's nothing to tell, so you can stop looking so solemn and give me a kiss. And if you do, I'll tell you something much more interesting."

"Bribing your way out of it," Laura said, her mouth against his. "What? You won the pools?"

"I'm taking you to Mexico for three weeks. It was Mexico you said you'd always wanted to see, wasn't it?"

"Now that," said Laura, "is what I call a stylish bribe. I might almost believe you loved me."

"You might even be right."

He was home and safe. Still, something would have to be done about Alice.

Part Three

9

On his ninety-sixth birthday, old Jack Craven summoned his lawyer and informed him that he wished to change his will. Gracedew was to be left to his beloved and only surviving cousin. Three hours after signing the documents, he died.

Matthew sat motionless beside the telephone, trying to take in the significance of what he had just heard. Malice or mercy? He preferred to think it was the latter which had prompted that death-bed recantation, and yet the old man could hardly have known how merciful the release would be. Possessed of an alternative, he could drop the pretence that he was pleased with the work he was doing and channel his energy and passion into saving and restoring the house. He could return to his history of Sir Thomas.

Excitement gave him a queer light-headed feeling. He walked about the room, trying to calm himself. Could he do it? At forty-two, on an uncertain income and Laura's shrinking dowry? With no provisions made, a vast amount of money would have to be found to meet the demands of the Inland Revenue. There were a few tied cottages, about fifty acres of good grazing land to be sold off. The better pieces of furniture, the Lelys, the Reynoldses and the Landseers had already gone, according to the lawyer. As for the upkeep—he remembered Alice's having told him that Charles Remington was paying nearly five thousand a year to heat Knaresfield. Still, Thomas Dobell's resources had been far from large when he began building Gracedew. Faith, energy and determination were the qualities required of him. They could and would be produced, now that he had a worthy cause.

There was relief in the thought that his affair with Alice could now come to a relatively painless end. Given her code of behaviour, they could now only be friends with a shared past. Laura need never know.

Laura. Laura who hated the country, who had told him a hundred times how glad she was that Gracedew would never be a part of their lives, confident that he shared her view—what would she make of the news? The suitcases were half-packed for the Mexican holiday which she was anticipating with such glee. No. It would be going too far to expect her to share in his excitement. The most he could look for was her understanding and support.

"Well, do you like it?"

Superimposed on the pretty girl leaning over the stair-rail in a white evening dress, he saw a stoutly mackintoshed figure trudging across the Gracedew fields. Poor Laura.

"I know," she said, blowing him a kiss. "Don't tell me. I'm to stop buying clothes. But it is pretty and you never know. There might be some lovely opera going on in Mexico City."

Brightly, sweetly, she babbled on. She had set her heart on going to Mitla now because of what Aldous Huxley had said about the designs being like petrified lace. And did he think they might get as far as Peru? Imagine Macchu Pichu with the sun coming up below you!

Matthew poured himself some coffee. She had never looked so happy. Still, it had better be done quickly.

"Come and sit down, sweetheart," he said gently. "I'm afraid we've got to have a serious talk."

"We aren't going? Is that it?" She came slowly down the stairs. "I thought it was too good to be true."

"We will go, darling, I promise you, but not this time. Something pretty extraordinary has happened." He poured her some orange juice. "Do you want a cigarette? I'll fetch you one."

"You know I never smoke at breakfast." She folded her hands in her lap. The pose and the white dress made him think of a younger Laura at her convent school. "Well? Good or bad?"

"Mixed. My old cousin's died. He's left Gracedew to me. The funeral's on Friday and I really don't think we can zip off to Mexico if we're to take over the house." He reached across the table to touch her cold cheek. "To tell you the awful truth,

Lorelei, I'm rather excited by the idea. Of course it's going to be difficult and I'm going to have to do the books or articles that pay best for a while, but it's worth it. Gracedew's such a beautiful house and it's something we can work at together, if you want to."

Laura flaked the crisp layers of a croissant and strewed them across her plate as she struggled to subdue a rising tide of panic. Was this the Matthew she knew and loved, the person who had always said he didn't give a damn about Gracedew and that there was no possibility of his inheriting it? She looked at his smiling face. No doubt about his feelings. He looked like a Nobel prize-winner.

"I don't even know exactly where Gracedew is," was the most she could manage in a stifled voice.

"Nottinghamshire. Hardly the back of beyond. It's only a couple of hours down the motorway."

She had been to Nottinghamshire once, for a hunt-ball. She remembered a dank and grieving house with passages like prison corridors, faintly pearled with moisture. Just like that horrible home of Grandcourt's first wife in *Daniel Deronda*, she had thought at the time. There had been long walks in stinging rain over blind green kale-fields, interminable discussions of unknown neighbours and the local hunt, silences punctuated by the rumble and chime of erratic clocks. And that, she supposed, would be her life at Gracedew, presiding over wet walks and shooting-party lunches, swimming in the grey waters of a Chekhov play until she drowned in melancholy. She had heard enough about Cousin Lucilla to guess what lay in store. But Cousin Lucilla had been more than twice her age.

She looked up at Matthew with a face pink and puckered by the effort not to cry. "Shall we have to live there all the time? I thought you liked being in London."

"Not so much as you do, poppet," he said with a smile. Her control began to slip, confronted with such inflexible cheerfulness.

"You could sell it. It's not as though it was your home. The old—he can't have expected that you'd give up your life to it at the drop of a hat."

"It was my home, Laura. You forget I spent most of my

childhood there and that I grew up expecting it to be mine. We may end by having to sell it if we can't make ends meet, but I don't want to think about that until we've given it a try."

Laura's response was to burst into tears. Matthew's temper began to rise. She could at least make an effort to show some enthusiasm or interest.

"Try to think about it a bit more positively, sweetheart," he said when the sobs appeared to be subsiding. "I rather like the idea of our going into it together, working to rescue a beautiful house, getting it back into shape, living another kind of life. It really isn't such an awful fate."

"I never wanted to live in the country," she said passionately. "I'd have married one of the Surrey locals if that was the sort of person I'd wanted to be. I loved you because you weren't. Can't you understand?"

"Perhaps you'd like to stay in Saint Anselm's Road while I try to run Gracedew, then? Would that suit your plans better?"

Irony was beyond her. She gazed at him with the look of the drowning swimmer who has just been thrown a rope. "We could make some sort of a compromise. But that seems so unfair on you."

"Oh, don't let that trouble you for a minute," he said, furious. "I'm only your husband. I'll just go and do something about the tickets. See you later."

"But Matthew! I'm sorry—I didn't—" The front door slammed. Peering out of the bay window, Laura saw her husband walking rapidly away down the street with his hands thrust into his pockets. There was no backward glance. She had not done well, she thought. He had looked for her support and all she had done was to cry and say she hated the country. It would serve her right if he never came back. She squeezed her knuckles into her eyes for a moment before sitting down to telephone the news to her parents. Listening to her mother's excited voice, she succeeded in feigning a pleasure she could not feel.

"Darling, it's just what Daddy and I have always wanted for you. I only wish Gracedew could have been nearer us. I never did like that London house of yours. So poky. I can't think why Matthew bought it."

"I'm quite fond of it myself. Still, I suppose we'll have to sell it. It doesn't sound as though we'll be able to afford to keep both."

There was a slight pause. "Laura, dear, your father's just saying that he doesn't want you to start using your own little bit of money on Gracedew. It's not as though it was your responsibility. I do agree with him."

"There's no need to talk as though Matthew was a thief. He's awfully generous. And it is my money to do as I like with."

"No need to start shouting, Laura. We're only thinking of your interests."

At least, Gracedew would put more distance between herself and her parents. That was a large point in its favour. She set herself to the task of finding others.

Matthew returned home at six to find his Laura bathed, bright-eyed and in one of her prettiest dresses, expressing a lively interest in Gracedew's history and his plans for it. Prepared to reason with and reassure her, he was relieved, but not entirely convinced. She had always been a good actress. Still, it was an admirable performance and one for which she deserved some credit. Whether her determination to be cheerful would survive even a week's experience of Gracedew was another matter. He was not very optimistic.

Rain fell heavily and without cessation on the day of the funeral, providing an excellent excuse for most of the mourners to absent themselves. A few had come to inspect Gracedew's new owner; no one had come to grieve for the dead. The address was given by Colonel Tresham, white-haired now and slightly bent, but otherwise remarkably unchanged from Matthew's memory of him. Alice had said that there was no love lost between her father and Gracedew's reclusive owner. The flow of rhetoric which boomed down the empty rows of pews was, presumably, prompted by some Tory sense of duty to uphold a gentleman and fellow land-owner. If his tributes were more enriched by adjectives than sincerity, it had to be said that he offered them very plausibly. As might have been expected from a man with thirty years of political experience behind him, Matthew reflected.

Sitting between Laura and Alice at the front of the church, he passed some time in comparing them, to the advantage of both. To his left sat his wife, dressed to suit a London wedding more fittingly than a country funeral, newly-shorn curls of flame lying on black velvet shoulders, high heels nervously fidgeting between the faded hassocks. To his right sat his mistress, pale and straight-backed in a dark tweed suit, her eyes resolutely fixed on the altar.

They had talked only once on the telephone since the news, with the clipped formality of strangers. There had been no discussion of further meetings, no reference to the past. He had in some shamefaced way begun to mumble something, but Alice had briskly cut across him, speaking in cool efficient tones of the funeral arrangements which she had offered to undertake. If she suffered, he was not to know of it. Looking at the vestry curtains, his memory unlocked a startling image of a small pink eunuch-like child, grinning, with her aertex shirt spread across her knees. Untimely desire stirred as he glanced sideways and caught Alice's sudden smile. It was likely that she had the same picture in her mind, or some more recent image from Ebury Street afternoons.

"Do look. The vicar's gone to sleep," she murmured.

"So he has." He smiled at his own egotism in assuming that he could read her thoughts. All women are Mona Lisas when it comes to the interpretation of smiles.

"Jack Craven was a man who valued privacy," Colonel Tresham declared with the look of a man who had just discovered an astonishing truth. "Few of us can say we really knew him. Speaking as one of those privileged few, I can say that Jack was a man whose friendship, when given, was given with a full heart."

"Right load of old rubbish, that is," Bates muttered to his wife in their pew at the back of the church. "I never heard him say a good word of Colonel Tresham in his life. Called him a pontificating old fool more than once."

"Hush up," Mrs Bates whispered as the Colonel glared down the aisle. "No need to go abusing the gentleman. You've had more pheasants out of his woods than I'd care to remember."

" . . . not a man to tolerate fools gladly. I remember a very amusing incident when . . . "

Matthew switched off his attention. 'Tis opportune to look back upon old times, and contemplate our Forefathers; he glanced up with affection at Sir Thomas, standing guard over the family pew, at Venice Dobell's sly merry face, so curiously like Laura's, chapelled high in a ruff of fretted stone. Venice, elusive as the city of her name. He thought of those early letters of their marriage which had so charmed him when he began his study of the family. Thomas had been her sweet Tom then, her honey love and her delight, until her dowry had been sucked into the cost of building Gracedew and Thomas' absorption with the house led him to neglect his wife. A train of lovers had gratefully entered the heated haven of Venice's body and Thomas, knowing it, endured and said nothing. Courage or cowardice? He could do no more than guess how much suffering was masked by the smiling stone relief.

Still, pain had been the framework of Thomas' age, the chance to gain a heavenly crown, the wedding-robe of all true Catholic believers. He had lost his wife, he had ruined himself trying to complete Gracedew, but he had died true to his faith and to himself. In that, there might have been some curious solace for all the despair. It must, he reflected, be the worst pain in the world to love a woman whose desire for you was dead. He glanced down to Laura's profile, sharply pale as the relief above her head. Should he learn from Thomas' tolerance, accept the fatal quirk of coincidence which had given him a wife who, like his mother, seemed to thrive on a succession of light affairs while always declaring that she loved only him? The future was suddenly full of threats. The preservation of Gracedew would depend largely on his earnings. Like Thomas, he would have to buccaneer, take the jobs that paid him best. There would be no chance of his being able to spend all his time here with her, and Laura, left alone, would fret, feel ill-used, look for a man to fill, for a time, his place. He closed his eyes.

"Gracedieu, grace of God, help me to keep her. Make her understand and love the house as I do. Teach her to trust me and be patient."

It was unfortunate that she remained so vehemently against the idea of children. A child would fill her time, engage and amuse her. A child who would have everything he had lacked, security, love, the certainty of an inheritance. Still, no use in dreaming. He could not force motherhood upon her as a kind of prison.

Laura's sharp little whisper broke in on his thoughts.

"Haven't they ever heard of heating at Gracedew? There'll be more than one corpse in this church before the service ends."

"It's nearly over, darling."

"Nearly! After two hours!" The whisper rose to an outraged squeak. Alice glanced towards her with a faint smile. Resignedly, finding himself observed, Matthew did what was expected of him and took off his coat to mantle his wife's shuddering body. Men didn't feel the cold—so women always told him.

"Ashes to ashes, dust to dust—" Warm rain spattered their shoulders as they huddled under the elms, city-white faces staring down at the grave. Tears pearled Laura's cheeks. Funerals, dead rabbits and Charlie Chaplin films—all had the same effect. It annoyed her. Why should she cry for that horrible old man? A good thing he was dead, except that if he was alive she would be in Mexico. No use in thinking about that. She had made her resolution. Love, enthusiasm, support. No weakness.

Warmed by a pleasant sense of heroism, she took stock of the woman who had shared their pew and who now stood on the far side of the grave. Her face was too long, her hair badly cut, but the eyes were clear and beautiful. She looked, Laura thought, just the sort of woman who would be capable of running a house like Gracedew. An old friend was how Matthew had described her, cunningly suggesting a woman of declining years. Alice Tresham did not fit into that category. It was not even possible to say that she looked well-preserved, Laura's favourite damning phrase. Realizing that Alice had noticed her stare and was returning it with a smile, she blushed and dropped her head.

The last mourners despatched themselves with indecent speed after the burial. The rain was by now falling in grey sheets and the prospect of a funeral feast (if there was to be one) at Gracedew furnished little joy for a drenched Sunday. The vicar, Mr Flower, shook hands all round and, rather pointedly, looked forward to seeing his new parishioners on Sunday at Matins. Invited to stay for a drink, he murmured something about lunch

198

with the Archdeacon, frightfully sorry, only time and roast beef waited for no man, before hurrying away with bent head towards his car. Lady Livingston, vastly sabled, was suffering from an imperceptible cold which she would never forgive herself for allowing them to catch. Charles Remington had some American art historians coming to look round the house. The air hummed with excuses and the purr of departing cars.

Abandoned, the Cravens shivered at the churchyard-gate under the rattling arc of Colonel Tresham's golfing umbrella. Conversation, however awkward, was enforced by such proximity. Matthew said that the address had been a most moving one. Laura remarked on the coldness of the church and the squeakiness of the organ and then, seeing Alice Tresham's expression of polite surprise, tried to redeem herself by saying that she had been spoilt by going to services at Brompton Oratory. Colonel Tresham laughed and said the young lady would have to lower her sights a bit. Laura gave an elegant shrug and said that surely Coventry Cathedral wasn't that far away. Alice wondered how this pretty urban creature with her spiked heels and tilted velvet beret was going to survive the longueurs of country life. Matthew had always told her that he liked a woman with a generous figure; she was disconcerted by Laura's rakish thinness. Tiny breasts. Small white hands with varnished tips—self-conscious, she squeezed red fists into her pockets. Suddenly, from nowhere, came a violent memory of Matthew at Ebury Street, his head buried between her legs, his tongue pointed and prying. The taste of him stung her mouth . . . .

"Well, we'd better go home. The boys haven't had their lunch yet." She smiled, too brightly, at Laura. "Awful bore, children. Think yourself lucky."

Laura slipped her arm through Matthew's. "I do."

"But you can't go," Matthew said, suddenly panic-stricken at the thought of the empty house. "Come in for a drink, at least." He was conscious of sounding more pleading than hospitable.

"Drink!" Colonel Tresham's laugh was like a small exploding cannon. "Lucky if you find a bottle of barley-water. I'm afraid my daughter's right. We should be off." It struck him that the girl looked a bit cold and depressed. Silly little fool, coming in clothes like that. Why Craven should have picked such a skimpy, whey-faced girl when he could have had Alice for a flick of his finger—there was no sense in it. Alice would have made a perfect job of running Gracedew. Still, the Cravens would be their nearest neighbours and he liked to think he was an hospitable man. He gave Laura a brisk pat on the shoulder.

"Come over when you've settled in. No need to telephone. Are we doing anything tomorrow night, Alice? We could get Charlie Remington to come over—"

"Oh, we aren't staying," Laura intervened. "Matthew just wanted me to see the house, didn't you, darling?"

"Actually, I did put a few things in a case for us," Matthew confessed. "I do think we ought to spend the night here after coming all this way."

Laura's face grew mutinous, but she said nothing.

"I'm so glad," Alice said warmly. "I did tell Mrs Bates I thought you'd probably stay. There's a bed made up, and I did a few flowers. And you'll find a bottle of wine and some food in the kitchen. Nothing very exotic, I'm afraid. Nottingham isn't exactly a gourmet's paradise."

"Wonderful Alice," Matthew said happily. "Where would we all be without you?"

Back in London, blast her, Laura thought, but she managed a smile.

"How terribly sweet of you, Alice. You shouldn't have gone to such trouble."

"Come on. It's the least I could do for my new neighbours." But still too much, she thought, watching Laura's eyes. If she doesn't know for certain, she certainly suspects something. Well, her victory. Why should she worry now?

"You'd better get going," she said harshly, afraid of betraying herself in some look or gesture. "You look half frozen. Give me a ring if you need anything."

"You see what a nice woman she is," Matthew said as they got into the car. "I do hope you'll be friends. She knows Gracedew backwards. She can probably give you a lot of useful tips."

"I'm sure she will." Laura turned a smile like a torch on him. "Yes, I thought she was charming. And looking so young for her age. Come on, Matthew. Start the car. I'm longing to see my new home.'' She awarded herself three points for a perfect response.

He forgave her ill-judged remarks about the church. She really was doing her best to please him. ''You should see this when the spring comes and all the daffodils are out,'' he said, navigating his way through the craters in the drive. ''It's absolutely ravishing.''

Laura looked through the window at black shrubs and pools of muddied leaves. ''Yes. It must be.''

Gracedew always looked its worst on a grey rainy day. As they got out of the car, Matthew saw Laura's face wrinkle with alarm as she looked up the lightless walls at the shuttered windows. The chimneys, even to him, resembled a row of gibbets pointing at the sky.

''I hadn't realized quite how big it was,'' she said. ''Oh Matthew, how are we ever going to manage?''

''Shush.'' He put an arm round her and produced what he hoped was a confident grin. ''Leave the miracles to me, Lorelei. We'll be all right. Look.'' He swung her round to face the lake. ''Isn't it pretty? There are waterlilies all over it in the summer. I'll take you out boating in a pretty straw hat. We'll have picnics.''

Laura looked down at the black oily water, the flat expanse of tobacco-coloured fields, the sooty trees with branches dangling in dejection. There wasn't so much as a duck to be seen. She wouldn't want to live on a lake like that, were she a duck. She turned away.

''What fun!''

''Fun?'' the house flung back in her face.

Mrs Bates opened the door to them, looking to Laura's apprehensive eyes uncommonly like a witch with her sharp black stare and hatchet chin. Age had been a shrivelling process; her legs and arms protruded like twisted brown sticks from the black wool dress purchased for the funeral.

''Terrible day for a burying,'' she said mournfully. ''Think of him lying in all that mud and slush, poor gentleman.''

''I don't think he'll notice,'' Matthew said, stooping to kiss her dry cheek. ''You look well, Mrs Bates. Not a day older.''

She allowed herself a smile. "You always were a terrible little fibber when you were a lad. I feel me years, Mr Craven. None of us any younger, are we?"

Matthew agreed that this was indeed a truth. "You haven't met my wife, Laura. Mrs Bates," he explained, "has looked after Gracedew with her husband for as long as I can remember."

"Forty-three years."

"Goodness!" Laura cried. Surveyed from the slant of her beret to the tips of her mud-spattered patent leather shoes, she felt that she had been found wanting in everything but youth, which was probably also against her.

"She's got a great look of your mother about her, hasn't she?" It was not clear whether this was an insult or a compliment. Brightly, she smiled.

"We never met, unfortunately." That was a stupid thing to say, but she was flustered and uneasy.

"Seeing as how she's been dead these ten years," Mrs Bates said, making the most of it, "I suppose that isn't surprising. From London, are you, Mrs Craven?"

"Surrey."

"Ah," Mrs Bates said. "South. Yes. Well. It follows, don't it."

"Follows what?"

Matthew nudged her. "Come along, darling. It's freezing here. Let's go into the library. I expect Mrs Bates wants to prepare lunch."

"Only pie," Mrs Bates said glumly. "Shepherd's."

"Just what I feel like." He was not going to allow any further shadows to be cast over the homecoming. "I hope you'll both be staying on to look after us. With the house the way it is, we'll be grateful for all the help we can find."

A chuckle rose from Mrs Bates' ribcage. "You will, 'n all. Still, I dare say Mrs Tresham will help you keep an eye on things. She took a lot of trouble making the house ready for you."

"So she told us," Laura said. She was growing rather tired of Alice Tresham's perfection.

"Oh aye? Still, doubtless you'll be wanting to make a few

changes. It won't be the standard of luxury you're accustomed to in London. Hampstead, isn't it?''

"Only just and not so very luxurious," Laura said, wondering from what source Mrs Bates had acquired what was evidently a deep mistrust of north London. Did she have visions of wife-swapping parties on Hampstead Heath, perhaps? Opium dens in the Vale of Health, marijuana beds on Primrose Hill? "It's not that bad, you know," she said gravely. "And we do live next door to the Methodist chapel."

"I wouldn't know about all that, not having been there." She opened the library door. "I never could understand why a sensible lady like Mrs Tresham wanted to go tearing down there every Tuesday to do her shopping. As though there weren't enough shops in Nottingham to feed an army. I'll call you when it's ready."

"Every Tuesday?" Laura exploded when the door had closed. "Well, at least she won't have to go to London for it now. Awfully convenient for you being next door. I can't think why you didn't marry her, really. She'd do everything so much better."

"It's over," Matthew said. "I never meant it to go on, even in London. There's no question of Alice and I being anything but friends now. She'll be yours too, if you'll let her." He took her rigid body in his arms. "Laura, it never was anything to do with what I feel for you. Alice is a nice kind woman and I've known her for years. She's more like a sister than anything else."

"That must have added spice to it. Incest as well." She realized that she was in an odd way pleased to have Matthew at her mercy for a change. It was tedious always to be the one who was forgiven. Besides which, Alice was neither young nor pretty nor, she guessed, particularly clever. As he said, a nice kind woman. There was no real threat. She could afford to be graceful about it. Removing herself from his embrace, she assumed her most madonna-like expression.

"Don't worry. I shan't make a scene. But I do hope there isn't going to be too much of a Rebecca situation here. I'm not going to be told how Alice did this and Alice did that every time I move a chair."

"I'm afraid there's bound to be a bit of that from Mrs Bates. Not that Alice is particularly marvellous—"

"Oh, but she is! So efficient. So thoughtful."

"But she has been over here quite a lot. And, well, she's—"

"Country. I know." Laura looked at her shoes. "Bloody brogues. You don't need to tell me. Doubtless, I'll learn."

He looked at her, thin, white, shivering, as out of place as a hothouse lily in a potato patch. "Of course you will. I've got a bit of learning to do myself. Writing isn't the preparation one needs for this kind of life." He smiled at her. "I did warn you it wasn't smart. I'm afraid you were expecting something more like your parents' home."

Laura thought of her parents' pretty sitting-room, harmoniously decorated in yellow and gold, the pleasant sporting prints, the spinet which no hand ever touched. (It was too valuable to be spoilt by being played.) She thought with some wistfulness of the fitted Swedish kitchen and of the light flowery bedrooms. Just at that moment, she would have exchanged all the grandeur of Gracedew for the middle-class comfort of Virginia Lodge.

It was true that some effort had been made to provide a welcoming aspect. The tables were decked with sprays of chrysanthemums and spiked laurel. The faded cushions were plumped out, the piano lid polished to a lake of ebony. She sat at the keyboard and tried out an arpeggio. Flat. Wandering over to the French windows, she looked out on a sea of nettles, their spiteful leaves hanging limp in the rain. Marianna of the moated grange. Oh God.

"Well, that's the first thing I'm going to tackle," she said purposefully. "It must have been a lovely garden once."

"There were huge fishponds out there when the house was first built. And the old house—" He pointed to a massive oak tree which darkened the windows from three hundred yards away—"stretched to there. Imagine! A palace!"

He was lost in dreams, beyond her reach. He couldn't even begin to understand her dismay.

"Hold my hand, Matthew."

"Poor Laura." He stroked her fingers. "Look, we will go

back after lunch today if you really want to. I just thought it would be nice to stay."

"It is nice," she said fiercely as tears escaped control and poured down her face. "I'm being idiotic. Got a handkerchief?"

Sniffing, she scrubbed at her face. "I don't want that old witch to see me looking like this. There. See? I'm fine. And of course we're going to stay."

Tenderly, he mopped up the remaining tears. "Darling Laura, I do know. Perhaps we can keep on Saint Anselm's Road for a bit. I don't want you to feel like a prisoner."

"We can't possibly afford to keep both," she said in a muffled voice. "Just living here will cost a fortune. And we haven't got a fortune."

"I know. Still," he decided, "we'll keep the basement and sell off the ground floor. And we'll have people to stay here for week-ends."

Who would want to come to such a sad derelict place, she wondered, but she smiled and said, yes, what a lovely idea. He was depending on her to be cheerful and happy. So she would be.

"Who knows? We might be able to get a grant. And if I do some more stuff for Will Lazlett . . . Ned Foley said he might be able to help if I had a good idea for a comedy series on the box—"

"No," Laura said. "You said this was going to be a turning point. You do your life of the Dobells. Perhaps I'll write a best-seller."

"Perhaps you will. Still," he persisted, "I will have to do some slave-labour. We're going to have to find an awful lot of money quite quickly. I'm not being extravagant about Saint Anselm's Road. I will have to spend a bit of time in London. Nobody's going to come hammering on the door with lucrative offers if I sit here."

She looked up at him. "I can't face staying here alone, Matthew. I'll do anything to help, but please don't start going away again. It's not so bad in London, but here—" She locked her arms round him. "I won't let you. I do love you."

He looked down at her bright hair. "And I you, more and more. We'll be all right, my love. And much closer, in a way.

Just us. No more dallyings for either of us. You're the only mistress I want.''

"Dear Matthew." She kissed him lightly on the lips and turned away bewildered by her own feelings. She did not really want it to be like that. No more frivolity. No more flirtations. No more games. The absolute intimacy and trust she had once passionately desired were now in her reach, and she did not want to have them, not in these conditions. The life of a retired couple stretched ahead, scrimping and saving to keep a house which, to her at least, seemed not to be worth the effort required. It was all very well for Matthew. Gracedew represented so much to him in the way of new hopes and plans. He might well be ready to settle into country life, to accept demeaning jobs when he could so thoroughly justify the reasons for accepting them. He might find fulfilment here. But, then, he was over forty. And, she thought sadly, it was beginning to show. Feeling the weight of his hands on her shoulders, she stiffened her back.

"I never," he said gently, "loved anybody so much as I love you. And that's the truth. You used to be afraid I'd run off and leave you. It's you, my darling, who may end by leaving me.''

"Nonsense. You know I won't." Guiltily, she turned to kiss him. "So don't say it." Indeed, he must not say it, for it was when he put himself in her power that her love wavered. Elusive and unpredictable, he was the man she loved and desired. Dependent and adoring, he became vulnerable. And to be vulnerable was, in her eyes, to be unmanned. Over his shoulder, she saw Mrs Bates standing watching them from the doorway. Disengaging herself, she gave a cool hard smile.

"I didn't hear you knock, Mrs Bates.''

"I didn't.''

"I think it might be better if you did," Laura said while Matthew stared at her. "If you don't mind.''

"As you wish," Mrs Bates said after a considerable pause. "Madam. Pie's up.''

10

Squeezed into a corner of James Erskine's newly acquired and coldly plastered penthouse conversion by Saint Catherine's Dock, Matthew looked down through a barrier of plate glass at the Thames, dead as the Styx below the brilliantly illuminated skyscrapers. London seemed like an anxious imitation of New York. All that was missing tonight were the whisky sours. Propped against the window, he surveyed his fellow guests with a prejudiced eye. The gay mob, as he really must learn not to call them, were here in force this evening. They were, as far as he could make out, the new rulers of the literary social circuit. Every time he encountered a new reviewer or a successful young writer at a party, the man turned out to be a homosexual. Not that he really had anything against them or resented the clannish way in which they operated; it was only that he felt like an alien among them. Standing on the edge of a group of young men whose conversation provoked each other, not him, to shrill bursts of laughter and a jingle of Saint Christopher medals, he thought that it was like being trapped in a nest of lethally elegant scorpions, each comment another poisoned flick of the tail. Conscious of his watchful silence, they opened up the circle, including him in their well-polished smiles, requiring his assent. He wondered what they would find to say about him after he had gone. Two years of absence from London life had made him curiously indifferent.

"Matthew dear, you're not allowed to stand about looking enigmatic." Lithe, curly-haired, ridiculously young for his forty-five years until you looked at his eyes, James danced towards him to refill his glass. "Tell us all the gossip. How were the bright lights of Hollywood? Who did you meet? Was it fun?"

The young men looked expectantly at him. He was required to entertain. He was not in the mood.

"It depends on what you call fun. I didn't have dinner with Douglas Fairbanks or Woody Allen. I did swim in a pool which had belonged to one of Zsa Zsa Gabor's ex-husbands. It turned out that they had three other writers working on the script. They ended by firing the lot of us and signing up the producer's son to do a rewrite. So I came back."

James registered sympathy. The young men turned away. Failure was so embarrassing.

"Poor dear, how awful! I must say I did have a few tiny doubts about it all. Still, they must have paid you quite well for the rights to the book." The Hollywood project had stemmed from a film to be made of Matthew's third and most famous novel. He had flown out there full of hope, seeing a miraculous solution to the endless problem of Gracedew's finances.

"I'm not sure what you'd call well. Three thousand for the rights and my travel expenses to be paid out of the film budget, eventually."

"Need a good lawyer?"

"The kind of lawyer I'd need to sue that gang might end by costing more than I've lost. Still, I've no reason to complain. Our old friend Ned's promised to sign me up to write a comedy series. That should pay the Gracedew bills for a bit, with luck."

James nodded and glanced away. One was sorry for Matthew, of course, but he ought to know better than to bring hard-luck stories out to drinks. But Matthew was never amusing nowadays, always talking about that dreary house. He really should snap out of it.

"Come and meet Alan Credell. He's written a marvellous send-up of the California jet-set life. We're publishing it this spring. You'd adore Alan. He's one of the wickedest men I know."

Matthew shook his head. "I really must be off. Jet lag. And I promised to call Laura at eight."

Should he suggest the telephone in his bedroom? Perhaps not. Matthew wasn't such an addition to the fun of the party.

"Dear Laura. How is she? Still writing her romances?"

"She wouldn't thank you for saying so. They really are quite good, you know. She's come on tremendously."

"I really must look at one of them," said James, who would

have died rather than be caught reading a Laura Craven book. One could only do so much for one's friends.

"Better than that, come and stay again. She'd love to see you and Robbie."

"My dear, I'd adore to come, but getting Robbie to budge from London at week-ends is like getting the mountain to Mahomet."

"Come on your own. We've pulled down the billiard room. And the arches have all been repointed." Not, he realized, that either detail could be of the slightest conceivable interest to James.

"I am awfully booked up, but I will be in touch." James smiled warmly. "Promise."

He would delay. As all their London friends did. Gracedew, for some reason which Matthew could not readily understand, was not a house to which people gladly came twice. They were always too busy. Well, it was not of consequence. He had little in common with his old friends, nowadays. The divergence in their styles of life had been too great, or the friendships too fragile. And anyway, he was happier to be at Gracedew on his own with his sweet Laura.

It would be good to be home again.

"Matthew back," was the only entry in Laura's once verbose diary of confidences and intentions for February the fourteenth of their second year at Gracedew.

There was nothing else to be said. It was a remarkable day in no respect. A Gracedew day. She woke at seven in the state of blank depression which she now considered to be normal. Primly slippered and wrapped in pink towelling, she went down to the graveyard dankness of the back passages to collect the milk and the morning paper. After unbarring the shutters to the grey glare of morning, she made the tea, scraped the remains of last night's baked beans into the dog's bowl, sliced the bread, spread the butter and returned with laden tray to where Matthew, grey-faced and comatose, snored among the rumpled pillows.

Bending down to kiss him, Laura found herself staring at the pink dome of his head and wondering for how long he had been deluding her by that curious side-parting. There was an odd yellowish tint to the grey, like lily pollen. She put down the tray.

"Time to wake up."

"Laura darling." His voice was warm, reassuring as apricot brandy. "You do look frozen. Come back to bed. Have a hug."

She folded stiff arms. "I don't need hugs. I'm not a child." She saw him wince at the coldness of her voice and reproached herself. How could she be so disagreeable on his first morning back? How much longer could she bear to be his darling child, the willing pupil forever trapped in eager adolescence?

"I'll run you a bath," she said, propitiating.

Matthew sighed. "Sweetheart, how many times have I tried to tell you that the heating uses twice as much fuel in the mornings? I do hope you haven't been having baths every morning while I was away. We really must—"

"Think about money. Alice Tresham has a bath every morning. I haven't heard you saying anything about her being extravagant." Why go on like this? She couldn't stop herself.

"Alice has a small house and a rich father. You did answer that dinner invitation?"

"Of course. I'm more efficient than you think." She stared at her reflection in the speckled glass above the fireplace. "One good thing about you going away. I always lose weight. Did you notice?"

"Darling, you're thinner and more beautiful than ever," Matthew said, as he always did. "I can't tell you how much I missed you while I was away. Do come back to bed, Laura. Just for a moment."

His eyes were full of love. Dear Matthew. Kind Matthew. If only she could slip back into the habit of love as effortlessly as he did after the weeks of isolation. It was so much easier for the returner than the waiter. But he didn't understand that. Never had.

"I really must get the breakfast."

The light went out of his eyes. "Of course. I'll help, shall I?"

Ready to burst into tears, she managed a bright smile. "No, you shan't. You're exhausted. Stay here and sleep a bit. I'll call when it's ready."

210

Burdened with the dreary knowledge of the disaffection she had no cause to feel—he was so good to her, so patient, so loving—Laura dressed, laid the breakfast, scooped from the hearths the dead ashes which Mrs Bates always ignored. Having retrieved some sense of virtue by these practicalities, she divided the post—hand-written letters to herself, brown bills to Matthew along with the garden and holiday brochures. Well, his life had been the more interesting lately—she deserved the treat. That the hand-written letters were all addressed to Matthew did not particularly trouble her conscience. Curiosity was a craving which demanded and had a right to satisfaction. She had been told by Matthew that she was charmingly immediate for so long that she believed it to be her most agreeable vice.

She noticed and did not appropriate a letter to Matthew from Alice Tresham. It would be more interesting to examine his diary later and see what reference—if any—was made to it. She frequently suspected that the affair continued. Mrs Bates had been quick to tell her that they had been seen having tea together in Nottingham. Nobody met nowadays just to have tea. She worked up a little fit of jealousy over the scrambling of the eggs and felt better for it. It took away some of the guilt.

After breakfast, Matthew worked on his history of the Dobells while Laura cleaned and scrubbed and prepared the lunch. (The third time that week Mrs Bates had failed to appear. She really must do something about it. A tactful word with Mr Bates, perhaps? Difficult to sack somebody discreetly in a village of this size.) As it was Thursday, she also did the washing and ironing while watching the Open University. The mysteries of applied mathematics were followed by a documentary about birds in Mexican folk art, reminding her of their aborted trip. How strange and beautiful a country it looked. No point in dreaming. There was neither the time nor the money for holidays now. Tears of self-pity blurred Laura's eyes, causing her to burn a hole in one of the sheets. So then there was sewing. Never a dull moment in country life, thought Laura, stabbing her finger through the cotton.

They had macaroni cheese for lunch. Cheap and easy. Matthew talked about a sit-com series he was planning to write to pay for the roof repairs. Poor Matthew, reduced to doing

211

hack-work. It sounded dreadful. She smiled and nodded and tried to hide her dismay.

"What about your work on the Dobells? I suppose this sit-com means you'll have to put it aside again?"

"Well, for a time."

"Familiar cry."

"No choice, alas." It had, indeed, been extraordinarily pleasant to spend a morning writing up his notes for the book to which he had intended to dedicate all his time. Two years of try-ing to run Gracedew had given him a sharper insight into how a house can come to possess a man. He had always understood Thomas' ambition. He was beginning to understand the despair which went with it.

"My mother says you're getting to be like Mr Casaubon," Laura said brightly. "Buried away in those sheaves of paper every time you come back."

Matthew winced. "I'm surprised to hear your mother even knows who Casaubon is. I can't say the rememblance strikes me as being very strong."

"Of course it isn't. She was only joking." Why must she always be hurting him? It was a hateful thing to have repeated. "Anyway, how many pages did you get done?"

He shrugged. Laura's obsession with quantity rather than quality had always puzzled him. "I don't know. Ten? Twelve?"

She put down her fork. "Do you know how much of my book I managed to write while you were away? Four pages. Four."

"Sweetheart, we're not meant to be having a greyhound race," he said wearily. "And don't you think it's quite nice that we should both be scribbling away here, side by side? We don't have to fight about it."

"Oh Matthew, I'm sorry. I wish I could stop being so horrible. Perhaps it's the weather. If I believed in a sun-god, I'd say he had a vendetta against this house."

"Poor darling. I shouldn't have left you here so long." He smiled. "I was thinking of going back to bed for an hour or two?"

"Good idea. You go and rest a bit." She jumped up. "I'll do some gardening before the rain starts again."

He looked at the window. "It's started already."

"Then I'll garden in the rain. Good for the complexion."

She wandered out and along the squelching gravelled paths which lay in the long grey shadow of the house. The lawns, at least, had been redeemed by the diligent greed of Colonel Tresham's sheep, who had done in one day what an electric mower would have been praised for achieving in a month. The grass looked soggy and uninviting, but blessedly flat. As to the rest, she preferred not to look at it. The garden was supposed to have been her special project. She had pored over books about Elizabethan gardens and done such beautifully elaborate drawings of how it might be made to look that her proud husband had framed and hung them over his desk. The drawings were a triumph; the garden had been a disaster. It mortified her every time she went into Matthew's study to see what she had intended to do and to remember how she had boasted of her expertise. She had spent the whole of last summer on the making of a knot garden round the sun-dial, neat plots of flowering herbs leading to an arbour at either end. Mr Bates had made a beautiful job of cutting the turf into lozenges and loops; for a whole week it had looked as pretty as a page from an illuminated manuscript. Only the herbs had all died and the arbours, bought by Laura as a bargain in the local garden centre, had clearly never been intended to last through a damp Gracedew winter.

Savagely, she wrenched at the sycamore sprouts in the gravel until it dawned on her that the rain would only bring up another crop the next day. And then the next. Matthew said it was worth the battle, but when the battle went on for month after month and no progress was ever made . . . .

"Oh, to hell with it," she said and threw down trowel and gloves.

She drove the Renault into Nottingham for the spurious purpose of replenishing the cheeseboard and bought herself a new dress for Alice's dinner-party. Looking in the mirror at the rich green silk which clung to her breasts and waist and hips like a serpent's skin, Laura grew vain and happy. She posed and twirled and shook her head to watch her red hair wave down the silk.

"Is it very expensive?"

It was. But very good value if you looked on it as an investment, the salesgirl cannily added. Years of good wear in a dress like that, and it wouldn't date.

"So you think I should buy it?"

She bought it. Matthew would surely forgive the rare extravagance. New clothes always put her in a good temper, and he would reap the benefit of that. She economized on the cheese and drove back through the drizzling dusk in a state of great satisfaction. Alice's dinner-parties were not known for being exciting events, but it was pleasant to think that she would shine.

Over tea in the kitchen, she let herself be persuaded into elaborating the plot of her new novel. It had been Matthew's idea. Now, he enthused and reformed her thoughts so tactfully that Laura would once have been deceived into thinking them her own. Not now. Lucky Laura with a husband who could spin ideas faster than a spider drawing out his web. She said so, smiling, fist clenched on the handle of the teapot.

"Well, it's the only thing that keeps you, my bright and brilliant one," Matthew said, laughing, affectionate, uneasy.

"Oh, I just write to make money. I can't write real books, like yours," she smiled, hoping to be contradicted.

"But darling, we all want to write stories like you," he said, evading truth with grace. "That's what you're so good at."

"Only because I'm not clever enough to do anything else." Bang went the teapot, spilling a thin stream over the cloth. Matthew mopped it up.

"I do wish you'd stop running yourself down. It isn't true."

"It is for me."

Matthew, she discovered, had typed out the morning's pages, arranged for the roof to be repaired, disposed of the weeds which Laura had scattered by the door. He laughed, all the same, when she confessed to her idle afternoon and the new dress. The pleasure and intimacy of their married life had always been in the daily disclosures made and forgiven; it was the aspect of her child-wife role which she least resented. Tolerance had always been Matthew's most endearing quality; it had proved the most enduring. They had their first glass of wine at six, as was their habit. During the night they would drink their way loquaciously through the best part of three bottles. Matthew held that in wine lay the secret of good health. Laura, once content with two glasses, now drank even with her husband and grew petulant if he filled his glass more often than her own. Either would have been disconcerted and distressed to hear themselves described as heavy drinkers, as they were by most of their neighbours.

Matthew had meant to speak mildly about her over-spending. Caught in the jab and flip of her chatter, he merely lit her cigarettes and nodded, wishing he loved her less, that she would understand, or try to understand, more. Reproached, she would only cry. For two days, perhaps, she would assume the look of a responsible and care-laden woman of twice her age while displaying a concern for economy which was maddening in its triviality. He would finish, as usual, by telling her to forget his criticism. Better, in the end, to have his Laura sweet and prodigal than to feed on lentils salted with her tears. So he smiled and listened and said nothing.

At seven, it was time to bar the shutters, draw the curtains, feed the dog, refuel the fires. Laura had a bath and changed into a ruffled shirt and jeans of tight-fitting velvet cord. The refreshed gift of her beauty was the aperitif she offered in consolation for the meagre cheeseboard. Matthew admired the shirt and made a joke about a lover's having given it to her.

"Don't be silly. Nobody gave it to me."

"Sure?" He never was.

"What do you want me to do? Make up a story? That's what I'm good at, isn't it? I met a man in Sainsbury's who turned out to be an oil sheikh in disguise. He took me to London in his Mercedes, drove me straight to Bond Street and said, 'Choose what you want, my darling. The riches of the East lie at your feet.' So I asked for a shirt." Laura made a moat of gravy around the cabbage castle on her plate. "I thought we'd agreed to give all that up. Having affairs. So why ask?"

"I was only joking."

"I'm about to die of laughter. Cheese?"

He caught her and put an arm round her waist as she swung past his chair. She stood still, staring at the wall. His hands slid up to touch her breasts. "Lovely Laura. Don't look so cross."

"I'm not cross."

"Let's go to bed early."

"There's quite a good play on at ten-thirty."

"Blast television. I'd rather play with you." His fingers twisted at her shirt-buttons.

"I'll just clear the plates away," Laura said.

Married bliss.

Cradled in blankets and faded quilts, with the heavy velvet curtains blocking out the glare of a spying moon, Laura helped him to pull off her nightdress. She let herself roll towards the hollow of the bed, to the warmth of his body. Passive and silent, she registered the ritual movements of desire, the squeeze, suck, lick, bite, the pressure against her thigh, the hot seeking thrust between her legs. The speechless craving for the response she would, and did, inevitably produce. The reflex action to a familiar stimulus, predictable as the shuddering dance of a clock-work toy when the key twists the spring. The sob of his release.

"Oh, how I adore you, my darling Laura!"

She turned her face from the tenderness of his smile, wincing at the pity which flooded her, helpless in the toils of a love she had once exceeded and now could no longer match. Sperm-smeared, self-hating, she lay prone. His hand touched her cheek.

"I love you. I do love you."

"And I love you, Matthew." Bestowing her affection with the nonchalance of a thankfully departing guest, she swung her legs out over the edge of the bed and pulled on her dressing-gown. "I'm just going to the bathroom."

"Of course." Dully, he listened for the sounds of Laura's purification, the gush of water, the soft anxious scrub of the flannel between her thighs. It was new enough to hurt him, this maidenly obsession with hygiene, the covert expression of a distaste which he had already sensed in her febrile manner and in the shrinking movement of her body from his when he reached for her. Well, he was probably making too much of it. She was always sexually uneasy when he had been away. It was only a phase, a quaint and even endearing form of modesty which was, no doubt, common enough. Desiring in the past, she would be so again.

"Nearly forgot the essential ingredient," she said with a

bright grin as she came back into the bedroom to curl up beside him in some show of intimacy and affection.

He sniffed appreciatively. "Nice. Rochas, isn't it?"

"Not the scent, stupid," she said, amused. "The Pill."

"Oh." The matter-of-factness of her voice chilled him. "Well, it's not the end of the world if you do forget it, my lovely."

"Oh, don't worry," Laura said. "I won't. I told you. I don't want children."

"Still, you might change your mind one of these days." He stroked her small flat belly. "Mightn't you?"

"Poor old Matthew." She kissed his cheek. "You must think I'm some kind of monster. Perhaps I am. I ought to want children. My mother says I'm unnatural."

"Nonsense. You're still almost a child yourself. There's all the time in the world."

He somehow managed, she thought, to make time sound like a life sentence. "Well, perhaps I'll change my mind, as you say," she said and rolled away to face the outer side of the bed. "Good-night Matthew. I'm glad you're back." He gave her back a light caress and turned away himself to stare into the darkness. Uncommunicative and desolate, the Cravens slept.

Matthew woke at dawn to see her at the window, a handkerchief crammed into her mouth to stifle the low whimpering of some private misery. Wearily, he reached for the paracetamol, preparing himself to spend an hour in solacing her. His hand on the bottle, he changed his mind and closed his eyes. There was nothing he could do for her except the one thing he was not prepared to do. He would not give up Gracedew to make Laura happy. Here was his purpose, his certainty, found at last, never to be abandoned. He had changed. She must learn to do so. She was not a child any longer. It was, he thought a little desperately as he finally got up to clasp and comfort his weeping wife, only a question of time.

11

A woman of spirit, independent means and good looks may enjoy a position of singular privilege in old county circles if she attends to the conventions with care. She need not hunt but should display a keen interest in the sport. Her household should be run with discreet efficiency, tending neither to lavish excess nor to parsimony. She may employ an odd-job man in her garden, but she will be seen to work in it herself. A couple of enviably rare plants will be well worth the trouble of their acquisition. Her dinner-parties will be small, cheerful, carefully planned. The food should at least seem to have been cooked by her.

If she can add to these assets the social talents of the good listener, the shrewd adviser and the sympathetic friend, she will seem too indispensable a part of her society to be criticized for laying some of its conventions aside. From the woman fated to be married off to any eligible local male, she can comfortably pass into the role of the woman whose wish for independence is respected. She can now lower her necklines and flirt without fear of criticism. She is the trusted female friend, the one with whom husbands can lunch and dally without incurring the wrath of their wives. She can do anything, except admit to her loneliness.

Whatever Alice Tresham may have felt when she lay alone under her patchwork counterpane in Chillingston Lodge, this was the public self which she had learned to present. Women liked and admired her; men enjoyed her uncommitting company and her combination of sympathetic humour with cool good sense. As the Cravens' nearest neighbour, it was inevitable that comparisons would be made between Alice and the young mistress of Gracedew. It was felt that Alice would have suited the role a great deal better than that tiresomely unco-operative Laura Dare.

They were prepared to overlook the time when Laura had appeared at the Quorn Hunt Ball in skin-tight leather jeans and scarlet open-toed sandals, murdering the parquet floors of Knaresfield with her three-inch dagger heels. They could not forgive her indifference to their kindness. They knew they had done their best. Mrs Harrison had taken her to two point-to-points, given her a cutting from her finest lavender bush—it was badly in need of thinning—and hinted that she might use her influence to have Laura appointed to the local Magistrates' Association. Mrs Tuckett had invited her to lunch and suggested that an extra morning helper in the Oxfam shop would be given a very warm welcome. Lady Livingston had gone to the trouble of having herself driven over to Gracedew, twice, in order to advise Laura on the most practical way to reorganize the gardens. She had, moreover, produced a jar of her own leather-book dressing for use in the Gracedew library.

They could not have taken more trouble to be friends. Laura's response had been a tepid gratitude which had not failed to give offence. She evinced no interest in the Oxfam shop or in becoming a magistrate. She had been untouched by suggestive accounts of old Mrs Craven's valiant support of the Women's Institute. She had made it clear that she detested blood sports and race-meetings. She had shuddered at the proposition that she should keep a horse. She had not even answered Mrs Tuckett's last invitation to a fund-raising coffee morning for the RSPCA. The final straw had been her announcement to Major Tuckett that she did not think Nottinghamshire society was up to much, a rash confidence which was publicized at the Tucketts' next lunch-party.

Gathered in the Tucketts' drawing-room after the meal, the ladies of Nottinghamshire vented the rage they had, with difficulty, suppressed before the husbands who were so irritatingly tolerant of Laura's shortcomings. Her pretensions were held up to scorn, her literary accomplishments derided. Write! Could they not all write such stuff if they had the time to waste? It was all very fine to have read Proust and to be able to tell them that Vinteuil had been based on Saint-Saëns. Very interesting, but look at her garden! And, my dear, her clothes! Poor, poor Matthew. Mournfully, they shook their heads over his fate, relishing the opportunity to feel wholly virtuous in being so thoroughly disagreeable.

On a distant sofa, vastly recumbent, Lady Livingston listened and sipped at her coffee.

"Oh yes, I can hear you all perfectly well, my dear," she said as Mrs Tuckett appealed to her to join the general indignation. "But you're forgetting one thing. Alice likes her. Alice is an excellent judge of character. Laura may have hidden strengths."

"Too hidden for my old eyes," Mrs Tuckett said. "You're far too kind, Gertrude dear. And Alice—well, Alice is an angel. We all know that."

"A very shrewd angel," Lady Livingston said. "If Alice likes Laura, it's a good enough recommendation for me. Gracedew isn't the easiest of houses to run, and Matthew certainly isn't the easiest of husbands. He's always leaving the girl on her own. And when he is there, I don't suppose she sees much of him. He's always buried in papers in his study whenever I go there."

"Can't exactly blame him for that," whispered sprightly Mrs Harrison, the wife of the Livingston estate agent. "He's probably sick of hearing about that pug and its ailments."

Lady Livingston leaned ponderously forward. "What's that about the rug, my dear? Persian, isn't it? Or does one say Iranian?"

"Pug, dear," Mrs Harrison pinkly cried. "Your sweet little dog. I was saying that he looks wonderfully well. Fighting fit."

"Biting fit, nasty little thing," Mrs Tuckett muttered with a glance at her left and recently savaged ankle. "Dear little fellow. Where would we all be without him? Oh, too fascinating, Gertrude. Our new postman's a communist."

Only Mrs Harrison discovered the link between the pug's teeth and a postman's shins, and tittered behind her hand as the conversation slipped away from Laura and dogs to the number of black postmen in Nottingham.

"Still," Mrs Tuckett said when Lady Livingston had gone. "It wouldn't surprise me if she ran off and left him. Very flighty bit of work. I wouldn't be sorry to see her go."

"But who would she go with?" Mrs Harrison, who would

gladly have eloped with anyone prepared to rescue her from a dull husband and two singularly unamusing children, sighed as she rose from her chair. "There really isn't anybody, Delia. It was horrid of her to say it, but you must admit that Nottinghamshire isn't exactly overburdened with delicious young men."

"Nonsense. What about James Mawson or Charlie Remington? I've seen Charlie hanging over her like one of those birds with big wings. Condoms."

"Condors. You really mustn't confuse them. Come off it Delia. You know he's been in love with Alice for years. And as for James Mawson—you must have heard what happened when Laura went to lunch with him and old Antony Makepeace?"

"No," Mrs Tuckett said with lively interest. "What?"

"James got tight and pounced on her in the kitchen. Laura went home in hysterics. Antony was simply furious. You know how possessive he is about James. It was," Mrs Harrison said pensively, "rather odd. I mean we all know James is as queer as six coots. I suppose Laura does look quite boyish in jeans."

"I've no doubt she encouraged him." Mrs Tuckett pinched in her lips. "I certainly don't intend to ask her here again in a hurry. I shall be civil, of course, but no more."

"Then you'd better start practising, my dear," Mrs Harrison smiled from the door. "She's certain to be at Alice's dinner tomorrow night. Mind you, I don't suppose Laura would notice if you were coldly civil or downright rude. She doesn't seem to hear insults."

Dressing herself for Alice's dinner after a virtuous day at work in the garden, Laura luxuriated in the thought that she would be the prettiest, the brightest and the best-dressed woman at the gathering. It was agreeable to be the centre of attention. It was delightful to escape from the oozing sadness of Gracedew, from the echo of her own footsteps on the long uncarpeted passages, from the rattle of wind in the ivy leaves as she hurried past the grim grey windows towards the comforting light of the bedroom.

"You'd better hurry," Matthew said with a glance at her slippers and straggling hair. "We've only got twenty minutes."

"I know. The shutters weren't done." She leaned towards

the dressing-table glass, her fingers smudging topaz wings above her eyes. "I suppose that awful Remington will be there. Your dear old school-friend. Do you think Alice fancies him? He always seems to be asked."

"Only to make up numbers," Matthew said. "I haven't heard that Alice fancies anybody."

She glanced round at him with a sly smile. "Except you."

Matthew straightened his tie and looked with a sense of dismay into the bathroom mirror where, in the hard light, the dark circles under his eyes made pools of ink. Whatever Gracedew had done for his sense of purpose, it had not dealt kindly with his looks. "That was a very long time ago, Laura."

She fluttered mascara-laden lashes at herself and smiled secret approval before slipping the dress over her head and smoothing its green sleekness down her hips. "Mrs Bates saw you having tea at the Camilou in Market Street." She spun round to point a lipstick at him. "Have at you, oh hypocrite. Now what's your defence?"

"That you look much too beautiful to start nagging," he responded with a smile. "Green suits you. Very Pre-Raphaelite."

"Too healthy. My cheeks look like tomatoes." She put the lipstick down and came towards him. The warm familiar pliancy of her body pressed against him as she lifted her arms up to lock them around his neck. "Kiss and tell. What were you up to?"

He laughed, delighted to see her in what he regarded as a healthy state of jealousy. "Having tea. And then we spent the rest of the afternoon in the Bedford Hotel, passionately screwing in front of a video sex film."

Laura's eyes grew enormous. "I don't believe you."

Still laughing, he slid his hands down her back to squeeze the roundness of her small buttocks. "Why not?"

"Damn you then," she said and slapped him, very hard, in the face. On startled reflex, he struck her back.

"Bastard," she said. "Bastard. God I hate you."

"I was only teasing you, Laura."

"Like hell you were. Fine. I don't care. You go and screw in the Bedford but don't be so bloody smug about it. And don't try to pass it off as a joke."

"I do love you more than any woman on earth," he said quietly. "I really don't want Alice or anybody else. Just you, my Laura. Is it so hard to trust me?"

"No." Her back towards him, she gave a muffled sob. "I wish I wasn't so disagreeable. If only I could be as sweet to you as you are to me. I do love you, Matthew, only—"

"Only what, lovey?"

She turned a desperate face towards him. "I don't know. I'd tell you if I did. I just don't know what it is. Oh well, come on. Let's go."

In the car he asked what she thought of their taking a holiday. They might go to Spain, or to Mexico, the lost trip. She said, in the small voice of a guilty child, that it would be very nice. If he was sure they could afford it.

He steered his thoughts away from the new roof. "Of course I'm sure. I'll book the tickets. We'll go in April." Silly of him. Of course that was all that was needed. The house had worn her down. A spell in the sun and a little frivolity would bring back the sweet careless Laura he had married. He could hardly blame her for getting depressed. Gracedew was not a cheerful house and there was no common ground between Laura and her neighbours. The temple of Nottinghamshire society had no niche prepared for a pretty, urbanized girl of Laura's tastes. Still, he thought treacherously as he glanced towards the pale glimmer of his wife's profile, Alice had managed to make a pleasant life here for herself.

Even Alice had not concealed her disapproval of Laura's hostile attitude to the county. She wondered aloud at the influence which Matthew had to exert in order to get his wife to do such simple things as the ordering of spring bulbs or the arranging of a dinner-party. He had, in loyalty to Laura, tried to minimize his part in the daily running of Gracedew. Alice had not been deceived.

"She isn't a child any more," she had said as they walked back to her car from one of their occasional meetings at the Camilou teashop. "You can't always be the arranger of her life. She won't love you better for it."

Under the glare of the orange neon lights, he had kissed Alice's warm cheek and tucked her scarf into the high collar of

223

her jacket with a pleasant sense of their old intimacy. "Dear Alice. You wouldn't. And I don't particularly enjoy doing it. But we don't always get the chance to choose our roles. If we did, well—"

"Well, nothing," she had said with her wide soft smile. "You love her. That's all there is to it. I only hope she's worth it."

"I wish I was more like Alice." Laura spoke from the darkness with the apparently oracular power of divining his thoughts which she frequently and unnervingly displayed. "You'd be much happier if I was."

He patted her hand. "Rubbish. I wouldn't have you any different."

"Promise?"

"Cross my heart."

She settled back in her seat with a sigh. "How terribly tolerant you are, Matthew."

"Idiot!" He laughed and swung the car into Alice's small gravelled drive with a sense that all was well again between them.

They were the last to arrive in Alice's bright and unexpectedly crowded drawing-room. Laura, as was her habit, gravitated like a drawn magnet to the fireplace and was immediately plunged into a discussion of the day's shooting at Knaresfield by Colonel Tresham and Charles Remington. Matthew glanced smilingly about the room and suppressed a momentary desire to flee. Old Lady Livingston was, inevitably, spread upon the most comfortable sofa between Antony Makepeace and the ferret-faced Mawson, nodding in complacent oblivion as they shrilly eulogized the food in their Italian holiday hotel. Coiled on the floor at Colonel Tuckett's feet and doing her best to imitate the dewy-eyed ingénue which photographs showed her once to have been, Jane Harrison turned her head to throw him an arch smile of welcome. Mrs Tuckett, he observed, was making a display of turning her big blue satin back on Laura, while showing a passionate and wholly unconvincing interest in Charles Harrison's account of his visit to a new garden centre. What could Laura have done to produce such a clumsy display of offence in the stupid woman? Dear Laura. She hadn't even noticed that she was being slighted.

None of the groups attracted him. He was content for the moment to watch his pretty wife as she widened her eyes at Charlie Remington and sighed over her inability to shoot. (He had, at last, managed to persuade her to suppress her loathing of the sport in company.)

"No finer sight than a handsome girl with a rifle on her shoulder," Colonel Tresham boomed. "I married a sporting woman and I've done my best to raise one. Alice was out with the beaters at eight years old and using a gun by the time she was fifteen. Damn good shot, too."

"Oh, Alice does everything well," Laura smiled.

"No reason you shouldn't shoot as well as she does. Charles and I can give you a bit of coaching, if you like."

Laura demurred with a smile. If only she had the time.

"Can't slave away in that house all the year round, a pretty little thing like you," the gallant Remington interposed. "Get Matthew to send you over for a day. Bring him along, if you like. He does shoot, doesn't he?"

Reluctantly, Matthew responded to Laura's plaintive glance and moved towards them. "Hardly, Charles. I take a pot-shot at a rabbit now and then, but it's more luck than skill if I hit one."

"It's all that reading. Buggers your eyes up," Colonel Tresham said amiably. "Pity, though. You could have a nice little shoot going at Gracedew. Plenty of birds around."

"Yes." He knew from the expectant pause that it was the moment for him to propose that they should come over one Saturday and try their luck. Like Laura, he feared rituals. The initial gratitude for an impromptu visit would pass from expectation to a tedious obligation. He had committed himself to rescuing Gracedew, not his neighbours.

"We've got one of your lot here tonight," Colonel Tresham said, seeing that an invitation was not likely to be prodded out by further hints. "Richard Leyden." He lowered his voice to a stentorian rumble. "Cousin of Alice's husband. He rang up on Thursday and asked himself to stay. Damned impertinent, I thought. Still, he seems a pleasant sort of young chap. Writes."

Matthew faintly grinned. "Do I sense condemnation in that?"

"All right if you've got the time," Colonel Tresham said gruffly. "I don't despise any man who cares about his work. Know him, do you?"

"Of course we do," Laura interrupted with her quick nervous smile. "He writes about literary psychology. You must remember his things in the *London Review*, Matthew. I shall be terrified. He's awfully clever."

Charles Remington looked at her dubiously. "I don't go much for these intellectual chaps myself. Always making trouble. Tell them you've got a country house and they look as though they'd like to shoot you. Damned Marxists. Is he a Marxist, this Leyden fellow?"

"There's nothing wrong with—" Laura began. Colonel Tresham gave her a friendly tap on the shoulder. "No politics at dinner, young lady. Stick to literature." He looked over her shoulder with a smile. "There he is. I'll get him over here to meet you. Dick, let me find you a drink. You've certainly earned one—he's been keeping the boys entertained while Alice was cooking," he explained.

Turning, Matthew saw a youngish man with curling brown hair and an engagingly broad grin. Far from handsome, his undeniable attractiveness had much to do with a look of alert intelligence, lightly worn. He could have been any age between thirty and forty.

He held up a glass. "Alice gave me some wine in the kitchen. As for the entertaining—they were doing most of that. I've been learning what a Marjuk does with a Gammet when he wants to capture a Warlock. Hope I've got that right. They're splendid boys. Awfully bright."

"Frightful little beasts," Colonel Tresham said with an affectionate beam. The extent to which he spoiled his young grandsons was the cause of some amusement to those who remembered Alice's disciplined upbringing. "You mustn't let them bully you."

"Oh, I think I've got the upper hand of them—just. Anyway, my compliments. They've come on a lot since I saw them in Malibu. More like Alice."

Colonel Tresham's smile grew wider still. "Do you think so? Just as well from what I've heard of Buck."

"Sure," Leyden nodded. "Buck was a very difficult man. I really used to admire the way Alice coped with him. But who doesn't admire her?" It was, Matthew thought, very smoothly added, just as she was coming to join the fireside group. Leyden's arm fell with easy intimacy around her shoulders. "Even more gorgeous than I remembered."

"Dick, you're far too young to be flattering middle-aged ladies." But not too young to succeed with them. Matthew watched a deep flush of colour spread down Alice's throat as she glanced at Laura with the gay complicity of a woman inviting another to side with her against a man. "Dick was famous for being the most flirtatious professor in Berkeley," she said. Well on in his thirties, then. "I bet he's been heaping you with compliments. Lovely dress."

Leyden dropped his hand with a laugh. "I'm certainly planning to tell her how much green suits her as soon as you introduce us. You didn't tell me you had such pretty friends, Ally."

Ally? Matthew pinched his eyebrows together. How ill it suited her; how little she seemed to resent it. Kissing cousins, perhaps? Intimates, certainly. He did not care for the idea, nor for the way Leyden was eyeing Laura.

"Married friends," Alice said with her straight clear stare. "This is Laura Craven, and her husband Matthew. You should have plenty to talk about. You're all writers."

"How pleasant—and unexpected." From Leyden's glance of cautious politeness, Matthew concluded that he was not alone in his ignorance. "I'm afraid I don't know——" he easily began.

"Oh, but of course I know you," Leyden said warmly, infuriatingly, extending a tanned, well-shaped hand. "You were writer-in-residence at Santa Fé about ten years ago, weren't you? I came to a splendid talk you gave on the nature of the English novel. Good, solid, old-fashioned stuff. I really liked it."

"Good." Matthew withdrew his hand and coldly smiled. Old-fashioned? "And I gather that you write about literary psychology. I rather thought that was Leon Edel's territory."

"Well, Edel's getting on a bit now and there's certainly room for more than one in the field. I've noticed that you English writers tend to be pretty sceptical about it, but I don't let that bother me," Leyden added with the ease of patronage. "You always take your time here about accepting new ideas."

"New?" He sought to devastate with polite incredulity. "You astonish me. In using Freud to analyze Auden?"

Leyden laughed. "Hardly. I've always thought Auden one of your most over-rated poets. Don't you find him very dated?"

Sensing trouble, Laura rashly plunged in. "Anyway, that's not fair, Matthew. Professor Leyden wrote that wonderful article about cerebral adultery. It wasn't anything to do with Freud. You must remember. I told you all about it and you said you wished you could have written it yourself."

"Did I, my love?" Remembering the occasion perfectly well, he was damned if he was going to admit to having expressed admiration, let alone envy of this bumptious American. His smile was thin. "My wife's a passionate consumer of literary reviews. I'm afraid I have to plead ignorance or forgetfulness."

"What the hell's cerebral about adultery?" Charles Remington broke in with a jolly laugh. "Pretty physical stuff, isn't it? Or am I being thick?"

"Of course it can be cerebral," Laura said impatiently. "It always has to start in the head."

"Or a bit lower down," Remington said, grinning.

Laura seemed not to have heard. "Two people looking at each other and just thinking what it would be like is just as bad as if they were in bed together. It's still a betrayal."

"Or a commitment," Leyden said, looking at her with bright, amused eyes. There was a small but pregnant silence. "Anyway, I'm glad you enjoyed reading it, or about it. And you write yourself?"

"Matthew's the writer," Laura said. "I just cover pages. My husband taught me all I know."

"Nonsense, Laura," Matthew said, smiling, embarrassed. She was never more dangerous than when she was humble. "You make me sound like some kind of Svengali."

She gave him a smiling green glance. "Well, aren't you?"

Leyden dispelled the awkwardness with a laugh. "A lady of as much modesty as charm, I see." He bent to light her cigarette and then his own. "I'm glad someone else still has this awful habit. I don't feel quite so much of a pariah."

"It's your last one, so enjoy it, my dears," Alice said gaily. "I'm not going to have the soup ruined for nicotine fiends. Anyway, it's out of date to smoke—didn't you know?"

"Just what my dear wife always says, bless her thoughtful heart," Leyden said with a grin.

"Oh, you're married, then," Laura brightly exclaimed. "And is she over here with you?"

"She is not." He exhaled slowly. "We split up three years ago. I'm talking about the times I go over to Sonoma to see my son. Well, somebody's son."

Colonel Tresham coughed. "It's going to rain tonight. They said on the wireless."

Laura went on looking at Leyden with bright, curious eyes. "You get along pretty well, though?"

"In fits and patches. So long as there's a telephone line between us. Most romantic marriages end up like that. Two months of heaven, ten years of hell."

Laura made a face. "What a depressing view of love. I don't think it's like that at all."

Propping his arm on the mantelpiece, Leyden looked at her with a smile. "Well then, let's have your views. Perhaps you'll convert me. What's love all about, Laura?"

"Hard work and small profits," Charles Remington said sourly. Perceiving that he had been ousted from his role as Laura's cavalier for the evening and that the hint of soup had led to no forward movement, he turned his attentions to Matthew. "How's Gracedew going, then? Got the new roof on yet?" His tone was cordially condescending. A rich man himself, he had been able to understand Matthew's interest in repairing and restoring the house, but not the slowness with which he was setting about it. Living in a society where everybody claimed to be impoverished, it never occurred to him that it might, in the Cravens' case, be based on more truth than was usual.

"Oh, starting stages," Matthew said. "No use in beginning work in winter." He spoke absently, watching the flush on Laura's animated face.

"No time like the present. Now what I'd do in your shoes is get one of these new wood-burning systems for your heating. They're not cheap to put in, but I've calculated that in five years' time . . ." He continued to explain the principles of his heating system until Alice gently and implacably pushed him towards the dining-room where the ladies were already placed and restless for attention.

Seated between Lady Livingston and Jane Harrison, Matthew struggled to seem engaged by each in turn while watching Laura and Richard Leyden across the table. He would have liked to know what Leyden was saying to make her laugh so much. It struck him that she rarely now showed spontaneous amusement in his own company. Perhaps it was a condition of marriage? On reflection, he was inclined to blame himself. While trying to keep the full weight of Gracedew's responsibilities from her, he found it increasingly hard to divert his thoughts from its problems. Even in writing, he found himself dwelling on Sir Thomas Dobell's finances with almost morbid fascination; his dreams were haunted by intolerant bank managers standing like prophets of doom on the brown mountains of his unpaid bills.

He could no longer even pretend to concern himself with the small dilemmas of Laura's daily dress, her anguish over what she called character-motivation in her novel, her quarrels with Mrs Bates. Recognizing the impossibility of convincing her that the finding of twenty thousand pounds for the roof was a more real cause for anxiety than a burned leg of lamb, he had taken the simpler course of silence, forgetting how much of their shared laughter had been the product of Laura's charming triviality.

Patiently, he attended to Lady Livingston's meditations on the advantages of cremation, a subject of which she seldom grew weary, and turned to the flirtatious Mrs Harrison.

"Well, your wife certainly seems to be enjoying herself with Professor Leyden," she said as Laura's clear laughter broke across the table. "She's looking so pretty tonight."

"Isn't she?" Glancing up, he was transfixed by Laura's eyes. They were slanted at him, but not in a glance which was intended to be met. She was—it was evident—discussing him, and her face was crimson. Whether from mirth or embarrassment, he could not tell. He stabbed his piece of meat with unnecessary viciousness. "What do you make of him?"

"Oh, he's very charming," Mrs Harrison said in a voice like cut glass. "When it suits him."

"What makes you think that?"

She leant close to him. "All that nonsense about playing with the children. I'll tell you what that was about. He came and took one look at us and cleared off with the first excuse that came into his head. But the minute you and Laura arrived—well, quite a different story." She nibbled delicately. "I gather he's quite a lady-killer. You'd better watch out."

He laughed. "Oh, Laura's perfectly capable of looking after herself."

"Dear Laura," Mrs Harrison said. "Such a pity we see so little of her. But I know she finds us all terribly, terribly dreary."

Matthew sighed. "Now, Jane, you know that isn't true—"

"What were you looking so miserable about at dinner?" Laura asked later, lying beside him in bed.

"Jane Harrison isn't the most enthralling company in the world. I wasn't miserable. Just a bit bored." He stroked her hair. "You were enjoying yourself. What were you talking about?"

"Lord, I don't know. Things."

"Very illuminating." He hesitated. "I was thinking how beautiful you look when you're laughing."

She gave a little wriggle of protest. "I wasn't laughing that much, you know. Still, I'm glad I looked as though I was having fun." Pause. "He said I looked Pre-Raphaelite. Lizzie Siddal."

"I've told you that hundreds of times."

She leaned across the pillows to kiss his forehead. "Dear Matthew. I know you have. It's just nice to hear it confirmed. That's all I meant. Anyway, he's going back to London in a couple of days. To his many ladies."

"A lad about town, then?"

"It sounded like that. Adoring students, I expect. He's spending a term at London University." She gave him an affectionate prod. "What you ought to be doing. I wish you were. Better than television sit-coms."

"What, screwing students?"

"No. Don't be so vulgar. Teaching."

Matthew yawned. "Wheeling and dealing in some wretched English department? No, thank you. I'm sure Leyden does it splendidly, but it's not my style."

"You don't have to call him by his surname. It sounds amazingly old-fashioned."

"I am. He said so, if you remember."

"Oh God, here we go. He was only teasing you." She rolled over. "I'm going to sleep. End of post-mortems."

A long time later, she said:

"Isn't Harmony Road a pretty name? That's where he's staying."

But Matthew was fast asleep.

The hangover which he always fondly supposed he was going to escape fell on him like a hard grey bolster the following morning. Dimly, he heard Laura getting up, scrubbing at her teeth, clattering a brisk army of coathangers. A ray of light jabbed his face like a flung knife as the curtains were thrown back. Flinching, he buried his head in the pillows. He felt frail and old and unready for a life which held only problems.

Dreams ungently gathered him back. He stood in a tangled garden, looking up at a ruined house, Gracedew, roofless, her windows gone, her walls greened by lichen and ivy. Behind the walls, out of sight, he heard a hurriedly suppressed laugh. Watchful, he moved closer, into the shadow of the walls where, unseen, he could listen. The laugh came again, clear and unchecked.

"It's all right. He won't be back until next week. Look. No one there."

Long red hair spilled down from an empty sill. A naked arm stretched to point out at the overgrown wilderness. Laura, or Venice Dobell? They seemed now to be one and the same.

"He wouldn't even notice if he was here. The house is all he thinks about. He did promise not to leave me alone here, but since he has—"

A man's voice—was it Richard Leyden's?—murmured

something. Looking up, he saw a tanned hand slide down her arm to stroke her fingers.

"He's such a fool," she sighed. "Such a fool."

The voices stopped. A man came walking through the grass towards him with long measured steps. He wore the clothes and the sad knowing smile of the man on the monument.

"Well, you know how it is, Matthew," he said. "What do you do to keep a house and a woman when both need more than you can give? I tried to keep both and I failed."

"It's not the same," he shouted. "Your wife was little better than a whore, Thomas. You never could have kept a woman like her."

Thomas Dobell shook his head. "She wanted company. I left her too much alone. Have a care when you write my story, Matthew. It is your own."

An old woman stood before him now. It's only a dream, he thought, but he could not wake. Fiercely thin and dressed in black, she stared at him with hard lightless eyes.

"You're no Craven," she said. "We never wanted you here. Go away."

There was no sound now in the ruined house. Distantly, a door banged. He glanced round.

"No need to look for her." The old woman's face cracked open in a grin. "She's gone. Left you. Like the other one. You never could keep women. Just like your father. Oh, but he wasn't, was he? Matthew the bastard. Little Jackanapes told you, didn't he? I remember now." She started to laugh, her cheeks puffed and pale. "Well, if you want to ruin yourself for a house that never should have been yours. There's no future. No child. Gracedew's days are over, my dear. You're wasting your time."

She leaned forward, choking him in a smell of dust and earth.

"Why don't you go away?"

"For God's sake, Matthew. It's twelve o'clock. They'll be here in twenty minutes."

Dazed, he blinked gluey eyes open to the sight of Laura in tightly clinging blue silk shirt and jeans, red hair tumbling richly down as she leaned over the bed to kiss him.

"Ouf! You're soaking." She drew back.

233

"Horrible dream," he said, apologetic.

"Hangover dream." Attempting to look stern, she folded her arms. "You did drink too much last night. You always do when we go to dinner with Alice."

"I know. Sorry." He sat up. "Who's the they?"

Laura perched on the edge of the bed. "Alice and Richard Leyden. She wanted him to see the house, so I thought we'd pull the stops out and give them a meal. You don't mind?"

"Of course not." He did. He disliked the idea of having Leyden in his home, of having to apologize for the shabby furniture, the fading portraits, of being forced as a polite host to overlook Leyden's flirtatious manner. Resentment, irritation, and the sour taste of last night's wine furred his mouth.

"I thought we could give them drinks in the Green Room," she said. "I put the heaters on. It's such a shame never to use it." Seeing his frown, she hurried on. "Well, the library is a bit dark and gloomy in winter. You said so yourself yesterday."

He contemplated the four of them perched in the vast echoing desert of the Green Room, crying platitudes across the jade acreage of threadbare Aubusson. Ludicrous picture.

"Splendid idea," he said. "You'd better change your clothes to suit the occasion. Floral and gallantly fading for the brave little wife. Pink, I suspect."

"Don't make fun of me," Laura said sadly. "I just thought it was a nice idea."

He felt guilty. "So it is, darling. Very nice."

"Oh, you'd better take a look at this." She held out a fat, prosperous-looking envelope bearing the Rackitt's trade-mark. "I didn't open it," she added unnecessarily but with an evident and touching sense of her restraint. "What on earth does Max want to write to you about—Kensal Rise fantasies?"

"What better subject?" Reality iced his sluggish brain as he skimmed towards the nub of the letter. The Freedman commission was his. Fifteen thousand pounds was not, he thought, a great price for the loss of a soul. Still, the Gracedew roof. He put the letter down.

"Laura, my love—"

She winced. "Bad news. They're remaindering my last novel and can't face telling me."

He patted her hand. "Nothing like that. I suppose I should have told you before. I didn't really think anything would come of it. I had lunch with Max when I came back from California. He said you'd told him we were a bit pushed for money."

She looked down at her hands. "You know what Max is like. He always worms things out of you. I didn't say very much."

"Oh, I'm not reproaching you. Our friend Max has come up trumps. Here. Read it and see what you think." He lay back against the pillows to watch her reaction. Eager curiosity gave way to puzzlement and then, hurtfully, a scornful little laugh as she dropped the pages back on the bed and folded her arms. Her voice was silvery, sharp as a needle.

"And who is Martin Freedman?"

It had not occurred to him that she would not know. Age gaps, of course. Why should she remember? Freedman had been a star in his own childhood, his heavy froglike face plastering the posters of Essoldo cinema foyers. The good thug, the lover who lost out to the villain. In England, he was almost forgotten. In France, where he now lived in luxurious exile, a devoted following of middle-aged *cineastes* still fed an old man's vanity.

"He was a sort of American Jean Gabin."

"I've never heard of him."

"He was rather splendid. I used to be a great fan when I was about fourteen."

"And Max wants you to write this book and then pretend it's by him?"

"It's a new Rackitt's project. Household names producing fiction on the subject the public associate with them. Freedman's would be a romantic thriller. Supermarket pulp. You know. There's a lot of money in it."

"For you?"

"For us."

"For the roof, you mean. If you get the money. Oh well, good-bye to another holiday and hurrah for the roof."

"We could have our holiday now, in France. Wouldn't you like that?"

"Courtesy of Mr Martin Freedman? No thanks. Chatting up

ageing film-stars isn't my idea of a holiday. I wanted one with you. By ourselves.'' She looked down at him with the detached stare of a child observing a trapped insect. ''How can you, Matthew? Telly sit-coms sounded bad enough, although I wasn't going to say anything. But this! Don't you know what it means? You'll be a laughing stock if it's known that you've done a book like this. It's not worth it. Honestly, it isn't.''

He winced. ''Thank you for that wifely response.''

She walked away to the door, hips swinging the constant invitation which seldom had much to do with her inclinations. On the threshold, she turned. ''I married a great writer,'' she said, ''and I end up with a hack. Wonderful. It must be every woman's dream.''

''Do you have a better way of finding the money?''

''I'd rather the roof leaked and you wrote a decent book. What about the Dobells?''

''I'll get back to it after this.'' He held her with his eyes, begging her to understand. ''I will, Laura. Believe me. I don't much want to do this. I just can't see another solution. It's only a couple of months out of my life. I've twenty years of writing left, at least.''

''If you give up Gracedew. There'll always be something to be done to the house, another reason to go away and earn some quick money. Only it never is quick.''

He had no answer. ''I can't give Gracedew up,'' he said. ''Don't let's start all that again. You know how I feel.''

''Oh yes. I certainly know how you feel.''

''You won't say anything to Alice or Richard Leyden, will you? It's not meant to be broadcast.''

''I wasn't planning to shout it from the rooftops, my dear,'' Laura said gently. ''After all, it's not exactly something to boast about. I'll go and help Mrs Bates with the lunch. Don't be later than you can help.''

Staring into the shaving-mirror at the soap-masked face of a clown, he wondered if it had always been the case that she had loved him for what he seemed to be? Had that been his power over her, his reputation? Remembering all the past times she had lain pleasure-drugged in his arms, whispering that she was his, all his, he forced himself to acknowledge the possibility. She had wanted him, but more than him, she had craved the privilege of being desired by a man whose name was known, of basking in the flattering sunlight of his own small fame. Take the reputation away, or diminish it, and desire became discontent. To be the wife of Gracedew's owner meant nothing to her. To be the wife of a successful man of letters meant everything.

Surely it couldn't be so simple, so cold an equation. With passion and fear, he rejected it. When the house was repaired, when summer came, when he was writing properly again; it was only a matter of patience and time. Perhaps he would ask some of his old literary friends to stay, let Laura see that he was neither forgotten nor despised, that her contempt was too quickly achieved. Or did she speak for them all? Uneasily, he gazed at his reflection.

12

"What a perfect morning," Alice said. "A real Gracedew day. Just like it used to be."

They sat in throned and uneasy formality, the four of them, in the room whose name gained a certain irony from the verdant patches of moisture which mushroomed from the walls. Morning light quivered on the long dusty windows, lancing golden bars over the undusted corners of furniture. From the library, too close for comfort, came a cheerful parade of plunked chords as Alice's sons played "Three Blind Mice" with unwearying pleasure.

"Sorry to cut off the concert, Alice dear," Matthew said, closing the door before pulling down the torn vellum blinds to plunge the room in a more flattering and dust-concealing ochre softness. Old rooms, like old women, respond more sweetly to dusk than to the glare of day.

"How delicious this is," Leyden said, trying to loll on a small upright sofa like a bandstand. "Perhaps I should just lapse into country life. It's all so soothing."

"So boring, don't you mean," Alice said, laughing at him. She was looking pink and happy and so unusually pretty that Matthew wondered if she was perhaps having an affair with Leyden. A revived one, perhaps? She had never talked much about her American marriage and it had never occurred to him that there might have been infidelities on her side. He did not much relish the idea, past or present. He had, he ruefully supposed, fallen victim to the idea that Alice had, in some beautiful Jamesian renunciatory way, committed herself to him. An error of vanity; she wore today the cream-fed smile of a well-laid woman. Nothing wrong with that. There was no reason why a good-looking woman like Alice should condemn herself to chastity. The perception, nevertheless, irritated him.

"Dick's like Laura," she went on. "Incurably urban. Country life's delightful until you have to put your feet in the mud."

"Absolutely right," Leyden said with a grin, but Laura, predictably, rose to the bait.

"That's not fair. If you'd seen me plodding out through the sludge to feed the hens this morning—"

"But I didn't," Alice said. "And I don't. It's no use, my dear. Even in gumboots, you look like a *Vogue* model. You just don't convince."

"If you mean I don't do any work, you're quite mistaken," Laura said sharply. "I just don't choose to make a frump of myself. Why should I?" Her pretty, sly eyes appealed to Leyden. "Alice thinks I'm frivolous because I like going to London and because I'd rather read books than weed gardens. I just don't think that houses should make prisoners of people. Not that I don't love Gracedew, but I don't intend to be ruled by it."

"That sounds reasonable." He glanced towards Matthew. "And what about you? You're away quite a bit, I gather."

He was quick to register the accusing note. "Only when I have to be. And hardly for pleasure."

"Oh, Matthew would do anything to keep the house going," Laura said. "It's his personal crusade, isn't it, my love?"

He shrugged. "I attach more value to the past than Laura does. Yes, I suppose keeping Gracedew has become my main concern."

"Above your writing?" Leyden looked at him with surprise.

"What is this, an interrogation?" He tried to laugh. "Yes. I think so. I really don't know any more."

Leyden smiled. "I suspect you of being a little obsessive. Still, you're a better man than I. Nothing gets put before my work."

"Love?" Matthew proposed, in a spirit of malice. Lust, he would have preferred to say.

"Love least of all," Leyden said with a laugh. "I'm with Professor Higgins on that. Put a woman in your life and you've nothing but problems ahead. But then, I'm a very selfish man."

"You certainly sound it," Alice said. "Except that there's not

239

a word of truth in it. I never knew a man who spent more of his time falling in and out of love than you, Dick. Mostly out.''

The likelihood of an affair diminished; she sounded altogether too cheerful and informed. Matthew noticed with some pleasure that Leyden seemed discomforted by her account of him.

"She always did exaggerate," he said, and turnèd his attention to the pictures. "I'd love to see round the house." He glanced hopefully at Laura.

"I'll take you," Matthew said.

"No Romneys or Reynoldses here, I'm afraid," he said, briskly leading the way through the coffined silence of the disused rooms. Leyden said nothing. The only comment he had ventured so far was that it was a pity to keep the shutters barred on such a beautiful day. Perhaps he was afraid of exposing his ignorance. Matthew found himself becoming increasingly irritated. Having requested a tour, the man could at least put up a show of admiration. He paused under a reproduction of the British Museum print of Gracedew and looked up at the soaring lines of the Dobell house.

"That's my secret dream. To get Gracedew looking like that again."

Leyden raised an eyebrow. "That's going to take some doing, isn't it? Do you have a grant?"

Matthew shook his head. "No such luck."

"Well, rather you than me," Leyden said with a smile. It was clear that he found the idea insane or ludicrous. Perhaps both.

"The book I've been working on recently is about the man who built that house, the Elizabethan one," Matthew said after a moment of wondering if he cared enough for Leyden's opinion to enlarge upon his plans. "Do you notice anything curious about it? Well, there's no reason you should. Have a look at this door, the triangles on the sides. Remember the window-ledges I showed you in my study. Triangles again. Do you see?"

"Vaguely. I've always known the Elizabethans were obsessed with geometric patterns. Sidney's sonnets are practically laid out on a graph in their rhetorical form, for example."

"You're on the right track. Thomas Dobell was a Catholic. Everything that's left of the original house is a celebration of the Trinity. He wanted to glorify his own name with a splendid

240

house. More than that, he wanted Gracedew to stand for his beliefs. What fascinates me is the ruthlessness of the enterprise. He used up his young wife's dowry. He sold her estates. He borrowed off his neighbours, destroyed his deer parks to get timber. He even married his daughter off to a rich Protestant merchant in the hope of getting more funds to complete it.''

"And did he?" Leyden shivered, wondering at his host's imperviousness to the icy draught in which they stood. Surely the story would have kept until lunchtime.

"No. His wife left him. His son-in-law betrayed him. Dobell was caught housing a couple of Jesuit priests by Walsingham's spies. The building was sold, unfinished, to a local lawyer, a Protestant. Dobell died at the stake a year later. It's his house which holds me here, not the Cravens'." He followed Leyden's pinched glance to the peeling walls. "Not that there's much of it left." He felt suddenly tired and depressed. The man looked bored and cold. It was impossible to convey his feelings. "There's no reason why you should understand."

Leyden shrugged as they walked on. "Well, I'm not you, am I? Dobell sounds a pretty dreadful character to me, but I'm on the wife's side. I'd be a bit worried, in your shoes."

"Why?"

"That my wife might behave in the same way." He glanced at Matthew and laughed. "Come on, I'm hardly being serious. Well, I'm glad to hear you're still finding time to write. It's been a long while since your last book. I hope our coming over hasn't interrupted your labours."

Matthew thought of the typed sheaves on his desk and then, with sudden revulsion, of Martin Freedman. "Not at all. I'm going to have to lay it aside for a bit anyway. Unfortunately, with a house like this, I need to make money. Well, most of us have to do some freebooting at some point."

Leyden surveyed him. "You don't have the look of a buccaneer. And if you'll forgive my saying so, you're not of an age to start being one. Seems to me it'd be a much better solution to flog Gracedew to Nottingham University or the town council and keep a couple of rooms for country week-ends. That way, you get the best of everything. London. Country home. Time to write. I said so to your wife last night."

With difficulty, Matthew produced a polite smile. "How kind of you to interest yourself."

"Oh, other people's lives do interest me," Leyden said coolly. "Laura didn't seem so against the idea as you clearly are. But it's not her house in the same sense, is it? It's your commitment, not hers."

He remembered that odd embarrassed glance across the table and understood the martyr's role she would have been playing. Treacherous Laura.

"True, but she knows how much I mind. She's been splendid about it."

"I don't doubt that for a minute," Leyden said. "I just wondered if she was happy."

It was difficult to hide his annoyance. Why was everyone so concerned with Laura's happiness? Where were her problems?

"I do my best to ensure that she is," he said stiffly. A flicker of amusement sparked up in Leyden's eyes.

"I'm sure you do. And keeping women happy isn't easy. You don't need to tell me."

"I don't intend to. Keeping Laura happy could hardly be described as a hardship." He wondered why Leyden brought out such a priggish strain in him. He never normally talked like this. He felt a need to apologize.

"No need," Leyden smiled as they entered the dining-room. "I'm just an envious man."

The two women turned towards them, thankful for an escape from each other's company. "Well!" Laura cried. "Where did you take him—Nottingham and back? We'd given you up for lost. The boys were starving, so we decided to go ahead with their lunch. Help yourself from the side, Dick. It's only shepherd's pie and two vegetables of the nominal kind. Phenomenally overcooked, thanks to Mrs Bates and her headaches."

Matthew frowned at her. She was talking too much and too fast. Nervous. Of what, he wondered? "When you've finished punning—we could have had Bates in to hand round the food. Didn't you ask him?"

She stared. "What, with just four of us?"

"Gracious, we're all used to helping ourselves," Alice said. "It's not a state occasion."

"He has to do something for his wages." Catching Leyden's speculative glance, he had again the irritating sense of being put on the defensive. He had wished only to demonstrate the luxury of Laura's life, to quell criticism.

"He does enough already, poor old chap," Laura said. "Garden, car, electrics, plumbing. It seems a bit hard he should have to buttle as well."

"I was hardly suggesting it as a daily onus."

Alice gave him a puzzled look. "It's so unimportant, my dear. You mustn't worry about things which don't matter."

"Anyway, the pie looks ambrosial," Leyden said, sitting between the women and filling his glass from the decanter of claret. "I was telling Matthew that I envied him for having such a pretty, clever lady in his life. And so I do. The only thing I can't understand is his ever leaving you alone."

"Matthew leaves me because he trusts me," Laura said. "Anyway, somebody has to look after the house. Can I tell them about your new commission, darling? I'm sure they'd be terribly impressed."

"I'd rather you didn't, Laura."

Alice gazed at him. "Why, what are you up to now?"

"Nothing. Laura's playing games."

Laura's eyes glinted. "Why be so modest? Matthew's off to France to work with an immensely famous film-star, never to be identified. Secret project. Super-agent Craven strikes again."

"Very intriguing," Leyden said. "I hadn't realized you were mixed up in the film business, Matthew. And you'll be staying here to keep the home-fires burning, will you, Laura?"

"But of course. I'm a well trained wife." Blandly, she smiled. "So let's toast the future. To Matthew's success in turning Gracedew into the Nottinghamshire Versailles."

Unwillingly, Matthew joined in the laughter. He was embarrassed and extremely angry. She had given him her word; to betray him was gratuitous malice, motiveless as far as he could see. Unless the motive was to stimulate Leyden's sympathy. It was clear that she had won it.

"Let's talk about something else," he said and launched into an enthusiastic description of his new digital recordings of Renaissance music. Leyden, he was pleased to see, looked restless, and when pressed, admitted that he had little knowledge of music. Matthew promptly began to compare Gibbons to Byrd. He went on to declare that a knowledge of music was the sign of a truly civilized mind. Alice, who dearly loved her piano, smiled and nodded. Laura, mistress of the slowest Chopin waltzes, looked soulfully into space. Matthew began to feel in a more agreeable frame of mind. The noisy eruption of Alice's sons into the room caught him complacent in mid-sentence.

"There's a lady outside," said the elder, Martin, pink and breathless. "She says she's your wife and Mrs Bates won't let her in."

"Quite right. You know perfectly well who Mr Craven's wife is," Alice said briskly. "Off you go and stop bothering Mrs Bates."

"We didn't bother her, Mummy. We told the lady she could come in round by the back door if it was urgent. So she did."

"Oh lord, am I causing chaos? I'd forgotten your English eating hours."

Matthew stared at the door in outraged disbelief. It couldn't be. It was. There she stood, swaying slightly on high-heeled black boots, slim as a snake in black leather jeans and a very tight polo-neck of shocking pink. Clarissa.

Her eyes blinked innocently under a raven's wing of bobbed hair as she came towards them. "Well, you do look pleased."

The silence had lasted beyond the limits of politeness.

"I must say," Clarissa remarked with her eyes fixed on Matthew like twin laser beams, "I do think you might show a little more enthusiasm. I'm not asking you to look thrilled, but you could manage a hello."

He rose to his feet. "Not thrilled. Not displeased. A trifle surprised. You'd better come and sit down. Have some pie. Some wine?"

"No wine, oh lord, no more wine," she said with feeling. "I'm floating in a bath of Nottingham's worst or I'd never have dared to come. But there we were, driving by, and there was the sign just begging to be followed. I couldn't resist it." She bestowed a dazzling smile around the table. "I was going to do a piece on dear old DHL's life in Eastwood. Much help they were, the Eastwoodians. They wouldn't even talk about him. They ought to be pleased that one good thing came out of that dump. I never saw such a dreary place. So we gave up and went off to cheer ourselves up in a Nottingham hotel—''

''Where's the other bit?'' Matthew interrupted. ''The we?''

Clarissa dropped him a grin. ''Hardly a lover, dear heart. The little photographer they sent down with me. I sent him packing off to London. So there's no we. Just me.''

''It seems quite enough.''

''Don't be vicious.'' She glanced away from him to Alice and the two silent and staring boys. ''They certainly didn't take after you, did they? I never thought of you having children. Hey ho, life's full of surprises. I never got round to it myself.''

''I think you're a bit confused,'' Alice said with a politeness which passed beyond parody. ''I'm not his wife. Those are not his children.''

Clarissa giggled. ''Trust me to get it wrong. Oh dear, now I've embarrassed you. I'd forgotten English women still blushed. It's sweet.'' She turned her attention to Laura. ''Sorry. Are you—but you looked so young. I didn't think you could be.''

''It doesn't matter.'' Laura held out a rigid hand which Clarissa failed to take. ''How nice of you to think of visiting us. But you should have written. We could have made a bedroom ready.''

''Oh, a sofa will do just fine for tonight, thanks,'' Clarissa said brightly. ''Well, what lovely manners. I don't suppose you think it's nice at all, but it's adorable of you to say so, Childy. You won't mind if I call you that? It's a compliment. Matthew always wanted child-wives, didn't you, my love? Until they grow up and get little minds of their own. That's quite another matter. You mustn't be wilful, Childy.''

Baffled, Matthew gazed at her. He could not decide whether she was drunk or nervous or simply, Clarissa-like, unaware of her glaring inappropriateness. He was, on reflection, inclined to take the latter view. She had probably been speaking the exact truth. All interest in him and his life had lain dormant until she had, unluckily, caught sight of the Gracedew turning. Ever

245

impulsive, she had blundered in with no thought of the effect she would have. Like Gatsby's Daisy, she remained guilty only of the carelessness which destroys lives without intention or recognition. And so, in some sense, she must always escape blame. It was an awkward situation for Laura, of course. Still, her ground, her husband. Given her considerable social graces, he had no doubt that she would manage it with style. And tomorrow morning, he would see Clarissa on to the London train. It was not his fault.

So Matthew watched his former wife, smiling, reminiscing and babbling on, supremely tactless, supremely unaware of it, while Leyden, leaning back in his chair, watched Laura as she carefully and slowly tore her paper napkin to shreds between her knees. Nothing else gave her away. Already attracted to her, he was touched by her anxiety to do well in a wretched situation which was none of her making, and angered by the perception that her pompous oaf of a husband was neither going to give her any credit for it, nor try to help her. He seemed if anything to be relishing his position while presuming on the good manners of his wife and guests.

He was filling the first wife's glass again, telling her that she looked wonderful, trying to draw Alice into the conversation. She, Alice, looked almost as miserable as Laura and quite as incapable of forceful action. They were caught, both of them, in that steel trap of English politeness which has so much to do with the fear of exposing raw emotions, so little to do with affection. Really, the whole scene belonged to some Edwardian tale of passion and social restraint. He felt like throwing a firecracker into the conversation for the simple pleasure of seeing it explode in his host's face. Instead, he smiled at Laura, trying to convey a sympathy which could not safely be expressed.

She's tougher than me, Laura thought. She wouldn't have let him bury her here. She was probably a better wife for him. A stronger character. She makes him laugh. Shared jokes. Not my jokes. It is not kind of Matthew. He is enjoying this situation, getting his own back. She still fancies him and he knows it. She doesn't look forty. She left him; there is something unfinished. I have a better right to sit at this table and I feel like a stranger but I must go on sitting here and smiling until he gets up. The rules of a stupid game which I do not want to play. I shall sip my wine very slowly and pretend I do not care. That is all I can do.

Clarissa was over her first unease. She had not been sure of what kind of a reception she was likely to be given; apprehension had been overcome by her curiosity about the house and her successor. On both counts, she was feeling relieved.

There had, in the past few years, been occasions when she had wondered if she had made a mistake in leaving Matthew. Jake's devotion had lasted only for as long as she could finance him. When the money ran out, he had given her a little talk on the beauty of candour before candidly explaining that she was insufficiently committed to the cause of equality to be a worthy life-companion. Clarissa had suggested that this sudden urge for truth-telling might have something to do with the arrival in town of Miss Alicia Tate, who was as rich as she was gullible. Jake had demurred—had he ever gone for women with legs like tree-trunks? Only when they had bank balances to match them, she had smilingly responded. It had been no comfort to be proved right.

Since Jake's departure, Clarissa had settled in Rome, where she'd been surviving on good looks, calculated affairs and a talent for pressing notable people to confide secrets to her in intimate situations. If a Clarissa Cunningham profile was seldom profound, it was always sufficiently scandalous to be read. Only to Clarissa did presidents and prime ministers garrulously unveil incestuous dreams and—in one celebrated interview—a predilection for lilac silk pyjamas; their unguarded intimacies were splashed across the pages of *Oggi* and *Paris Match*.

It was not fulfilling work. There was, on the other hand, a pleasant sense of power in knowing that her jabs at the under-bellies of the great could cause such squeals of pain. (Who, as one victim sourly observed, would cast their vote for a man said to wear the slogan ''Cupid's Pet'' on his underpants?)

It had paid off. She could now afford the luxury of writing the occasional less meretricious piece for *The Observer* or *The Sunday Times*. Her flat overlooking the Borghese Gardens was smart and pretty; her friends were, for an hour or two, amusing; her clothes were paid for; her travel came courtesy of an old friend in Alitalia. But there were times when she was too tired to charm and too anxious to not to have to try: these were the occasions when she wondered if she had made a mistake, if life in an English country house would, if dull, have been blessedly secure.

Well, now she had seen it and could thank her stars that she had escaped. Gracedew's exterior was enchanting, but what a wretched mess those Victorians made with their improvements! That grim varnished panelling and all those tatty red baize doors with draughts coming under them like death's fingers—imagine trying to heat such a room with a miserable one-bar fire of which the dog appeared to be reaping all the benefit. One didn't need to look far to guess that the Cravens lacked cash.

She smiled at Laura. "Delicious bread. I bet you made it yourself."

"Supermarket," Laura said, looking past her. "But thank you."

Clarissa continued to observe her through narrowed eyes while delicately nibbling at the bread. Pretty, sharpish, nervous. She evidently doted on Matthew, hung on every word he said. Poor old Matthew. He probably needed the reassurance. He hadn't aged well. And he hadn't written a decent novel in years. A bit of a has-been, really. She could feel quite kind, sitting here and gently flirting with him while that stupid Tresham woman gawped at her. The man looked interesting. She hadn't managed to catch his name.

She leaned towards Matthew and looked deep into his eyes. "Lovely to see you again. Really, it is. I'm very offended you never brought Childy to visit me. Ex-spouses shouldn't be enemies. It's too silly."

"Perhaps." Matthew laughed. "To judge by your writings, we'd have been lucky to find you. Delhi, Dakota, Durban—you seem to lead the life of a meteor nowadays."

"Have pen, will travel. It's not such a bad life," Clarissa said. "You're a fine one to talk. Still, I have done pretty well for someone who was told by her husband that she couldn't write. I got fifteen hundred for the Gandhi piece. Not bad for a couple of days' work. Childy writes a bit, doesn't she?"

"Laura writes extremely well."

She gave him a bland smile. "And so she should, with such a

248

good teacher. Do you like being a pupil, Childy, or have you had enough of home education?''

''Perhaps she's in no need of being taught,'' Leyden interrupted and stood up. ''Now Laura, are you going to show me round the garden before Alice and I leave? You did promise.''

''Did I?'' She flushed. ''It's such a mess. There's nothing out at this time of year.''

Was she going to be so stupid as to reject a chance to escape, he wondered? ''I really would like to see it,'' he persisted gently. ''Matthew was telling me Gracedew used to be one of the biggest houses in England. It'd be nice to see it from a distance, get some idea of the layout.''

''Oh, Matthew could tell you far more about that than I.'' She rose, her eyes returning to her husband with a look of timid appeal which infuriated Leyden. ''Shall we all go? It is such a lovely day.''

Clarissa stretched out her long legs and smiled. ''I haven't come equipped for country rambles, Childy dear. I'm going to stay and chat to Matthew.''

Alice pushed her chair back. ''In that case, I'll take the boys down to the village. Sweetshops are more in their line than gardens. Shall we meet up in about an hour?''

''Fine.'' Leading Leyden to the door, Laura turned with a bright smile. ''Do enjoy yourselves.''

''We will,'' Clarissa said with a broad grin. ''One way or another.'' Her laughter followed them out.

In the hall, Alice turned quickly to put an arm round Laura. ''Oh, she shouldn't have come. Poor you. I did think you managed it splendidly.''

''I certainly don't intend to be upset by Clarissa,'' Laura said. ''There's nothing to it. Matthew's putting a good face on things. That's all.''

''Still,'' Alice said hesitantly. ''I wouldn't trust her. She is rather a bitch.''

''I never imagined otherwise,'' Laura smiled. ''Don't worry. I can look after myself. And I shall. Are you coming, Dick?''

Her spirits appeared to die at the threshold, confirming Leyden's suspicion that she minded a great deal more than she was prepared to admit to Alice. Pacing along the bright gravelled paths at her side, he contemplated and rejected a dozen ways of expressing his thoughts as he watched her pretty red shoes kick slowly through the loose stones. He had found her a delightful companion at dinner, full of malice and laughter. She struck him now as defenceless, young and unhappy. He tried and failed to picture her life in the big empty house when Craven was away.

"What do I do? Nothing very exciting. If I'm feeling virtuous, I ask Mr Flower—he's the vicar—to lunch. I write my book, take the dog for walks, dust the books in the library, rearrange the kitchen, watch television. It all passes the time of day in Venezuela, as they say."

"Don't you have friends to stay? Your parents?"

"We don't see much of each other." She gave him a wan smile. "Matthew and they aren't exactly hand in glove, and my mother hates cold houses."

"Perhaps you should see more of Alice," he suggested. "She's very fond of you."

"Is she?" Laura did not sound greatly enchanted. "You know she nearly married Matthew, I suppose?"

He shook his head. "We've been out of touch for years. And Alice isn't much of a one for life histories. Still, that shouldn't affect you."

"Oh, if it was all over." She gave him a sideways glance. "Those sort of things never are. Alice would have made a much better job of running Gracedew."

Leyden grinned. "Don't fish. I'm not going to answer you. Still, you must get plenty of writing done when you're alone."

"I don't very much like the kind of writing I do any more," she said abruptly. "I used to. When I started, it was just so exciting to see my name in print, to be able to call myself a novelist. But when you go on turning out that same kind of thing again and again, it's — well, a bit dispiriting. Boring subject. I'm going to take you to see the railway castle." Running off the path, she jumped from a concealed wall to stand below him with a smiling face. "Come on. It's only a few minutes. I haven't been there for ages."

Looking down at the pale triangle of her face and the red ropes of her hair unlooped by the wind, he found in her again what he had wondered at the night before, the rare blend of a pure face with the knowing eyes, the provocative smile and stance of a Renaissance courtesan. Lucky Matthew Craven.

"Well, I hope your thoughts are complimentary," Laura said. "Do you always stare at women quite so hard?"

He jumped down to stand beside her. "I was playing the alphabet game. You were Burne-Jones and Botticelli last night. Today you're Crivelli and Carpaccio."

"And I feel like Daumier and Doré—gruesome. Still, yours sound much nicer. I'm flattered."

"You're very easy to flatter."

"Meaning I'm susceptible?"

"Meaning I find you beautiful."

She leaned forward and kissed his cheek. "I do like you, Dick."

He laughed. "I like you. A lot."

"Good," said Laura.

He had perceived her as frail and delicate; he was surprised by the rapidity of her pace, a long easy stride which he had to struggle to match as they crossed the empty bone-hard fields overhung by the lean gradient of hillside. Rooks spread up in rustling arrow-lines over the sparse and distant coppices. A curtain of cloud fell across the fields towards them. "Gracedew weather," Laura said. "You're going to be frozen without a coat. Anyway, here we are. Look."

Above them, glaring down from the hill like some curious antique monster, was the fortified tunnel. No longer used, it had fallen into a state of total disrepair. The ivy which had once traced skeletal fingers over the lancet windows now cascaded down to block the tunnel's mouth. The turrets, half-buried in earth and grass, poked out from the undergrowth like twin periscopes, sedately wreathed by bindweed. The hill had quietly taken its territory back again, made the tunnel a part of itself. In ten years or so, there would be little to show that the tunnel had ever existed.

"Matthew said we ought to write to the Victorian Society about it," Laura said. "But then it would have all been renewed and polished up. I like it just as it is. Nature getting her own back. It's like a cautionary tale."

"Cautioning who?"

"Us," she said simply. "Gracedew will go this way in the end. A beautiful romantic ruin. Once it's ruined us." She smiled at him. "Still, it's a noble way to go."

"It makes me think of all those extraordinary temples buried in Mexican hills," Leyden said as they walked on into the scrubby meadows flanking the river. "Buried worlds with only a broken ridge or a slight change of contour to show they ever existed."

Laura stopped and gazed at him. "Were you there? Did you see where *Under the Volcano* was written? Oaxaca, was it, or Cuernavaca? And the sinking opera house, and the Yucatan, and Palenque? Tell me. Please tell me."

He was laughing at her eagerness. "I really wish I could take you there," he said. "Do you think your husband would let you run off for a holiday with me while's he's in France?"

"I'll ask him, shall I?"

"Perhaps not." Leyden looked back at the grassy turrets, splashed with red by a feeble burst of sunlight. "I do like the *Nightmare Abbey* aspect. I could almost expect Scythrop or one of his lady-loves to peep out of one of the windows."

"Or Mr Cranium taking a tumble—oh no, that's *Headlong Hall*. Bother, I always get it wrong," Laura wailed and put her hands over her eyes. "Oh damn! Damn!"

It was a moment before Leyden realized that Peacock's novels had nothing to do with her distress. Her cry was an appeal. Gently, he put an arm round her shaking shoulders. "Come on now. You mustn't worry, Laura. Nothing's going to happen. She should never have come here. It must be horrible for you."

"It's not even that," she sobbed. "It's this. I hate it. I hate being stuck here and never seeing anybody and always being alone and having to pretend all the time that I'm happy. And the thought of having to go on like this year after year and nothing ever changing. I know Matthew loves it. I know he can only earn money when he goes away, but he doesn't understand how lonely it is. He's never here long enough to know."

Holding her in his arms, Leyden found himself torn between inclination and apprehension. If he told her, as he felt strongly tempted to do, that she had better leave her husband, she might well read into it a suggestion that she should come to him.

Certainly, she would suppose that he might help her. Feeling her body pressed against him almost as though she was naked under the skimpy silk, he was full of desire. To pursue that physical impulse would be as fatal as the other. The consequences were larger than the need, but the need was strong.

"How nice you are," she sighed, looking up at him with grateful eyes and parted lips.

"Not nice at all," he murmured as he bent his head to kiss her.

"I can't think where they are," Alice said as she came into the dining-room. "Gracious, are you still here? It's past four o'clock."

Clarissa stretched her arms above her head and yawned. "What's the hurry? There can't be anything to do in the country on a Monday afternoon in the middle of winter except to watch television or chat. Why don't you sit down and relax?"

"It may surprise you but I do have work to do," Alice said. "Write letters, get the tea ready, make sure my father's all right, write my weekly piece for the local paper—"

"You as well? I'd never have guessed."

"Only fashion for middle-aged ladies," Alice said, reddening. "I doubt if Matthew's ever seen my efforts. My father says they're awful rubbish, but they pay me quite well."

"I never knew the Colonel was a judge of prose," Matthew said.

"He isn't. But he has opinions."

"Rather a poor one where I'm concerned," Matthew said.

"Not altogether surprising."

Clarissa opened her black-rimmed eyes very wide. "Why, what has Matthew been doing? I thought he was the backbone of the county."

"Past history. It wouldn't concern outsiders."

"But I don't feel in the least an outsider," Clarissa protested. Alice raised her eyebrows.

"Don't you? How surprising." She pushed open the window and leaned out.

"Any sign?" Behind her back, Matthew frowned at Clarissa

who was clearly preparing further to investigate the past. "Well?" For Alice was strangely still and quiet. "Seen the ghost of Sir Thomas?"

"No." She pulled the window shut with a bang. "It's all right. They're coming. They must have been out in the park. I'll go and fetch the children."

"I wonder what she did see?" Clarissa traced a circle round her crumb-and-ash-strewn plate. "She was red as a plum—did you notice that when she turned round?" Her fingers scratched at his sleeve in a gesture which Matthew remembered having always found curious and irritating.

"Probably something to do with her hormone balance. You make too much of things." He leaned back and out of her reach. "Do try to be nice to my wife, Clarissa. Stop all this Childy business. It isn't kind."

"Oh, I'll be sweet as apple pie, don't worry," she smiled. "But I think your little Laura's perfectly capable of looking after herself. You shouldn't be so—hello, Childy dear. Had a nice stroll?"

From the doorway, Laura surveyed them. "She's quite right, Matthew. I can look after myself very well. I don't need protecting. I'm just going to see them off. Don't bother to move. You look so comfortable here."

The door slammed shut on them. "Ouch!" Clarissa said. "Rotten timing. Well, too bad."

"Not good." He stood up. "You stay. I'd better go and join in the farewells."

"Oh, duty!" Clarissa mocked his retreating back. "Well, well, what a good little husband it is."

He turned to give her an unsmiling look. "I love her," he said. "And I mean to keep her. And now, for the love of God, shut up."

After dinner in the lodge, Colonel Tresham retired to his lonely bed at the manor, leaving Alice and Leyden to sit on beside the fire in her pleasant drawing-room. It was the Colonel's habit to draw the evening out until nearly midnight; a television programme about nuclear disarmament had brought about his uncustomarily early departure. (The idea of disarmament was anathema to a man whose view it was that Britain could only keep Hun and Russkie at bay by converting herself into a gleaming arsenal.)

Alice smiled at Leyden. "Poor old Pa. It's years since he left politics but he still has to hold forth like the voice of Britain. I really should have checked the programmes. Only *Barchester Towers* tomorrow, thank goodness. Even he can't be upset by that."

"I didn't think you showed much heart for disarmament yourself," Leyden said. "You ought to think about your sons. It's not a very cheerful outlook for them with Pershings and Cruise."

Alice lifted her wonderfully clear eyes. "And what are you doing for CND, Dick dear?"

"I don't have to do anything," Leyden grinned. "I'm very ably represented. My students have all been demonstrating since they were in nappies, so far as I can make out. How about your neighbours? Are they for CND? Laura, for instance?"

Alice laid her sewing down in her lap and looked at him. "Fourth time."

"What?"

"That you've introduced Laura's name. I know it's tempting to rush in and play Galahad. Don't. You'll only give her ideas."

He returned her earnest look with amusement. "They might be quite good ideas. I told her she should see more of you."

"She wouldn't have relished that one much," Alice murmured. "But you know quite well what I mean."

"No, I don't."

"I saw you," she said. "In the garden."

"Oh. Kissing, you mean." He laughed. "How perfectly terrible. What a crime! A married woman. Did you never kiss a married man? Truth now."

"Only divorced ones. Anyway, I won't say any more. I see you aren't going to listen."

"But I hate half-finished subjects," Leyden said. He got up to turn off a news announcer in earnest spate. "She doesn't seem very happy."

"Only because Clarissa turned up."

"She was crying when we were out in the park."

"Clarissa's only there for a night. She'll get over it. She's not a baby."

"It wasn't Clarissa she was crying about. Not really."

"Stop interpreting the situation to suit yourself," Alice said sharply.

"Yes, Nanny Tresham," Leyden mocked her intonation. "I'm not going to give up. Anyway, I'd be doing you a good turn. Matthew would suit you a good deal better than Laura, don't you think? Gracedew's more your style than hers."

"Oh, style." Alice shrugged. "You mean I'm an efficient housekeeper."

Leyden perched on the arm of her chair and leant down. "You did have an affair with him though, didn't you?"

Alice looked down at the half-patched pile of children's clothes in her lap. "I wanted to marry him."

"Do you still love him?"

She did not answer immediately. "I'm fond of him," she said at last. She dropped her head back to stare up at him. "Don't present yourself as my accomplice, Dick dear. What you feel about Laura or she feels about you is no concern of mine. I don't want to know any more. I've said what I think."

"Forbidden fruit?"

"I'm not forbidding you. How can I?" Her eyes narrowed. "You haven't fallen in love with her, have you?"

"Of course not." But his hesitation was sufficiently marked for Alice to doubt him. "Anyway, I'm off tomorrow morning. It's highly unlikely that I'll ever see her again."

"Unless, of course, you pursue her. Matthew's going away."

He tried to read her expression. "Are you suggesting—?"

"I'm not suggesting anything," Alice said. "But I do know you better than you seem to think."

"I'm beginning to wonder how well I know you."

"Quite as well as I wish you to."

Lying in bed, Alice wondered how determined a pursuit he was intending to make and whether she should do anything further to dissuade him or to warn Matthew. Arguably, it was always better not to interfere in other people's lives. It was also in her interests not to do so. He had worked that out already, shrewd Dick. Laura and Dick, Matthew and herself. It was a

256

pleasing picture. How odd it was that after all this time, she should still love him so much, still have the feeling that with her, his life could have been a happier one. It still galled her to sit at Gracedew as Laura's guest, and to feel how much better she could have arranged it all. Poor Laura; she would be having a dreadful evening. It would be more than understandable if she felt like getting her own back, having a fling. And then—and then?

"Mummy. We can't go back to sleep and the hot-water bottle's cold."

"Coming, darlings." Slippers, dressing-gown, motherhood, reality. "Do stop shouting. I said I was coming." No use in wasting time on dreams.

At Gracedew, dinner had passed off better than Matthew could have anticipated. Laura had produced a superb cheese soufflé; Clarissa had been all admiration and sweetness. She could, when she liked, be very amusing. Her stories of drawing-room politics in Rome were maliciously funny and she was a sufficiently good mimic to bring to life her unknown cast of characters. It occurred to him, watching her quick gestures and her vivacious smile, that Clarissa had probably been singing for her suppers for a goodish while. She had become extremely competent at it. He did wish as the meal went on that she would refer less often to their shared past, but it was, after all, the past and she could not be accused of sentimentalizing it. There was no real harm in her telling Laura how they had met or how she had detested Chester Square, or how funny it was to think what she had been like then. Did he remember those awful political posters? She had no time left for that sort of nonsense now. Kids' stuff, idealism. Really, at the end, one had to be practical.

"Lord, how young and idiotic we were," Clarissa sighed.

Laura smiled at her. "You're hardly ancient now. I'd never guess you were over thirty."

Clarissa snapped a glittering smile at her. "Dear Childy. Insincerity is the best form of flattery, but it has to be a little bit plausible. I'm nearly forty, and I'm sure I look it."

Matthew made a polite mumble of dissent. She spoke only the truth. She still had the arresting quality which had first caught his eye, a bright wickedness, an infinitely suggestive smile. She had, nonetheless, gone a bit over the hill. The fluttering eyelashes were only a temporary distraction from a fine net of lines; the neck, that long, wonderful, serpentine ripple of cream, was a little stringy. At a distance, she could pass for a girl. At arm's length, at the end of the day, all of the years showed.

Clarissa caught him in the act of scrutinizing her and winced. "It's not that bad."

"I was looking at your necklace," he lied.

"Why? Do you want it back?"

He looked at her, startled by the sharpness of her voice. "Did I give it to you? I'd completely forgotten. It's rather charming."

"It suits you," Laura said. "Matthew's awfully clever at choosing jewellery."

"He hardly needs to be," Clarissa said dryly. "You'd look pretty with a piece of tinfoil round your neck."

It was, he thought with proprietorial pride, the truth. Laura was looking very beautiful. She had, unusually, done nothing to alter her appearance for dinner, probably out of tact towards Clarissa who had no clothes into which to change. It was not a question of cosmetics or of dress. She wore a protective aura of radiance which gleamed in her eyes and smile. He rather hoped that Clarissa would go to bed early. Laura in the fire-light, rosy with desire and pleasure. Under the table, he pressed his legs against her, eager to convey his need for her.

Laura moved her legs away and stood up. "I've got a bit of a headache. I think, if you don't mind, I'll go to bed."

He could have smothered her with kisses for such a ready understanding. "It doesn't sound a bad idea. Perhaps we should all make a move."

"Oh no," Laura said. "You stay and talk to Clarissa. It's only ten. See you in the morning. Breakfast's at eight."

The door shut. "Well!" Clarissa said as Matthew slumped back in his chair. "You do look enchanted by the prospect. I didn't know my company was that dreary."

He recalled himself to the obligations of a host with an effort. "Not even an enemy could accuse you of that. What will you have? Whisky or brandy?"

"A drop of whisky." Her eyes glinted at him. "If you'll join me."

"Why not?" He poured them each a sparing measure. Clarissa lifted hers in red-lipped smiling salute.

"To you. Just like old times, isn't it?"

"Hardly. You were on Pepsi in those days. Bar the wedding festivities when you passed out."

"Not very gentlemanly of you to remember that. I must be thinking of someone else. Awful how confused one gets."

"Still, not surprising. You've had a full life, from the sound of it."

"Pass," Clarissa said with a grin. "Anyway, I'm full of admiration for yours. Lovely house, pretty wife—"

"And no decent books."

She shrugged slim shoulders. "We all have to make money as best we can."

"I wish I could persuade Laura to look at it that way," he said with a sigh. "She's keener on the idea of the great writer than the great house, unfortunately."

"With a bit of perseverance, she might end up with both. Lucky Laura." She leaned forward to light her cigarette from a guttering candle. "I must give this up soon or I'll go the same way as your mother. Which reminds me, you never did answer my letter. I thought you'd be rather intrigued."

He narrowed smarting eyes against the sour rings of smoke. "By what?"

"The chance to meet your real father, my dear. I've been dying to tell you. He's rather fun. And fascinated by your connection with me. Very boring of you never to tell me about it."

"Or prudent. One of your lovers, was he?"

Clarissa smiled. "Do you really want to know?"

He shook his head. "No, on both counts. Not interested."

"How very unenterprising of you. I can easily arrange it if you change your mind. I'd love to be the one to bring you together."

"Sweet of you."

"I was born to do good," Clarissa sighed.

"You haven't done badly, by yourself."

"Thank you, darling. All right. I'll change the subject. What do you think my chances are of getting an interview with Gaddafi? I've always wanted to see North Africa and Libya's better than nothing."

Dutifully, he applied himself to the subject of Clarissa's career. It was twelve o'clock before she declared herself to be ready for bed.

Wishing her good-night at her door, he found her body suddenly in his arms. Her mouth was on his, her tongue probing for a passage past clenched teeth. He had never minded the taste of cigarettes in Laura's kisses. Clarissa's mouth had the taste of despair.

"Just to remember me by, darling," she said, drawing back to look at him from the darkness of her room. "Coming?"

He met her smile with another. "No. You really haven't changed, have you?"

"I don't intend to." Her smile widened. "Your loss. Good-night. Sweet dreams."

He would certainly have to make sure of getting her on to the morning train. She was, as she had always been, disturbing and utterly untrustworthy.

The light in their bedroom was still on, but Laura was soundly asleep, her mouth curved in a contented smile, her hand curved under her cheek. He looked down at her, envious of her peace, hating the thought of having to leave her again when they had had so little time together. He wondered if he should not over-rule her objections and take her with him. It would do her no harm to see how hard he had to work to find money for Gracedew; it might make her a little more sympathetic. Her words of the morning still rankled. A hack, she had called him, ignoring the necessity which forced him to take the jobs which paid him best. Even Clarissa had showed more understanding than that.

Still, the house could hardly be expected to run itself. The Bateses were willing but too old to be relied on with confidence. A month or so on her own was really not so very much to ask. She had her book to write. It was no fault of his if she insisted on making a hermit of herself.

Watching her smile, he wondered whether it was prompted

by some memory of Leyden. It had been a very long walk. Plenty of time for confidences, the expression of discontent. Just as well the man was going away. He wouldn't care to leave her on her own with a character like that in the vicinity. Leyden was not the kind of man to let marriage stand in the way of his desires.

He heard a faint tap on the door. Laura stirred.

"Matthew? The window seems to have jammed. I can't shut it. Do you think—"

"You'll find some blankets in the cupboard. "Good-*night*, Clarissa."

Her footsteps retreated along the passage. He undressed rapidly and slid down into the bed beside Laura. His hands pushed up her nightdress, kneading her into protesting wakefulness as he pulled her towards him and drove into her. He came almost at once, while Laura was still murmuring confusedly from her dreams. He kissed her cheek.

"Darling Laura."

Her eyes blinked open. "Oh. Matthew. I thought—"

"Yes?"

"Nothing. I'm so sleepy. Good-night."

Dissatisfied, he turned away.

Part Four

13

Matthew had been gone a week. A pale scattering of snowdrops was the only foretaste of spring, drooping their heads like bashful novices. Rain greyed the windows and plopped through holes in the roof into an army of buckets and saucepans. The lawn was a squelching marsh hedged in by dank thickets of laurel. The last of Laura's pet goldfish floated swollen in the stone pond until, unable to contemplate the reminder of her neglectful care any longer, she told Mr Bates to take it out and bury it in an unmarked grave. Less sentimental than his mistress, the old man threw it in the dustbin.

Sometimes, sitting alone in the library at night after the Bateses had gone home, she remembered the ghost Matthew had seen here when he was a child. A woman. A servant who had hanged herself. Why couldn't he have kept the story to himself?

The silence of Gracedew was never so absolute as to allow her peace of mind. There was no reason why the floors should creak in empty rooms, why a window should blow open when there was no wind. Not that she believed in ghosts. She had no rational grounds for her fear; she still found herself leaning forward and listening intently for something which seemed about to develop from the creaks and rustles of the watchful night.

Sometimes, too restless for sleep, she wandered up and down the long passages between the rows of Craven portraits. They were waiting for her to take her place beside them on the walls, to watch as unwearyingly as they did, while the moonlight quivered down through the windows in an atmosphere full of them, where nothing of her found a place. She did not want to find a place among the hard-faced women in black and muted greys, hands folded below their waists, eyes measuring her and finding her wanting.

She managed to complete another chapter of her book, but the characters had grown predictable and dull, kept going only by the forward jerks of an over-familiar plot. Loosely based on Victorian Gracedew, she had garnished it with sexual intrigues and the confrontation scenes dear to her publisher's market-conscious heart. She had planned to make this one different, subtle, allusive, richly literary. It had ended as another formula novel, calculated to sell four to five thousand copies. It was, she thought, a measure of her antipathy towards the house that she could bring no enthusiasm to the subject. It lay dead as a corpse on the pages.

She thought with longing of the book she had so wanted to write, about herself, about Matthew, about real life, not these wooden creatures dressed up as flesh and blood. Matthew had advised her to give it up after being shown the first chapter.

"Sorry, darling. You wouldn't want me to pretend. It just doesn't work. The narrative's flat, the characters aren't credible."

"What do you mean, not credible? They're you and me."

"If this man's meant to be a portrait of me, I can't think why the hell you married me."

"I was only trying to be honest."

"Leave that to the school of Erica Jong." He dropped the pages in her lap. "Stick to what you're good at and leave the contemporary novel to me."

"You haven't got a special right to our lives. It's my material, too. I've lived it."

"But only one of us can write it," he said. "I don't want to have an argument. I've told you what I think. Sorry, Laura."

It was, she thought, another symptom of his possessiveness. He could let go of nothing. Everything had to belong to him. His house. His wife. His women. His story. One day she would find the courage to rebel.

Or to leave him. Shocked, she looked up. She had let the thought come out. Leave him. Could she?

Alice, always cheerful, always concerned, rang two or three times to suggest that they might go to a play or film together, or would she like to come over to supper? She managed to sound properly grateful while resisting the invitations. Alice was not to be easily put off.

"Are you sure you're all right? When's Matthew coming back?"

"I really don't know. Some time in early April."

"He'll be here for Easter?"

"I think so. If not, I'll spend it with my parents. I haven't seen them for ages." She had no intention of doing any such thing, but neither did she relish the idea of a Chillingston Easter lunch with the Tucketts and Charlie Remington.

"Well, I'm here if you need me." There was a slight pause. "You've still got the basement in Saint Anselm's Road, haven't you?"

"Yes."

"I was thinking—Dick was looking for somewhere. I could mention it to him, if you liked. Perhaps he could get in touch with you."

"Why not?"

"Well, don't work too hard, my dear," Alice said and rang off, with a serene sense of having fulfilled her neighbourly duties.

Rain. Rain. Rain. A wall of greyness, penning her in. She polished the silver, inspected the progress of the spring bulbs, looked up the films in the local paper. James Bond and two Westerns. The world was against her. It occurred to Laura that she had never yet seen Matthew's history of the Dobells and that she might take a pleasant morning off her own work to look at his. He had no business to hide it from her. Books were not like diaries. As his wife, she had the right to know what he was doing. Busily justifying what she felt to be a mildly improper act, she took the key from under the blotter in his study and unlocked the little mahogany drawer into which she had often seen him pushing the manuscript. Comfortably sprawled in his writing chair, she began to leaf through the pages.

An hour and a half later, she put the manuscript down with a disagreeable sense of shock. It had often struck her that there was something curiously personal in her husband's attachment to Sir Thomas. He was always defending the reckless extravagance which had gone into the creating of Gracedew. Love was worth much, he said, but Thomas' courage had lain in risking the love of his wife for the sake of the larger thing, the house which stood for his beliefs. She saw now that he had been telling her not about Thomas, but himself. His history had become a novel. The characters were, unmistakably, drawn from Matthew and herself.

Nervously, she stubbed a cigarette out in his ash-tray. No wonder he had been so determined to establish his right to make what creative use he pleased of their lives, or that he had been so reluctant to show her his work. It was good. She would acknowledge that. He had always said it would be his best book. She turned back the pages with a kind of horrified fascination to look again at the sentences which had been most wounding. Wincing, she read them again. Venice and Laura. One woman. Here they were, all the faults in her character which he had said were so endearing, minutely described with all the tenderness he might have shown to an insect trapped under a microscope. The book was, to her understanding, a defence of his obsession, the house, presented in such a way as to make a hero of himself and a callous bitch of her. The objective reader would be all on his side.

And yet, the dedication. "To Laura, my beloved wife." She could find no irony in that. Perhaps he had not understood how much the book would hurt her. It was just possible that he had made unconscious use of her, that he had been concerned only with analyzing and justifying the heroic folly of Thomas Dobell, and himself. Perhaps. With this intimate revelation lying in front of her, she was beginning to wonder if she had any real under-standing of Matthew's character. The Matthew of the novel was a stranger she seemed to know, talking of his beliefs and passions in a way her Matthew never had. He had taken possession of her. She saw now that she had been given the keys to everything but himself. Only now had the last room been opened, and it was full of shadows.

Someone was knocking at the door. She stood up quickly, half expecting Matthew to walk in.

"Yes?"

Mrs Bates appeared, wearing the expression which signalled one of her headaches. "I've bin looking all over for you. Never thought you'd be here, in Mr Jack's room."

"Mr Matthew's room."

"Names sticks," Mrs Bates said. "Mr Matthew don't mind me calling it that. I'd like a word if you've a minute to spare."

"Of course." It sounded ominous. She drew confidence from the large expanse of desk before her. "Well? What can I do for you?"

"The last month and a half's wages would do for a start, thanking you," Mrs Bates said briskly. "We don't live on air, you know."

"Surely Mr Craven paid you before he left?"

"I wouldn't be asking if he had, would I?" She folded her arms. "Four hundred and twenty pounds owing. And Bates was wishing me to tell you that Mr Remington's paying Dobson seventy-five a week. Dobson don't do half the work Bates does, and he's only a young lad on his own."

Laura traced a nervous pattern on the blotter. Damn Matthew. He should have warned her, at least. "I know sixty a week doesn't go far nowadays—"

"Forty after tax."

"That's all we can afford. We aren't as rich as Mr Remington. Gracedew isn't a big estate like his where you can run the costs off the farming. You know we had to sell all the cottages. Nothing comes in. And the outgoings really are terrible. If it wasn't for you and Mr Bates being so splendid—"

"Flattery's nice, but it don't pay the wages," Mrs Bates said. "We does what we can. Although I can't say it's easy. The mileage I've done on those stairs. Not that it wasn't bad in old Mrs Craven's day, but there was six in the kitchen when we came and as much food as we could wish for. Mrs Craven, she always looked after us. And Mr Jack, he never let a week go by without the Friday envelope."

"I'm sorry," Laura said. "Honestly, I am, but I don't have the money. I've got about two hundred pounds to live on until the end of April and two cheques made out for the electricity and telephone. And that's all I've got. I can't do anything until Mr Craven comes back."

Mrs Bates looked at her with eyes like coal chips. She had promised Bates that she would be pleasant about it, use no harsh words to upset the young lady, but her head was aching as

269

though she had a pickaxe in her skull and the sight of Laura lolling like a duchess behind the desk, saying she wasn't going to lift a finger to help them, was more than flesh and blood could stand. Her in her fancy silk shirts and French trousers. That's where the money went. Watching her glance down at her long pink nails as she reached for a cigarette, Mrs Bates felt her control snap.

"I always said we'd regret your coming here. Working our guts out for a pittance and all for a chit of a thing who doesn't know an apple and a pear apart until she's told. We'd never have had this kind of trouble with a lady like Mrs Tresham."

"I'm so sorry my husband didn't think of you when he was getting married," Laura said sweetly. "What a pity you didn't write and let him know how you felt. I'm sure he would have changed his plans."

Mrs Bates saw the prudence of returning to more stable ground. "All I'm saying is that obligations is obligations. We've always done our best. We owed it to the house."

"And to the family." A good line to take, that, she thought.

"Family?" She gave a sharp little laugh. "Not the word I'd be using. You won't pull any wool over my eyes with that talk. Family my foot."

Laura stared at her, wondering if the woman was mad. "What on earth do you mean?"

Mrs Bates looked down uneasily. She hadn't meant it to slip out. Maybe he hadn't liked to tell his wife. Still, if that was the case, he wouldn't like the idea of anyone else knowing. It was worth a try.

"Well," she said. "I'm sure I wouldn't want to be delushioning you, but I heard Mr Charles say he weren't no son of his years back when he come here after his wife ran off with that continental. And Bates always told me there wasn't enough blood to spot a hankychief between Mr Jack and Mr Matthew. And he had it from the horse's mouth, so to speak. Not that we didn't all play along with it. Still, you wouldn't want everyone knowing. It'd be awkward. Best to get things sorted out and not a word said."

"Blackmail."

"Just straightening things out." She smiled agreeably. "You

have a little think about it. I've made up the fire in the library if you want to sit where it's warmer. Like a churchyard in here in winter.''

The door closed. Numb, Laura leaned back in the chair. Not a word, not a hint in all the years of their marriage. She had been told only that his parents had been divorced, that his mother had been unfaithful, nothing else. Now, at last, she could understand why inheriting Gracedew had meant so much to him. It wasn't just a legacy, it was a legitimizing. As the acknowledged heir, he became a Craven. It was to the final burying of his past that she had been expected to sacrifice herself.

He had not written that justification into his novel.

Reflecting on his concealment of the truth, she found his behaviour inexplicable. She tried to imagine herself discovering that she had another father, and decided that she would not mind it at all. Certainly, had it been the case, she would not have hidden the facts from Matthew. She had always told him everything. That was how it should be, in a good marriage. Well, a marriage. However angry she felt, she was still his wife. She must do what she could. Thomas Dobell's wife wouldn't have lifted a finger to help. She, Laura, was a better person.

She rang her parents. Her father answered.

''Hello darling. I've just had rather a good round on the course. Two birdies. Not bad for sixty-five, eh?''

''That's wonderful,'' Laura enthused, remembering that birdies were good and might have put him in a receptive mood. ''How's Mummy?''

''Oh, pegging along. You coming down to see us soon?''

''I will try,'' she promised insincerely. ''You know how it is with houses. You get so bogged down.''

Mr Dare made sympathetic noises and noted that she sounded uncharacteristically depressed. ''Matthew's there, is he?''

''Not exactly. He's in France. Doing a book.''

''Bloody fellow's always buggering off somewhere,'' Mr Dare amiably remarked. ''Nice life. Always being left on your own. I wouldn't stand for it. Still, none of my business. But I do think you ought to come and stay for a bit. What about Easter?''

''Oh, I—I'm going over to Alice Tresham's,'' she lied.

"That's the woman your husband was running about with, isn't it?"

"I told you, Daddy, she did the running. He just ran. It was years ago."

"Never trust old flames, if you want my advice," Mr Dare said sagely. "They don't die down, you know, just smoke a bit."

"I expect you're right." She took a breath. "It's not that I'm worried about. Daddy, do you think you could lend me five hundred pounds?"

The voice of kindly paternity grew suddenly guarded. "Five hundred? But you can't be short of money, Laura. You were, if I remember, very generously provided for. Rather more generously than most girls of your age. You surely aren't trying to tell me there's none left?"

"I've got two hundred pounds in the bank and the couple who work here haven't been paid for six weeks."

"Well, I'm afraid that's Matthew's problem," Mr Dare said briskly. "I always thought he was irresponsible. You get on to your husband, my dear. That's the answer. Two hundred pounds—what the devil have you been doing? Dressing at Dior? More to the point, what's Matthew been doing? Dammit, Laura, a husband's meant to look after his wife's finances. I've always seen that your mother's account was in credit."

"It's not quite the same," she said weakly.

"I'm very sorry to hear it. Very sorry indeed." There was a pause, so long that she wondered if he had fallen asleep until a cough announced his wakeful presence. "Look here, my dear, of course I'd like to help, but I really don't think it's wise. We don't want Matthew thinking of his wife's family as an open purse, do we? Rather humiliating for you both, anyway."

"It's a humiliation I could well—"

"What?"

"Nothing."

"I must say that in your shoes, I'd—"

"Yes?"

"Sorry, my dear, your mother's saying the lunch is getting cold. You take a firm line, Laura. Stand up for yourself. It's high time you did."

The wires clicked and fell into a detached purr as Mr Dare trotted away to feed upon Laura's folly and his wife's roast beef. His daughter replaced the receiver and looked at it thoughtfully. His reaction was quite what she would have predicted and she had no trouble in guessing what he had been about to say. Her marriage had not pleased them and the one parental visit to Gracedew had robbed them of the idea that Matthew had come into a property worth boasting about. Mrs Dare, nurtured in a hothouse of unspotted cleanness, was baffled by the shabby grandeur of Gracedew and tortured by the lack of central heating. Mr Dare had missed his midday sherry and had lavished hyperbolic praise on the only remaining Elizabethan fireplace in his anxiety to overlook everything else.

Gracedew was held to be a disaster; the non-appearance of grandchildren heightened their sense of dissatisfaction. A surprising delicacy had prevented them from voicing their feelings to Matthew, and Laura had capitalized upon it, leading them to assume that the choice was quite as much his as her own. Only she knew how much he wished for a child and how, year after year, she had continued frantically to oppose that wish. And why, she asked herself, was she so committed to denying a single cell from Matthew's body a chance of life in her? It was not a question which she had cared to face. Now, rather grimly, she acknowledged that she dreaded the thought of anything which would bind her further to Gracedew. And to Matthew. Not, she hurriedly amended, that she was thinking of leaving him, but if the circumstances should arise—she looked down at the smiling image of herself on the desk—a fading photograph of their first Italian holiday.

It had not always been so.

Fuck me full of you, she had whispered in the hot nights, drawing him into her like a hungry parasite, a succubus, feeding on him. She had wanted his child then, looked at the first brown blood-spot of the month with a feeling of deprivation, when now she grew frantic with alarm if it came two days late. Poor Matthew. How he would love to imprison her with children, a jolly brood of little Cravens to keep her in the home and present a future for Gracedew. A few more nails in the coffin of his hidden past. Well, God bless Marie Stopes.

The telephone vibrated sharply into life at her elbow. Probably her father again, to lecture her on extravagance. She picked it up with reluctance.

"Laura? Dick Leyden here. Alice just called to say you might be able to help me find a place to stay for a couple of months. I thought I was fixed up in Harmony Road for the whole term, but the family who own this house decided that they need it for themselves. I really don't want more than a room and an electric kettle—I'd pay, of course."

"In that case, you're the answer to all my problems," Laura said as gaily as she could. It would not do to sound too desperate. "How do you like the idea of Primrose Hill, bedroom, kitchen, bath and garden, at the knockdown price of fifty a week? Would that do?"

"I thought you were perfection," he said. "And now I know it. It sounds wonderful. You're sure it won't put you out?"

"Absolutely not. I don't suppose, if you liked it, I mean—could you pay in advance?"

"Sure. Stop me spending it," he said. "Still, I'd better see it first. Perhaps I could give you a meal and we could settle the details then. When do you come to London next? I'd love to see you anyway."

"I hadn't been going to—Matthew's away, you know. I really shouldn't leave the house empty."

"That's a shame. Surely one night wouldn't do any harm. Look on it as a business venture if you have to make excuses."

"Oh, I don't have to account for myself to Matthew," she said, annoyed. "I could come on Thursday."

"Done," he said promptly. "Do you like Mexican food?"

"I'm prepared," she said promptly, "to like anything that isn't an omelette. I seem to have been living on them."

"It doesn't sound too wonderful," he said. "We'll do better. Seven o'clock, fourteen Harmony Road." He paused. "I like your voice. Alice does tend to bay a bit when she's excited. I used to think it was part of being English. I can't imagine you baying. Nice laugh too."

"Go on," Laura said, happily. "I do like compliments."

"I'll save the rest for Thursday," he said. "Don't bring a nightdress."

"Don't what?" She must have misheard.

"No nightdress. I'm going to bed with you after dinner."

"You are?"

"That's my fell intention. Still want to come?"

"Certainly I do. I'm perfectly capable of refusing you."

"I'm sure you are. But I'm full of hope."

"Don't be. Hopeless case," she said cheerfully. "Seven o'clock it is."

Replacing the telephone she walked across the room and peered at her face in the mirror. Her eyes looked back at her, green, wide and clear. "Well, well," she said. "Now you're for it, my dear. If you incline. I rather think you deserve a treat."

"Well, well," said Dick Leyden. "What a success you seem to be."

"We seem to be," she said sleepily, turning her head on the pillow to look at him as he leaned away to turn off the light. "I wish you wouldn't. I'd like to lie and look at you all night."

"You're a sweet girl." He slid a hand down the fluent curve of her back. "But you should have told me you hated Mexican food."

"I liked the bread."

"Did you sleep with Matthew in this room?"

"Do you mind?"

He yawned. "I'll try to get used it. Nice toes you've got, but they're cold. Good-night, Celia my sweet."

I shall scream, Laura thought in the tranquil breathing silence which followed. I shall throw myself out of the window. I'll tell him I never want to see him again. I'll drive back to Gracedew right now.

"How pretty you are," he murmured. And Laura, to her great surprise, turned meekly on to her side and went to sleep without another word.

In the morning, lying in the bath, she said: "Is your wife called Celia?"

"Fairy," he said. "Frightful name. Suits her. Laura's much prettier."

Smiling, she pressed on. "I only know one Celia round here. Perhaps it's her. You said good-night to her."

"Christ, I must have been drunk," he said. "Did I really?"

"It doesn't matter." She looked out of the corner of her eye to see whether it did to him. He was looking into the mirror with the concentrated stare of the half-shaved man.

"She's a woman I've been to bed with a couple of times," he said flatly. "I suppose it's likely that I will again. I certainly can't rule it out."

"I don't see why you have to tell me," Laura said, digging pits in the soap with her nails. "It's of no consequence to me whether you do or not. I'm not your wife."

"Perhaps you should be," he said, bending to rub at her cheeks with the flannel. "Look up. That's better. Nice and pink. You look even better without make-up. Like a little girl. A nice pink water-sprite." He leaned back against the door with a contented smile. "How very pleasant this is. Pretty bathroom. Pretty Laura. I shall like being in Saint Anselm's Road. You'll have to come and keep house for me."

"Services are not *compris*. Still, I might visit. A landlady's duty."

"Quite. Any chance of Matthew putting in appearances here?" he asked as they were dressing.

"I suppose he might when he's back. It wouldn't matter, would it? You're such a respectable tenant. You've even paid his wages for him." It was best, she thought, to keep to a slightly flippant note. "Well, I'd better be off."

He put his arms round her. "No, you don't. I haven't any work to do that can't wait until this afternoon. Let's go walking."

"Lovely. Where?"

"Where the mood takes us. We'll explore. Show me the London I've never seen."

Laura laughed. "It was never like this with Matthew. Just fun."

"I can't imagine life not being fun with you in it," he said. "Come on."

Laura took him to a street-market in the East End where Leyden bought her a black velvet hat with an ostrich feather trailing from the crown. It smelt faintly of cats and certainly was not worth five pounds but, to please him, she wore it. She caught sight of them both reflected in a shop-window and thought what an agreeable couple they must look to other people.

"Now what am I going to give you in exchange?" she wondered.

"Just a kiss," Leyden said.

Later they walked up to Primrose Hill and found themselves at the centre of a children's kite-flying competition. Laura was charmed by the tugging scarlet dragons and bearded emperors scudding sideways, soaring high above the glass-sided towers of Marylebone. Leyden watched with amusement as she spun on her heels to follow the erratic flights of the multi-coloured monsters overhead. "You seem such a different person here," he said as they turned away down the hill. "I'd say you were a born Londoner."

"Perhaps I'm just happy to be with you."

"Did she stay long, the first wife?"

"Only until the next morning. I don't know why you think Clarissa upset me. I couldn't have cared less."

"That's not how it struck me." He glanced at her. "I thought you were being given pretty fair cause for distress. Perhaps you're used to it. Matthew didn't strike me as being the unfaithful type. Is he?"

"Not particularly. He used to be. I don't think I care any more whether he is or not. I suppose that means I don't love him any more." She waited for a response. None came. "What about you? Don't you ever get jealous?"

"I've never had cause to be," he said. "You'd best be warned. I'm usually the one who leaves."

She was chilled by the detachment in his voice. "Thanks for the encouragement. You mustn't overwhelm me."

He bent to kiss her. "Don't sulk. How nice you taste. Let's go back. I want to be in bed with you."

Lifting her mouth against his, she could not stop herself from questioning him. "Have you slept with an awful lot of married women?"

"None so pretty as you."

"Did they stay married?"

"The sensible ones did. Well, an affair shouldn't be a total commitment, should it?"

"No, I suppose not."

Driving back to Gracedew that evening with the sun in her eyes and the memory of his flesh warm on her skin, Laura was overcome with panic. This was not like the affairs of her past. She had always been the one to finish them, but not as an act of virtue. Desire without love grew stale in the very moment of its gratification. Now, remembering Leyden's smile, his voice, his delighted pleasure in her body, his words of love, his hints at other women, another Laura-excluding life, she recognized the imperative need to stop this affair immediately before her feelings ran out of control. She had had her fun. There was no real danger yet. She would not tell Matthew. She would not see Dick again.

Gracedew rose before her in the lilac dusk, serenely harmonious, a harbour from the turbulent sea into which she had so nearly hurled herself. The smell of earth and chestnut buds sweetened the air. She leaned over the balustrade at the front of the house to watch two swans sedately gliding across the lake, their long necks undulating with the limpid grace of a dancer's arms. That was how love should be, calm, harmonious, painless. This love would bring her nothing but pain.

She walked around the garden paths, pushing away the memory of her walk here with Richard Leyden, arranging in her mind's eye the pretty graceful things she would do to please Matthew. Here a tulip tree of pale half-cupped blossoms, there a border of madonna lilies. A *hortus conclusus* of all the virtues which she would practise. The evening wind brushed her and she stood still, remembering the quick light touches of Leyden's clever hands about her body, finding her out, knowing her, possessing her.

Matthew would be away for at least another month. It was such a long time since she had felt so happy, and so young.

"Beautiful evening, Mrs Craven." She turned to see the bent figure of Bates standing under the elms. "Had a good drive down?"

"Not bad." She smiled at him. "Nice to be back. I was thinking I'd never seen it looking so lovely."

"Oh, Gracedew has her moments. It'll be better when the roses are out. That's the time old Mrs Craven always said was the best. I was thinking we might put a few Icebergs in the front this autumn."

"I don't want to think about autumn," Laura said with a theatrical shudder of horror. "Country houses should have nothing but summers."

" 'Twouldn't do much for the garden," Bates said dryly. "We could do with a drop of rain."

"More? We've had nothing else for months."

He looked at her with kindly amusement. "Bit warmer down in the South, I expect. Surrey, isn't it? It takes a bit of getting used to Midlands weather. I've been here sixty years and I'm still fretting at the way the winters cling on. The wife now, she'd not have it any different. Put her on a beach in Spain and she'd be complaining of the heat from morning to night."

"You'd better take me instead," Laura said. "Oh, I've got your wages. I'll go to the bank tomorrow. I'm so sorry about the delay. I didn't know anything about it."

"You wouldn't have if I'd had my way," he said. "I didn't want to go bothering you while Mr Matthew was away. I think it was one of her headache days." His netted eyes peered up at her with an expression of fatherly interest. "You've been a bit peaky yourself. Dare say you don't eat enough when you're on your own."

"Enough to get by. I'm hardly fading away, Bates."

"Still, it'd do you good to get away a bit more," he persisted. "You ought to go to town more often. I can keep an eye on the place. I was just about running it for old Mr Jack near the end, you know."

And not too well, from the sound of it, Laura thought, but she smiled and said: "Indeed I do. His left hand and his right."

"Well, I'm fond of the place. It's home to me."

"I was a bit puzzled by one thing your wife mentioned," Laura said as they walked under the chirping branches towards the house. "About Matthew. Something about his not being a real Craven."

Bates shot a keen glance at her from under the white tufts of his brows. "You don't want to listen to Jean's gossip," he said. "She's always bin a bit of a chattermouth. It don't mean much. Don't you go fretting yourself with what she says."

"She said you knew quite a lot about it."

"Nowt worth remembering," he said steadily. "I don't hold with back-talk myself. Judge by what you see, not what you hear's what my dad used to say." He stopped at the library door. "I'll be getting along. Good-night, Mrs Craven."

There was a note in the hall from Alice to say that she was sorry to have missed her and to call and let her know if Dick had taken the rooms. Prying, Laura thought uneasily, and she walked quickly past the telephone. In the library, she settled down to read, grew restless, and decided to ring up Matthew. A girl's laughing voice answered the telephone.

"Yes please? You want Martin?"

"Mr Craven, please. It's his wife calling."

"I'm sorry. I don't quite—" She broke off in evident confusion.

"His wife," she repeated. "Laura Craven." A murmur of voices was followed by a click, a whisper.

"Laura. Darling, how lovely to hear from you. I was just thinking about you."

"Very discreetly. I don't know who that was, but she obviously had no idea you're married."

"Oh, that was only Sophie, Freedman's girlfriend. She's a bit vague. I do wish you were here, darling. You'd love it." He dropped his voice. "Freedman's pretty dreadful, but the place is rather a knockout. Jasmine and bougainvillaea everywhere, more lobster than I ever ate in my life, parties every night. All I need is you."

"For such a life who'd want a wife?" Laura inquired acidly. "Nice of you to think of me, though. I do appreciate it. How's the book going?"

"Oh, coming along. It shouldn't take more than a month and then back to my lovely Lorelei and Gracedew and all delights. Well, what have you been doing? Writing away? I expect old Remington's been making the most of my absence."

"He rings up now and again. Listen, Matthew, since you forgot to pay the wages, I had to do something about it. I've let our bit of Saint Anselm's Road for a couple of months. Fifty a week, all in advance. You don't mind?"

"Of course not. How very clever of you, darling. Where did you find the tenant?"

"Alice did. Richard Leyden was looking for somewhere and, since he seemed quite suitable, I said yes."

"I see," Matthew said slowly. "Well, I suppose that's all right. I'm not sure he's the tenant I'd have chosen. I didn't much care for him. You might have asked me first."

"There wasn't time, and Mrs Bates was being pretty disagreeable about the money."

"I can't think why. She's perfectly well off. Well, I expect Leyden's better than nothing. Say you love me, darling."

"Love you," she muttered at the wall.

"Come on."

"I love you," she wailed. "Only, oh Matthew, I—"

"That's better. That's my Laura. Anyway, back soon, my love. Don't call too often, will you? The charges went up again last month."

"In that case, why don't you—"

"Good-bye, darling."

Telephone conversations, Laura decided, were the worst form of communication ever invented. She closed the shutters, fed the dog, put on an old dressing-gown, made herself an omelette which she washed down with stale cooking wine before curling up by the one-bar electric fire to watch the news. The day already seemed to have happened to a different person. She was Laura of Gracedew again, chaste, loyal, retiring. A trusted wife, a keeper of hearths. Yawning, she watched the camera lights flash over the lenses of Robin Day's inquisitorial glasses as he unsparingly exhibited his boredom to a discomfited audience questioner.

"Next. Lady in the yellow beard—sorry, lady in the yellow muffler."

Laughter. Laura wriggled her toes forward to warm them at the fire. What was the fun of discussion programmes when you had no one to discuss them with? The telephone rang. Alice, almost certainly. She lifted the receiver and felt a grin edging across her face like a sunbeam as Dick Leyden spoke into her ear.

She tried to pinch in her mouth, to sound severe.

"You sound a bit sad," he said.

"Pining for you, of course," she said, giving up. "No, watching the intrepid Day. Glad I'm not having to face him."

Beauty might silence him. I'd like to see something which could, bar an exit in mid-sentence. Lovely seeing you, Laura. You might come and sample some other country's cooking on Monday."

Listen, Dick, I've been thinking. I can't see any future for us and I'm not so very unhappily married and I can learn to live with Gracedew. I do think, for my own sake, it's better that we shouldn't see each other again. Yes, that was what she should say.

"What a nice idea," she said. "And I'll bring you some flowers."

"I must say, Laura, you're quite a delight. I thought about you all afternoon. In some rather carnal way."

"Tell me." She leaned forward to turn off the television.

"Think about it until Monday," he said with a laugh in his voice. "Food for the imagination. It might help the omelettes along. Good-night, angel."

The restaurant was an unlucky choice. She had been to it perhaps twenty times with Matthew. The waiter who led them to the table asked after Mr Craven with what she thought was an impertinent air of solicitude. She was conscious of Dick Leyden's ironic observation as she blushed and hedged.

"You're missing him."

"I'm not." She studied the familiar menu. With Matthew, she had always chosen the fried mushrooms. "I'll have the onion soup."

His hand covered hers on the table. "It's all right, Laura. There's no sin in loving one's husband."

"I don't," she said fiercely and then, ashamed, tried to modify. "Well, not as I did. Not in the same way. Gracedew changed all that. I'm very fond of him of course."

"You sound remarkably like a Victorian Miss. I'd be ready to bet you love him more than you'll ever let on to me. And very proper too. You shouldn't apologize for it."

282

"I wasn't." But I do want you, she thought as he looked at her with smiling eyes. "I married him in another kind of life."

"You're adaptable. Most women are."

"I don't want to adapt. I want—I really don't know what I want. Not Gracedew."

He stroked her fingers. "Perhaps I was sent to teach you."

"I don't want a teacher." She leaned back. "What did you do this week-end? Anything nice?"

"Work. A couple of dinners."

"Who with?"

"People."

"I didn't imagine you were dining with polar-bears," Laura said crossly. "I mean, who? Celia?"

Leyden frowned and took his hand away. "Look," he said. "You're free to do as you like. So am I. There are no commitments, not yet. So let's not have any inquisitions."

"I was only asking." Laura felt the corners of her mouth beginning to quiver. "I didn't mean to pry."

"I know." He touched the downcast curve of her cheek. "I'm not going to pretend I don't see anybody else, but I don't particularly want to talk about it. Cheer up. You're certainly my prettiest dinner-partner by a mile and a half and there's no one I'd rather be with tonight. I hope you're going to stay until tomorrow."

"I could," she said recklessly, "stay for a couple of days. I can always say I was visiting a friend."

He signalled to a waiter. "Best not. We don't want you causing too much of a scandal in the shires."

It was, Laura thought after her fifth assignation with him, a relationship more rich in suggestion and more empty in hope than any she could have devised for the express purpose of tormenting herself. She was extraordinarily happy; she was unbearably miserable. She fed upon fantasies while recognizing that Leyden neither shared them nor wanted any part in them. He called her charming, delightful, adorable; she understood that she could seem so only by appearing to match his independence. If she suggested meeting him more than twice in a week, she came up against a barrier which was like a slap in the face. He wanted only a part of her life; she must seem always to wish only to be a part of his. The terms were unspoken but clearly understood. She was too unsure of him to transgress them.

She knew herself to be behaving crazily. It was probable that Leyden would leave her as soon as Matthew returned, if not before; it was certain that her frequent absences were the subject of lively discussion in the local country houses. It was better not to wonder what was being said by Lady Livingston and the Tucketts. If she did not ask and refused to communicate, she could keep apprehension at bay, and advisers. She wanted advice from nobody; it was too easy to predict the kind she would get. They would tell her to give him up. She was not prepared to do so. Not now.

A part of her was in love with him. Another part of her stood back and watched with fascination the desperate stupidity of her behaviour. Astonished, she listened to herself declaring her love, pleading with him to ring her up, to tell her when they could next meet, edging him towards the commitment which he would not give. In her moments of detachment, she understood that she was behaving in a way which was likely to drive him away. She wished to, and could not, change.

"If only I could learn to love you less. Will you ring up this evening? I'll be back at ten at the latest."

Kissing her upturned mouth, he sighed.

"Oh Laura, dear Laura, how awfully determined you are. I'll ring, of course, if you want me to. But do you think, just for an hour, we could talk about books or houses or plays or even fucking? But not, my darling, always about love and the future."

She had retained just enough prudence to know when persistence became destructive. And anyway, she had the solace of knowing that if he did not love her alone, he loved her best. He continued to see and, she painfully recognized, to go to bed with other women, but he spoke of them in a reassuringly diminishing tone. It was she whom he took to dinner; the others all took him. Didn't that prove, well, something?

It was funny, she thought, that it should have taken this experience to make her understand what Matthew must once have suffered with Clarissa.

*   *   *

Max invited her to lunch one day, ostensibly to discuss the progress of her novel. She arrived at the usual Hungarian restaurant fresh from Leyden's arms, rosy on the memory of him. She knew she was looking pretty without troubling to glance at the mirrors on the walls. The smiles of the seated men as she walked by gave a fair enough reflection.

"I see you're taking a leaf out of your own books, my dear," Max said acidly as she took the chair opposite his half-consumed plate of pike quenelles. "Unpunctuality is charming in a romantic heroine but just a little irritating in a lunch guest. Thirty minutes is pushing it. The first course was delicious. I'm sorry you missed it."

"Since I'm not terribly hungry I'll manage to bear the punishment. Poor Max. I am sorry." She threw a dazzling upward smile at the waiter and noted its effect on the next-door table with satisfaction. "Just a green salad and some radishes please."

"And a steak," Max said. "I detest eating alone. Regard it as an act of altruism."

"I really don't—"

"Medium rare," Max cut across her. "Don't argue, dear."

"I know which side my steak's buttered." She saw that he was not in a joking mood and hurried on. "The book's going awfully well. Don't worry about it."

"I'm not in the least worried about it," Max said tranquilly. "It's you who are bothering me, my dear, and that's putting it mildly."

"Oh? How intriguing." She felt crimson searing her face to her ears. "But I can't think why. I'm fine."

Max neatly spread a posy of butter curls across his roll. "I've known Matthew for a good many years now," he said. "I like him. We don't have much in common, of course, but we get on well when we meet. He seems to be very fond of you."

"Nobody fonder than absent husbands," Laura said dryly. "Still, I've got you to thank for that. You produced Martin Freedman."

"Keep your voice down or shut up, sweety," Max said. "We're not having a public relations lunch. I gave Matthew that job because you said he was desperate for money. It's not the sort

of job he ought to do and I don't suppose he'll do it very well."
His small eyes glinted at her. "I did it for him and for you. I
respect what you're trying to do for that house. You're
preserving a tradition."

"Like Mr Kipling's cakes. Yes, I suppose so."

"Let's be honest, Laura," he said, leaning plumply forward.
"You're never going to be a great writer, but Matthew may be
if he doesn't throw away his time on bloody stupid things like
sit-coms for Ned Foley. What he needs from you is a bit of
support. If he can get a decent sum of money out of this book
and if you're prepared to work at the house and your marriage
instead of flittering around north London, you can get that place
in order and see that he writes something worthwhile again."

"I never would have guessed you were a frustrated agony
aunt."

"Cheap." He tapped her cheek. "Don't like advice, do
you?"

"I'm not sure I need it," Laura said with a smile she felt to be
uneasy. "I don't understand what you're saying."

"I'm telling you about Richard Leyden," Max said. "Don't
open your eyes at me. You may be discreet but he isn't."

"Just because I see someone for a couple of dinners!" she tried
to laugh. "How ridiculous!"

"I'm not bothered with your morals," Max said. "You can
fuck him upside-down in an aquarium for all I care. I'm talking
about Matthew. Don't hurt him. What you do is your affair, if
you'll forgive the pun, but you didn't have to pick the man
who's proposing to your husband's ex-mistress. You can't
imagine Celia Rivers would keep her mouth shut? She's making
a laughing stock of you and Matthew. Ask Leyden."

"He hardly ever sees her," Laura rashly exploded. "And from
what I know of Celia, she probably did the proposing. I can't
imagine Richard wanting to marry a middle-aged actress with
the brain of a peahen. I'm not going to listen to this any longer.
You don't know what you're talking about."

"I'm only telling you what's being said," he replied. "You
may think of your friend as a quiet literary fellow. You'd better
understand a few more things about him. He likes money, for
one thing. And Celia Rivers isn't poor."

"I detest gossip," Laura said, pushing her salad away.

He nodded. "I don't wonder. You needn't worry. I won't say anything to Matthew, but don't take it too far. Your friend Leyden isn't going to stay around to help you when the shit hits the fan. And it will. Too many people know what's going on."

"Lovely radishes," Laura said coldly. "I always enjoy coming here. It's so relaxing."

"Point taken," Max said with a grin. "So, the novel's coming along well? Ready by May?"

After lunch, she walked up through the leafy afternoon calm of Soho Square's shadows, to drift like a dead thing with the current of the traipsing crowds of tourist strangers. The news that the affair was already drinks-party gossip was rather horrible. The thought of Dick proposing to that old rat-bag Celia was ludicrous. She wished now that she had not reacted so sharply; the wiser course would have been to make a show of blank disinterest. Celia was old, but she was awfully rich. He couldn't. Or could he? He had said once or twice that he was in the market for a rich wife. It had been a joke, only a joke. She winced as a stocky young woman crashed into her, treading heavily on her toes before giving a high shriek of recognition.

"Laura! How amazing! It is you, isn't it?"

She gazed at the plump pink face which was beaming friendship at her under a cluster of tight brown curls, and finally recognized it as belonging to Susie, the ex-Screeby's publicity girl. Seeing no escape, she smiled.

"It must be telepathy. I was just thinking about you," Susie babbled merrily. "Doesn't Screeby's seem years ago? You've been married. I've been divorced. Time and the river. God, Selfridges is hell. I can't find a single decent dress over size twelve. They seem to think that anybody larger only wears striped shirt-waisters. I wish I was your shape. You're thinner than ever." She pressed an arm round Laura. "You need feeding up and I need to sit down. Which adds up to a cappuccino round the corner. You're not in a hurry, are you? You can't be if you're in Oxford Street."

It seemed easier to comply than to start fabricating excuses. "Lovely idea," she said and allowed herself to be dragged alongside Susie's voluminous parcels towards Manchester Square.

"Well, you certainly seem to be thriving on country life," Susie remarked as she relishfully scooped the sugared froth off her cup and licked the spoon. "Or is it love?"

"Perhaps both," Laura said, contemplating the imprudence of confiding in Susie. "I just wish life wasn't so horribly complicated."

"Ah, so it is love. Well, you always were a romantic," Susie said. "It certainly suits you. Who is he? Anyone I know?"

"You might. So I won't tell you."

"Very irritating of you, but probably sensible," Susie's eyes gleamed with interest. "You're not going to leave Matthew, are you?"

"I suppose I might."

"Well, can't say I blame you. I always said it would be tricky. Got a good solicitor?"

Laura blinked. Susie's matter-of-factness was rather dreadfully combined with the sweet crunch of biscuits. "I hadn't thought that far. I suppose I should."

"He will if you don't," Susie said through a mouthful of macaroon. "Don't be noble. It doesn't pay. Well, I'm quite relieved. I saw that thing in *Paris Match* yesterday and I was just thinking, poor old Laura. But it's quite good. It means nobody will blame you. If he's carrying on like that, the last thing anyone will say is that it's your fault."

"Why, what did *Paris Match* say?" Laura asked as Susie's hand reached out to sweep the plate clean.

"It's not so much what it said as how it looked," Susie said darkly. "Pictures. You'd better get a copy. Perhaps I shouldn't have mentioned it." She stared at Laura critically. "You look a bit upset. Shall I get you some water?"

"No. Really. I must go. I have to be somewhere at five. Lovely seeing you. We must keep in touch." She dropped a handful of coins on the table, a kiss on Susie's cheek, and ran out into the street.

She finally tracked down a copy of the magazine in the underground. Waiting among the weary shoppers for the whistle and wail of the northbound train, she flicked through the satined pages until she found herself staring at a half-page photograph of a dinner-party in the home of Martin Freedman.

The focus of the picture was on Freedman, but there, sitting, or rather lounging between him and her husband, was Clarissa, with one bare arm draped over Matthew's shoulder. Hurriedly, she turned to the print. Clarissa got a good press. *Séduisante,* they called her. *Séduisante* was what she looked. *La séduisante première femme d'un milord et écrivain anglais, très bein connu.* Martin Freedmam was given the role of Cupid in this happy reunion. The reporter was prepared to predict that *la séduisante* Clarissa was ready to be tamed at last, by the man who had first won her heart. It was very much in the *Paris Match* style. Of Matthew's existing marriage there was not a word.

She tore the article out and put it into her bag before throwing the magazine away. The funny thing was that she couldn't decide whether to laugh or burst into tears. Really, it was incredible. Clarissa and Matthew. He could not have done anything more designedly hurtful and offensive. Only some small part of her mind would admit that she had been given exactly what she wanted, a perfect justification for her own behaviour. She could be as outraged as she pleased and have public opinion on her side. And she did wish to stand well in the world's eye. If only it had not been Clarissa.

Reflection produced the thought that grief over Matthew's faithlessness would serve her purpose with Dick Leyden far better than an onslaught about Celia. That was tiresome nagging; this was a good tragic role. She had long ago learned the advantages of seeming vulnerable. She paused on the corner of Saint Anselm's Road and stared into the gritty evening wind until her eyes were streaming with pain, but by the time she reached the house, she was crying in earnest and had lost any idea of strategic manoeuvre in a tide of apprehension. It was, terribly, possible that she could lose them both.

Leyden held her quietly against him, stroking her hair, soothing her. "Poor little Laura. Poor sweet. I'll get you some wine. There, drink it up. Poor love. What is it? What's the matter?"

As if she were a child. As she had been to Matthew. She pulled away.

"I'm all right. Really."

"You look it."

She nodded, grinned, sipped at the wine and started to cough as the sobs rose to block her throat. "It's Clarissa. He's gone back to Clarissa." She pushed the page into his hands. "I feel so stupid. I never thought—it's so silly of me to be like this."

"Not silly at all." He glanced down the page. "How very unpleasant. I thought the French trip was all about saving Gracedew."

"So did I. I suppose they fixed it while she was staying."

"Better not to speculate." He looked at her thoughtfully. "Are you planning to do anything about it?"

"There's nothing much I can do."

"I'd say there's quite a lot." He pushed the telephone towards her. "Why not give Alice a call? Or your parents. I don't think I'm quite the right person to advise you."

"I don't see why not." She stared at the telephone. "Max said at lunch that you wanted to marry Celia Rivers. Do you, Dick? I might as well have all the bad news together."

"What a useful little spy you are. No. She did drop a few hints but I wasn't interested. That doesn't mean I'm thinking of marrying anyone else."

"Oh, I wasn't thinking of anything like that," Laura hurriedly asserted. "I was just curious."

"I'll bet. Dear Laura, how awfully transparent you are."

She made a face at him. "And how complacent you are. Do you think everybody's dying to marry you? I do love you though."

"And I you. Still, perhaps Gracedew's where you should be. Gardens, tea parties and a nice nursery full of little Lauralets— oh, don't start crying again. Please. I was only joking."

"It's not funny," she wept. "I know I should be like that, but I'm not. I don't fit anywhere. I'm no good at being a country wife. I'm not clever enough for the likes of you."

"Your husband isn't a stupid man. Stop running yourself down."

"I'll just get myself run over."

"Here. Have a kitchen knife. Quicker."

"I know. I'm going over the top again." She managed a smile. "If only I could get away somewhere. I need to sort myself out. Don't look so worried. I'll be all right. I always am in the end.''

Leyden looked down at her. Her eyes were red and swollen. Mascara made black puddles on her cheeks and her teeth were chattering like a drawerful of spoons. He felt helpless and annoyed and upset. He had neither wanted nor expected to become so attached to her. Irritating she certainly was, but her graces were numerous. She made him laugh. She was sexually enchanting. She was good company. And she loved him. The thought of returning to his promiscuous but mildly unsatisfactory life in California without her was, he suddenly realized, very depressing. He thought of the grey shadowed house in the suburban back streets of Santa Monica, so orderly, so silent. He thought of Laura, pretty, engaging, anxious, so sweetly frantic in her desire to please, so comic in her little fits of drama and petulance, so soft and desirable in bed. It might work. It was worth the risk of hurting her. It seemed that there was nothing to keep her here.

He lifted her hands to his mouth. "I'm going back to the States earlier than I expected. Next week in fact. I can go with you or without you. Think about it."

She gave him a pale and wondering look and slowly drew her hands back into her lap. "I can't just abandon the house."

"I'll tell Alice. She'll look after things perfectly well until Matthew comes back. She'll probably rather enjoy it. All you need to do is to pack a suitcase and get hold of a couple of hundred pounds. I can find you some sort of work out there if you want. As for writing, you can do that anywhere."

"And I'd live with you?"

He was slightly irritated by her failure to respond. "You can sleep on the beach if you'd rather. Obviously, I can't offer to marry you."

"It would be a sort of experiment?"

"You said you wanted to get away."

"I don't know what to say," she murmured. "It sounds so awfully irrevocable. I'm frightened."

"Then stay. I'm not pressing you."

"Would you mind if I stayed?"

"I'd like you to come. Think about it for a couple of days."

Oh God, help me, she silently besought, as she stared fixedly at the jar of catkins on the gingham tablecloth before her. What do I do? I've dreamed of him saying something like this for weeks. Now all I can do is say I'm scared. Scared of going. Scared of staying. I ought to refuse. He's still not committing himself. He'll drop me when he's bored. But if he goes without me—I'll never love anyone like this again. And Matthew's all right. He's got Clarissa. If the leaf drops off that branch on a green square, I'll say yes. Let it be as simple as that.

"Well?"

"I'm thinking." She fixed her eyes with intensity upon the leaf as it shivered at her breath. She found herself hoping that it would not fall, that the moment of decision would never come.

14

Matthew hunched against the pale sweet-smelling pigskin upholstery in the back of Freedman's Jaguar as it gleamed slickly down through the Porte d'Orléans exit from the *périphérique* between the buzzing lines of Citroens and baby Renaults. Freedman's plump, silk-gloved hands slipped round the wheel, guiding the long bonnet in and out of the queue like a vicious scarlet proboscis.

"Great car, this," he said for perhaps the fifth time since they had left Mougins early that morning. "Best buy I ever made. I guess I told you how I got it off Berni Lucci after we finished making *The Contract*, Matt?"

"I think you did mention it." In the passenger seat, Sophie wound down her lipstick, glanced at her sleek pretty reflection in a hand-mirror and said: "It is such a wonderful story. It is the way that you tell it, Martin. You make all the voices so well."

"Do, dummy. Six years and you still talk like a goddamn foreigner."

"I was not employed for my linguistic abilities," she said pertly.

"Just for your pretty tongue," Freedman said, pulling off a glove to wiggle a forefinger in her mouth. "Sweet, sucking, finger-licking Sophie—don't bite me, you little bitch."

"I'm hungry. Can we have lunch at the Closerie, Martin darling? It would be a celebration for finishing the book."

"I booked already. We're lunching at one and meeting Rawlings at three, at his studio. Okay by you, Matt?"

"Fine. I just hope the picture's as good as Clarissa suggested. I'd hate to think you'd driven all this way on a wild-goose chase."

"She doesn't strike me as being a woman who makes

mistakes," Freedman said. "A real shame she couldn't have stayed on. She's a wonderful person, Matt. You don't seem to me to have a proper appreciation of her qualities."

"Perhaps I know them too well, having been married to her."

"You should have heard her talking to that magazine reporter about *High Summer*. I never heard anyone give such a sensitive account of Duvalle's role. She could have been there beside me when I was making it. Straight to the centre—pow! She'd make a great film critic. That man was just knocked out by her."

"Matthew told me she had never even seen the film," Sophie observed. "She was just pretending, from what Matthew had told her. You are so naïve, Martin. She wanted to impress you. She is looking for a rich husband."

"Never seen *High Summer*?" Freedman shook his head. "I don't believe you. She knew it backwards. She could describe just how I was looking at any point in the film."

"You'd believe anything from a pretty woman," Sophie said with a yawn. "Ask Matthew."

"We did talk about it a bit," Matthew compromised tactfully. "But she could have seen it already. I wouldn't let it bother you, Martin. Truth isn't Clarissa's most shining attribute."

"Well, I thought she was a great girl, just great," he said truculently. "I would marry her myself if I didn't think you were booked for a second round."

"Don't be noble on my account. You seem to forget that I'm a happily married man."

"There's no such thing," Freedman grinned. "Take it from me. I'm an expert on the subject."

"You think your wife will have seen that article?" Sophie inquired with interest. "You will not be very happily married if she has."

"Oh, Laura knows a bit of gossip when she sees it," he said easily. "And anyway, she never reads *Paris Match*."

"You are too sure of her, I think."

"Why shouldn't I be, after seven years?"

"Seven year itch. It's a real danger point," Freedman said. "I know, I've never got past it."

"Seven years. Just imagine to be with one man for seven

years!" Sophie wriggled in her seat. "I would go crazy."

"So would the man, sweetie," Freedman said with heavy humour. "Would you take her on, Matt?"

"Sophie's a delightful companion," he smiled. "Think yourself lucky."

"Is that what they call it?" Freedman pinched her bare brown knee. "You don't know what she costs me in clothes. She nearly ruined me on our last trip to Paris. No dresses this time, Soph, just the picture."

"But I do need some new shoes, darling. Just a little pair of sandals. I will get some cheap ones, I promise." Her brown eyes fluttered a wink of connivance at Matthew. "You have seen my gold sandals. They are so old. Tell him."

"Her shoes are very old. And she's seen some very pretty ones in *Elle* magazine. And they're only four hundred francs. A real bargain." Stifling a yawn, he stared out at the long grey suburban streets spattered with spring rain. April in Paris. How infinitely preferable to be spending April at Gracedew. He wished he had not allowed Freedman to bully him into coming on this expedition. The book was finished. He could have been on the morning plane from Nice. Home by tea-time. Instead of which, another long, expensive and relentlessly boring restaurant meal with Freedman and his pretty, tough, little mistress lay ahead. Another two hours of the sycophant's role, laughing at Freedman's jokes, supporting Sophie's endless demands for admiration, while he watched the old film star's eyes dart over the tables in search of a glimmer of recognition and waited for the meal's predictable conclusion in barter with Freedman's scrawled autograph on a photograph of him grinning at the manager in exchange for twenty per cent off the bill. Embarrassment had become deadly familiarity. Apathy rather than corruption had deadened his sense of disgust. He had resigned himself to being seen as a minor satellite in the Freedman orbit.

Not that life at the Villa Sylvia (Freedman's third wife, Sylvia Schwartz, had left little other than her name in the house after their much publicized divorce in 1976) had been entirely disagreeable. To some, it might have seemed a holiday in Paradise. He had been given his own private suite of rooms, free use of a snappy little Alfa Romeo sports car. A smartly uniformed maid had been appointed to bring him breakfast by the pool, to launder his clothes, to tidy and polish everything from the typewriter to the toothpaste tube. He had even been permitted a degree of privacy. Freedman had soon made it clear that he was readier to offer advice than to assist in writing the book which would go out under his name. It had been surprisingly easy to gain permission to spend his mornings working peacefully in the cool grey shade of his room with nothing but the distant splashing of Sophie and her friends in the pool and the steady chirrup of cicada wings to disturb him.

The rest of the day had not been so good. No wonder that he had put on half a stone. The drinking began at midday and went on until early morning, bar a brief respite during Freedman's afternoon nap with Sophie. A gregarious bully, Freedman liked to be surrounded by people who drank as hard as himself. To command his respect, it was necessary to out-drink him. Sophie had long ago shrewdly produced a liver complaint which excused her; Matthew had been imprudent enough to drink two bottles of Sancerre on his first day. Hangovers had become as much a part of daily life as the nightly vomiting up of shellfish, cream cheese and Napoleon brandy. He had managed to accustom himself to going to his desk with a mind that felt like a dehydrated sponge, from which a minimum of three thousand words a day had somehow to be dredged up. The need for money and to escape as quickly as possible from the glossy unpleasantness of the Villa Sylvia had been urgent enough to generate the necessary degree of mechanical efficiency. Three times thirty-two; ninety-six thousand words; the space of a month; the length of a book; the money for the house; the securing of a future for Laura and himself at Gracedew. Fifteen thousand pounds, payable on delivery to Max at Rackitt's. That was the price for the awfulness of the past four weeks.

Well, not quite. One thousand down, fourteen to go. It was an unwritten code in Freedman's set that one should seem rich enough to be indifferent to money. On at least four occasions he had found himself in the position of being expected to pay a sizeable restaurant bill for a party of eight. Freedman's crude jokes about the meanness of the English, combined with the coolly speculative stares of the guests, had made any attempt at resistance impossible. Clarissa's arrival, ostensibly to do an interview with the old film-star, had produced an additional financial burden.

He had not been entirely surprised by her appearance at the Villa Sylvia. It was his own fault for having told her where he was going on the drive from Gracedew to the station. He had not meant to do so; she was a sufficiently professional interviewer to have squeezed the information out before he had realized the danger.

"Martin Freedman, eh," she had said. "I haven't seen an article about him for years. I wonder if you'd—"

"No," he had said. "I'm there to do a writing job, not to look after Freedman's public relations."

Discouragement had never hindered Clarissa in her career. She had turned up at the villa a week after his own arrival, with a commission from *Paris Match* and with none of his own anxiety to disguise the fact that she had once been his wife. She had gone rather further than that, hinting at a lasting intimacy between them which might lead to a reunion. Furious though he had been, it was not easy to say of a pretty woman and a fellow-guest that she was a consummate liar and that he would as soon think of taking up with a black mamba.

She had set out to make herself charming, and there was no doubt that Freedman had been charmed but not, unfortunately, to the extent of paying her running costs. That had been his privilege, and Clarissa at forty was a good deal more expensive than Clarissa at twenty-four. She had, quite unrepentantly, been sponging off him for the past two weeks. In return, she had kept Freedman amused and out of his way. In her own fashion, she had given him his money's worth. And she had got what she wanted, a two-hour intimate interview with Freedman on marriages and mistresses.

He wondered why she had been so insistent that Freedman should see this picture and that he should go along as part of the entourage. Perhaps she had meant it as a kindness. Given her own way of life, she might well suppose that he would enjoy a free trip to Paris and a splendid meal. She did not know him very well.

Two weeks of her company had provoked no nostalgia, only

a desire to escape the present. And yet she had been looking remarkably good. The Villa Sylvia uniform—bikinis for the day, silk shirts and jeans for the evening—showed her supple body off to perfection. The sun had coloured her skin to the rose-gold of a Caravaggio boy. Seeing her sprawled on a cane chair by the pool, toasting her body while her face bloomed pale as a camellia in the parasol's shadow, he had wondered why it was that he felt no desire for her. He had found the answer when Clarissa opened her sloe eyes and gave him a thin smile of complicity and invitation. She was sharp and witty, attractive and available, but love was as dead now as it had been on the day she had left him. And since sex without love seemed an act of sadness, he had walked away.

Partly from lack of volition. Partly from the memory of Laura. Sweet, green-eyed Laura. He had found himself missing her appallingly towards the end of the month. Clarissa was good company, but he craved the intimacy, the nearness of a familiar body when he fell asleep. The habits of marriage. The comfort of familiar love. It was, he thought ruefully, something on which he found himself depending more as he came into middle-age. He had lost the sense of an unknown body as a new-found land, there for the discovery and conquest. He had found his perfect kingdom. He wanted no other. Still, he thought, a wise husband would make no such declaration to his wife. If Laura should ever sense the degree to which he depended on her—well, she had probably looked at his manuscript by now. It was the nearest he would ever come to expressing the absoluteness of his love for her.

"She was there when you rang this morning, Matthew? Your wife?" Sophie timed her entry into his thoughts in a way which had never ceased to surprise him in a female so wholly self-engrossed. "I heard you calling."

"Probably with her parents. She said she was thinking of visiting them."

"Ah," Sophie said with a little nod. "She is not the mouse, then. The mouse who plays, you know. When the cat is not there."

"Oh, that mouse." He smiled. "Afraid not. She's too busy house-keeping."

"She will be very bored."

"That," he said mildly, "is why I wanted to go back yesterday."

"A day won't make any odds," Freedman said. "If she's as sweet as you say, she won't mind your being a day late. And if she's not sweet, she'll stay long enough to grab the cash. My wives were sweet as pecan pie until they got their pretty little fingers on the dough."

"It is true," Sophie affirmed. "They did not behave very nicely to poor Martin. Not like me."

Freedman let out a bellow of laughter. "You're the worst of the lot, Sophie, and that's the naked truth."

"*Mais que tu m'embêtes, cheri,*" Sophie said coldly. "For that, you will give me a lobster for my lunch."

"Good idea. We'll join you. Up to *langouste*, Matt?"

"Who could refuse?" Not a paid follower.

They left the Closerie des Lilas at three-thirty, by which time Freedman was in rollicking good humour. Two and a half bottles of Chablis had washed down lobsters so succulent that Matthew's disgust at seeing them prised out of an aquarium for the boiling-pot had not outlasted his first mouthful. Sweet cold Suderaut and a delicious froth of lemon soufflé had contributed to the general sense of hedonistic pleasure; the admiring glances of two middle-aged fans at the next table had wreathed Freedman in smiles. Sophie had succeeded in extracting the hundred franc notes necessary to go and buy her sandals; Matthew was to provide company for Freedman and a discreetly supporting arm across the boulevard to the Rue des Fourches.

"Some street. It's a fucking alley," Freedman said with disgust as they squeezed between the tall walls of blank grey brick spattered with bird-lime. "Can't be much of a place to paint in, poor old devil. He must be down on his luck."

"Well, there hasn't been a Rawlings exhibition in years, and I doubt if his style attracts many commissions nowadays."

"Still, if he's broke, he'll make less of a hassle about the price." Freedman gazed up the spindly iron staircase which was the only visible entrance route to Rawlings' studio. "Christ. Do you think we'll make it?"

"It doesn't look as though there's much choice. We could always go and help Sophie choose shoes."

"Hell, we're here, aren't we? The things I do for art," Freedman grumbled, but it was clear that he had no intention of giving up. Lack of determination was not among his vices.

A small figure had appeared on the iron platform at the top of the staircase. A birdlike cry, presumably an invitation, floated down to the alley.

"Oh well, let's get on with it," Freedman muttered and started up the stairs.

It had been years since anything had been heard of Rawlings. Matthew had been astonished by the news that he was still alive. Remembering the photographs he had seen of Rawlings at the peak of his career, a smooth-faced society artist whose paintings of the wives of baronets and stockbrokers had briefly earned him the name of England's Sargent, he wondered if the old man was aware of the shocking contrast which he now presented, unshaven, in a threadbare, food-stained jacket. An incongruous jauntiness in the beret and shifting smile suggested that Rawlings had managed to retain to himself, at least, some image of success. He had under-estimated Clarissa; it seemed clear enough now that she had wished only to do the old artist a good turn.

"That's one hell of a climb for your clients," Freedman said loudly, mopping his cheeks with a silk handkerchief. "Lucky I'm in good shape. We've kept you waiting. Terrible traffic."

"And irresistible lobsters at the Closerie." Rawlings grinned like a playful pike. "You have been under surveillance. I can see all the boulevard from my crow's nest."

"You've been painting the street?"

"Just looking. The street is my company when I am working." He rubbed his hands and smiled. "Well, come in, Mr Freedman. Mr Craven."

Puzzled, Matthew looked at him. "We've met, then?"

Rawlings' grin widened. "She told me you would come. I have been most curious to meet the man she talks about so much. And you are here to buy my painting?"

"Uh-uh." Freedman tapped his chest. "Here's your man. I just hope it's as good as the lady promised. I'm no expert, but I'm a fair judge of quality."

Rawlings opened the door. "It is my best. The place is in rather a mess. I should have cleared up for you. Still, we can drink. What'll you have?"

"Business first," Freedman said in a voice which barely smothered his dismay. "Well, you've certainly got a fine view."

Little could be seen of it through the grime which lay thick as a fingernail on the great grey window at the far end of the studio. Matthew's eyes flickered from the crumpled bed half hidden behind a curtain to the grey damp-blistered walls. Of work in progress, there was no evidence beyond a heap of rags and a few brushes soaking in a jam-jar. The canvas on the easel was blank.

"Well," Rawlings said, "if you gentlemen won't drink with me, I'll do the honours to hospitality alone. I didn't have a Closerie lunch." He scuffled briefly behind the curtain and produced a half-empty whisky bottle. "No glasses, I'm afraid. Sure you won't join me?" He tipped the bottle to his lips and drank noisily. "First of the day. Always the best. Now—I'll tell you about the painting before you look at it. Just to whet your appetite."

"No need for that." Freedman propped himself against the door, fearing for his suit with the peeling walls. "Clarissa's a good publicist. But she said that the sitter's anonymous. Now that bothers me. A face without a name isn't much of a proposition."

Rawlings took another gulp. "The charm of mystery, Mr Freedman. Call her Beauty if you like. But a name isn't part of any deal I'm prepared to make."

"Simple enough. No deal." Freedman glanced at his watch. "We're meant to meet Sophie in half an hour, Matt."

Rawlings put a yellow claw of a hand on his sleeve. "I can assure you that her anonymity will not affect the value of the work. You should at least know why the lady has never been named. I want to tell you the picture's history."

"Okay." Freedman clipped and lit a cigar. "Make it short."

Rawlings curled himself up on the end of the bed, the bottle, now almost empty, between his knees. "I have never married," he said. "I adore the company of women, but in measured doses. For the artist, like the photographer, it is not a bad thing to flirt a little with his subject, to make the woman feel desirable. And if she is just a little in love, she will do as she is told and the picture will be much easier to work on. Perhaps better.''

''Point made,'' Freedman said irritably. ''Marriage would spoil the fantasy. So you had mistresses instead.''

''Masters and mistresses,'' Rawlings said with a sharp little smile. ''I always thought it was frightfully conventional to tie oneself to one sex. Still, putting that aside—when I was thirty, and I wouldn't want you to ask how long ago that was, I had a very enjoyable little affair with a young woman I shall call E. She had only been married for a year. There was a need for discretion. I had a charming studio in Tite Street. She lived in Chester Square. It was all very convenient, and great fun. She thought up some story of charity committee meetings to keep her husband happy, and every Tuesday and Thursday she came along to the studio. I would have a delicious little meal ready—I used to adore cooking. She always brought a bottle of champagne.''

Freedman stubbed out his cigar. ''I thought you said you'd keep it short.''

''I'll précis it,'' Rawlings said. ''She got pregnant. I offered her the money to take care of it. She refused. She said she had some physical problem. It was likely to be the only child she would ever have and she wanted it. Do you think I could have one of those wonderful cigars? I'm meant to have given up, but they do smell quite delicious.''

Freedman laughed and shook his head. ''Keep talking. I'd hate to be the instrument of your fall from grace. So what did you do?''

''I begged her to be sensible. There were some rather dreadful scenes. It seemed she had decided to get a divorce and marry me. I told her it was out of the question. I couldn't stop her having the child, but I certainly wasn't going to marry her. I told her that it would be better if we stopped seeing each other. She wanted the painting back that I had done of her. It had not been commissioned. I refused. She left in a fury. Two weeks after that, her husband visited me. He said that she had told him everything and that he had decided to accept the child as his own. Nothing would ever be known. And then he said that I must return the painting as a matter of principle and honour.''

''And you kept it.''

"Naturally." Rawlings smiled. "It was the best bit of work I had ever done. Why should I give it away to satisfy some dull little man in the Foreign Office? Is something wrong, Mr Craven?"

Matthew stared with sick apprehension at the sly flickering smile and the watering red eyes. Clarissa's great discovery; he wondered how she had managed to stay away. Wherever she was, he could be sure that she was relishing the thought of his discomfiture. "Do go on," he said bleakly.

"So I kept the picture," Rawlings said as he shuffled across the studio. "But I gave my word. I would never identify the sitter. I would never acknowledge the child. I would take Iago's role. Nothing would be said from that day on. So you see, Mr Freedman, why it is out of the question that I should give you the lady's name." He bent to pull a cloth away from a canvas propped against the wall. "Beauty is unveiled."

Freedman let out a whistle. "Did the husband see it?"

"I could hardly prevent him. He was rather upset."

Matthew walked across the room to stand before the canvas in silence. So Charles Craven must have stood all that time ago in the artist's studio, unable to speak as he confronted a wife he never had and probably never did so see again. Whatever Rawlings might say, he must have been infatuated then to paint her as a sated Venus. Elizabeth Craven lay naked, spread-eagled on a bed with the light from a side window falling to dapple her face as she stared indolently out. Her legs sprawled wide, casually exposing the white inner curves of her thighs. The body of a concubine at rest; the face as he remembered it, helmeted in black curls, eyes slanting like willow leaves. So she had looked when she came breathless and late to the station, the smell of sex warm on her skin, brought from some lover's bed. Freedman's moist lubricious stare filled him with anger and shame. The thought of her decorating a wall in the Villa Sylvia, a feast for curious eyes, was intolerable.

"How much do you want?" Freedman asked.

"Twelve thousand." He smiled agreeably. "Don't let me put you to the embarrassment of haggling. There is only one price."

"Hell of a price," Freedman commented. "Still, it's quite a picture. A picture to screw under, I'd say." He laughed.

Rawlings said nothing. His eyes watched Matthew under a pale shield of lashes. "Do you like the picture, Mr Craven?"

"I'll buy it," he said, quickly, not looking at Freedman. "Will you take a cheque if it's post-dated by a week?"

Freedman's fleshy mouth opened in a gape of astonishment. "Hell, Matt, are you crazy? That's going to mop up most of your share."

"I know. And Mr Rawlings knows my reasons."

The artist giggled. "But of course. Clarissa is such a clever arranger of life. I knew she would send you. Curiously, it was your mother she reminded me of when we first met and found you were our common bond. If I was twenty years younger—she is so amusing."

"Damned if I can see what's so amusing," Freedman said.

Matthew knelt to replace the cloth over the painting. "It's very simple. Mr Rawlings was playing a little game when he said that he couldn't reveal the sitter's identity. He wanted to tell me the story and to see how I would react. I think it comes as no surprise to him that I wish to buy the picture."

Freedman blinked. "You mean you know who she is?"

"Oh yes. I know."

"Fuck me," Freedman said. "If I bought pictures of everyone I knew, I'd be out selling cabbages in the market. Well, your funeral. I'll leave you to the wake. See you at the Dôme in half an hour." He held out a cigar to Rawlings. "Paint me another one like that and I'll give you a crate of them." His heavy steps receded down the stairs.

Matthew wrote the cheque rapidly and held it out. He had no wish to prolong the visit or to allow Rawlings the indulgence of some false sentimentality. They had met as strangers and so would part.

"There you are. It's a fair price for your best work."

An uncertain smile flickered across Rawlings' face. "I should give it to you, I suppose, in the circumstances. Unfortunately, times being hard—"

"I said, it's a fair price."

"Still, I wouldn't want you to think too badly of me. It wouldn't have worked, Matthew. You can't imagine your mother living somewhere like this. We wouldn't have survived as a couple. It was a great romance for her. She would have hated the reality."

"Bearing your child must have seemed real enough." He sounded perhaps too harsh; he could not bring himself to be kind. It was impossible to superimpose on the seedy figure beside him the handsome successful young artist with whom his mother had lain all those afternoons ago. The word "father" seemed void of meaning. He wanted the man to give him the picture and let him go, but the hand on his sleeve was as inescapable as that of the Ancient Mariner.

"We've got a lot to talk about, Matthew. You look very like Lizzie—Clarissa never told me that. Same eyes. Let's go and get a drink round the corner. Your friends won't mind waiting for a bit."

He shook his head. "I'd rather not. There really isn't much to be said. You can justify yourself. I can seem to agree, condone, whatever you like. It doesn't alter anything. It doesn't make us friends. We can't be. It's too late. The picture matters to me. Nothing else about this occasion does. It should be significant. It isn't."

Rawlings dropped his hand. "If that's how you feel. I thought somehow—"

"It would all be different? You thought after telling a story like that, I'd want to weep in your arms? I might shed a tear or two for my mother. She may have suffered. I very much doubt if you did."

"I did what I thought was best," Rawlings said stubbornly. "And I'm not prepared to say I was wrong. You'd never have got that house if she'd stayed with me, you know. Clarissa said—"

"Clarissa's a lying bitch. She didn't set up this meeting from the goodness of her heart, I can tell you that."

"Perhaps not." Rawlings looked so shrunk and dejected that he was moved to something near pity. The man had embarked on the occasion in a spirit of malice. It was possible that he had dreamed of it ending in some other way.

"Look," Matthew said. "The man I knew as my father is dead. He wasn't particularly bright or remarkable. He had none of your talent, but he gave me his name and he loved me. To

305

accept you now in his place would be like betraying him, even though he's dead. I don't want to do it. Do you understand?''

Rawlings put the picture in his arms. ''I don't have a choice, do I?''

He caught Freedman up on the boulevard.

''Sorry to have deprived you of your masterpiece.''

Freedman shrugged. ''Guess I can stand the loss. It wouldn't have gone too well with the Bonnards. Still, I'm having a hard time making out why you did it. I thought this commission was a case of make or break for you.''

''I needed the cash.'' He felt some need to explain what must have seemed an act of insane extravagance. ''The woman in the picture is my mother.''

Freedman nodded without any show of surprise. ''I thought you seemed pretty upset when he told us that story. You didn't have to buy it, though. He must have had it there for years and nobody any the wiser. And it's not the kind of family portrait you'd be wanting to hang up at Gracedew.''

''I'll probably put it away in a cupboard and look at it once a year.'' He smiled at the sluggish, slightly stupid face, lined by the unaccustomed problem of thought. ''I doubt if I can join Sidney Carton on the scaffold in saying it's a better thing than I have ever done, but it was what I had to do.''

''Well, you're an odd man,'' Freedman said. ''Your wife's going to kill you for turning up with empty pockets. Thought of that?''

''She'll understand.''

''She's a remarkable woman if she does.'' He laughed. ''I'll say one thing for you. You're quite an optimist.''

He flew into Heathrow the following day, with the picture wrapped in his coat and the manuscript dangling from an arm in one of Sophie's pretty boutique bags. It seemed appropriate to the sleek sheaf of sex, sun and scandal which was to be ennobled by the name novel. Novelty was all it lacked.

Buying the picture had been a way of buying himself off the hook of corruption. Thomas Dobell had forfeited his life for his redemption. Beside that, twelve thousand seemed a small price to pay.

306

Max was waiting for him at the barrier, his pendulous, sallow face looming like that of a latter-day Tiberius above a chattering group of schoolgirls.

"You travel pretty light," was all he said.

"Habit." He put the bag in Max's hands. "It's more me than Freedman, but I don't suppose that matters."

"So long as we've got the name. I don't mean to diminish yours, Matthew."

"But Matthew Craven doesn't move a title off the super-market shelves at quite the same rate."

"Afraid not." He peered into the bag and gave an approving nod. "Nice and solid. A hundred thousand words?"

"Ninety-six. Action packed."

"Good fellow. Pity I can't get them all producing at that rate."

"It's wonderful what an overdraft will do."

Max laughed. "Nothing that fifteen grand won't put right. What have you got wrapped up there—a souvenir of Cannes?"

"A Rawlings nude."

Max raised his eyebrows. "I didn't know he'd done any. That must have cost a pretty penny."

"Twelve thousand. So if the cheque can be sooner rather than later, I'd be grateful."

"You're off your head," Max said amiably. "You've blued all that on a bloody picture? What about the house?"

"I've got a few ideas." He grinned. "Don't look so appalled. Everything's going to be fine."

"I'm glad to hear it. Do you want a lift? I've got a car in the park."

"I'll take the tube. I want to get back to Gracedew this evening. I thought I'd give Laura a surprise."

Max nodded slowly. "You don't like the idea of coming along to a party this evening and going down tomorrow? We've got a few people coming to meet James Faverty. He's got a novel coming out this week. I think you'd enjoy meeting him. He's a nice boy. Bright."

Matthew shook his head. "I really should get back. I sent Laura a telegram to say I'd be back tonight. And anyway, our London base is rented out."

"Richard Leyden left last week. He's gone back to California,"

Max said after a slight but perceptible pause. "Or so I heard. I gather that actress friend of yours took his departure rather badly. Celia Rivers."

Matthew looked at him in surprise. "Bit old for him, surely? Leyden can't be more than thirty-eight. What an odd coincidence." Still, the news came as a relief. He had suffered a few nights of unease over the thought of Leyden in Saint Anselm's Road, the possible temptations for his London-loving Laura.

"Small world," Max said with a glance at his watch. "Well, I'd better be off. I'll have the cheque in the post as soon as I've checked the manuscript. Lucky you don't have an agent. Speeds it all up." He held out a hand. "I'd like to come and see what you've done to the house when you've a week-end free. Or perhaps we could have a bite at L'Escargot when you're next in London. Keep in touch, won't you?"

Hissing northwards on the Inter-city past a skim of fields and the strutting lines of pylons, Matthew reflected with some puzzlement on Max's manner. He had never much cared for the man, but there had been an awkward kindness in him today which had been both baffling and touching. He had always been very decent to Laura, taken her out to meals when she was on her own, increased her advances when she was short of money. Not like Screeby's. Catch them ever paying a penny before it was legally due. That wretched little Fellowes would be pestering him for a new book soon and again he would have wearily to explain that books of the kind he wrote didn't pay the Gracedew bills. Nor, alas, would the Dobell novel. Glumly staring through the window, he pondered the house's future.

The door at the far end of the empty carriage opened. Without any great pleasure, he saw Remington and Harrison, the Livingston agent, elbowing their way towards him.

"Hello, Matthew. Mind if we join you?" Without waiting for an answer, they took the places opposite him. A gentleman is always glad to see his friends in transit. "You look well," Harrison said in his loud jolly voice. "Had a good holiday?"

He decided against explaining how little of a holiday it had been. Writing could never seem like real work to his country acquaintances.

"Not bad. I was just racking my brains for some bright ideas about Gracedew. Any suggestions?"

"Oh, you're going to stay on then?" Remington looked surprised. "I rather thought now that—ideas, eh," he said, as Harrison prodded his foot. "Pity you had to sell the land and cottages. There's the answer, if you'd got them. Charles was just telling me the problems he's been having with the tenants at Livingston. Gertrude's a frightful old skinflint, but the place does manage to keep itself."

"Just," Harrison said. "But who'd want to live like Gertrude? The last time Jane and I had dinner with her, we got boiled potato parings for soup followed by something not too far removed from whatever it is she feeds the pug on."

"No flies on Gertie," Remington said with a roar of laughter. "Last time I used her telephone, she charged me double and said she had to take the quarterly rate into account. There's the answer, Matthew. Rob the poor and you might end up rich."

"Come on. You're hardly in the category of the under-privileged." Harrison protested. "The land at Knaresfield must be worth a couple of million."

Remington's face lengthened. "Show me the lawyer I haven't used to try to break that bloody trust. I can't touch the Gains-boroughs and I can't touch the land. The fact of the matter is that my father was round the bend when he drew up those documents. He never should have been allowed to do it." He stared gloomily at Matthew. "At least Gracedew's a manageable size. What do you do with two hundred rooms and all of 'em ugly? For two pins I'd move out and build a bungalow in the garden. It'd probably be a damn sight more comfortable."

"You could, of course, and without paying," Harrison said. "I'm always reading about these conversion jobs. One stately home equals ten luxury flats. It's not a bad idea. It does mean the place is kept alive."

"Catch Gertrude doing that," Remington said. "Still, it's a thought. One does get a bit sick of being a steward for the nation when the nation couldn't give a damn. What do you think, Matthew?"

He reflected. "I'd rather let the place go to ruin. I've read about those conversions, too. You don't have any control over what they do. They can rip out the staircases, put in jacuzzis, paint the walls orange. I don't think I could bear that to happen to Gracedew.''

''The last of the romantics,'' Remington said, not unkindly.
''Well, you may be right. It's a pretty house.''

Harrison started another track of conversation with a long story about a racehorse which he owned as part of a syndicate. Matthew kept an attentive smile on his face and returned to Gracedew's future.

There had been an article in the magazine provided for his flight about an Irish castle whose owner kept it going by transforming it into a medieval banqueting hall for six months of the year. Nothing on that scale could be done at Gracedew—the prospect of feeding two hundred people at night in shifts was intolerable. It might, however, be possible to organize some kind of an entertainment in keeping with the house which would attract tourists and help to pay for the upkeep. But what? Well, what more splendid tribute could there be to the courage of Thomas Dobell, he suddenly thought, than to create the joust at which Thomas had planned to tilt before his queen when the house was completed? The moment of glory which had never come. He would take the part of Thomas. Laura needed only the costume to become Venice, whom she so resembled. They could hire one of those extraordinary groups who delighted in pretending to be Elizabethan noblemen. It might even be possible to devise some kind of *son et lumière* on the lake. An aquatic masque with dolphins and tritons? He pulled himself back to reality. The aim of the enterprise was not to bring about his final ruin. The organization required would be immense; the financing would need a miracle of faith. Still, he could borrow. Everybody had told him that his only hope was to make the house pay for itself. Let them back their wisdom with money. Laura's father, for one. And Remington, for all his talk of impoverishment. He might be good for a couple of thousand if it were made to seem a safe investment.

The more he thought of it, the more attractive the idea became. He had often talked to Laura of his feeling that the house should bring them closer together, working for a common goal; here, it seemed, was the way to do it. The admission of the spent twelve thousand could wait a bit. First, he would fire her with his scheme. Perhaps he would take her to a restaurant in Nottingham that evening, give her the treat she deserved. Knowing Laura, she had probably been dining on tinned soup for the past month. A recompense was called for, a pretty present, perhaps a new dress.

The train hissed forward, dragging its snaking grey coil across the Trent. Peering out of the window, he could see the rosy west front of Gracedew half buried behind the trees. He was startled by the strength of his emotional response to it as the place where he belonged, whatever happened, however intractable the problems. Here, in this soft Midlands landscape still untouched by the stealthy expansion of the city across the familiar fields surrounding Chillingston and Foldham, was his home, his life, his certainty. It was curious, he thought, that he should be so full of hope and confidence. Perhaps the meeting with Rawlings had not been such a bad thing. He had faced the shadows of the past. Ahead, there was only light.

He took a taxi from the station and paid the driver off at the foot of the Gracedew drive, preferring to stroll at his own pace beneath the swaying candles of the chestnut trees. Rain dropped softly from the low sweep of branches. A covey of ducks whirred up from the lake. Ahead, the tall chimneys of Gracedew ranged like quiet sentries across the golden pillows of low blowing cloud, the watchdogs of his castle. The wind sighed at his back. The past lapped softly at the present. He had only to half-close his eyes to see Sir Thomas now.

He blinked at the discovery that there was indeed a figure standing under the distant archway, no phantom but a girl in a lightly fluttering dress. She raised an arm in signal. He waved back and began to run, splashing through the puddles like a schoolboy.

"My dear Matthew. You looked at me for so long I thought you'd seen a ghost." Alice held up her face for him to kiss. "Didn't you recognize me?"

"The sun was in my eyes. I thought—" He broke off with a smile. "How lovely to find you here." But it was not what he had wanted, to find her here now, when all he desired had been locked in his expectation of his darling girl, her arms outstretched to harbour him. He was too impatient to be polite. "Where's Laura? In the house?" He touched her cheek. "Dear Alice, you'll think me a monster, I know, but I'm going to abandon you for half an hour to look after yourself. You'll forgive me, won't you?"

"Oh Matthew!" She looked up at him with a pale stricken face which held him still. "You don't know? I did write. Perhaps I got the address wrong. Laura said she was going to tell you herself, but she was in such a hurry. I suppose there wasn't time. You haven't heard anything?"

"She's ill? She's had a crash? What is it?" He tried to speak calmly. "It can't be any worse for being said. Tell me."

Alice dropped her head for a moment, then raised it to look him straight in the eyes. "She's left you. She went to California last week with Dick Leyden. That's why I'm here." She put her hands lightly on his shoulders. "Oh Matthew, I am so sorry. I feel so responsible. It was because of me that he came here in the first place."

"It's not your fault."

At least his voice sounded normal. He struggled to take in what had happened. She had gone. Just like that. Leaving him to a house of emptiness and silence, to the blank where there had been Laura. To the vacant cupboards, where her pretty dresses had sidled up to squeeze out his suits, to the untenanted chair at her desk. To the tick of clocks, to the habits which, in solitude, lost all point. The moment had come which he had laughed about so often with her, the moment when she would leave him. He remembered her laughter, the merry confidence of her shaken head. "You know I won't. Silly Matthew. I'll never leave you." Never, she had said a hundred times. And he, like a fool, had believed it. If he had only stayed. If he had only been less sure of her love.

"You mustn't start reproaching yourself," Alice said gently. "What happened, happened. You can't unmake it."

There was an awful finality in the way she said it which cut through the last feeble strands of disbelief like a meat-cleaver. He did not want Alice's common sense. He could not face the idea of walking into that emptiness.

"I'd better go," she said. "I'll call you tomorrow."

He caught at her hand. "Stay."

"Do you really want me to?"

He nodded. "Please. Just for a bit."

She put her arms round him, her face warm against his. "Oh Matthew. My dear Matthew," she murmured. "She wasn't worth it. She didn't understand. She never felt about Gracedew as you did. I know it's awful for you now, but one day, perhaps, you'll see that it isn't the worst thing that could have happened."

He held her away, staring at her face, so serene, so full of kindness. His angel of mercy, waiting to rescue him, to be given the role she would fill so well. The understanding companion, the perfect wife. Oh Laura, Laura.

"I suppose we may as well go in," he said.

15

Nothing quite like it had ever happened to Gracedew village. Heads had been shaken at parish meetings, doubts querulously expressed, but the spirit of adventure and enterprise seemed, as the vicar wonderingly observed to his wife, to have infected them all.

Incredulity and indignation had been the feelings dominant among those who had grumblingly attended that first meeting a year ago when Mr Craven had announced his plans. A three-day Elizabethan event to raise money for the house? The proposal had been greeted by nudges, titters and curiosity. The news that they were required to appear in costumes of the time had been met by baffled silence. Mr Craven had not been deterred. Smiling encouragement, he had outlined his plans. The children were to perform dances and sing madrigals; their elders were to represent any characters of their choice. He had drawn up a list of possibilities to give them ideas. Interest, waning at this point, had risen perceptibly with the next proposition. If, he had said, the scheme proved successful, Gracedew would not only become a tourist attraction but a provider of employment. The stable-yard would be converted into a handicraft and garden centre. The old dairy would become a cafeteria. Work was not easy to come by nowadays, he knew. If they were prepared to put their backs into helping to make a success of this first experiment, he would undertake to employ at least six people on a permanent basis at wages directly related to the annual profits. And if there were any suggestions or objections, he'd be glad to discuss them at the next meeting.

There had been a good deal of laughter and scepticism, but it became clear during the next two weeks that the villagers had on the whole approved of the idea. There was a strong residue of loyalty to the Craven family among the older inhabitants; nobody wanted to see the house go down. There was commiseration, too. Mr Craven had put a good face on things but he had been looking pinched and sad since his wife had gone. He wasn't so standoffish as they had thought, just a bit strange and shy. Not surprising, said the older villagers. Look at the way he was brought up. It all went to show.

It was worth a try.

But who, from that first meeting, could have predicted that the matrons of Gracedew would come almost to blows over who was to be Amy Robsart and who the sly Lettice Knollys? (It had been the vicar's thankless job to point out to both aspirants that they were a little old for the roles they craved: offence had been promptly registered by absence from next Sunday's service.) Who for that matter could have supposed that burly Mr Cartwright would make a remarkably convincing Earl of Leicester or that prim Mrs Bates would be ready to pad herself out as an ancient Doll Tearsheet? Everyone knew the ways of the Lord were passing strange, but they had never seemed more hilariously so than in the revelations made by the choosing of characters. Mr Flower himself had been puzzled by the degree of kinship which he had come to feel for the sour Protestant parson, Solomon Bundy, in whose glum guise he had been walking among the crowds these past two days. As for Mr Craven: well, Mrs Cartwright had not been the only one to have been given a shock when she first saw him in full dress as Sir Thomas Dobell. It was as if the figure in the monument had walked straight off the wall.

It had taken a year's hard planning. And it had, against the general expectation, paid off. There had been five hundred cars and eight coaches on the first day, more on the second than the first, and on this, the third day, the car park was reported to be blocked from end to end by eleven o'clock. They had worked together for this success, and the weather had matched their generous spirit, providing three days of cloudless summer skies and the kind of warm lazy glitter on the land which goes with the crooling of pigeons and the clap of cricket bats. The thunder of the charabancs had become a music almost as sweet to the villagers' ears. Luck, but well-deserved, in the vicar's opinion. Nobody could have put more effort into the operation than Gracedew's owner. He was a man with a vision. No obstacle had deterred him; no problem had proved insurmountable. Scepticism had been met with a good-humoured smile, protests with persuasiveness, refusals with grace and resistance. It had frequently struck the vicar that Sir Thomas Dobell, himself no mean plotter and cajoler, could hardly have outdone his younger representative in those skills.

He smiled at his wife as she carefully buttonholed her mouth with lipstick in the shadowy bedroom glass. No need to point out that the wife of an Elizabethan priest would not have been adorning her face with cosmetics. "How nice you look, Beth. It's a charming costume. I shall be sorry when we're back in our old clothes again."

"More than I will. I never knew hessian prickled so much." She tweaked out the grey folds of her skirt and pushed the white cap back from her wide placid forehead. "There's Mistress Bundy, ready for the day."

"I was thinking," he said as they went down the stairs. "It's very unchristian of me, but I do think that Matthew Craven is a happier, perhaps even a better man, without his wife. I grieve for him, of course, but—"

"I can't think why. Of course he's better off," she briskly answered. "Nothing unchristian about saying that. Everybody thinks so. You should hear Mrs Cartwright on the subject. It's that nice Alice Tresham who's done it. She's the one who's changed him. Just the sort of woman he should have married in the first place."

"Alice Tresham." The vicar, who prided himself on being a reflective man, mulled over this idea with interest. It was true that Alice Tresham had been spending a great deal of time at Gracedew and that she had played a major part in organizing the events. He had heard that much of the fund-raising had been done by her. A capable, pleasant, orderly woman; yes, she would make a good châtelaine.

"But you're a little premature, Beth dear. He's still married."

"It's well over a year since she went. He must act some time. But you do agree that she'd be a splendid candidate?"

He laughed. "What organizers you women are. He may quite like leading the life of a bachelor."

"Stuck all alone in that dreary great mausoleum?" She laughed incredulously. "How could he be? Think of old Jack sitting there, mad as a hatter, for all those years. And Matthew's only in his forties."

"He could have people to stay."

"It's not the same thing. No, no, what he needs is Alice," Mrs Flower said sagely. "I only hope he knows it."

Lady Livingston moved with ponderous deliberation through the milling crowds towards the refreshment tent, a gaily striped pavilion which held out some promise of refuge from the glare and noise. Alice had said something about raspberry sorbets; the prospect invited on a hot afternoon.

A knight in red and black armour trotted briskly past her, the feathered plumes swinging and bouncing from the back of his helmet on broad mailed shoulders. He turned to look at her with a grin.

"Cheer up, Guenevere."

Guenevere? That woman of loose morality? She drew herself up. "Keep your comments to yourself, young man."

"Oh, bugger off," the knight said and snapped down his helmet. Across the soft pat of retreating hooves boomed the genial voice of the announcer:

"Those who wish to see Sir Roger de Coverley defend his name against Sir Philip Sidney should now make their way to the jousting ground. Three minutes to go. Those wishing—"

A deeper frown travelled across the oceanic smoothness of the illustrious features. "Too ridiculous," Lady Livingston murmured aloud. "Don't they know anything about history?"

"But my dear, it's all such fun! You mustn't take it seriously!" James Mawson had emanated beside her. "Of course it's all wildly wrong, but isn't that just the charm? It really was brilliant of Matthew to dream this up. I'm enjoying it all immensely, despite being trampled underfoot by the eager throng."

"It certainly appears to be popular," Lady Livingston grudgingly acknowledged. "Not what one would dream of doing oneself, of course."

"You don't think it inspirational? Antony and I thought we might offer a little modest competition with a Georgian evening. A chamber orchestra and a *fête champêtre* in the garden. Not for the masses, of course. One does rather quail at that."

"One does indeed. Although financially, of course—Matthew told me he's expecting to take a profit of six thousand."

"Just enough to pay the heating bills for a year at Gracedew, I should think." James turned to look at the house. "It's delicious, of course, but I do feel so thankful not to have a home that big. Not as bad as Knaresfield, of course. Livingston always seemed to me so perfect. Such a manageable size. But then you've done it all so cleverly, Gertrude. When one thinks what somebody like you could have done for Gracedew."

"It's a case of being up to it, really. Dear Laura simply wasn't. Not her fault. It's a question of who you are."

"Awfully perceptive of you. And so right."

A happy smile wreathed Lady Livingston's face. Perhaps she had put it rather well. She must remember to use the phrase again. Being up to it. Yes, that was what it was all about. She broadened her smile into an invitation. "I was feeling rather tempted to look for the raspberry sorbet Alice mentioned. Perhaps you'd like . . . or are you going to watch the joust?"

James contemplated the possibility of explaining the charm of the burly-shouldered knights to the old cow and regretfully decided against it. Antony had been frightfully disagreeable lately and the little courtyard flat at Livingston could, if he played his cards well, be a useful bolthole. Anxious to please, he must strive to seem charmed.

The reserved table was already occupied by a number of reassuringly familiar personages in sensible everyday clothes. Lady Livingston was rather tired of looking at young girls whose idea of Elizabethan costume was to show a good deal more of their bosoms than was pleasing on a hot afternoon. She sailed towards the table with James floating attentive in her wake. Their faces brightened with a welcoming expression which quite restored her good humour. Dear Delia Tuckett, able to smile again now she had her new teeth. But Jane Harrison's dress! One really couldn't go about in puff sleeves and sashes in one's forties. *She* never had.

"Well, what a lovely surprise, Gertrude dear," Mrs Tuckett cried. "Now Richard, do get Gertrude some of the sorbet. I thought you said you wouldn't be able to come, dear."

"I certainly wasn't going to pay. Matthew very thoughtfully sent me a complimentary ticket." She sank with a small gasp on to the proffered seat. "Well, this is all very comfortable and pleasant. I must say, I'm thankful to be out of the mob. I've never seen so many blacks. It's like being in Africa. Too extraordinary. Where's Matthew?"

"He was walking with Alice in the rose garden when I last saw him," Jane Harrison said. "Rather promising, I thought. Antony and I are taking bets on it."

"On what, my dear?"

"The marriage date. Now Gertrude, don't pretend to look surprised. Alice practically lives at Gracedew now and you know how she adores the house. You must admit she'd make Matthew a wonderful wife."

Antony Makepeace cocked his head on one side like an intelligent old parrot. "We've got ten pounds on it. Alice engineered the whole thing, of course. It's screamingly obvious."

"Not to me, I'm afraid," Lady Livingston said without warmth. She liked to be the originator in speculations about her neighbours and their affairs. She knew herself to be unusually perceptive. "Engineered it. What *do* you mean?"

"Richard Leyden was brought down here by her, wasn't he? And put next to Laura at dinner. And who was responsible for his renting the Cravens' flat? Who came rushing in to pick up the pieces? You always said Alice was a shrewd woman, Gertrude."

Lady Livingston demurred. "I never meant that she was calculating. And I really can't accept that Alice arranged all this in order to—well, to get Matthew. It makes her sound so unpleasant."

"I'm on Gertrude's side," James Mawson said. "Alice simply isn't clever enough to plan all that. And why would she want a man who'd already treated her frightfully badly?''

"To get her own back, dear," Antony said with a giggle.

There was an uncomfortable silence as Colonel Tresham emerged from the crowd to peer down at the table. "I thought I might find Alice here. Anyone know where she's got to?''

"Alice? Goodness." Mrs Harrison's expression of innocence was badly overdone. "I'm sure I've seen her about."

"Well, if she turns up, tell her I'm off home. Had enough of the jamboree."

"I don't think it's Matthew she wants so much as the house," Mrs Tuckett said when he was safely out of earshot. "It does seem such a sensible solution. And I don't suppose she's too old to have another child."

"And what about Laura?" Mawson looked round the table. "We seem to be overlooking the fact that Matthew's got a wife already."

There was a momentary pause before Mrs Tuckett rallied. "Well, hardly. I know you and Antony adored her, but I can't bear to think of the way she behaved. I'm sorry to sound unkind, but she really was a dreadful little thing. No feeling for the place at all. She couldn't have cared less about it."

"It's really a question of being up—" Lady Livingston began with happy certainty. James Mawson—he could be most irritating—cut across her.

"You can hardly blame her for that, Delia. Gracedew isn't everybody's idea of heaven. I think we ought to be very grateful to dear Laura. She was fun. And you must admit she's given us a lovely lot of gossip."

"Oh well, if you're going to be frivolous about it," Jane Harrison snapped. "I find life quite as much fun without her. Just because she was decorative."

Mawson gave her his sweetest smile. "Jealous, dear?"

Charles Harrison pushed back his chair. "Now look here, James—"

"I think Alice would suit him very well," Lady Livingston said firmly. "But it won't come to anything. She's a dear girl but she's not clever about men. She made the same mistake before with Matthew. Men don't marry because they're grateful. And they don't choose the most suitable candidates, alas." She spooned a dollop of pink ice between her lips and sighed appreciation. "Quite perfect."

"And why do you think they marry, Gertrude?" Mrs Tuckett asked with interest.

"Sex," said Lady Livingston. "Laura had sex appeal. Alice has everything else." Carefully, she wiped a rosy smear from her chin. "Well, that was most reviving. Is anyone coming with me to watch the jousting?"

Dutifully, the assembly rose to follow her out, stifling their amusement as well as they could.

"Too extraordinary," Mrs Tuckett said to her husband. "What can have happened? I always thought Gertrude was so frightfully strait-laced."

"Up to the neck." Major Tuckett searched for an explanation. "I wonder if she's taken to the bottle."

"I know she likes a glass of whisky before she goes to bed." Mrs Tuckett gazed with speculative eyes at the broad retreating back of Lady Livingston. "No. I don't think she's drunk. She always waddles. No, it's clear there's more to Gertrude than meets the eye."

"Not sure I could cope with more than I see myself. Poor old Livingston. Don't wonder he died young. Tiny little chap. Bit like a flea and the elephant, really."

"Perhaps she just wore him out." Mrs Tuckett laughed merrily. She had never quite forgiven dear Gertrude for allowing the pug to place a permanent scar on her ankle.

Doreen Bates turned to observe Sir Antony Makepeace and James Mawson as they supported each other across the muddy tracks surrounding the jousting ground. "Right pair of old queens they are. I never knew how Mrs Craven could stomach going to lunch with them. Look at Mr Mawson now, ogling and smirking at the riders fit to bust himself. Disgusting."

"Here's your favourite," Bates said. "Quick or you'll miss him with all the chat."

Elbowing her padded breasts to unnatural heights, she smiled up at Sir Philip Sidney, young, moustached, triumphant, cantering forward for the admiration of the crowd while his opponent stood glumly rubbing the mud off his hose.

Passionately, she clapped her praises. Sir Philip did not notice. He was looking moodily at the beer tent and wondering how long it would be before he could take a break.

"Do you remember when we saw John Travolta in that silly film at the Odeon, John? He's got quite a look of him from the side. Lovely physique. So manly."

"Must be all those taps he pulls," Bates said. "He works in The Chillingston Arms on Saturdays. I never knew he went in for this sort of stuff."

Her face fell. "You do know how to take the romance out of life, John. What did you have to go telling me that for?"

"Stop you making a fool of yourself. You've watched him for three days solid, my duck. He's only a lad. Nowt there to put stars in your eyes."

"I know that." She hunted about for the words to express the funny little feeling of excitement she got from watching the show. "I don't believe in the others, but he looks so real. He makes me think of how it must have been here in the old days, like in that Henry the Eighth they had on television. And then I think of it now, and poor Mr Matthew walking about in those big empty rooms and nobody to carry it on and everything falling to bits. It's not what was meant to be. It's not what they built it for."

Bates looked at her in silent amazement. He had never heard her speak with such passion about anything other than her health and her father's will. "It's not what Gracedew was meant for," she repeated, screwing up her face. "I don't grudge the work as some might, but what's the use when there's no future in it? There's no joy in the house."

He squeezed her thin arm. "Don't take on so, my duck. It'll all work out for the best. You've told me yourself how much better it's been since Mrs Tresham started to put things in order. If he's got the sense, he'll marry her. She's past breeding age, I shouldn't wonder, but she's got the two lads. There's a future there, if he'll take it."

"He won't though. Not while he's still mushing after the other. Photographs all over his desk and a right to-do if I forget to dust one. He won't even have her old face-creams thrown away. Married to a memory, he is."

"He'll come to terms with it. He'll have to," Bates said with more certainty than he felt. "Mind you, I don't blame her for going like she did. It wasn't a life for a young girl. You could see she wasn't happy."

Mrs Bates' face hardened into righteousness under the bright mask of rouge. "Oh, we all know you've a soft spot for a pretty face. She'd only to smile and you were all over her. You should have taken a bit more notice of the way she was carrying on after he went away. Powdering and prinking and prancing about like a cat with the cream, telling me how she wanted to make the house all nice for Mr Craven's return. She didn't pull the wool over my eyes with that talk of business in London. Business. He should have taken a horse-whip to her. That would have lammed some sense into her."

She was turning out just as he'd always feared, a puritan hatchet. The mother all over again. And no stopping her, neither. "It's the getting away with it you can't take, isn't it? You'd want him burning her pictures. I don't suppose you'd be the last to bring him the matches."

She looked away. "You're always against me. Can't open my mouth. Can't have a thought of my own. It's allus got to be the man who's in the right of it in your family. Just like your old dad."

"Let it rest, woman. I'm not saying you shouldn't have your views. It doesn't go to say I've got to share them, though."

But Mrs Bates' attention had been diverted to fresh grounds for disapproval. Her nails skewered his arm. "Will you look at that Gracie Cartwright. Showing her all and grinning fit to bust about it. All that talk about her being a secretary. She looks more like one of those striptease dancers."

"It's allygorical. She's meant to be a nymph or summat. And they've covered the necessaries."

"It's obscene." She glowered at the semi-naked back of Miss Cartwright. "She'll go to a bad end, that one."

Bates grinned. "She'll make a fair treat of the journey, though. Come on, Doreen. She's nobbut a pretty lass enjoying herself. You're only young once."

Sir Philip Sidney—she couldn't bring herself to think of him as the boy from The Chillingston Arms—had left the field to join the group of young men who circled round Gracie, smirking and laughing and making jokes. She remembered herself at Gracie's age, a shy ugly gawk of a girl going about in her sister's hand-me-downs, the outsider whose rare evenings out had always been as the wistful invisible third, gooseberry and hanger-on. Bates had only asked her out for a bet. Millie Lewis had told her that and she hadn't disbelieved it, although Bates had always said Millie was a liar. Well, she'd been lucky, she supposed. He'd been a good husband. No mucking about. Millie's husband had gone off with a dancer. Which all went to show that it wasn't enough to have a head of golden curls and a waist you could put your hands round.

Sir Philip had edged his way to the front of the group. Got his arm around Gracie now. They didn't waste much time nowadays. She turned her back on them.

"I was thinking," she said, "of how old Mrs Craven used to be able to go round this garden knowing everything in it, Latin and all. This one never troubled to tell one rose from another. You could have planted nettles and she'd not have noticed."

"She wasn't bred to it. She'd have learned in time."

A small sniff was her answer. Well, no use in arguing with Doreen when she'd made her mind up. She'd never liked the girl. It was true that she had not fitted the role of the lady of the manor so well as Mrs Tresham would do, but then she'd been such a pretty wild thing with her quick light ways and her chatter. They'd had a good laugh about that herb garden she'd wanted him to set out. No more stable than a will o' the wisp in her enthusiasms and ideas, but she had lit the place up for a time with her funny clothes and her laughter. He'd often wondered if enthusiasm wasn't worth more than efficiency at the end of the day, but that was to make excuses for her failings. And there hadn't been much laughter towards the end. No, she would never have got a real grip on the place, made it work. Mrs Tresham was the one for that. Gracedew wouldn't founder with her at the helm.

John Patterson paced slowly across the uneven cobbles of the rear courtyard, an unlit cigarette gummed to the corner of his mouth, a heavily pencilled notebook in his hand. His feet moved neatly toe to heel, measuring out the square while his eyes scanned the upper line of the building for broken gutters and crumbling bricks. She had warned him not to expect the place to be in such a carefully preserved state as Knaresfield. There was a lot to be done. The north-facing wall would probably have to be pulled down and rebuilt. The windows would have to be replaced. None of that Victorian junk could stay. The clients of Coutt & Gross expected authenticity. They would be offered a fair semblance of it.

Alice Tresham had come to the Derby offices of Coutt & Gross a month before the joust with the proposition that they should take Gracedew on as their next major conversion job. It was, she had explained, her own idea. She had very much liked what they were doing with Mr Remington's house and knew how pleased he was with the arrangements. She would prefer that Mr Patterson did not deal directly with Mr Craven who might have some initial reservations about the scheme. Mr Craven was, she had said with a smile, not quite so business-like as Mr Remington. He might be alarmed at first by the amount of modernization required and by the prospect of sharing his home with strangers. Patterson had been quick to reassure her. Coutt & Gross were known for being highly selective in their choice of clients. The conversions, while conceding to the expectations of the buyers, would be in the very best of taste. The communal jacuzzi and the gymnasium would be unobtrusively situated. Fitted cupboards would not disturb more than a fraction of the original panelling or mouldings. She had cut him off in full flow with the curt assurance that she knew exactly what was involved. It was simply a question of convincing Mr Craven.

Her interest had been evident, but Patterson had been slightly at a loss to understand what her involvement with Gracedew was. It was clear that she was not Matthew Craven's agent. What then was she? The future wife of Mr Craven, he had been given to understand, but she counted on his discretion. And he had, of course, promised it. She had struck him as a woman of good business sense, the sort of person he liked to deal with. Her grasp of market values appeared to be sound. Her readiness to compromise had augured well for a satisfactory relationship. He had agreed to come and look over the premises while keeping a low profile. She had suggested that a visit during the three-day Elizabethan event could be made without his arousing any curiosity.

So here he was, feeling slightly ridiculous as he struggled to take notes while remaining unnoted, but feeling too an almost schoolboyish excitement at the lucrative vistas which such a handsome property opened up for Coutt & Gross. They could make at least four decent flats out of the courtyard block and there had been a strong suggestion that they would, if they played their cards well, get a generous chunk of the main house as well. At, say, a hundred thousand pounds a flat, Gracedew became a very appealing proposition. He only hoped that Mrs Tresham's future at Gracedew was as secure as she appeared to think.

The knights had stripped off their armour and gone back to Leicester, followed by an unwieldy caravan of horse-boxes. The tents were down from their frames, the temporary barrier ropes unhitched. A few litter cans still squatted like yellow beacons in a sea of trampled clay and gusting paper, but Gracedew was, by slow degrees, taking back her privacy. It was, Matthew realized, the first time in three days that he had been able to hear the scream of wheeling swifts, the staccato flutter of wings in the beech-leaves as dusk dropped down.

He leaned beside Alice on the balustrade overlooking the lake to gaze down on the deep reflection of the house. The ducks paddled slowly in to cluster under the willows as the fire of evening dulled down to sullen blackness. Peace at last.

She turned her head to smile at him. "I'm exhausted. How about you?"

"A bit drained." And ready to be alone, although he could not find the heart to say it.

She put a hand on his arm. "Well, it worked. You've started to get the house back on to solid foundations. It's going to survive."

"I couldn't have done it without you." He kissed her cheek and turned his head away as she raised soft lips. "Dear Alice. You've been marvellous."

"You know how I feel about Gracedew. And about you. With love, it's all so easy."

And so terribly hard without it, he thought. This had been the evening when he had promised himself he would act, make the kind of commitment which he knew she expected and which would be welcomed by everybody. He had already taken the first step. A small ring, a ruby flanked by the conventional two diamonds, lay discreetly in its box on his desk. Not an engagement ring, of course, but significant enough to be binding. The prelude to a sensible, a rational attachment.

And one which would be regarded by most men as their good fortune. She was looking gravely, if a little sedately, beautiful in the heavy Elizabethan dress, her pale blonde hair trapped in a net of pearls, her handsome shoulders squared by padding. Desire had gone but he could dispassionately admire her good looks. He could even relish her clever complementing of his own black and gold costume, his masquerade wife. He knew what a striking couple they made. Many people had remarked on it. Several of the tourists had presumed that she was Mrs Craven and he had been too gentlemanly, or too apathetic, to set about refuting the error. He had, as so often during this past year, seemed by his silence to acquiesce. And now, having allowed supposition to grow into anticipation, he must do what was expected of him. Her tranquil silence called for it.

She shivered slightly. "I should have brought a shawl. Shall we go in?"

"In a moment. I rather like being here at this time of evening. It'll be over in five minutes."

Resignation would be the wisest course. He had been given every chance to see how well she would run the house, and him. She would be practical, deft, organizing, tactful. He would be allotted his time for writing just as he would be allotted his time for having the vicar to drinks, for entertaining Alice's jolly sons, for paying the wages, for having his pre-dinner drinks. Like Isabella Mary Craven, his Alice would order the home by the homilies. A time for everything. All things in moderation. Everything in its place.

It was churlish to resent the prospect of an efficiency which he had so often pressed upon Laura as a goal towards which to strive.

"I was thinking," Alice said, very sweetly, not looking at

him, "how wonderful that portrait of Isabella Craven would look in the Green Room. It's so dark in the library and there's such a lot of light in there. I moved it this morning, just to try it out. I think it's rather a success."

"I liked it where it was. That's why I put it there."

"You don't think it's a bit hidden away?"

He smiled. "Certainly I do."

"Then why?"

Because it's my house, he felt like saying. But it wasn't worth the effort. Charmingly, tactfully, she would persist until his resistance had worn down. "I'll think about it," he compromised.

"And perhaps the picture of your mother could go in its place."

"Absolutely not."

He had made a grave mistake in letting Alice know anything about the Rawlings portrait. Not that he had told her much beyond the fact that he had met the artist and paid rather a lot of money to acquire the picture. She knew none of the details of the encounter. Her interest and perplexity derived from the understandable supposition that the portrait was a typical Rawlings, a three-quarter length oil painting of a woman placed in one of the settings through which Rawlings so cleverly promoted the status of his sitters. It remained his resolute intention that neither she nor anyone else would lay eyes on the canvas now safely hidden away in a box-room trunk.

"Anybody would think it was a *Playboy* pin-up from the way you keep it squirrelled out of sight," she said when it became apparent that he had nothing to add to that flat negation. "It does seem a little peculiar to pay all that money and then hide the picture away where nobody can see it. Still, I won't go on. I know you don't like talking about it." Her eyes continued to question him.

"I don't, much."

"Laura never knew about your birth, did she?" she resumed after a pause. "I always find that strange. It seemed such a candid relationship."

"We talked about most things. That never came up, somehow."

understand?''

He saw what she wanted. No, Alice, it's you I trust. Laura never understood me as you do. It was curious how much reassurance even a woman so apparently serene and confident as Alice required for contentment.

''I'd rather not talk about Laura this evening,'' he said. ''Sorry. I don't mean to sound rude. Only—''

''I know. It still hurts. Poor Matthew. You've done awfully well. Everyone says so.'' She seemed to be giving him time to respond, but he had nothing to say. ''I suppose you'll be starting proceedings soon. After all, it's over a year now and she's still with Dick. She couldn't expect much of a settlement in the circumstances.''

He suppressed an irritation which he felt ill-equipped to justify. Her concern was too apparent. Everything she said jarred on his nerves.

''What do you mean by circumstances? Has something happened? Have you heard from her?''

She stared. ''What on earth makes you think Laura would write to me? But I imagine she's still with him.''

''I know she was six months ago. I haven't heard a word since then. I did write once or twice, just in a friendly way. There's no reason we shouldn't try to maintain that. Friendship, I mean. She might even be glad of it. I remember you telling me how lonely you were in California.''

''Only after Buck had gone.'' She was frowning. ''I can't see why Laura should be in need of friends. You're too forgiving. She treated you terribly badly. She couldn't have gone at a worse moment.''

''There's never a good moment for that sort of thing.''

There must, mustn't there, come a day when he would stop reproaching himself, stop the endless train of ''if onlys'' by which he might have stopped it from happening, stop the harrowing up of a past which grief could not change? He had not known how much he would miss her. He could not have anticipated that the pain would still be as acute, over a year later. He still found himself moving too quickly to answer the telephone, thumbing through the morning letters for the familiar upward scrawl of Laura's hand, turning to embrace a warm body in some sleepy memory of the night smell of Laura's breasts, Laura's thighs. He still could not bring himself to put the photographs away, or to abstain from the masochistic solace of reading her old letters. Greedily absorbing those declarations of love and her desire, he could, for a while, deny the reality of her absence.

He must. As he must accept the responsibility. He had made his commitment to the house, assuming that her interests lay with his. He knew that she had never been happy at Gracedew, that she had felt superfluous, out of place. He had given too little time to her feelings, offered her the state of independence as loneliness, not freedom. There had been so many mistakes. He had been wrong to suppose that time would make an Alice of her, cruel to leave her so often alone. Complacency had blinded him. Only with hindsight could he clearly read the signs, the hieroglyphs of her despair.

Too late. He put his arm round Alice's shoulders. "Poor love, you are cold. We'll go in. I've something to give you. Oh, by the way—" He had almost forgotten to ask her. "I ran into an acquaintance of yours in the stable yard. He was taking notes. He wouldn't tell me what for, but he mentioned your name. What is it—something to do with the tourist shop?"

Alice seemed to hesitate. "I think that would have been Mr Patterson," she said slowly. "He's a surveyor, I want to talk about that to you some time. It's a little plan I've been hatching."

"A surveyor. Who does he work for? Not Coutt & Gross, I hope?"

"Stop being so inquisitive." She gave him a reassuring smile. "I'll tell you tomorrow."

"I'd rather be told now. You were talking about Knaresfield the other day. Saying how clever you thought Remington had been to arrange it. I seem to remember a Patterson being involved in that." Her silence increased his alarm. "He was. I remember the name now. Christ, Alice, you don't suppose I'm going to let that happen to Gracedew?"

"All right then," she said. "Yes, he works for Coutt & Gross. It's the only rational solution. We—you can't want to

330

live in the whole house, Matthew dear. Charles has been a different man ever since he took the decision to divide Knaresfield up into flats. And he says they're an awfully nice bunch of people. He gets free use of all the facilities. They even agreed to let him keep the dining-room for big parties."

"Wonderful. And they've completely wrecked a house which has been in his family for three hundred years. Is he really happy about that?"

"Goodness, how disagreeable you can be," Alice said. "I was only trying to help. My father thought it was an excellent idea."

Cheaper than having to help subsidize the place himself if the desired marriage took place, Matthew thought. "I'm sorry," he said. "You'd better tell Mr Patterson to put his notes away. I thought you understood how I felt about the house."

"I'm thinking of the future. You can't afford to be romantic. There's no sense in relying on things like jousts or paying-guests to finance the house. Conversion's the best solution. Honestly."

"Perhaps." The familiar inertia crept over him, the reluctance to prolong the conversation (it could never with Alice be termed a quarrel) which would only be allowed to close when she was sure of victory. "Do you want me to see him?" That would please her.

Her wide, beautiful smile glowed her approval. "Will you really? I know I should have consulted you first. You aren't too angry with me?"

"I can't imagine ever being angry with you." It was, he thought, very strange that he could be as brave as a slayer of giants over something like the organization of the joust and yet find no strength to argue with this quiet, inexorable woman with her unwavering certainty that she knew what was best for him and for the house. Still, his submission or his statement seemed to have pleased her for she leant forward to kiss his cheek.

"Dear Matthew, I'm longing to see what the surprise is."

"Come and see. I think you'll like it."

They walked hand in hand to the door. Inside, the telephone blindly wailed for a response.

"Blast. It's probably old Delia Tuckett. She left her bag in the pavilion." He went towards it. "I'll get rid of her. Why don't you go through to the library and put some music on?"

She turned at the library door, her hand to her lips. "Be quick."

He picked up the receiver with a mixture of irritation and relief to have postponed the moment, however briefly.

"Hello?"

"Matthew? It's me."

He was almost sure it was her, but the voice was hardly more than a whisper in the crackling of the wires. "Laura? Laura?"

"Are you alone?"

He tried to sound normal. "How lovely to hear you. Not quite alone, no. Alice Tresham's over here. Just for a drink. She's been helping to run a sort of fund-raising event here."

"I know," she said to his astonishment. "Mr Flower told me. I came from the station this evening, but I didn't want to burst in on you. Not being exactly an invited guest."

"Darling Laura, you'd hardly be a guest. Are you at the rectory now? I'll come and get you."

"Wait," she said, sounding rather odd. "You haven't heard what's happened."

"Is Leyden with you?"

"Look," she said. "I know I've got no right to ask favours, but could you try to get Alice away? I do want to talk to you. It's urgent."

"I'm not having—I'd rather not have your lover here."

"Nobody's asking you to. The last I heard of Richard he was in San Francisco."

Richard? Had he left her? "Why leave him behind? He might have enjoyed the trip. Nostalgic pleasures."

"I'm not explaining it very well. I'm not with Richard Leyden any more. It happened about two months ago. He said he'd realized we were too different for it to work out."

"I thought the bastard was supposed to be in love with you."

"I think he was, for a bit. And then he met somebody else. Only I—" She stopped.

"Yes?" The Scarlatti sonata rose to a crescendo. He put a

hand over the receiver. "Turn it down, Alice, will you? I can't hear. Yes. Only you thought—"

"I'm four months pregnant. And I haven't got any money left. Max sent me enough for the air fare. Matthew, I don't know what to do."

"Have you told your parents?" He remembered as he asked that the Dares always went to Portugal in June. Probably just as well. The reaction from that shrine of convention would have been fairly galling to her pride. "It's not important. Look, I'll be along in half an hour to pick you up. There's plenty of food here. I'll make you a meal and you can go to bed early. We'll talk about things tomorrow. All right?"

"Yes. Better, anyway. I'm so sorry. I've messed everything up. Perhaps I shouldn't have come." He heard the choking sound of a suppressed sob. Bloody Leyden.

"Don't be an idiot. Where else should you have gone?" He hesitated. "Just remember I love you. Everything's going to be fine. Don't worry."

She was crying when he put down the telephone. Slowly, he went down the passage to his study, to get the ring intended for Alice. Slowly, he took it out of the box. Pretty, unostentatious, conventional. Not the kind of present he would ever have given to Laura. It would suit Alice admirably, as she would have suited him had he not been committed elsewhere. He had recognized that commitment from the moment he first heard Laura's voice. Passionately and unequivocally, he wanted her back. It would be up to him to see that she stayed.

And the child? Another illegitimate heir for Gracedew? He could hardly fail to be struck by the irony of the situation. And yet, treated in the proper way, it was a chance to redeem the mistakes of the past. By taking the child in, treating it as his own, ensuring its security, he would be making the greatest possible demonstration of his love for Laura and, in some way, escaping the bitterness he still felt about his own childhood.

And, after all, had he not longed for an heir?

He put the ring back in the box and left it on his desk.

"So much for your telephone technique. You've been gone for the whole side of a record," Alice said before she looked up at him from her chair. "What's up? Seen a ghost?"

"Laura's here. Leyden left her when she was two months pregnant. Charming fellow, your friend."

She stared at him. "Here? In the village? How extraordinary. And what does she propose to do? Have the child here?"

"She sounded pretty confused. I doubt if she's worked anything out. I told her I'd pick her up."

"Gracedew seems to be living up to its name. A refuge for runaway wives. How lucky you kept the London flat. That's the best answer, I should think, until she's had the child."

"The place where she had the affair with Leyden? I'm not sure I agree."

"You think she'd mind? I suppose she might. What about Ebury Street? I'm hardly ever there."

"She knows about Ebury Street. You and me, I mean."

Alice raised her brows. "I must say, you're very particular about her feelings. I can see that it's pretty awful for her, but nobody asked her to go and get pregnant. Perhaps she did it on purpose."

"I doubt it. She never wanted children."

"She could have changed her mind. Women do. Anyway, my dear, I think I'd better remove myself from the scene. The surprise will have to keep for a day or two." She smiled as she came towards him. "I've got a feeling that I know what it is. Shall I guess?"

Briefly, he closed his eyes. "Dear Alice, I'll give it to you with pleasure and love, but I'm not terribly sure that you're going to want it any more."

A foot away from him she stopped and stared at his face. "Matthew, you can't be going to be such a fool as to take her back? Hasn't the past year taught you anything?"

"Only that I love her. I don't know what's going to happen," he said. "I've no overwhelming certainty about the future, but I know what I shall try to make of it."

"I see." She looked down at her large well-shaped hands and folded them into each other as a faint tremor became visible. "An heir for Gracedew. Well, it's more than I could have managed. If you're prepared to take on the responsibility, I suppose it's quite convenient from that point of view." Her eyes, when she had gained sufficient control of herself to raise her head, were blank with grief. "I wish you luck. I do think you're making a terrible mistake. She always hated this house. She'll go again when she's used you up."

"It's a risk I'm prepared to take. Still, I'll let you know how it goes."

"No need."

"Still—" He would have like to put some grace into their parting, but the words had dried on his tongue. Any phrase he offered would sound false. A foot from each other's bodies, they were locked apart, unable to communicate from the worlds of their separate desires.

"You're making a mistake," she repeated, plaintively.

"Perhaps."

He sat on for a few minutes after Alice had gone. The mistake, as he saw it, would be to return to the old pattern of life. The last year had shown him how much he needed Laura. Her need for him had been strong enough to bring her back. It was up to him now to see that love not only triumphed but endured. His dream of restoring the house of Thomas Dobell had been a splendid one but he had been taught the price of achieving it. He understood his hero better now. By looking at himself, he could see the flaws in Thomas, in the willingness to sacrifice love to personal ambition, to risk all for something which, without love, was worthless. If he and Laura were to be happy, he must put the marriage before the house, learn to separate trust from complacency, recognize that her needs were equal to his own. God only knew how they were going to survive. Still, God's house.

Driving slowly between the lighted cottages towards the rectory, he saw a figure running towards him down the road, arms flailing, hair flying up like a sheet of copper in the glare of the headlights. He braked, jumped out and caught her in his arms.

"Idiot. I nearly ran you over. Oh Laura. Darling Laura."

"I couldn't wait. I thought you'd never come. And then I heard the car and—do you hate me very much?"

With her hair against his face and her mouth on his and the moon bright as a silver button over the trees?

"Come on," he said. "Get in the car and I'll take you home."

"Home." Her head on his shoulder, she looked up with a contented sigh as the tall row of Gracedew's chimneys came into sight. "All as it was, is now and ever shall be. Nothing's changed."

"Nothing that matters," Matthew said.